THOSE WHO CHOOSE EVIL

ALSO BY KATE FLORA

The Thea Kozak Mystery Series

Chosen for Death

Death in a Funhouse Mirror

Death at the Wheel

An Educated Death

Death in Paradise

Liberty or Death

Stalking Death

Death Warmed Over

Schooled in Death

Death Comes Knocking

Death Sends a Message

———

The Joe Burgess Mystery Series

Playing God

The Angel of Knowlton Park

Redemption

And Grant You Peace

Led Astray

A Child Shall Lead Them

A World of Deceit

Such a Good Man

Those Who Choose Evil

THOSE WHO CHOOSE EVIL

A JOE BURGESS MYSTERY
BOOK 9

KATE FLORA

ePublishingWorks!
love what you read.

Released July 2025
ISBN: 978-1-64457-710-3

ePublishing Works!
644 Shrewsbury Commons Ave, Ste 249
Shrewsbury, PA 17361, USA
www.epublishingworks.com
Phone: 866-846-5123

ONE

It was a habit Burgess had developed years ago. A nocturnal one. At the end of a shift or if he needed some space with his thoughts, he'd swing by the park. Sometimes he'd stay in his truck and think. Sometimes he'd get out and walk into the park. He liked the smell of the earth, sometimes of fresh cut grass, sometimes the fall scent of decaying leaves or, in winter, the sharp bite of cold air mixed with the salty tang of the sea. It was the place where, maybe five years ago, he'd found a young teenage hooker, naked, badly beaten, and left to die in the winter cold.

She'd survived and after some setbacks and missteps, had gone on to train as a massage therapist. Now Alana Black sometimes came to dinner with him and Chris and the kids. She thought it was hilarious that she'd gone straight and ended up with a cop for a friend.

Tonight, even though a late November frost had turned the grass silver under a full moon, tempting him to a nocturnal walk, he was too tired to bother. A bad night's sleep and a long day at work had worn him out. He was planning to head home, where Chris would have saved a plate of dinner for him, but his truck had other ideas. When he told it to go left, it went right, rolling to a stop where he always parked when he wanted to check the park. Bad enough that his teammate Terry Kyle could read his mind. Now his vehicle was doing it?

Swearing, he grabbed his flashlight—the big, bright one that could sweep the park—and stepped out into the crisp night. Moist air had gathered around streetlights in nebulous halos and the frozen grass crunched under his feet. In the distance, an occasional car up on the highway sped past but down here he was alone. After a day of constant human contact, it felt good to be alone. Maybe his truck just knew?

His back to the highway, he stood looking out into the darkness, filtering out the traffic sounds behind him and focusing on anything that might not sound right. He might be annoyed at the way the universe decided things for him, but he was pretty sure he was here for a reason. Cops had instincts. They had gut sense. Just like he sometimes believed in divine intervention, Burgess believed that his city sometimes spoke to him. Tonight it wanted him here; now he needed to know why.

Strobing his flashlight beam from side to side as he walked slowly into the park, he listened to the night, and there it was. A small sound, like the mewling of a kitten or the sobs of a weary child. Something out there was crying for help. He closed his eyes and focused on the sound, trying to tell where it was coming from, and thought he got a bead on it. He headed in that direction, pausing every few steps to listen again.

Another cry and then silence.

It might be some nocturnal animal. Might be. But Detective Sergeant Joe Burgess had been a cop for a long time and he'd heard hundreds, maybe thousands of cries of distress. He thought this was human. He continued his walk, stop, listen. But the sound had died away.

He stopped again, turning in a slow circle, and called out, "Hello? Is there anybody out there? Hello?"

The night only gave him back silence. He shook his head, trying to tell himself he'd imagined it. That the ghosts of too many years were distorting his senses and throwing up boogey men where there were none. Standing in the frosty grass, his feet were getting cold and his fall jacket wasn't heavy enough. Soon it would be time to switch up to colder weather gear. Burgess believed in being prepared for the weather. There would be a warmer jacket back in the truck.

He could go back and get it. He could also go back, start the engine, and drive home to good food and a warm and sleepy Chris in his bed.

Burgess turned, the breath he'd huffed out in irritation steaming around his face. His city had called him here but if it wasn't going to show him what it wanted, he was going home. As he turned back the way he'd come, he heard it again. Small and faint, and visions of the night he'd found Alana Black, beaten and bloody, came back to him. Whatever or whoever it was, he had to know.

He turned and restarted his slow walk, listening as he headed deeper into the park. "Hello?" he called. "Hello? Is anybody out there?"

This time the sound was clearer. A voice. A female voice, very faint and weary. She said, "Help me."

Surer of the direction now, he headed toward the voice. Toward her. Flashlight swinging from side to side, illuminating the darkness of bushes and the crisp gleam of the grass.

She was lying on her side next to a battered, rusty trashcan. Bloody. Naked. Her thin white body almost unreal in the silver moonlight.

Burgess hurried toward her, pulling off his jacket to cover her and getting out his phone. He gave his location and called for an ambulance. For officers to secure the scene and for evidence techs. He didn't know if this was a place where she'd been assaulted or whether she had been dumped here, but there might be something.

Assured that help was on the way, he knelt beside her. "Police offi-cer," he said. "I'm Joe."

Her body was more bruises than unbruised flesh. Dark purple ridges circling her wrists and ankles said she'd been restrained. A prisoner. Held against her will while she had struggled to escape. She was young, probably not much more than his daughter's age. Nina was sixteen. Despite the bruises, he could see that she was pretty, with long, wavy dark hair and delicate features.

"You're safe," he said, keeping his voice low and gentle. "I'm a police officer. My name is Joe. Help is on the way, and you're safe." He took her hand in his and repeated, "You're safe."

Her eyes opened briefly. Eyes that were a startling emerald green. "Please," she whispered. "Please don't let them find me. Don't let them take me back."

7

TWO

As personnel surged around him, attending to the girl and the scene, Burgess made the call he made far too often—a call to Chris to say he was tied up at a scene and didn't know when he'd be home. Even though she'd known when they met that Joe was a cop and belonged to his job, there was always that tug between duty and family. There would be until he retired or his family abandoned him. So far, the balance mostly worked, though sometimes the ties got frayed.

He tried to do better. Chris and the kids deserved it but so did the citizens of Portland, Maine, who depended on him and his colleagues to keep them safe. For now, having made the call, he tucked thoughts of his family away for later and joined the EMTs who were putting the girl on a stretcher.

"She's a mess, Joe," one of his favorite EMTs said. "Looks like another of Burgess's waifs."

Did people really call them that, he wondered? He had heard it before. But work the streets of a small city for many years and of course you'd collect people. The unparented children. Those lost to drugs and drink. The frightened immigrants trying to integrate into a new culture. What he hated most were the children. He'd outright told his boss, Lt. Vince Melia, "no more kids." His heart couldn't take it. But the city and its denizens ignored his plea. As long as he wanted to be a detective in the personal crimes unit, life would throw kids in his path and Burgess would suck it up, try to throw patches over the vulnerable spots in his job-toughened hide, and work to get them protection and justice.

He looked around at the techs searching the area, and the small, pale figure on the stretcher. Then he looked back toward the road where he'd parked, and at the tangle of roads surrounding the park. It wasn't an obvious place to dump someone. More likely that she'd come here on her own, fleeing from whoever had held her captive, and gotten this far before she collapsed. But had she come from a building nearby? Jumped from a vehicle? And how far was this far? She seemed too fragile to have traveled far, but fear is a powerful motivator. It could have driven her beyond the capacity of her emaciated body, and, when collapse seemed imminent, taken shelter here where she hoped for the safety and cover of bushes and the dark.

For now, he'd leave the techs to do their work here and follow the ambulance to the hospital. See what he could learn from them, and when he'd be able to speak with her. They would be protective, of course, and that protection would war with his need for information. Sooner was always better, and each side was sure it knew best.

He snagged Wink Devlin, who was directing the techs, and asked if he could grab Dani Letorneau to come to the hospital with him to photograph the girl. Photographs were something else hospital personnel would object to, and a serious violation of the girl's privacy, yet absolutely essential for a prosecution when they found whoever had done this. *When*, not *if*. The damage had to be recorded now. Bruises healed. Scared victims stopped cooperating. Disappeared. Were intimidated into silence.

"Dammit, Joe," Devlin said. "Roast chicken. Blueberry pie. Mrs. Wink in an amorous mood, and we get this?"

Burgess said he was sorry. He was. Wink liked being called out to scenes. At home, he was too often under pressure to retire, an idea that terrified him. But everyone had their cozy domestic nights. For that reason, he hadn't called out the rest of his team. Let Stan and Lily have a quiet night with tiny Autumn. Let Terry and Michelle enjoy an evening with the girls. There was always tomorrow, and plenty already on their plates.

"You can have Dani. I'll send her along in a few minutes," Wink paused. "She's coming along great. When I do retire, you'll still be well covered."

"If you go, I go," Burgess said. "Can't imagine how we'll do this without you. You serious this time?"

Devlin shrugged. He wasn't young and the work did take it out of them. The thing about crime scenes was when they were discovered, you had to go. Couldn't mutter, "Call me in the morning" and sink back into sleep. "Dunno," he said. "The cold. It gets to me more."

To all of them. And Burgess here without a coat. He stepped away and continued his scrutiny of the surrounding area.

"Here," a voice beside him said, pulling him back. "Your coat, Joe."

He took it absently, about to put it on, then realized it was now part of his evidence. If there had been hairs or fibers or anything on the girl's body, they might now have been transferred to his coat. He folded it over his arm and headed for the Explorer to put it in an evidence bag. Then he drove to the hospital.

Cops spent a lot of time in hospitals, either injured themselves or bringing in injured victims or suspects who needed to be mended before they could be questioned. It was a familiar place in the way a dentist's office is familiar. You have to go there and you usually dread it. He parked near the emergency entrance beside a "no parking" sign and headed inside. The only people who would enforce parking here were the police or hospital security, and they knew him and his vehicle.

The girl was just being wheeled in through the door, so he followed her into a cubicle and stayed inside when the curtains were drawn.

A moment later, the curtains parted and two women came in. Dani Letorneau, carrying her camera, and his favorite ER doc, Dr. Sarita Cohen. She was a small woman, and so heavily pregnant she had to stand on tiptoe to reach the patient. She smiled at Burgess and Dani, and said, "I see this girl is in good hands. What happened?"

"She's in good hands now that she's with you," Burgess said. "As for what happened? We have no idea." He reconsidered, because that wasn't true. "Found her down in the park. Naked. Dumped or fleeing, we don't know yet. All we know is what she said before she became unconscious, which was not to let them get her or take her back. That's all we've got. I'm hoping she'll revive soon and we can learn more."

Dr. Cohen nodded and started attending to the girl, snapping out her orders to the waiting nurses like a drill sergeant. "We'll do our best," she said over her shoulder. "You know she's in bad shape."

He did know. Knew also about the resilience of the young, which gave him hope for this girl.

Time passed. Dani, carefully working around the medical crew, got her photos. She didn't say anything. Dani was a pro, but she hadn't yet perfected the cop's opaque face, and what she was seeing was upsetting. Finally, she lowered her camera and said, "I'm done, Joe. You'll have these in the morning. Do you think——"

She broke off. No reason why he should know more than she did about the likely outcome. "I'll see if Wink needs me. Otherwise, I'm going back to 109 for a bit."

"Can I give you my jacket?" he said. "It's in the car. I used it to cover her, so——"

Again, no need to continue. So much communication was unspoken among those who worked so many scenes together.

She nodded.

Before he followed Dani out, Burgess asked Dr. Cohen, "Any thoughts on when I might be able to talk to her?"

"Hard to know, Joe. We know so little about her and don't have any labs back. I'd say not until morning, if then. She's been starved and beaten and who knows what else. Sometimes, cases like this, they're too far gone to save."

She hesitated, wanting, he knew, to give him hope. After so many years of being the one who gave the hope, the reassurance, the promises of justice, it always felt strange to have someone care for him. Yet Dr. Sarita Cohen did. "Joe," she said, "you should go home to your lovely family. Get some sleep." She smiled. "But you won't, will you? You're pretty bad at taking your doctor's advice. How are things going, anyway? Feeling more lively?"

Not long ago, when he'd been feeling so tired he'd labeled himself a dinosaur lumbering toward extinction, she'd prescribed thyroid pills.

They were helping. Just slowly. And Joe Burgess was a naturally impatient man.

"She has the most amazing eyes," he found himself saying. "Emerald green. Like nothing I've ever seen before." That description sent his mind whirling again. He wouldn't go home. He'd go back to 109 and search missing girls online. The raven black hair and startling green eyes were rare enough they might lead to something.

"It's amazing," Dr. Cohen said. "But I can literally see you getting an idea, ready to charge into action. It's…well, you'll think I'm silly for saying this, and I am not a silly person, but it's like you've been plugged in."

"You're not a silly person," he agreed. "When is the baby due?"

"I've got another month. Not sure I'll make it. I'm already so off balance I feel as though, if I tipped over, I could never get up on my own." Another of her quick smiles. "Like an overturned beetle. How's your son doing? Into any more scrapes?"

"Not this week. Not Dylan and not Nina. They've both had their turns. I think Ned is a bit jealous. Maybe trying to figure out what he could do to outdo them. Kids." He shook his head. "I never imagined any of this for myself."

"Yeah. You've kind of been the victim of a very twisted stork. Not so many men who find teenagers dropped down their chimneys." She was paged, and shook her head. "Sorry. Gotta go. You be careful out there, hear me? I like to hope I've stitched you up for the very last time."

"A hope I share. Can you have them call me if she wakes up? I really need to jump on this fast. I think there may be other girls involved."

They went their separate ways. Before he left the hospital, Burgess stopped at the nurse's station to request that no one except police and hospital personnel be allowed access to the girl and that they call police if anyone asked about her. He left the same message with hospital security. Then, having done all he could here, he headed back to police headquarters to do some online searching.

THREE

Once he'd put his searches into play, Burgess decided to go home. There wasn't anything else he could accomplish tonight, and Dr. Cohen was right—it made more sense for him to be rested so he could tackle the situation in the morning.

His city was quiet tonight. The cold had sent many of those who'd normally be hanging out on steps or in parks into shelters, though there were always those determined loners who couldn't stand being around other people. He spotted some of his regulars as he drove home. He still missed one regular, his old friend Reggie. They'd played high school football together. Gone to war together. Only one of them had come back whole. Burgess still looked for him even though he'd been there when Reggie's body was pulled out of the sea. Landscapes had different resonances for people, depending on the paths their lives had taken. His city was a landscape of damage. Or crime. Of the cruelty people inflicted on one another.

For someone else, an artist perhaps, the city might have been shades or shapes. For another, perhaps newly arrived, the city might be a landscape of possibilities. For another, a place where dreams and plans had failed and life had become colorless and without hope. For his late mother, surely the one who set him on his path to become a detective, it had been about observation, about slowing down enough to see what was around her. Sometimes as he drove these streets at night, seeing things no one ever noticed, he could still hear her soft voiced, "Look, Joseph," calling him to come and see something.

Joseph looked, and it was always something worth seeing.

Ahead, he saw a small black shape crossing the street and slowed to allow a cat to pass and slink into the shadows. Better a cat than a rat. Rats—of the animal and human variety—were so damned resilient. And they were everywhere.

He snapped on the radio, hoping for some music to pull him out of this maudlin mood. Lucked out with some Creedence, a song that rocked him the rest of the way home. He parked beside Chris's small white car and Dylan's ancient black Subaru, checked that he indeed had a warmer jacket in the truck, and headed inside.

The driveway was getting crowded, but it was a relief, with his crazy schedule, that Dylan could now drive himself and Nina to school. Watching your child learn to drive must be something like watching them learn to walk—an experience he'd missed with his three. Walking had happened before the stork Dr. Cohen referred to had dropped two damaged children and the son he'd never known about down his chimney. Now his solitary bachelor life was full-on family chaos. Chris was stressed but delighted. He was still stunned.

Inside, he saw that the construction to convert the first floor into two bedrooms and a family room was nearly done. The additional chaos of having his house torn apart, and the lackadaisical pace of a fellow officer moonlighting as a carpenter who had treated the renovation like he was doing Burgess a favor, had done nothing for his mood or his energy. Joe Burgess was a growly old bear, and while bears didn't have spots like leopards, they were also resistant to change. It would be good for the kids to have some space of their own, and he knew from experience it was better to have your kids underfoot than out doing who knew what.

Of course, he knew what, didn't he? He knew way too much about the trouble kids could get into.

Thoughts about Nina's current unsuitable boyfriend wanted to intrude. Like he knew about trouble, he knew too much about what could happen to girls. But not tonight. He slammed the door on those thoughts and went upstairs. From habit, he took off his shoes on the landing and headed inside.

There was a light on in the kitchen, and a place set for him at the table. He got his dinner from the oven and sat down to eat. Chris wasn't only lovely to look at, she was a wonderful cook and seemed to enjoy feeding her brood. Enjoy feeding him. It meant far fewer drives through the golden arches or hastily gobbled something and coffee from Dunkin. It meant he'd lost weight and gained energy. It meant he was a lucky man. He reminded himself to tell her that. Again.

Finished, he put his dishes in the dishwasher, undressed in the bathroom, took a quick shower, and headed to bed and the still marvelous fact that in that bed he'd find Chris, curled in her little sleeping ball. He could snuggle up to her warmth and let the day fall away.

He'd had at least half an hour of sleep before he got a call from the station. There was a man who'd come in wanting to file a missing person report. The guy had been squirrelly—their words—and strangely vague about the girl who was missing. He'd said she was his nanny. Then his stepdaughter. Then a houseguest. They'd taken the report and gotten the guy's information, but it didn't feel right. They had the plate number of the man's car and would send Burgess the info. The event had been recorded.

He debated. Return to sleep and wait until morning or go back in now and see what he could learn.

Not really a debate. When the trail was hot and the case was already occupying his mind, he wouldn't really sleep. He might linger in bed, eyes closed, hoping that would be enough to rest his body, but he had cop's habits and cop's instincts. There was something out there to be explored and it was better not to wait. Besides, despite his aging dinosaur nature, he still rose to the thrill of the chase. To the excitement of learning something that would propel a case forward. Reluctantly, because Chris's warmth was hard to leave, he slid back the covers, got some clothes, and dressed in the bathroom.

He left a note on the table, explaining his absence and thanking her for the dinner, and headed back out into the night.

FOUR

The video showed a thick-set, middle-aged man with a lot of wavy graying hair. He wore a paint-stained green hoodie, worn work boots, and Clark Kent glasses but wore the clothes like a disguise. He seemed aware of being filmed and kept his body turned sideways. His voice was deep, with a trace of accent that wasn't Maine. He'd given his name as Glen Briscow. In his statement, he said he needed to report a missing girl. Young woman. His nanny. His…uh…his stepdaughter. His houseguest. She'd gone missing and he and his wife were concerned about her.

His description of the missing girl was equally vague. He'd given her name as Margaret, Maggie, and Meg. Said she was sixteen. No, nineteen. No, twenty-one. About five foot four, he thought, though maybe she was shorter than that. Probably weighed about one twenty, although she might have lost weight recently. Brown hair. Well, dark brown. Well, really almost black. Sorta black. He wasn't sure how that would be described. Blue eyes. No. Wait. Her eyes were more greenish.

She'd been gone about ten hours, which was unusual for her. She usually stuck close to home. He'd fumbled for a last name, offered several possibilities, then settled on his own. Yes. Her name was Maggie Briscow. He also fumbled his address, giving several different house numbers and street names. Said they hadn't lived there very long, he was still getting oriented. Couldn't recall his phone number. He didn't have a cell, just a landline and it was new.

No wonder they'd called him, Burgess thought. *This guy was draped with red flags.*

"We've got his plate number, though, right?" he asked.

"Yeah. It felt off, so I sent a rookie out to watch, see what vehicle he left in. It was a 2013 silver Subaru Outback with racks on the roof."

Burgess waited.

"And yeah, we ran the plate. It came back to a 2010 Toyota Prius. Not registered to anyone named Briscow. Couldn't find any vehicle registered to a Glen Briscow, though we did find a 2013 Subaru registered to a Margaret Briscow. You'll want that address." He passed Burgess a pink message note. "And the name and addy of the person who owns or owned the Prius is there. No record of the plates being returned."

So, what? The guy takes the time to switch the plates on his car but not to get his story straight? Was he someone who dealt in stolen cars? But if he was the one who'd kept this girl captive, why show up like this and ask about her? Because she knew too much and finding her was more imperative than staying hidden?

He asked them to grab some shots of the man and leave them on his desk, then took the message slip and headed out. He'd swing by the hospital first, make sure Glen Briscow or someone else hadn't tried to get to the girl. Then he'd check out the two addresses he had. By morning, if they got lucky, NCIC might have some names of missing girls for him.

If cops said things like, "aha, the plot thickens," it would have applied here. Actually, his teammate Terry Kyle sometimes did say that, though it was usually an ironic observation.

Someone—a woman, not a man—had been at the hospital making inquiries and been sent away empty handed. She was described as middle aged, middle sized, and unremarkable. The best he could get was shoulder-length brown hair and glasses. Gray sweatshirt and black leggings. Sweatshirts and leggings were kind of a uniform among female Maine residents. Besides, if you weren't unconscious or bleeding, no one paid much attention to you unless you pitched a fit and started throwing furniture around the lobby. Evidently, she had not done that. He checked with the nurses on the girl's floor. No one had tried to see her. She was still unconscious and being monitored carefully.

Nothing more he could do here. He went to check out the addresses he'd been given. The address Glen Briscow had given for his report didn't exist, the computer said, and when he drove out to the address of the vehicle registered to Margaret Briscow and peered through the windows, the furniture was covered with sheets and there were no signs of habitation. No vehicles in the driveway. He checked the mailbox. No mail but no rust or spiderwebs and the door didn't complain when he lowered it. Despite the deserted house, it appeared the box was in active use.

He wanted to check on the Prius at the address the Subaru's plates had come from, but it was half an hour away in another town. He wasn't keen on making the drive when there were things to do here, nor on waking people up just to ask about their license plates. He or someone on his team could swing by in the morning. Swing by rather than making a phone call because face to face, when possible, was always better. They were good at reading voices but the facial expressions and body language could be invaluable.

If he wasn't going to get sleep, he needed coffee. Cops drank a lot of coffee, much of it pretty bad. But he knew where to get a decent cup, even at three a.m. Coffee, and because he had to be honest with himself, a really good croissant breakfast sandwich. He got both, then drove up to the Eastern Prom, parked, and had himself a little cop's picnic and a ponder. Gradually, the black changed to ever lightening shades of gray and a shy morning sun began to illuminate the bay. Time to head in to work.

Still too early to call Chris. He'd do that later. Right now, he was curious about the owners of the Prius and of that vacant house. Eager to see Dani's photos from last night. Wondering whether it was too soon to hope for anything she might have found on his jacket. There was no emergency. This wasn't the first twenty-four of a homicide. No need for her to spend the night processing evidence that could be processed in the morning. It was, though, the first twenty-four of a horrible case of child abuse.

And truth? To Burgess's mind, it was always an emergency. Always urgent. It was easy for evidence, witnesses, or bad guys to disappear while the cops were still fumbling around on first. Probably why he was so worn out when other cops his age were fresh as daisies and retired.

Clearly, today his cynicism was ascendant. Having had good coffee and good food, he should be in a better mood. They told him there was therapy for that. And pills. He wasn't interested. Some fool had even suggested a gratitude diary. He supposed there were things he was grateful for. His family. His team. Good boots and a warm jacket in winter. People who actually believed in cooperating with the police. He didn't need some book to write that down in.

As he sat at his desk, poking through his computer, the room gradually filled up around him and the noise level grew. When a voice behind him said, "Fill me in, Joe," he turned to find Terry Kyle only two feet away. Kyle could do that—move through a room like a weightless shadow. Kyle was holding what he figured were Dani's photos.

"Yeah, stopped at the lab on my way in and Dani had these for you."

"Not much to tell," he said, but he got up and headed for the conference room. It was quieter there. No one to overhear. There were people in this department who seemed to prefer gossip to crime solving and he wasn't eager to feed the gossip mill.

They closed the door and sat at the table, not far from the movable whiteboards they used when they were sketching out their information. Suspects. Facts. And suppositions.

"Stan in yet?" Burgess asked.

"Haven't seen him," Kyle said. "He'll find us. The kid hates to be left out."

The kid was Stan Perry, the youngest member of their core team. Perry was in his thirties. Not really a kid anymore. But his undisciplined habit of larking off on side investigations of his own sometimes led to trouble, and ulcers for Burgess and Kyle. They also sometimes led to great discoveries. Since his daughter Autumn was born a few months ago, and he and Lily had married, young Stanley seemed to have settled down, but he was now newly challenged by the task of balancing an all-consuming job and a family. It was a balance they all shared, and one that was impossible to always get right. When crime called, they answered and sometimes the folks waiting at home for dinner or a talk or even a date got pissed off.

Kyle leaned back in his chair in a listening position and said, "So tell."

"I was driving down by the park last night—"

"As you do."

"And something told me I had to stop and walk into the park."

"As it will," Kyle intoned.

The call and response not of minister and congregation but of cops beginning to sort what they knew.

"I thought I heard something. Someone in distress. I followed the sound and found a girl there. Naked and cold. She'd been badly mistreated. Dehydrated. Emaciated. In real bad shape. She was covered in bruises. And the deep, raw ones around her wrists and ankles said she'd been restrained. She looks to be about fifteen, but that's only a guess."

No questions yet, so Burgess continued. "I wrapped her in my coat and called for help. She's over at the hospital now. Still unconscious, last I checked. Dr. Cohen says it may take a while before we can talk to her." He didn't add, "if at all." Their hospital was good but there had been caution in Dr. Cohen's assessment.

"Unconscious when you found her?"

"Nearly. She did speak briefly. She said 'please don't let them find me. Don't let them take me back,' so we can assume there's more than one person involved. People who, for some reason, were holding her against her will."

The door opened and Stan Perry came in. He looked, as he always did these days, like he needed a comb, a shave, and a good month's sleep. There was baby spit down the back of his shirt. He closed the door, crossed to the table, and sat. "What did I miss?"

Burgess gave a quick recap and moved on.

"While I was home, just asleep, the station called. Some guy had come in trying to file a missing person report. But he was dodgy. All over the place. So they grabbed the license plate off the Subaru he was driving, which turned out to be from a Prius."

He stopped. "So far, everything about this Glen Briscow is fake. The address he gave us doesn't exist. There's a woman named Margaret Briscow who does own a 2023 Subaru but it's registered to an empty house. The Prius is registered to a man up in Gray." He shrugged. "Hospital says a woman came in late last night, looking for a girl. Whether it was our girl or not, they don't know. She didn't have ID. The girl from the park didn't have ID, I mean, and I told the hospital not to let anyone near her. Woman tried to push for information but didn't get any, and she went away. No good description of her. So—"

He reached for the stack of photos and pulled it toward him. "That's all we've got."

"Dumped there or running from someone?" Kyle asked.

"Can't know for sure but I'd say running. Her feet were all cut up. And there have been those strange folks here and at the hospital looking for her."

They looked through Dani's photos, the girl's bruised white body made more vivid by the flashes. The night beyond seemed looming and sinister.

"Jesus!" Kyle said. "There's definitely a story here. So what next?" There was a muscle working in his jaw that said what he wasn't saying: that Kyle was the father of two young teenage girls and cases like this hit close to home.

Burgess listed some next steps. "Who owns that Prius and do they know the plates are missing? What can we learn about that empty house? Who owns it and why is it empty? They had to know about it, had to monitor it to use it to get the Subaru's registration, I'd think. Maybe we can track down the dealer who sold the car? Maybe, though a long shot, there are prints on that mailbox? Is Glen Briscow in the system somewhere? Or the man who's using that name? We've got a couple photos from the desk camera. Maybe find the woman who was at the hospital on their surveillance video and do a photo match search."

He shrugged. It was often like this. They started out looking for a lot of needles in a lot of haystacks. Sometimes they got lucky. Sometimes their haystacks multiplied until they were facing an entire field. It was the job. But right now, with all of his team reasonably healthy and raring to go, he felt the beginnings of the excitement of the chase. Something had happened to that girl. Something another human or humans had done. And they were going to find out what and why and who.

"I'll take researching that house," Kyle said. "And the Subaru. Kinda feeling like some time at my desk today." He grinned. "Who knows? I might even grab a little nap."

Right. Like Kyle ever napped on the job? He was just saying what Stan Perry was thinking.

"Crap! I wanted the desk job. But okay, I'll check out the Prius," Perry said. "Take a nice little ride out into the country."

Kyle started stacking up the photos again, then stopped. "Hold on. There's something. I'm gonna get my magnifying glass."

He was out and back in a flash, then pulled the top photo closer and held the glass over it. Burgess and Perry leaned in as Kyle pointed to something small and shiny on the ground near the girl's head. "Looks like a necklace or a locket of some kind. Did Wink and Dani collect it?"

Burgess didn't know. Neither had mentioned it but he'd left the scene before they finished to go to the hospital.

"I'll check," Kyle said, and left.

Burgess took the glass and went over the other photos, but it appeared only in the one, mostly hidden by a tuft of grass about a foot from the girl. It wasn't like them to have missed it, but it had been dark and the ground sparkled with frost. It could be important. If the techs didn't have it, he'd have to go back. Back soon, before the park was filled with walkers and bikers and the homeless who spent the hours when the shelters were closed on the benches. Now that the sun was up, a bit of sparkling gold would attract someone's eye.

Kyle returned, shaking his head.

"I'll check it out," Burgess said. He went to his desk, grabbed his coat, and headed out. He'd barely gotten out of the garage when his phone rang. The hospital. There was a woman there claiming to be the girl's mother and demanding to see her child. What should they do?

"Stall her until I get there," he said. "Under no circumstances is she to go near the girl without an officer present."

He hung up, hoping they'd follow instructions. Sometimes they did; sometimes they didn't. It was a busy place.

Dammit. He still had to get down to the park. Find that necklace, if it was still there. He flipped on his lights and stepped on the gas.

He parked where he'd parked last night and sprinted toward the spot where he'd found her. When he was about fifteen feet away, he saw a man stop, lean down, pick something up, and stuff it in his pocket. He sped up, caught up with the man, and said, "Police, sir. I just saw you put something in your pocket. Can you show me what it was?"

Not a man. A boy, maybe sixteen, who ought to have been in school. He smirked at Burgess and said, "Nope. Sorry. Finders keepers, okay."

"Not exactly. This is a crime scene and you may have just picked up something that's important evidence."

Kid just stood and smirked. Burgess suppressed the urge to slap the smirk off his face. Guys his age could be so stupid about who they showed attitude to. Back in the dark ages, when he'd been sixteen, sassing a cop would have gotten him gut punched and probably kicked as well. The world got better and the world got worse. He was aware that a small crowd was gathering around them but ignored it.

"I think you've got a gold necklace in your pocket, and if you do, you need to give it to me."

"Nope. Not gonna."

Fuck. The clock was running. He couldn't count on the hospital keeping the girl safe, and he was stuck here with a snotty little brat. He said, "What's your name, son?"

Got the expected, "None of your fucking business. I didn't do anything."

He said, "You've got two choices. Give me the necklace, or I'll call patrol and you can sit in a cell until I have time to deal with you. And your family. And your school, since that's where you ought to be right now. Your choice."

Burgess watched the kid's body tense as he considered whether he could outrun a heavy old cop. Saw the shoulders relax as he made the right decision. Kid said, "Aw, fuck it," reached in his pocket, and pulled out the chain. Instead of handing it to Burgess, he dropped it on the ground, then took off running. The crowd that had gathered, likely hoping for a confrontation, scattered. Cops did little these days without an audience eager to see them get it wrong. It was a hell of an incentive to do the job.

Burgess wasn't going to chase him, but he'd got the kid's face in his memory. One strike against him. He'd better not show up on the department's radar again any time soon. He tucked the necklace into an evidence envelope, wrote the necessary details, then headed over to the hospital.

FIVE

He went first to the information desk, where the friendly volunteer there directed him to a woman sitting in a chair in the lobby. He didn't immediately go to her. Instead, he called the nurse's station on the girl's floor and confirmed that she was still unconscious and no one had been allowed to see her. Then he crossed the room and sat down across from the woman.

When she put down the tattered and dated magazine she hadn't been reading, and looked over at him, he knew immediately the woman was at least a relative, if not the girl's mother. Same thick, raven black hair and startling green eyes. Unlike the girl's pale and vulnerable youth, though, this woman, despite careful makeup, looked her age. She also looked hard and angry.

She was carefully dressed in tailored black slacks, a fitted camel cardigan over a cream-colored blouse, and neat black ankle boots. Her hair was coiffed and her jewelry understated and expensive. Nothing about her appearance suggested a hurried departure after getting a concerning phone call.

He needed to know who had made that call.

"Detective Sergeant Burgess, Portland police, ma'am." He pulled a chair closer and sat where he could observe her. "May I have your name, please?"

Her dismissive shrug was a practiced gesture. "I don't see why my name is relevant to anything, Officer. I just want to see my daughter and for some reason, the people in this place are refusing to let me. And—" She huffed out the "and," paused, and said, "And you need to tell me why."

Like him, she was someone used to being in charge of the conversation.

"Your name, ma'am," he repeated. "And some form of identification, please."

"Look. I haven't done anything that warrants police intruding into my business," she said. "Just tell that bozo behind the desk I'm here to collect Colleen."

She wasn't going to collect anyone. Not for a while. Maybe never, depending on what the story was.

He repeated his request for her name and some identification. After a few more huffs, and some meant-to-be-withering glares, she opened her handbag and dug around. After considering and rejecting a number of cards, she pulled out a driver's license and thrust it at him. A Connecticut license that even to a rookie would have screamed fake.

Keeping up the charade, he took out his notebook and copied the information. The name was Amanda Chambers McGovern. She was forty-eight years old. She lived in a southern Connecticut town. She was five feet six and had green eyes and black hair. Probably the age and physical characteristics were real. Or close to real. He doubted that the name was.

He handed it back. "Thank you, Ms. McGovern."

She tucked it away and zipped her bag shut, preparing to rise. "So, are we done here?"

"Ma'am, we're just beginning," Burgess told her. "You say you believe that your daughter is a patient in this hospital?"

"Of course she is. I know she is. And I don't understand—"

He held up a hand to stop her. "Your daughter's name is?"

"I told you. Colleen."

"McGovern?"

She nodded.

"How old is your daughter?"

She had to think about that. "Fifteen."

He wondered why she had to think about that. "And she lives with you at this address?" He read off what he'd written down.

"Of course she does."

"When is the last time you saw her?"

Again, she had to consider. A lot of time spent on her appearance, less on her story. "Two days ago."

"Morning? Evening?"

She shrugged in irritation. "What difference does that make?"

"Just answer the question, please, Ms. McGovern."

"Morning."

"So, the last time you saw Colleen was two days ago at your home in Connecticut? Is that correct?"

She nodded.

"And what was Colleen's condition at that time?"

"What the hell does that mean? Her condition? Are you asking if she was pregnant or something?"

"I'm asking whether she was healthy. Well-nourished. Not physically harmed in any way."

"Well, of course she wasn't harmed. Alan and I aren't monsters. Colleen can be difficult sometimes but no one hurts her. We don't believe in that."

It was such an obvious lie. No healthy teenager got into the condition of the girl he'd found in the park in only two days.

She sounded uncertain, though, as if his questions were giving rise to questions of her own. Beneath her belligerent responses, Burgess understood that this woman was scared. Scared and worried about police involvement. Her mission was clearly to grab the girl and get away as quickly as possible. He hoped to learn why.

"So, you last saw your daughter in the morning two days ago? Is that correct?"

He got a nod. "And you haven't seen her since?"

No answer.

"Has she been in contact with you during that period?"

Again, no answer.

"Does your daughter have a phone?"

A shrug. "She says she lost it."

The woman was beginning to fidget in her chair.

"Did you know her whereabouts during that time?"

A reluctant "No."

He could practically see thoughts skittering through her mind as she searched for an answer that wouldn't make her appear to be a negligent parent. Not wanting to give her time to formulate some lies, he pressed on.

"Is your daughter in the habit of disappearing for days at a time?"

She shook her head vehemently. "Of course not."

"Is she a habitual runaway?"

No answer. He made a mental note to be in touch with the police in Connecticut in towns near the ones on that fake license. See if this family was known to them. Harder with a fake name, but if the daughter was a runaway? With an appearance so distinctive?

"How did you know to look for your daughter here, in Portland, in this hospital, so far from home?"

A long silence. Her fingers knotted in her lap. Her eyes kept shifting around the room, looking anywhere but at him. She couldn't say her daughter had called. Not after she'd said the phone was missing. She finally said, "We got a call."

"A call from whom?"

"Just someone. Just…look, it's none of your business. I'm her mother. I'm here to collect my daughter and take her home, to her own doctor, where she can be taken care of properly. And you …you and this hospital…have no right to keep me from doing that."

"I'm sorry to be sharing bad news," he said. "But at this point, she's in no condition to be released."

"Oh sure," she said. "I know how hospitals work. They see that we have great insurance and want to hang onto Colleen and run up the bill. Well, sorry. That's not happening."

Right. Until now, they'd had no idea even what the girl's name was, never mind where she was from or what kind of health insurance her family carried. The hospital still didn't and all Burgess had was a bunch of lies. Despite this and other suppositions, at no point had she shown any concern or even curiosity about her daughter's condition. Had the mysterious "they" who had called said the girl was okay?

Everything about this situation was very wrong. There was no way this woman could be allowed to remove her daughter from this hospital, this city, this state. Nor to even visit the girl without a police officer present.

She said, "Are you refusing to let me see her?"

"It would be helpful to us if you could identify the unknown girl who was brought in last night."

"Unknown girl?" She stared at him. "Colleen wouldn't tell you her name? Or give you our contact information? That's just like her, really. She can be so stubborn."

All output, not input. She hadn't heard what he'd said about the girl's condition. Burgess shook his head and put on a serious expression. "I'm afraid you are unaware of the gravity of the situation."

"Of what situation? Look, Colleen is a great one for spinning a story. She might have told you anything. She's...uh...she's given to rather fantastical tales sometimes. She probably got off a bus, realized she'd gotten herself into another scrape, and made up some story about being kidnapped or homeless or something so someone would give her a bed for the night. It really shouldn't be your problem. I can take it from here. I've got the car and I'm ready to settle her bills and drive her home."

This woman was lying in so many ways. Burgess wondered if she thought he was some rube country cop she believed she could bamboozle.

Sometimes, in situations like this, he felt like the real Joe Burgess was somewhere up by the ceiling, hovering there, watching the interaction between an angry, defensive liar and a bulky, late middle-aged cop with a scarred face and untamed graying hair. The man by the ceiling watched the man in the chair, the man who always hoped to see caring and concern and too often saw anger and indifference. He also felt the stirrings of a real mystery here, not that the girl's condition hadn't suggested that already.

"I'm sorry," he said. "The girl who was brought in last night, your daughter if she is in fact your daughter, is in no condition to be released. She's still in the earliest stages of being evaluated."

"Oh, spare me the drama. I'm sure Colleen's fine."

She said it firmly but again there was a wariness behind the words, as though for the first time this woman was considering the possibility there was more going on than a willful and errant child. Instead of backing down, though, or asking more questions, he watched her become more resolute.

"I'm taking my daughter home with me. Now."

"And I'm afraid that's impossible."

"You aren't a doctor. And you can't expect me to take medical advice…" A pause, "Or childrearing advice from some boondocks cop."

The people of Portland would be surprised to learn their city, largest in the state and a cosmopolitan scene that was drawing new residents from all over the country, was considered the boondocks. Burgess had been about to offer to allow the woman to see the girl, assuming the medical staff approved, and as long as an officer was present. Now he waited to see what she'd do next.

She got out a phone, waved it at him, and said, "This is ridiculous. I'm calling our lawyer."

Burgess nodded and got out his own phone. Keeping a wary eye on the woman, he stepped away and called the department's attorney. He explained the situation and said they needed an order to protect an abused child from being removed from the state. She'd know what to do. Then he called social services and asked for a social worker to be assigned to the case. All the while, the woman across from him was yelling into her phone at someone on the other end about how she needed to speak with Alan right now, it was urgent, to hell with his meeting. She needed his help. The whole situation with Colleen was going to hell and it had to be dealt with now.

At least it appeared one thing she'd said was true: that the girl's name was Colleen.

People around them were staring like it was theater. Which, given how much about the woman was fake, it sort of was.

Alan must have gotten on the phone, because the woman turned her back and lowered her voice. Not low enough. Burgess, with decades of overhearing what he wasn't supposed to hear, moved closer, snapped a photo of her, and listened.

"Godddammit, Alan. The girl's gotten away and now she's in some podunk hospital up here in Maine and they won't even let me see her. The big cop who's in charge says 'she's in no shape to leave.' I mean, what the fuck? It's supposed to be a safe place, right? Just somewhere they can impose some discipline. Teach her she can't run around like a crack whore just because she doesn't like you. Like us."

She listened, shaking her head, and said, "But how can I do that? Just leave her? She might not be your child, but she is mine. I mean, what if he's telling the truth? What if she's actually injured? What if she needs to be in a hospital?"

She listened again, lip caught between her teeth. She didn't like what the man was saying. Said, "How are they going to do that?" Waited, then asked, "Well, what did he say on the phone? You talked to him. What did he tell you?"

A pause. Then, "No. I won't calm down. I am not hysterical and I am not being difficult. The cop asked if she was injured when she was home...Oh, I said two days ago. Of course I said no. But what if they...what if she really is--"

A pause while she listened. "But I don't see how. Look, Alan, I just need to bring Colleen home and we'll figure something out."

A couple of nods, some murmured, "Okay" and "Sure," and "But." Finally, she said, this time so low Burgess almost couldn't hear it, "Of course I didn't use my real license, Alan. That's why I got it. I'm not an idiot, you know."

After a couple of bright, chipper farewells, she wheeled back to Burgess. "I would like to see my daughter now."

Burgess by the ceiling and Burgess on his phone merged into one suspicious detective. He waved toward the chairs they'd been occupying. "Sit down, please. We're not done here."

SIX

He fumbled in his pocket for the necklace, planning to ask her about it. It was in his hand as he turned to look at her.

She'd remained standing and seemed to have reached some decision. She shook her head. Said, "In a moment. I need to find a ladies' room first. It was a long drive and all that coffee and I—" She looked around. "And anxiety about my daughter. Do you know where?"

Like he was the information desk. But despite his suspicions, he couldn't really detain her, so he directed her down the hall, then followed at a discreet distance. Stopping near the restroom door, he pulled out his phone again and called Kyle. Said, "I need you here. Got a woman claiming to be the girl's mother, and there's a lot about her that's concerning, including a fake license."

Kyle, as always, just said, "On my way." They could discuss things further when he arrived.

Women came and went from the bathroom, but no sign of her. One, scruffy and furtive, worn hands curled before her chest like a small rodent, actually paused to stare at him as she passed. Something off about that. Like maybe the woman in the bathroom had asked her to do something? The staring woman had an eager, expectant look but didn't try to lure him away.

He was getting impatient, about to invade the bathroom, to hell with propriety, when the fight broke out in the lobby. Two men, both intoxicated and belligerent, piled in through the door, squared off, and started swinging at each other and shoving furniture.

A woman screamed.

A child wailed.

The hospital had security, but he was a cop and he was close, so he headed toward the lobby.

He grabbed the nearest man, yelled, "Police" in his ear, and the guy subsided like a popped balloon. The other man made for the door just as Kyle entered. "Grab him," Burgess called.

They sat the two men down in chairs and Burgess said, "What the hell was that about?"

First man flashed a nearly toothless grin, swiped at a trickle of blood from the corner of his mouth, and laughed, his breath a fetid wave of alcohol fumes. "Lady gave Moira buncha cash for us to cause a disturbance. Was we good?"

Was it good to damage furniture and frighten children? To make a scene in a place where people were already so stressed? What fucking world did this guy inhabit? Of course Burgess knew what world. The one his father had inhabited. Broken furniture, beaten his mother, and frightened his sisters. As an escape technique, though? Whoever this woman and her Alan were, they were people indifferent to anything but their own interests.

Fuck, Burgess thought. He told Kyle, "Keep 'em here," and headed for the bathroom. This time he didn't wait in the hall but charged right in. Aside from a woman applying eye makeup, who ignored him as she leaned into the mirror, the room was empty.

God, he thought as he walked back to the lobby. *Fooled like that? He was no better than a rookie.* Burgess up by the ceiling watching gave a cynical nod. Burgess lumbering down the hall pushed down a wave of anger. He always hated to lose. Hated it even more when his carelessness had let it happen.

They grabbed what they could from the two drunks, including some information that might help them locate Moira, then headed for security to see what they could learn about the woman's whereabouts.

No sense in rushing out to the garage. She'd had enough time to get away.

Video showed that as soon as Burgess had turned toward the lobby, she'd peeked out, seen him moving away, then booked it in the other direction, heading to the parking garage. Video showed her getting into a shiny, dark sedan and driving out too fast for the tight confines of the garage. On an otherwise impeccable vehicle, the plates were smeared with dirt in an attempt to make them unreadable.

They grabbed a screen shot of the car's plate. Rocky Jordan, their computer maven, might be able to work with it. A few letters and numbers, at least. But, like the faked license, it showed that whoever this woman and her Alan were, they definitely had something to hide. Something that involved the damaged girl upstairs and the mysterious "him" she'd referred to on the phone. He was beginning to formulate some ideas about what might be going on.

"Someone's gonna make a grab for the girl," Kyle said. "Or finish her off."

What Burgess thought, too. "Not on our watch," he said.

He reminded Kyle about the nondescript woman who'd come to the hospital late last night, asking questions about a girl who'd been brought in. And about the man at the station. A couple—if they were a couple—who'd had information that wasn't public knowledge. He turned to the security guy who was helping them and asked to see the video from last night.

Despite her scruffy appearance, the woman moved confidently, seemed aware of where cameras were placed, and had done her best to avoid them. Still, there were some shots they could grab, something else to study when they got back to 109. The woman must have parked on the street because there was no video of her in the garage or the outside lot.

"I'm not comfortable leaving her," Burgess said. "The girl. Not when so many people are interested in her."

Kyle nodded. "And we know how busy security can get. We've got to put someone on her room."

"Or an army."

Kyle tilted his head as though considering that. "Wouldn't it be nice. Burgess's army has a nice ring to it."

They thanked security, gathered their photos, and left.

"Before we go, let's take a look at the girl," Kyle said. "You've seen her but I haven't. I want the picture in my head." He shrugged. "And then go back to the park. See if anyone saw anything last night. It all helps. Cold night or not, there are always people around."

Which it did. You could look at crime scene photos 'til the cows came home, but it wasn't the same as viewing the victim. Or as going back to the park and standing in the spot where the girl had been found, surveying the environment. And seeing what the city had to tell them.

Upstairs, he and Kyle checked in at the nurse's station, then went to the girl's room. Lying there, unmoving, she looked small and fragile and almost as pale as the sheets, a look sometimes described as 'deathly pale.' The only color beyond the striking darkness of her hair was the vivid purple of her bruised and torn wrists.

He'd been too busy to consider it before but now Burgess was seized with the fear that she might not recover. That maybe she'd been held too long, or the conditions had been too harsh. That despite her desperate attempt at escape, it had not been enough.

He stood at the foot of her bed, listening to the hum and hiss of machines, and made the promise he always made to victims: that he would get her justice. Usually, those victims were dead. The promise felt even more solemn, somehow, made to this girl.

He usually succeeded. Not always. No cop had a perfect record, and the ones they couldn't solve often haunted them for life.

He wondered how her mother, or whatever relative to her that woman was, would have reacted to seeing the girl like this. It wasn't something that could easily be shrugged off. It was a powerful and heartbreaking visual. Was she so cold she would have been unaffected? Would she have seen this only in relation to herself?

Unwonted, he heard her confident, dismissive voice telling him that her daughter was an opportunistic liar, given to fantasy, to telling elaborate lies. How would she have dismissed this?

He turned to Kyle. "She deserves all that we can give her."

Kyle nodded. No need for speech.

They went to their cars, drove to the park, and got out. Burgess led the way to the spot by the rock and the trash can where he'd found the girl and related the story about finding the necklace this morning. As Kyle shared his cynicism about human nature, Burgess included the story of the little "finders keepers" weasel who'd tried to run off with it.

They turned slowly, surveying the area around the park. Mostly highway and city streets. Even in the middle of the night, someone would likely have spotted a staggering, naked girl on the highway or near a street. Yet she'd gotten there somehow. No way a naked girl could have hitched a ride. But could she have stowed away, maybe in the back of a truck? Or had she escaped from somewhere nearby?

"Maybe she had a coat?" Kyle suggested. "A coat. A blanket. Something that would have covered her, made her look more like one of our homeless."

"Unhoused," Burgess said. "I think that's the new PC term."

Cops, seeing scarce department funds going for diversity classes rather than training and equipment to keep themselves and the public safe, got kinda cynical about terminology. Not "illegal," but "undocumented." Heck, many people were undocumented. It wasn't like the state kept good track or anything or everyone carried ID.

"Let's just walk around a bit. See if we run into anyone who was here last night. Not winter yet, despite the cold. People would have been out."

They separated, Burgess heading toward the highway, Kyle toward downtown, doing the slow step, look, step as they went. Sometimes the smallest thing could be a clue.

Maybe a hundred feet ahead, there were three men huddled on a bench, clothed in the motley layers the unhoused used to keep themselves warm. Burgess knew one of them, a man name Buddy, who had known his late friend Reggie. He walked up to them and exchanged greetings.

One of the men, a bearded redhead a bit younger than the others, lurched to his feet. "You wanna sit, Detective?" he asked.

Burgess remembered his name. Leon. And that Leon was prone to get into trouble. To help himself to things that weren't his. Said, "No. Thanks, Leon. I'm fine standing."

His eyes circled the group. "Hoping you might be able to help me with something."

They waited, and he gave it a beat before he said, "You've maybe heard we found a young girl here in the park last night? In real bad shape? You hear anything about that?"

The redhead said no. The man Burgess didn't know shook his head. The unknown man and Buddy put a little distance between themselves and redhead.

Buddy said, "Heard about it. Real young girl, right? Nekked, I heard. All beat to shit." He nodded to himself. "Bad times we live in, Joe. I wouldn't no way want to be young again." He considered. "Except maybe for the aches and stuff, ya know?"

"You got that right," Burgess agreed. "So what did you hear?"

He didn't press, although he thought Buddy's "heard" was actually something he'd seen.

"Heard she came running down from the highway. Up there." Buddy pointed up to 295, where traffic was zooming past. "Man said she jumped." He considered. "Jumped or fell, is what I heard, off the back of a pickup."

Again, Burgess waited. Minds like Buddy's, dimmed by years of alcohol and hard living, worked kind of like Magic Eight Balls and could take their time to summon up the facts.

After a bit, Buddy rubbed his stubbly chin, a raspy sound against calloused fingers, and nodded. "Guess she had a blanket around her and she dropped it while she was running." He shrugged. "That's all I heard."

"Nobody following her?"

"Not that I seen," Buddy said, forgetting he was supposed to be reporting what someone else had seen.

"Any idea what time this was?"

Buddy grinned and tapped his wrist. "Fergot to put my watch on this morning, I'm afraid. And yesterday morning, comes to that. Time don't matter much down here, so long as we make it to whatever church that's serving supper in time." Another pause. "Different days. Different churches, ya know?"

"Some of 'em better than others?"

37

"Sure as hell are."

"That blanket," Burgess said to the group. "Anybody notice what happened to it?"

The redhead, Leon, shuffled within the confines of a blanket, shook his head a few times, and reluctantly unwrapped. Without a word, he offered the blanket to Burgess.

Burgess folded it over his arm, then looked toward the highway. "Can you show me where you found it?"

Leon studied his feet again, made like he was going to speak, then shook his head, and Burgess understood what was unspoken here. The girl hadn't dropped the blanket. She'd fallen unconscious and Leon had helped himself.

Burgess stomped hard on his rising anger. It wouldn't help here. This was definitely going to be a day when humanity disappointed him at every turn. The kind of day he'd developed the hide of an alligator to withstand. Girl runs from her captors, collapses in a park, and instead of getting her help, some useless excuse for humanity follows her and takes the only cover she has for himself. Leaving her totally exposed on a freezing night.

Buddy and the unknown man put more distance between themselves and Leon.

Before Burgess left them, he said, "Anything else I should know?"

All he got was a chorus of shrugs.

"You think of anything, you let me know. Okay?"

Now three men weren't looking at him. Maybe there was something more but he wasn't getting it right now. They probably figured they were off the hook, but he'd be back.

He turned and walked away to look for Kyle.

Kyle was standing by the rock where the girl had been, a small, bright-eyed woman beside him. Kyle looked at the blanket, shook his head, and didn't say anything. He didn't need to.

"So, Joe, this is Betsy..." Kyle hesitated and bent toward the woman. "Remind me of your last name, ma'am."

"Craig," she said. Her voice was very small and soft.

"Betsy was down in the park last night. On cold nights, she sometimes comes down with blankets and coats in case anyone needs them."

"And it was the first real cold," she said.

He wondered where this was going. If this woman had come upon the girl, she wouldn't have left her lying there. So he waited.

"It's not much," she said apologetically. "But Detective Kyle says you never know what will be helpful. Only I am kind of embarrassed to mention it. Except for the girl. What he told me about the girl. I wish I would of found her when I was making my rounds. But he says she was there by that rock, and when I walked past around midnight, there wasn't anyone there."

He filed away the information that the girl hadn't been there at midnight, wanting to ask whether she wasn't uneasy, a small woman alone walking the parks at night. He decided she'd be offended. She might have a calling, and who was he to challenge that, he who had a calling of his own? It was dangerous. And for some, the need to do good kept them from worrying about danger. He shifted to wondering what she might have to tell them and waited.

"Tell Detective Burgess what you saw," Kyle prompted.

The woman looked up at him. With her black cap and bright eyes, she reminded him of a small bird. She nodded.

"It was actually later. I'm sorry. Closer to one, I think. Way past my usual time. But my daughter and grandson were over earlier, so I got a late start. I was here, near the rock. I use the rock as kind of a marker. I start near the rock, walk the park until I've given out all the coats and blankets I can carry, then go to the car, get more, and walk the other way." She indicated clockwise and counterclockwise circles with her hands. "I'd just gotten back from my car with more blankets and such when I heard a vehicle door slam up on the highway. It's not a place someone ordinarily stops unless they have car trouble. That hour, if they're out at all, they're bent on getting home. Anyway, I looked up and I saw a man outside the truck, walking along the side of the road like he was looking for something that had fallen off the truck.

"That went on for maybe four or five minutes, mostly with him pacing beside the truck like he was waiting for something. Then another car stopped. Silver. A little station wagon? Probably a Subaru, though a lot of cars look alike these days. They conferred. After a bit, they climbed over the railing, came down the bank, across those access roads, and into the park."

Burgess had found the girl around two. She'd been in plain sight, here by the rock. If she'd been here at one, or earlier, Betsy would have seen her, so she must have hidden from someone looking for her somewhere else, then gotten this far and collapsed.

The woman looked down at her feet. "I feel silly, saying this, since I'm out at all hours and among some pretty rough people, but there was something about them. About him. Even at a distance, he gave off a vibe that made me uneasy. I have to learn to read people. A bit like you, I guess. Quick reads about safety. I...I didn't finish my rounds, like I normally would. I went straight back to the car and drove home."

She took a breath and raised her eyes, looking from Kyle's face to his. "I think you will understand this, Detectives. There are some people in our world who are absolutely evil, and I can feel it. It...it surrounds them like a cloud. A dark cloud. Or an aura. Something." She sighed. "I know. You probably think I'm another one of your crazies, since I'm down here in the park doing dangerous things. But I've always been able to spot evil, ever since I was a little girl. And that man was evil."

SEVEN

He and Kyle both nodded. Most cops did believe in evil. Did understand that some people are genuinely, irredeemably bad and are indifferent to, or take genuine pleasure in, the suffering they cause. They could sense it, so why not believe she could?

"We understand," Kyle said. "You were smart to go home."

"Before you left, did you have a chance to observe the woman?" Burgess asked.

"I'm sorry. But no. I…I'm sorry, but I was scared and I left. And the thing is that not much scares me."

Was it only a sense she'd gotten, or something she'd seen or heard? Burgess asked.

"Just a sense. But a powerful sense."

They collected her contact information and let her go.

"Sweet Jesus," Kyle said, as they watched her small departing figure. "You go to bed one night thinking about getting a decent night's sleep and wake up to a mess like this." He paused and looked at Burgess. "Except it called you out earlier."

"And if it hadn't, they would have found her or the girl would have died."

"Long shot, but I wonder if patrol noticed anything? Noticed that truck or that car?"

"We've got their photos, the woman and the man. Assuming they're the same ones who went to the hospital and came to the department. It's a place to start," Burgess said. "Their photos and that car registration. You get anywhere with that, yet?"

"The Subaru? Or the Prius? Or the house the Subaru was registered to? You mean before my fearless leader called me away to deal with some brawling drunks? I was just getting started. I'm happy to go back to that now."

Kyle looked at the blanket, which Burgess was still holding. "I don't want to ask, do I?"

"Depends on whether you still have much faith in human nature."

"I do try."

If it had been Burgess saying that, Kyle might have agreed that he was very trying. But this was the reverse and Kyle didn't try Burgess's patience. He was the world's best teammate.

Something for Burgess to write in his gratitude diary.

"Besides the woman, Betsy, did you find anything?" he asked.

Kyle mock-glared at him. "The woman's not enough?" He shook his head. "Nope. I'd say it was quiet night last night, but we both know better. You coming back to 109? Want to grab coffee first?" he said.

He patted his lean stomach. "Too busy for breakfast this morning. The girls were arguing and Michelle was annoyed with both of them. Being peacemaker before I'm fully awake isn't easy. And—"

Long pause, but Burgess knew what was coming. It was not an uncommon story. Kyle was living with, and in love with, a wonderful woman who wanted to get married. He wanted to marry her but was gun shy after his first awful marriage. Michelle was helping him raise his two girls but wanted a child of her own. With all they saw, and the demands of his job, he was wary of bringing another child into the world, knowing what a crappy place it was. Now that his girls were teenagers, with all the issues that brought, the tension in his household was rising exponentially.

"And I told Michelle I thought a Christmas wedding would be nice," Kyle finished.

Families created such complicated balancing acts. Burgess had proposed to Chris a year ago, yet, despite accepting his proposal, she still refused to marry him. She jokingly called herself Mrs. Almost Burgess. Unless that was Almost Mrs. Burgess. He didn't find it funny. Everyone assumed they were already married and he was running out of patience for her to make an honest man of him.

Sometimes it was easier to lose himself in a case where he'd be so caught up he didn't have time to dwell on how annoying his domestic situation was. And then, because he was scrupulously honest with himself, he'd also have to reckon with the damage constant exposure to darkness and violence did to him and to his family. Sometimes he wished he could take a stiff brush, stick it in his ear, and clean out the inside of his head.

"Coffee would be good," he agreed. "And food. I also missed breakfast." The number of meals he missed, he ought to be thin.

Before they walked back to their cars, Burgess took a few photos of the rock and the ground where he'd found the girl. It was a thing he did—record the empty space where the victim had been as a visual reminder of how their challenge would be to fill in that space with details.

———

Fed and caffeinated, he and Kyle went back to 109. He gave the blanket to Dani, who frowned at a chain of custody that had the blanket going, presumably, from their unconscious victim to an unhoused man named Leon Vernon to Burgess.

Dani, watching him fill out the details, said, "Does that mean what I think it means?" A pause, then she answered her own question. "I guess it has to, doesn't it, or else we would have found it with her or when we searched. People." A long silence. Dani was young still, and not entirely jaded.

"I'm sorry," he said.

"You must have been so mad," she said.

"Disgusted," he said. "I always think I'm immune to being surprised by people's awful behavior, and then I'm reminded of it again."

In the bad old days, guy did something like that, the cops would have set him straight. Leon and that weasel kid. Now there were so many people who needed to be set straight it would be a full-time job that left no room for actual policing.

Yeah, he was not in a good mood. These days it was harder to be cheery and upbeat when he'd missed a night's sleep.

People who knew him would likely say he'd never been cheery and upbeat. He waved a hand toward the blanket. "I'm hoping it will tell us something," he said.

"If it's there, we'll find it, Joe." Dani said. "It's a nice blanket. Vintage. My grandmother had some like this. Ugly brown but super warm thick wool. She called them her camp blankets."

He'd almost forgotten the necklace in his pocket. A delicate gold chain with the letter *C*. He pulled it out and completed an evidence form for that, too.

Dani was still watching, an anxious look on her face. "We missed that?" she said.

"Under some grass that was heavy with frost. We all missed it. Terry spotted it in one of your photos and grabbed the magnifying glass. I went back for it this morning. Almost lost it, too."

The minute he said that, he regretted it. Being a stickler for having cops adhere to the rules had earned him the title of "meanest cop in Portland," but he didn't want her to feel criticized. He had no complaints about Dani and Wink.

He told her the story of the snotty kid.

"Bet he's still looking over his shoulder," she said. "Nobody messes with Joe Burgess."

"Would that that were true," he said.

They shared a laugh and he left the lab and went upstairs, wishing what she'd said *was* true. There were people in this case who were definitely messing with him. Top of the list was that woman this morning who'd thought she could just waltz in and take the girl away. At least she'd given them a name. Colleen. If she hadn't been lying about that, too.

Stan Perry wasn't at his desk. Probably still on the trail of that Prius and its plates. Kyle was immersed in his screen. Burgess stopped at his desk, tucked most of the photos into his drawer, and carried the ones of that car and its smudged plates to Rocky Jordan. If Burgess got a kick out of being on the real-world trail of bad guys, Jordan got a similar thrill from using technology to catch them. Portland was lucky to have someone who wanted to be a cop who also loved the internet searches, scanning videos, breaking into devices and finding ways to get information the baddies thought was hidden or destroyed.

Jordan swiveled in his chair when Burgess came in. "Hope you've got something for me, Joe. I'm feeling underutilized today."

Burgess had never known anyone before who declared themselves to be underutilized. Many, if not most, people longed for that situation.

Only that wasn't true. They might long for breaks in the action, but no one wanted a boring job.

No one worth their salt. Who had a job worth doing.

Michelle and Chris might wish their men would give up active detecting in favor of the safety of desks, but he and Kyle would go mad. Did they really want two bored, deeply unhappy and restless men on their hands? Chris would probably say yes. Then reconsider and say no. He couldn't answer for Michelle.

He laid the photos down on the desk and gave Jordan a quick recap of the story. He finished with, "Looks like Connecticut plates."

Jordan leaned in and studied the photos. Got a magnifying glass and studied some more. Said, "I'll see what I can do," so Burgess left him to it, but the techie was smiling as he bent to the task.

Maybe the police could adopt a new motto: **Want to Banish Boredom? Come Serve and Protect.**

As a recruitment strategy, it had possibilities. These days, they needed possibilities. The ranks were down and constant criticism and public scrutiny of everything they did, along with the rising possibility of lawsuits, had made the profession unattractive.

The instinct that had kept him alive all these years was also good at protecting him from his department nemesis, Captain Paul Cote. Somehow, he knew Cote would be lurking by his desk, waiting for all the details of this new case. And damn! He'd left some of the photographs at his desk. Luckily, only the ones from this morning's trip to the hospital and not the ones from last night. And at the back of a drawer. It was irritating to have to live defensively in his own department.

Cote was his superior up the food chain, and therefore theoretically owed deference and duty, but he was also notoriously careless with information and had an ugly tendency to dwell on the violent, sordid, and sexual. They called those people who gathered at accidents and crime scenes "blood maggots" and Burgess thought the label fit Cote as well.

Burgess figured Cote had been toilet trained too early and it had damaged him forever. Something had. In any case, Burgess wasn't inclined to share photos of that poor girl's naked body with Cote if he could help it. Those photos were in the conference room, buried in a stack of papers.

The captain could ferret them out if he was willing to take the time, but he preferred to snoop on detectives' desks and in the murder books.

Burgess ducked into the conference room and pressed his back against the wall where Cote couldn't see him if he peered in the door. Cowardly, maybe, but he did it anyway. When he heard Cote say, "Tell him I want to see him," to Kyle, he gave it another minute, then returned to his desk.

"Captain Cote wants to see you," Kyle said as he passed. Nothing more, but they both knew Kyle's real message was "stay out of sight."

He had reports to write and thinking to do, then he would see what he might learn about those photos and whether he could find any matches. As he thought further, he realized that Rocky Jordan would be happy to scan the photos of the man and woman from last night and the woman this morning into the computer. Probably also happy to do the photo matches, and Burgess was eager to see the results of that.

He grabbed the rest of the photos from his desk and carried them to Rocky's office.

"I'm good, but I'm not that good," Jordan said, turning away from his screen.

"Just couldn't stand the thought of you being underutilized. So when you get a chance, can you scan these people in? I want to see if photo match can come up with anything."

He was turning to go when he hesitated. He went back and spread the array out beside Jordan. "This guy," he pointed at the man who'd filed the incoherent missing person report, "came in in the middle of the night and wanted to file a missing person report. It was so sketchy they called me. We suspect he's involved somehow with the girl we found down in the park last night."

Rocky made a note or two and waited.

Burgess pointed to the woman who'd gone to the hospital trying to get information about a girl who had been brought in. "We believe she was with the man earlier, down in the park. Witness says they seemed to be looking for the girl. Seems like then they split up on separate missions to see if they could locate her."

He got out his phone and showed Jordan his photos of the woman from this morning. "And I interviewed this woman at the hospital this morning. She claimed to be the girl's mother and insisted on seeing her, so they called me. I interviewed her and got a bunch of lies. Then she took off. It's her plate you're trying to read. I'll send you the pictures."

Glad that Jordan was on the case and that with his skills he'd get answers if there were some long before Burgess could, Burgess went back to his desk.

He wrote his reports for last night, for early this morning in the park, wrote up his interview with the woman claiming to be Colleen's mother at the hospital, and then what they'd learned from various witnesses when he and Kyle returned to the park. Then, because he'd asked even though he thought the NCIC missing persons information wouldn't be useful to identify the girl they'd found, he checked the responses.

The limited information he'd been able to include in his query was broad and therefore likely to bring many responses. It had.

He began to go through them. It was depressing how many missing young girls there were and how it spoke to their vulnerability. There were no reports that fit the girl maybe named Colleen who was over at the hospital, but another one caught his eye. It was a month old. Another fifteen-year-old girl, this one from New York. Described as unmanageable and a chronic runaway. The parents had reported her missing after pressure from her school when she'd failed to show up for ten days. Pressure from the school. Pressure from the local cops. A sense that the parents weren't being forthcoming. Her name was Melanie Porter. In the photo, she looked scared and lost.

He wrote down the relevant information. Thought he'd make a call to the local police, see what their take was. Because there was something about it. That cop's instinct again. He considered what he'd overheard the woman say on the phone. "What did he say?" and "It's supposed to be a safe place, right?"

What and where was it, this supposedly safe place? Was it a place where parents sent their incorrigible children? A place where the children were starved and beaten and physically restrained? If there was such a place—and yes, he was letting his speculation run wild here—did the parents choosing to send their children there know what it was like or had they believed it was a good, safe place?

Maine was a large, rural, sparsely populated state, especially once you got north of Augusta. He had to wonder—had someone set up shop somewhere offering to reform people's errant teenagers? Someone whose methods were harsh and dangerous, who perhaps lied to the parents about the nature of the place. Sold them on a kind of rural summer camp where the kids were calmed by hard work and communing with nature. It wouldn't be hard for those who wanted to profit from "reforming" teens to operate under the radar.

Talk about looking for needles in haystacks. But what if that's where this girl he was reading about was? Where the girl over at the hospital had been? Or it might just be that Detective Sergeant Joe Burgess, with his head full of the awful things people did to each other, was allowing his dark imagination to go wild and making something out of nothing. He had to do more digging, even if it led nowhere.

He needed to look at more missing girls and see if any pattern emerged. He stared unseeing at his screen. It looked like his case might have just gotten far more complicated.

EIGHT

He was pulled from his musings by Captain Cote, who invaded his consciousness by appearing at his side, settling his bulk on Burgess's desk, and saying, "I need to be updated about this business with the unidentified girl."

Of course he did. There might be something salacious about it that, like a dog with a bone, Cote could carry back to his office and gnaw on.

Burgess gave his usual deflecting response. "Just sent you all my reports on that, Paul. Kyle's working on some research regarding a person who may be related, and Perry's out in the field, following up on some stolen plates that may also be connected. It's early days yet. We're still getting a handle on what we're dealing with."

Nothing more. Keep it close and keep it lean was their rule, especially where Cote was concerned. The man could ask, and Burgess would answer as well as he could without giving too much away. It was a ridiculous way to do business when they were all supposed to be on the same side, but Cote had an infuriating habit of spilling details they wanted to keep close to the press, as though the press was his team and Burgess and the other investigators a mere annoyance that had to be tolerated.

Still, the food chain was the food chain and deference was owed. He waited to see where Cote would go.

"Young girl?" Cote said.

"We believe so."

"She hasn't——"

How could Cote know they had a case and not know anything about it? He would say it was because Burgess and his team were tardy in writing their reports. Burgess would say it was because Paul Cote didn't like to be bothered with details, except those that caught on the tips of his curiosity, and so didn't bother to read reports or ask open-ended questions that would actually bring him up to speed.

Burgess took a deep breath. He wasted far too much time and energy working around Cote and worrying about the harm he could cause. As a lumbering old dinosaur, and in this case one that hadn't gotten any sleep last night, he needed to pace himself. Save whatever energy he did have for the work that mattered.

He gave Cote a quick summary of the situation, leaving out the kinds of details his team would understand but Cote wouldn't—like the fact that he had heard his city calling him down to the park last night—and including the information about the woman claiming to be the girl's mother but refusing to be forthcoming with essential information. About the lies she'd told and their belief her license was a fake.

Intending to take Cote further down that road so they could work the other angles in peace, he said, "What caring mother lies about every relevant detail including when she last saw her daughter, and carries a fake license? You know anyone who carries a fake license?"

Cote agreed that it was suspicious. He said, "And the girl was naked?"

"She appeared to be running from someone or somewhere," Burgess said. "We haven't had time to canvass around the park yet. The…uh…regulars aren't especially good informants."

Oh, Joe, what a liar you are. He hoped Cote wouldn't read his report with the information about Leon, Buddy, and the woman who gave blankets and coats to the homeless. He wasn't sure what Cote would do with the detail about Leon stealing the girl's blanket. Said, "We've got a lot to follow up on. Photos of the woman…women…at the hospital last night and this morning. The man who came in in the middle of the night to file a missing person report." He paused. "You heard about that?"

Cote nodded. Said, "What have you got from the girl? Isn't she your primary source of information?"

Burgess put on his bad news face. "She's in bad shape, Paul. Very bad. Unconscious. Looks like she was starved and beaten over an extended period of time. Open wounds on her wrists suggest she was restrained. Doctors are pessimistic about whether she'll recover." A pause. "Girl the age of my daughter. It's heartbreaking the way people use, abuse, and discard each other these days, Paul. I keep hoping… after those little Hispanic girls…for no more."

He gave it a beat for Cote to recall the case that had had them all reeling with the horror of it.

After too long a pause, Cote nodded.

"It's not the world we grew up in." Which he said because Cote liked to claim he was years younger than his actual age and Burgess liked to stick pins in that bubble whenever he could. He said, "We're hoping this is an isolated case but I'm looking at missing children and—" He sighed. "And who knows what will turn up, right?"

After waiting for more, which Burgess wasn't giving him, Cote shifted his weight off Burgess's desk and went away. A minute later their immediate boss, Lt. Vince Melia, appeared. He didn't park himself on the desk. Instead, he summoned Burgess to his office and said, "What've we got?"

Before he could start filling Melia in, he sensed someone behind him, and heard Kyle's voice from the door.

"Sorry to interrupt, Vince," Kyle said, coming in and sitting down beside Burgess. "Joe, have you heard from Stan?" To Melia he said, "Stan went to check on that Prius whose plates were illegally attached to a Subaru." Recognizing that wasn't enough, he added. "Guy driving the Subaru came in in the middle of the night to file a missing person report. The plates on his car were from a Prius."

"So sketchy they called me in," Burgess said.

He looked at his watch. "He ought to be back by now. He knows we're waiting for his information." He swiveled in his chair to look at Kyle. "You think something's wrong?"

Kyle hesitated, then nodded. "I do."

"You call him?"

"Yup. No answer."

Burgess was getting a bad feeling about this. This whole business. He'd pretty much had a bad feeling about it since instinct sent him down to the park last night. Now Perry's absence was amping things up.

Melia shook his head. "You don't think Stan's just—"

"He's pretty much stopped doing that," Burgess said. "It's not impossible…just less likely."

"And you two want to go and see what's up?"

"We do."

"Fill me in first."

So Burgess and Kyle shared all they'd learned so far. "Rocky's working on some bad photos of the license plate on the car the woman claiming to be the girl's mother was driving. Fake license, lotta lies, and mud smeared plates on an otherwise clean car. Then he's gonna do some photo matches, see if we can identify any of the players." Burgess paused. "We'll keep you up on it, Vince."

Which Melia knew they would.

They adjourned to the conference room, where Burgess tried to call Stan and got no answer.

"We've gotta check it out," Kyle said. "The old Stan might not respond if he's chasing something, but the new, reformed Stan Perry answers his phone. He's got a wife and kid who might be calling, never mind the meanest cop in Portland."

"And son, that will be you some day."

"I don't have the right personality for it."

Burgess headed for his desk. He grabbed his coat and his phone. Said, "I can train you." Then, "We'll take the Explorer." He waited while Kyle got his stuff and they headed down to the garage.

As they headed north on 295, he said, "What does your gut tell you, Terry?"

"Besides that I missed lunch?"

Which reminded Burgess that he had also missed lunch. Coffee and a breakfast sandwich didn't count. But it was Kyle who burned through his food fast. Kyle so lean and wired that much of the time he seemed to vibrate, even when he was sitting still. He said, "Besides that."

"That we are all going to regret the instinct that sent you down to the park."

Burgess thought it was true even though it meant the girl would have died. Died or been found by the mystery couple and taken back to more of the same mistreatment. And then probably died, given the state she was in. There was a lot of room for regret in their business, much of the time regret about things they couldn't help because they were part of the job.

It was a gray day, the kind that never resolved into a storm or sunshine, but hovered overhead with a sky like a dirty old quilt. As he aged, he found himself more sensitive to the lack of light that came with winter. More sensitive to the months of gloomy gray and brown before and after the snow came. He knew how to dress for the weather—his years on patrol had taught him that—but the last few years the cold could get to him despite the care he took.

He changed the subject. "So, you're really thinking about a Christmas wedding?"

"I'm really thinking about running away to Tahiti. The girls are difficult, at least my younger one is, and despite my excellent interviewing skills, I can't get her to tell me what the problem is. Michelle is difficult. That doesn't take interviewing skills. She wants marriage and a baby, which I do, honestly, plan to give her. Marriage, at least. The idea of returning to diapers and sleepless nights again isn't appealing. Even the cat is being difficult and I don't care what is bothering her."

Kyle sighed. "I'm becoming a perpetual downer. I think I'm starting to hate myself. A bottle and a solitary life are starting to look good again."

"You don't mean that," Burgess said. "You love your girls and you love Michelle. I don't know if you love the cat. And we both know where the bottle will take you."

"I don't love the cat. But the girls love the cat. And the cat, with that ability they possess to identify and annoy the person who doesn't like them, gets into my lap every time I sit down."

"My kids always wanted a dog," Burgess said. "Now, we've got Fideau, and, like with your cat, he definitely thinks he's my dog. Chris thinks it's funny. He is a pretty good dog, though. He's come through a couple times when I needed his help."

"He's a very good dog," Kyle agreed. "Must be some search and rescue training in his background. How he ever ended up with that thug is a mystery."

As with many police officers' pets, Fideau had become Burgess's dog when his owner was arrested.

They drove in silence for a while. Sometimes, when he was alone, Burgess used drives to ponder. Consider what he knew about the case and what direction to go next. If they were together, he and Kyle might play verbal ping pong, knocking ideas and possibilities back and forth to strategize about the case. Today, with too many question marks and not enough information, they were silent.

They drove past stubbly fields that had been hayed or harvested. Past dooryards with sagging Halloween decorations and rotting pumpkins. Pots of dry, brown chrysanthemums. Houses where the plastic stapled over the windows for warmth was already blowing loose. It had been a wet and windy fall. As they passed, he wondered what it would be like to live in the opaque cave that plastic created from November until April. Wasn't winter already depressing enough?

He knew, though, from growing up poor, the lengths people went to to save money.

They followed directions to a small, tired, white farmhouse with a sagging barn. They parked on the edge of the road to protect any tire marks there might be in the muddy driveway. At the edge of the drive-way, a tarp covered car was parked.

"Think that's the Prius the plates came from?"

Burgess shrugged and looked down. Tire tracks showed there had been a lot of recent vehicle activity as well as a lot of footprints around the Prius. There was no sign of Stan Perry's car.

"I'm getting a bad feeling about this," Kyle said, articulating what Burgess was feeling.

"Yeah. Let's check under that tarp first."

They walked on the grass along the edge of the driveway to the vehicle and lifted the tarp. It was a Prius and it didn't have plates.

"Let's see if anyone is home."

They knocked on the door. Waited. And knocked again.

As they waited, Burgess realized that they hadn't gotten any information about the registered owner of the Prius, only the name and address. That had been one of Perry's tasks. If he'd learned more about the owner and written a report, they hadn't seen it. More likely, Perry had gladly abandoned any internet searching before he left 109 in favor of being in the field. That had led him here. Now there was no one in the house—at least no one answering the door—and no sign of Perry.

Burgess turned and studied the driveway. One set of muddy tire tracks led to the door of the barn. He looked at Kyle. Said, "Barn."

In the dusty barn, they found Stan Perry's car under a mildewed tarp. Looking, if you were to peer through the fly-specked, cobwebbed windows, like it had been there forever. They photographed the tarp, then pulled it off and examined the car, including the trunk. No damage to the car. And no sign of Perry.

"Some days I feel like Fenimore Cooper's pathfinder," Burgess said, as he squatted to get a better look at the driveway. Two sets of heavy men's shoes or boots and a faint set of drag marks leading from the barn to the tarp-covered Prius.

Burgess photographed the tracks, then they made their way along the grass back to the Prius. They pulled off the tarp and peered into the car. In the rear hatch area, there was a big, dark bundle.

They tried the doors. The Prius was locked.

It only took a moment to decide that exigent circumstances meant it was necessary to use a pry bar on the trunk. Kyle waited by the car while Burgess went back to his Explorer for the bar. He handed it to Kyle and said, "You may do the honors."

Kyle pried open the hatch. Together they leaned in and pulled the heavy bundle toward them.

There were so many moments like this in their lives. Moments of anxiety about what would be on the other side of a door, in that alley, in that closet, somewhere out in the night. While other people who'd chosen safer jobs might turn and walk away, discretion being the better part of valor, cops rarely got that choice. Moments when their "I don't wanna" was as strong as any three-year-old's. But they stayed and carried on because "you gotta" trumped "don't wanna." Your colleague is missing, you go look for him. You find a suspicious bundle, you examine it, never mind what such bundles might have held in your past.

As though they were one, he and Kyle took a long breath in, exhaled, and Burgess reached for the mouth of what appeared to be a huge black canvas bag. He undid the rope that tied it shut. The opening revealed a head. Stan Perry's head. Then his body as they shoved the bag down to free him. All the while both silently praying, "Let him be alive."

NINE

He was alive. Unconscious, but alive.

"What the fuck?" Kyle said, as they wrestled the rest of Stan Perry out of the bag and cut the ties on his wrists and feet. "They didn't want to kill him so they just left him to die? When we find these assholes, I am going to—"

He stopped, because however strong the impulse was, they didn't get to do the things they wanted to when they encountered something like this. He stepped away and kicked a tire. Then stepped back. Said, "What do we do with him? Call an ambulance? Take him back to Portland with us?"

It was a complicated situation. What they'd normally do was call in their crime scene people to process this car and Stan's car, collect the bag, all that, but this place was out of their jurisdiction. Burgess studied Perry's still figure. "Maybe he's drugged," he said. "No sign of injuries beyond that wound on his head."

"Beyond the wound on his head?" Kyle countered. "Head wounds can be deadly."

"So, you call it. I'd put him in the Explorer, cover him with a blanket, and take a look at what's inside that house. What's a little more breaking and entering, right?"

So yeah, maybe sometimes they got to do what they wanted to do.

Kyle shrugged, and the two of them carried Perry to Burgess's vehicle, arranging him carefully on the back seat and covering him with a blanket. They collected the bag he'd been stuffed in, and the ties from his hands and feet. Put all that into evidence bags. Then they returned to the house. When they turned the knob, they found the door wasn't locked.

In many places, an empty house would be a locked house, but in rural Maine, plenty of people didn't lock their houses. Or they locked the front door to show they weren't home but left the back door unlocked. There were a lot of country customs that differed from city ones.

Cautiously, Burgess turned the knob and stepped into a dated kitchen. Goldenrod appliances, linoleum floor, chipped maple veneer cupboards. There was a car key on the table. Toyota. Maybe for the Prius. Two brown placemats. Plates and silverware. Two glasses with gold flowered patterns on them. It all looked frozen in time, like nothing had moved for at least thirty years. Or like the set for a play where in a moment the curtain would go up and an elderly woman in a house dress and apron would appear.

But the place was clean and neat, not dusty, and didn't smell or look abandoned. Mr. Coffee on the counter. No dishes in the sink but some in the draining rack.

"This isn't right," Kyle whispered.

"No. It isn't. Let's check the rest of the house. Maybe they just went out to run an errand."

"Conveniently long enough for someone to attack Stan, hide his car, stuff him in that sack and leave him in the Prius? And what's up with the car key on the table. It's not like they borrowed it and then returned it. They only took the plates."

"Unless 'they' are the people who live here."

"Golly," Kyle said. "A genuine mystery."

"Oh, this whole thing is a genuine mystery," Burgess said. "You want upstairs or down?"

Kyle looked at the stairs and grimaced. "Down."

"Right. Make the old man with the gimpy knee climb the stairs."

"Climbing stairs will keep you young. I read that somewhere."

"Small chance of that, unless you've got a time machine."

The stairwell was dark, so he looked for a light switch and flicked it on. One of those bulbs so dim it was practically useless. People bought them because they were trying to save money. They'd be better off saving their limbs. Shrugging, Burgess climbed the stairs. Worn. Uncarpeted. Creaky. If there was anyone upstairs, they definitely knew he was coming.

Straight ahead was the bathroom. To the left and right, rooms with closed doors he expected were bedrooms. He checked the bathroom. Like the downstairs, clean, dated, and empty. Turned to the room on the right and opened the door.

There was a faint, unpleasant scent in the air. One he tried not to recognize.

A bedroom, as expected. The unexpected was that there was someone in the bed.

He stepped toward the bed, saying, "Police, sir. Are you okay?"

Then he stepped back again, because the figure in the bed had once been a very old man. Now it was a very dead old man. The room—and the house—didn't reek of death because this man had been dead a long time. Long enough to be almost desiccated. The scent was only faint, though earlier it must have been strong. An open window was keeping the room very cold.

Jesus. Yes, up close, the death smell was stronger. But there was no sign of secretions from the body on the sheets. They were crisp and clean. Which meant someone else lived here, someone who maintained the house and, ugly thought that it was, also maintained the body. He got out his phone and took a bunch of pictures.

He heard Kyle's feet on the stairs and stepped out of the room.

"What?" Kyle said.

Burgess waved a hand toward the room he'd just left. "Body," he said. "Dead a while."

Kyle stepped past him into the room. Came out. Said, "Oh, crap. Now we've got to call the staties." Because this was definitely a death that needed to be looked into, even if it was from natural causes. And

Portland police only had jurisdiction in Portland. This scene belonged to the state police.

Burgess's cop brain immediately started throwing up reasons why someone wouldn't report the death, besides the obvious homicide. Chief among them? To continue to receive pensions and social security. To continue to reside in a place they didn't own.

But considering those possibilities was not going to be his job, because this wasn't his scene, his body, his jurisdiction, his problem.

But oh, yes, it was definitely his problem, and one that was going to be a mess. One of them had to stay here to deal with this, but they needed to get Stan Perry back to Portland. Get him medical attention. Yet without Stan, how was Burgess going to explain why he'd entered the house?

Crap. He never thought he'd say it, but he wished one of these days they'd get a nice, simple, straightforward homicide where the guy or gal confessed or was found at the scene, holding a knife or gun, muttering, "I didn't mean to do it."

They finished checking the upstairs, the clean bathroom and empty, neat bedroom, then went downstairs and out into the yard again. Burgess asked, "Were Stan's keys in the car?"

He hadn't noticed. Hoped Kyle had.

"Nope."

"Maybe in his pockets? If we get lucky. I'll check the car. You see if Stan has them."

Burgess didn't feel particularly lucky, given their situation. He went back into the musty barn, kicked the tarp aside, and checked the car for keys. Found them tucked under the driver's seat, which was odd. Maybe whoever attacked him and hid the car here meant to come back for it. Not good to be found with an injured cop stuffed in a bag or a tarp-covered police car shut up in your barn.

He backed the car out of the barn, closed the door, and backed up to his vehicle. They transferred Perry to the backseat. Covered him with the blanket again.

Burgess handed Kyle the keys. "You get Stan back to Portland," he said. "I'll call the staties."

"You could make that anonymous," Kyle suggested. "From a pay phone."

"Are there still pay phones?"

Kyle fished around in his jacket pocket and held out a phone. "You can use this," he said. "Burner."

"Seriously?" Burgess said.

"Seriously." Kyle nodded. "I thought it might be useful someday. I've never used it, but I keep it charged and keep it with me."

They stood in the cold while Burgess considered. A biting wind had come up and he was grateful for his warmer coat. He thought about the enormous hassle of dealing with the state police about why he was here and revealing the details of his own investigation. Considered the risks of concealing their interest, when down the road this case might mean they'd need state police cooperation. Thought about how he'd feel if the staties did this to him. Decided using the burner was the better course. For now. They didn't have the hours explaining and handing off this place, and the dead man inside, would take.

He didn't much like himself for that decision.

He held out his hand for the burner. "Okay. I'll use it. You get going. I'll wipe things down, then make that call. See you back at 109."

"Unless you see me at the hospital."

"Young Stanley is tough."

"And we'd both hate to have to tell Lily he's in the hospital."

"That we would."

Kyle drove away. Burgess went to remove traces of their presence. Let the staties puzzle over all the tire tracks and footprints, just as they had. And why it appeared someone had used a pry bar on the Prius. And where its plates were.

He did take a few minutes to examine the second bedroom. It appeared to be occupied by an older woman. A large woman. Back in the kitchen, he looked at some paperwork on the counter. Grabbed two names: Elvira Clemens and Tobias Jones. He photographed a phone bill and an electric bill.

Then, longing for a shower and a way to wipe what he'd seen from his brain, he wiped away their traces and headed back to Portland instead.

TEN

He made that call from the road, putting on a strong Maine accent and dropping his voice to its lowest register. He said, "There's a dead body at…" Gave the address, then added, "You might wanna check it out," and hung up. Yeah. He'd be pissed if someone did this to him, but on the other hand, it was important that that body be dealt with properly. He wouldn't be surprised to learn, when he dug into these people, that the woman who lived here had been collecting the dead man's benefits for a long time.

Back at 109, he dropped off the items he'd collected in the lab, then sat at his computer to see what he could learn about Elvira Clemens and Tobias Jones. He started with the registered owner of that Prius. Wasn't surprised when it turned out to belong to someone else. That person's name was Edwin Hall. The registered address, though, was that same farmhouse. So either a relative or someone they—or she—had allowed to use the address.

He kicked himself for not checking the mailbox. Maybe it was a maildrop for someone who didn't want their actual location known. They knew from the registration of the Subaru's plates they were dealing with someone with a penchant for using other addresses to hide their own. He sidetracked into a search for anything he could find on an

Edwin Hall. An unfortunately common name. Even Edwin Hall Maine gave him a lot of possibilities. Nothing from Edwin Hall and the name of the town where the Prius was registered. He leaned toward the screen, scanning the photos of myriad Edwin Halls, hoping for something that would give him a lead.

In the end, bleary eyed, he could tell you that Edwin Halls came in all ages, shapes, sizes, and colors, but none of them looked like anyone he could confirm was related to his case.

He switched to searching for Tobias Jones. Fewer of them, although the surname Jones definitely made his search harder. Like Joseph Burgess. He belonged to a vast tribe. They could have had annual Joe Burgess reunions. There were no cars currently registered to Tobias Jones and he didn't hold a current driver's license. He did, however, own the farmhouse.

Burgess wondered if there was a will. Or if there had been. If the man's death was concealed so that Elvira Clemens would have a place to live? Use his pension and social security to pay taxes and insurance on the house? These days, with direct deposit of such things, until a person's death was confirmed the money would just keep coming. The government was fast on the draw after a death certificate, though. Body barely cold before they were clawing back benefits.

Was he being too harsh with respect to Clemens? Maybe she'd cared for Jones for many years and felt owed? Maybe she was his sister, but he'd inherited it all? Plenty of maybes. Had he just closed the door on many of them by handing the situation over to the state police?

Despite being in conversation with no one but himself, he shrugged. Truth was he didn't need any more mysteries on his plate.

He called Kyle for an update on Perry's condition and when they might return.

Kyle didn't even bother with his usual "Kyle, investigations," just said, "He's fine. Soon as they finish stitching him up, we're on our way back."

Returning to his screen, he started a search on Elvira Clemens. A car registered in her name. A ten-year-old Corolla. A driver's license with a photo that confirmed that she was a heavy woman. Her age was given as fifty-seven. She was nearly six feet tall, so that second set of footprints dragging Perry across the yard, which he'd assumed were male, could have been hers. He should know better than to make assumptions. Hers and whose?

He decided to do a criminal history check on her and bingo. She'd done time twenty-five years earlier for killing her husband.

Was it possible the late Tobias Jones was a second husband and Clemens was a black widow? If indeed that body in the bed was Tobias Jones.

He searched marriage records and there it was. Ten years ago, Jones and Clemens had married. The groom, a widower, was seventy-eight at the time; the bride, a widow, forty-seven. He needed to know more. What had been the nature of her crime? Had there been children of either Jones or Clemens?

He started with the earlier killing Clemens had been convicted of, immersing himself in old criminal records and newspaper articles. He got on the phone with New Hampshire state police, trying to track down someone with a memory of the earlier case. Eventually found someone who told him that the person he really needed to speak with was a retired New Hampshire detective who'd worked on the case. His informant said the man was solitary and didn't like to be bothered, but he'd take Burgess's information and pass it along so the guy could call if he wished. He'd just hung up when Kyle and Perry returned. Perry sported a bandage and looked worn out; Kyle, unbandaged, looked worse.

He finished his call, made some notes, and summoned them into the conference room.

"Eight stitches," Perry reported. "Lily's gonna have a fit and I'm going to hear another lecture about how the father of an infant shouldn't have such a dangerous job."

"Which we hear all the time," Kyle said. "Even though our kids aren't infants. Kinda goes with the territory."

Burgess looked at his watch and at his team. They looked kind of ragged. "Late lunch on me," he said, and named a place they all liked. He didn't get any pushback. They needed to eat, and a quiet place with good food would help with what they all had to discuss. Plus, they wanted to get out of here before Cote came snooping. They needed to share what they knew and put the story together. They also needed to put their lieutenant in the loop.

Burgess figured he could update Melia when they got back, so they headed out.

The hostess, who knew them, gave a quiet corner booth at the back and said she wouldn't seat anyone near them if she could help it.

Once they'd ordered—it was definitely a day that called for meat and this place had huge and amazing burgers and potato wedges—Burgess said, "So fill us in, Stan. What happened out there?"

Perry shook his head, winced, and said, "What if I say I don't really know?"

"Just what you do know then."

They all knew head injuries could mess with memory.

"So I got there. Parked on the road and walked up the drive. I knocked on the door. No one answered and there was nobody around. No car, I mean, except for the Prius under that tarp. So I was checking it out. Had the tarp off. I'd photographed where the plates were missing, and I was taking a picture of the vehicle identification number when something crashed down on my head. I looked down. I saw feet. Large feet. Two sets. And then, as the cliché goes, everything went black."

Perry looked sadly at his iced tea. "I sure could go for a beer right now."

"Not with a head injury." Kyle and Burgess said it together, like they were a pair of indulgent uncles dealing with a nephew who didn't quite get it.

"Christ, guys, I know that. I didn't order one, did I? It's just, you know, I feel like such an idiot, getting sneaked up on like that."

"You never saw or heard a car?"

"Nope."

Burgess thought about the thick wet grass along the driveway. It would have done a good job muffling approaching footsteps. He thought about the layout of the house and barn. Could the attackers have been inside and just not answered the door? He said, "After you knocked, did you look in the windows, see if you could spot anyone inside."

"Where I could. No one in the kitchen or living room, and that's about all I could see. That kitchen's something else. Like from a 1960s TV show."

So the attackers had been somewhere else. Or upstairs. Burgess thought when he got back, he'd take a look at Google Earth and see what it could tell him about the buildings and surrounding land. He couldn't fault Perry for not being observant when he hadn't been sufficiently observant himself. He'd never even looked behind that barn. In his defense, once he'd found that body, it had been important to get out of there.

He and Kyle filled Perry in on what they'd found in the farmhouse. The dead man in the bed. No sign of anyone else, but plenty of signs of regular habitation. They told Perry how they'd found his car under a tarp in the barn and found him, zip-tied hand and foot, in a heavy canvas sack in the Prius.

Perry shook his head. It was lot to take in. "Guess I'm lucky you guys came looking for me, huh?"

"You are," Kyle said.

"You didn't notice any other cars," Burgess said. "Did you notice any footprints in the drive? It was very muddy."

Stan Perry rubbed his forehead, as one did when trying to recall a fuzzy memory. "There were tire tracks. And footprints leading to the door. And to the barn. I was gonna check the barn next, when I was done with the car, but then...I never got the chance."

Their food came, and conversation paused while they ate.

When their burgers were gone and the potato wedges only a memory, Burgess told them what he'd learned about the people associated with that house. That Elvira Clemens and Tobias Jones were married. The house belonged to Jones. It would require the medical examiner's confirmation, but they suspected the dead man in the bed was Tobias Jones. The Prius was registered to someone named Edwin Hall. And that twenty-five years ago, Elvira Clemens had gone to prison for killing her first husband.

"I've got a lot of old news to wade through. And someone needs to see if they can learn anything about Edwin Hill, who registered that Prius at that house. For instance, does he have a Maine license? See if we can learn what the connection is between him and Clemens. I'm waiting on a call back from a retired detective who worked on the Clemens case. Though the guy I spoke with said it was unlikely I'd get that call back."

"Uh…so you guys just left that house with the dead man in it?" Perry said.

Burgess and Kyle exchanged looks.

"Body belongs to the state police," Burgess said. "We don't have jurisdiction."

Perry nodded. A small nod so as not to jar his damaged head. "And we didn't want to get swept into their investigation and have to explain what we were doing there. Or have them muck up ours."

"You got it," Kyle said. "Joe didn't want to spend the rest of the day trying to explain why he was there. Why he went into the house. Why he used a pry bar on the Prius. Why the victim of an assault…by which I mean you, Stan…wasn't there."

He shot Burgess a look. "You don't want to know the rest."

"Think I can guess the rest, can't I?"

Burgess and Kyle nodded.

"So where do we go from here?" Perry asked.

"Terry's going back to researching the registered owner of that Subaru. You're going to see what you can learn about Edwin Hall. And I'm going to figure out how much I can tell Vince when I bring him up to speed. Oh, and I'll call the hospital, see how our girl is doing. Then one of us should take a look at that empty house Margaret Briscow claimed was her address and talk to the neighbors. And whether there's anything on record about a man named Glen Briscow, which is the name the guy gave when he came into the station to report a missing person."

He stopped. "It's a lot. And I am sure there's more coming at us. Let's hope we can find more information about the players we've identified so far and see where that takes us."

The check came and Burgess paid the bill.

"Thanks, Dad," Perry said. Then he paused. "That's funny. You know. You used to be a single guy and it was a joke. Now we're all dads."

The three dads headed for the door.

ELEVEN

Before he returned to his desk, Burgess went to Vince Melia's office. Melia was his lieutenant, and a very good one. While they might bob and weave when updating Captain Cote about their investigations, they were straight with Melia.

He stuck his head in and said, "Got a minute?"

Melia nodded, so Burgess entered, shut the door, and sat.

"This looks serious," Melia said. "What's up?"

"I've been bad," Burgess said. "Very, very bad."

Melia waited. He trusted Burgess not to be bad and his trust was rarely misplaced.

Burgess summarized the events of the morning. Stan Perry's trip to the farmhouse to check out the vehicle whose plates had been on the Subaru driven by the shifty man who'd come in to report a missing girl. How Stan had fallen off the radar, not answering his phone, and they'd gone to look for him, which Melia already knew but it needed to be part of the story. He described what they'd found when they got to the house. Perry's missing car. No sign of Perry. Then finding Perry's car hidden in the barn and Perry unconscious, with a head injury, in a sack in the locked Prius.

"Jesus!" Melia said. "Is Stan okay?"

"Eight stitches and a fuzzy memory. But he's tough. He won't be sent home."

Which was how Burgess and Melia both liked their people. Care for them, yes. Baby them, no.

Melia said, "And?" Because there was clearly an and. Warily because he didn't yet know in what way Burgess had been bad.

"Kyle and I went into the house to search for whoever might have attacked Stan. Oh, backtracking, we did knock before we started looking for Stan but no one answered. This time, the door was unlocked so we went inside to look around. It was…"

He hesitated, recalling the vintage kitchen, the table set for two. "It was like a stage set, Vince. Like it was all fake, except that it looked like someone lived there. Dishes drying in the rack. Food in the fridge. Half a pot of coffee."

Melia held up his hand like he was about to ask a question.

"The coffee was cold," Burgess said. "So we split up. Kyle took the downstairs and I went upstairs. And found a dead man."

That brought Melia halfway out of his chair. "You what?"

"In one of the bedrooms. In bed. And old man. He'd been dead a while. More desiccated than decomp. But the room was clean. The sheets were clean. Someone was taking care of that body rather than reporting it. Maybe for the benefits. Maybe because it wasn't a natural death."

Melia nodded. "So the bad thing you did. Was it not reporting it, so it wouldn't muck up our investigation. Or not reporting it because we'd have the staties underfoot going forward?"

"Couldn't not report it, could I? So I kind of chose a middle ground."

"Which was?" Melia hesitated. "Am I sure I want to know this?"

"I think you have to. So you can have our backs in case this hits the proverbial fan."

"Oh. Thank you very much, Joe. I love all that stuff hitting fans and love even more having your backs. At least it's not Stan this time."

"Too true. All young Stanley did was get himself hit over the head and stuffed in a bag in the trunk of a locked car. Kid's bound to need years of therapy. Maybe have to retire on a disability after so much trauma."

"Nobody on your team is that much of a pussy. Or you'd be retired ten times by now."

Burgess nodded. "More stitches than a baseball. Anyway, it turns out, much to my surprise, that Kyle had a burner phone. So I wiped the place down and, on the way home, made an anonymous call to report a body."

"And the very bad thing is not sticking around to get yelled at by Maine state police detectives?"

Burgess nodded. "Just thought you ought to know."

"Where are we with the girl? How is the girl?"

"I have to call over there and find out. But as for who did this? We've got a lot of avenues to pursue but we're getting nowhere fast. This one is going to be a slog." Burgess shrugged. "But you know my team. We're good at slogging. Things might look like an historic Kennebec River logjam right now, but we'll pry things loose and get the case flowing again."

"I love your optimism. And your metaphor." Melia paused. "Or is that simile? No. That would need like, wouldn't it." He shook his head. "Like I really care."

Burgess stood. "Well, I tried pessimism but it didn't get me very far. I'm just about ready to start my gratitude diary. Why, look at today? I am so grateful that Stan is okay and that we followed our guts and went to look for him."

"The famous cop's gut. I wonder if we're supposed to be feeding it some pre or probiotics?"

"Think we feed it information." Burgess sketched a wave and headed back to his desk.

As usual, when he had a case that captured the public's attention, his desk was so covered in pink message slips it looked like a bottle of Pepto-Bismol had spilled on it. He triaged them the way he always did. Urgent. Needs attention. Might need attention. Needs to go in the circular file.

When he was done, his desk was neater and he had three piles of messages awaiting his attention. He started with Urgent. Dani

Letorneau wanted him to drop by the lab when he got a chance. He always put Dani and Wink in the urgent pile. Dr. Cohen over at the hospital wanted him to call. He knew that even though the girl was in intensive care and no longer part of her caseload, Sarita Cohen always kept tabs on certain cases. Two messages from names he didn't recognize that purported to have information about his investigation. A message from the retired detective who'd worked on the Elvira Clemens case. So much for the man not wanting to be bothered.

And a call from his son Ned's school. Concerned that Ned was in trouble, he put that one first. Both his son Dylan and his daughter Nina had tangled with the administration in their school and he'd needed to sort things out. He hoped Ned, feeling left out, hadn't done something troubling of his own. Ned's exuberance in the wrong place or time could lead to trouble.

His call took him not to the principal's office but to the guidance office. In truth, he hadn't known that middle schools had guidance offices. As the saying goes, you learn something new every day. In his world, it was usually something bad, but he could hope.

The guidance counselor gave her name as Emma O'Brien and thanked him for calling back. "I'm hoping you can help me out with something," she said. She hesitated, as people often did when talking to the police, then rushed on. "Ned and his classmates are working on a career fair and he volunteered you to come and talk about becoming a police officer. He says that's what he wants to be when he grows up. Um…"

He heard her take a breath. "I know you're very busy, Detective, but it would mean a lot to Ned."

"Happy to, if I can," he said. "When is this event?"

Another "um." Another breath. She said, "Tomorrow evening."

Right. Let's give people plenty of notice. It might be grouchy on his part, but Burgess would bet some of the other parents being asked to participate had had more than a day's notice. Maybe not her fault. Maybe someone had bailed. Maybe Ned hadn't offered him up until today. He said, "What time? And is it at the school?"

"Seven. And yes, at the school. I'm…uh…sorry about the short notice. Ned's teacher says he didn't mention you until today and then he said you were probably too busy. So…can you?"

"Ms. O'Brien, given the nature of my job, my schedule is often not my own. Right now, I'm in the middle of a very complicated case. Best I can say is that I'll try to be there, and if I can't, I will try to send another officer in my place. Hope that's all right?"

"Absolutely fine, Detective. Fine. We…I appreciate it. See you tomorrow. I hope."

Burgess disconnected, then called Dr. Cohen. He went to voice mail, which didn't surprise him. The ER was usually crazy busy. He said he was back in the office whenever she found time to call him back. Then he stuck the phone in his pocket and headed down to the lab.

Dani and Wink were both bent over something spread out on a table, studying it with magnifying glasses.

"Ah, Detective Burgess. Kind of you to favor us with your presence," Wink said.

"You two say show up, we generally try to comply," he said. "Unless we're off in the hinterlands rescuing one of our team."

"Stan okay?" Dani asked.

"We think so. Eight stitches in his head. Expect he came back to work because it was easier than facing Lily."

"Speaking of heads, it's still hard to wrap mine around Stan being married and a father," she said. "He was such a wild man."

Burgess nodded. "So what's up?"

"What's up is this," Wink said, pointing to the object they were examining. Burgess recognized the blanket he'd gotten down in the park from Leon, the one they suspected had been wrapped around the girl. He pointed to a small dish where little bits of something, some plant, had been collected. "Hitchhiker plant. Dani thinks it's an unusual one. Maybe one that will give us some possible places where the girl was held. We're going to send photos to a botanist at the university, see if we can get an ID of the plant."

"Hitchhiker plant?"

"Plants that spread their seeds by attaching them to people and animals to give them a better chance of survival," Dani explained.

"Haven't you ever come back from a walk with a bunch of little prickly things stuck to your pants or your socks?"

Of course he had. He'd just never heard the term "hitchhiker plant" before. "Hope he or she comes up with something. Let me know." He turned to leave, then turned back. "Anything else?"

"Not yet, but we're working on a lot of things," Dani said.

Wink just gave him the look that said he should stay in his lane and they'd take care of theirs.

Burgess nodded and went back to his desk. No call back yet from Dr. Cohen. He looked again at the two numbers without messages. Whoever they were from had only asked for Burgess to call and left a number. He knew their assistants would have tried to get more. He pondered. Try one of these numbers or call the retired detective? He'd been told the man was prickly and wasn't likely to call him at all. Not someone to be kept waiting if he was willing to talk.

He made the call. Got a raspy "This is Flanagan. This Burgess?"

"It is. Thanks for calling me."

"Yeah. No problem. Not sure I can help much, but go ahead and ask your questions."

Burgess gave a quick summary of the events that had led them to the farmhouse and raised their curiosity about Elvira Clemens. Normally, he'd play it close to the vest about what they'd found, but Flanagan was a fellow cop and knowledge of the circumstances might help with what he was willing to share. Cooperation between police departments could take many forms. Total cooperation. Total stonewall. And the whole area in between. He described finding the man who might be Tobias Jones in bed in the house.

"So that's where we are. We've got a badly malnourished and severely abused girl at the hospital who was running from something. We've got a man inquiring about the girl who was driving a Subaru with plates from a Prius. We traced the Prius to that farmhouse, which belongs to Jones. We've got a couple of other names connected to this thing. Edwin Hall, who is the registered owner of the Prius. A man who gave his name as Glen Briscow, and a Subaru of the right color and year registered to a Margaret Briscow."

Burgess stopped himself. This guy didn't need to know everything they'd seen and done. Just the outline. He wondered where to start. Just ask an open-ended question and let Flanagan take it from there. "So that's the background. What can you tell me about the earlier case involving Elvira Clemens?"

The man snorted. "You got all day?"

"If that's what it takes. We've got that abused girl, a child really, who may die, and a cast of characters who are mostly phantoms."

"What about the girl's family?"

"We found her naked. No ID. A woman showed up claiming to be her mother, but her license was fake, and her answers were lies."

Flanagan made an agreeing sound. "Don't know how helpful any of this will be. I assume you've read the newspaper reports?"

"I have."

"So, twenty-five years ago, Elvira Clemens was a bombshell. She was tall. She was blonde. She was built. Men swarmed around her. She came from a poor family. Raised in a trailer. Father deserted the family. She decided early on that she was going to use the one thing she had going for her—her looks—to give herself a better life. She wasn't inter-ested in love. She was interested in money."

He stopped. Coughed what sounded like a longtime smoker's cough and continued. "Vera…that's what her family called her…eventually met a man named Edwin Hall. He was an up-and-coming developer. Rich family. Good connections. He wanted a wife who'd be arm candy for the events he had to attend and thought Vera fit the bill. Hall put money into her. Straightened and whitened her teeth, lightened her hair, got her a trainer to shape her body. Found someone to teach her how to dress. The whole nine yards."

Another pause. Another cough. "Hall, see, figured since he'd made her, he owned her. You know how those guys are. She wasn't a woman he loved, she was something he'd built, like one of his developments. Behind closed doors, if he'd had a bad day, she had a bad day. Usually, situations like that, we'll have been called in many times before one of them kills the other. Not this time. There wasn't a peep. No rumors. Nothing. Until the night she shot him."

Even though he was on the phone, not speaking in person, Burgess found himself leaning forward eagerly, waiting for the rest of the story.

"She was the one who called us. Told dispatch she'd shot her husband because he was beating her and she thought he was going to kill her this time. And yeah, when we got there, she was all beat to shit. One arm broken. There was blood everywhere. She was still holding the gun. Oughta have been self-defense. But you know how these things go. We do our best and then the justice system takes over."

A snort. "Justice system? Plenty a times, I called it the injustice system, especially when people are connected. His family were fat cats and she was jumped-up trailer trash. But she was stoic. Just took her punishment. And of course, by the time it got to trial, she was all healed up. Plus, she was a bad witness. Took the stand in her defense and was just kinda sullen and hostile and that didn't sit well with the jury. So she got manslaughter. Eight years. Served seven of 'em before they let her out. Hell, guys who get drunk and run over a kid get less than that. Not that I have an opinion or anything."

Burgess knew how it was. Even said the same thing about the justice system. "Were there any children?" He thought he knew the answer and Flanagan confirmed it.

"One. A little boy. Oh. The victim …if you can call him that…was Edwin Hall. Son was Edwin Hall after his daddy. Only five at the time. When she went inside, he went to live with his father's parents. The same parents who'd made their son a twisted, entitled monster. When she got out, she tried to get her kid back, but he was a teenager by then, and used to the perks of being raised by rich folks. It was sad. Kid definitely followed in his daddy's footsteps, only he didn't keep it behind closed doors. We were scooping him up regularly before his eighteenth birthday and he always got a slap on the wrist because the judge felt sorry for a poor boy whose mama had killed his papa."

Another cough. "Did I mention the parents could afford great lawyers?" A snort. "Don't imagine I have to tell you that. Anyway, he got into bigger trouble once he was an adult. By then he was running scams. Starting businesses to rip people off. Then he fell off our radar. Musta moved someplace else, became someone else's problem. Heard she moved to Maine. Nothing after that. From what you tell me, even if her husband died of natural causes, she'd be likely to not report it after what happened to her here. Know what I mean?"

75

He did. It was a sad story. Burgess wondered if, when Edwin Hall had worn out his welcome in New Hampshire, he'd moved to Maine and rejoined his mother? If he'd continued to run scams, and what those scams might be. He said, "I don't suppose you have pictures of her, of the deceased husband, of the kid?"

Flanagan snorted again. "Course I do. Some cases, you know, you kinda keep with you. Or pieces, anyway. I've kinda been waiting for the day when that kid—not a kid anymore, of course—gets into big enough trouble that it makes the news. It's only a matter of time. She may be the one who went to jail but he's the bad seed." He coughed, then said, "You got a fax number? Or I can email 'em to you. That's prob'ly better. I don't even know if my fax works anymore."

Burgess shared his email, thanked Flanagan for his time, and moved on. At some point, those photos would show up and they might be helpful. While he was studying his message piles, his phone rang again. He'd expected Dr. Cohen, who was usually quite persistent when she wanted to talk to him. But it wasn't her. It was a nurse on Colleen's floor.

After she'd identified herself, she said, "I'm not sure what to do, Detective Burgess. The information desk says there's an attorney here with what he says is an order to release the girl to him, and he says he's got an ambulance waiting downstairs."

TWELVE

Oh crap. He needed to confirm that the department's attorney had gotten the protective order he'd asked for so this couldn't happen, and also catch up with human services, which could be lackadaisical even when the situation was urgent. Also get the hospital's attorney involved.

"Call Security," he said, "and make sure no one approaches the girl until we can get some people over there, then call the hospital's legal office."

He called his attorney and asked for a copy of the protective order.

"Oh, dammit, Joe," she said. "I haven't gotten to it yet."

"Well, you may have just lost us the case, and the primary witness. There's an attorney over at the hospital with an order that he says gives him the right to take her."

"Crap. Okay. I've got the paperwork here. I just need to run it past a judge." She must have recognized how feeble that sounded. She said, "I'll send someone to the judge and go over to the hospital myself to wait for it. And I'll call the hospital's attorney."

"You have the photos?" he asked.

"I do."

"Hospital reports?"

"Not yet."

What in hell were they waiting for? The girl almost died and the nature of her injuries said there were human actors involved. He kept that to himself and asked, "What about human services? They're supposed to be involved."

"Crickets," she said. "I'll have my assistant make a call."

He hung up, not feeling optimistic, and immensely frustrated that he had to keep all the balls in the air because everyone else kept dropping them. He wanted to be a good detective, not a good juggler.

He looked around for Kyle, found him in the conference room.

"There's a guy over at the hospital. Attorney. Says he's got an ambulance waiting and an order allowing him to take the girl."

"I thought—"

"Me, too. But evidently, we are the only ones who are concerned that if this girl leaves the state, she disappears, and we'll never know who did this to her or whether there are other girls, or girls and boys, involved who are still at risk. Or whether she will be safe. Our attorney says she's on it now. Which may be too damned late."

"So we go over there and do our best to stall things?"

"Exactly."

Kyle smiled his most evil smile. "That might almost be fun."

As they headed for the truck, Burgess's phone rang. Dr. Cohen.

"Joe. We've got bloodwork back on the girl. Colleen. It's some miracle she found her way to the park. She's got so many drugs in her system, and needle marks suggesting she'd been being drugged for an extensive period of time. Not needle marks like an addict. Needle marks like she was forcibly injected."

He filled her in on the attorney waiting to take the girl away. "I need your report on what you've uncovered," he said. "All your reports. Take them to the hospital's attorney. We may need to make the case that it would be medically dangerous to move the girl at this point. Can we do that?"

"We absolutely can. I'll jump on that right now. For once, we're having a quiet day in the ER. Of course, the moment I say that, all hell will break loose, right?"

"Always does for me," he agreed. "Kyle and I are on our way."

Burgess thought about what the woman claiming to be the girl's mother had said. That she'd last seen her daughter two days ago. If that were true, then it had been the parents who'd kept her prisoner, restrained her, injected those drugs, and inflicted those bruises, so if this attorney was representing them, whoever they were, he was complicit. Could an attorney be an accessory? He didn't know.

Burgess was glad he'd recorded that conversation.

He hadn't brought Dani's photos but he had some on his phone.

As always, when he was in a hurry, everyone on the road in front of him was having a meandering day. Years ago, he'd dubbed people who didn't drive with purpose "Meanderthals." Today, they were out in force. Finally, unable to stand it even though the drive was short, he went for lights and sirens. Sometimes that worked, scattering them. Other times, panicked idiots slowed down even more, unable to figure out what they were supposed to do. He often wondered what part of "pull over and wait" they didn't understand.

They parked in his usual spot and he and Kyle got out. "See if you can locate that ambulance, find out where it's from, who is paying for it, where it's supposed to take her. Oh, and first, while I engage him, can you get some photos. People connected to this case have a habit of not identifying themselves."

Kyle nodded, and Burgess headed inside.

He found the man in question—the expensive clothes, briefcase, and furious face that screamed attorney—pacing by the information desk.

Burgess approached the man. "Detective Sergeant Burgess, Portland police," he said. "And you are?"

"Pissed off that this two-bit hospital can't even understand a simple judge's order," the man said.

"It's from a Maine judge?" Burgess asked.

The man glared at him. "Connecticut. The girl's state of residence."

"You have proof of that?"

The man demonstrated considerable charm when he replied, "The fuck do I need proof for?"

Burgess suppressed a smile and said, "You show up in a Maine hospital with a document purporting to give you the authority to remove an unidentified patient in critical condition who is the subject of a criminal investigation, you don't expect people to ask for proof? For documentation regarding the petitioner's relationship with the patient?"

He held out his hand for the document the man had been waving around.

Like a child who didn't want to share a toy, the man put it behind his back.

"You really going to make me call for backup?" Burgess said. "Just to see a document? Because if I don't see that document and you don't provide satisfactory answers to my questions, that girl is going nowhere."

He waited to see if that would sink in. Sometimes people's faces are mirrors of their thoughts, even if they mean to be inscrutable. This guy was mad enough to bust a gut and didn't like having his authority—or more properly, his pomposity—challenged by a mere small city cop. After a minute, the man shook his head. "I'm not showing you anything. It's only the hospital that needs to comply. You've got no rights here."

Interaction with Cops 101: You don't tell a cop he's got no rights. Not unless you're a judge and it's a criminal proceeding, and probably not even then. Burgess said, "Fine. But if I don't see it, my attorney doesn't see it, and the hospital's attorney doesn't see it, you get nowhere. Maybe there will even be a judge involved, because this girl is the victim of a vicious attack and we need to know what happened to her. That and to confirm her identity. So can I assume you've got documents proving who this girl is and establishing her relationship to whoever petitioned the judge?"

The man was looking uncertain, like he'd gotten a bullshit story just like Burgess had from the woman claiming to be the girl's mother and been convinced this was just a walk in the park. Show up. Get the girl. Get paid. Except probably he got paid first. That was how attorneys worked.

Out of the corner of his eye, Burgess saw Kyle taking the man's picture. Something the man missed because he was intent on arguing.

Burgess said, "You do understand that the girl has been badly abused over a significant period of time and is still in critical condition, right? She's not just some package you can toss in an ambulance and drive away. Whatever your paper says, this hospital cannot release her unless it is convinced that she's safe to transport and you've brought an appropriately staffed ambulance."

He honestly didn't know if what he was saying was true, but after decades of being on the receiving end of attorney's BS, he'd gotten pretty good at slinging his own.

Instead of choosing to be reasonable and persuasive, the man shook the paper at him again and said, "You can save all your crap for someone who cares. I've got the authority and I'm taking her."

At that point, the hospital's attorney and the department's attorney arrived, their arrival signaled by the strike of their heels on the tile floor. Two tall, tough women in smart suits. As he watched their approach, the man said, "Two broads? That's all you've got?"

Burgess wondered under what rock the petitioner—maybe the parents, maybe someone else who needed to secure the girl to cover their ass—had found this guy. Calling professional women "broads" was the stuff of old, bad noir films. He turned to greet them. Nodded at the waiting attorney, and said, "I'd introduce you, but he refuses to give his name or show the petition."

Before he stepped back to let them handle it, he said, in a lowered voice, "I need to see that document. Who purported to have a claim on the girl. Who this jerk is. Where he intends to take her."

He stepped back, saying, "All yours."

The two women moved in like a pair of sharks cornering a seal. Burgess wanted to stay and watch, but he needed to know what Kyle was learning out there in the parking lot.

He found Kyle standing beside the open driver's door of an ambulance. Actually, of a vehicle that looked like a retired, long out of service ambulance. It had the shape, lights, and a fading logo but no one with any wits would mistake it for the real thing. While Kyle engaged the driver, he went around and opened the back. There was no equipment. No gurney with mattress and blankets. No seats for the attendants. Just a filthy mattress on the floor with some chains and metal rings that could be used to restrain an occupant's hands and feet.

Jesus! He wondered if the attorney had even set eyes on this vehicle.

He used his phone to take some pictures of the interior, then of the license plate, and joined Kyle. There was another man in the passenger seat, a huge man, scarred and tattooed, his hair held back by a folded bandana. He was ignoring Kyle and the driver and playing a game on his phone. Burgess snapped a quick photo, thinking, as he did so, that this whole case was a lot of photographs and little more. Photos and license plates. He reminded himself that every case was different. Sometimes it took a lot of legwork to get answers.

Beyond the ambulance was a shiny black Mercedes. It also had Connecticut plates. Figuring it must belong to the attorney, Burgess photographed that as well and forwarded the photos of both plates to dispatch with a request to run them.

As he watched, Kyle shook his head and stepped back. The driver slammed the door, fired up the engine, and drove rapidly out of the lot.

Kyle looked at him. "They're getting away. Do we care?"

"Nah. We've got pictures of the interior. We've got the plate. They're just some hired thugs brought here to handle the girl." He showed Kyle pictures of the vehicle's interior.

Kyle exhaled and swore. He looked sad. "They really thought they could get away with this?"

"If the hospital hadn't called us, they might have. I'm going to see what's happening inside."

"I'll be there in a minute," Kyle said. "Got something I need to do out here."

Burgess had an idea what that something might be.

He headed inside, both to update the hospital and department's attorneys and to see how the conversation was progressing.

Not very well, it appeared. The two women and the man were still facing each other and their expressions said little progress had been made by either side.

Burgess joined them. Addressing the Connecticut attorney, he said, "Did you make the arrangements for the ambulance?"

"My client did."

"So you aren't aware of the condition of the vehicle?"

A shrug. "It's an ambulance. Was I supposed to examine it to ensure it met your standards?"

"The hospital's standards," the hospital's attorney, Meg Sullivan, said. "What's the story, Joe?"

"Christ," the man said. "Is everyone in this podunk state on a first name basis?"

Kyle had joined them. He said, "Did you know the word 'podunk' is of Algonquian origin?"

Kyle knew the oddest things.

Ignoring the man, Meg Sullivan held out her hand for Burgess's phone, which displayed the inside of the ambulance. She frowned, said, "You have got to be kidding," and passed it to the department's attorney, Lucy Brackett, who also frowned, then turned it so the Connecticut attorney could see it.

He made a grab for it and Burgess blocked his hand. "You can look but don't touch. This is the situation you've been attempting to put an extremely fragile patient in. No gurney? No medical supplies. And chained to the floor?"

The man leaned in and studied the photo. "Nah. No way. You're just trying to pull the wool over my eyes. That isn't an ambulance."

"Exactly," Burgess said. "Yet that's what you had waiting out there. Care to explain?"

The man shrugged. "Nobody told me." Then, suspiciously, "You said 'had.' What do you mean?"

Burgess shrugged back. "They took off."

"I'll just hire another rig. Obviously, the company was trying to cheat my client."

"Sir, you aren't taking our patient anywhere," Meg Sullivan said. "There's a lot more ground to cover than the quality and staffing of a vehicle." She held out her hand. "Let's see that order. At this point, we don't know the girl's identity. Your client's identity. Or what evidence you have to establish a relationship."

The man glared at her. Then at Lucy Brackett and at Burgess and Kyle. Glared. Didn't hand over the paper, still keeping it behind his back like a taunting child. After a moment of indecision, he said, "We aren't done here," bent and picked up his briefcase, and walked out the door.

"What the hell was that?" Sullivan said. "I can't believe it." She stopped. Shrugged like she was responding to some inner conversation, and said, "Lucy, we'd better make sure there's paperwork in place to keep this from happening again."

The two of them headed for Sullivan's office.

Burgess looked at Kyle. "So he won't get far, will he?"

Kyle shrugged. "No idea what you're talking about."

They stepped out the door so they could survey the parking lot. The man was standing beside the shiny Mercedes, yelling at the phone in his hand. He said, "I said I need a fucking rental car at the hospital and I need it right now."

A pause. Then, "What do you mean, which hospital? You telling me this fucking podunk town has more than one?" Another pause, then, "Hello? Hello? Are you still there? I said I need…" To no one in particular, he said, "Unbelievable. The fucker hung up on me."

Burgess and Kyle left him to his dilemma, walked to Burgess's truck, and drove away.

THIRTEEN

The Mercedes registration led them to an address in Connecticut, though not to a name, as it was registered to a business. The plate on the fake ambulance, unsurprisingly, had been stolen.

"I'd say the plot thickens," Kyle said, "but it's already as thick as pea soup. These folks sure like to play license plate roulette."

"And they're pretty desperate to get their hands on the girl. Wish I could have had a look at those papers. At least I have a photo of the lawyer. That, and the address from the Mercedes, might lead us to someone."

Burgess swerved to avoid a man absently wandering into the street. After they passed, he realized the man was barefoot. And the day was freaking cold. He was a compassionate guy but he was also one on a mission. He radioed for patrol to scoop the man up, then drove on. "We need to sit down and assess what we have," he said. "See if our collective minds can decide what our next steps should be."

He braked for an unleashed dog whose owner was back on the sidewalk, bent over a phone screen. He stopped, backed up, and rolled down his window. "Ma'am?" he called.

No response from the woman with the phone. He raised his voice.

"Ma'am? Your dog is supposed to be on a leash. It ran into the street and I nearly hit it."

She glanced over at him, shrugged, and returned to her screen. Her indifference pushed a set of buttons that had already been pushed too much today.

Burgess considered calling animal control. She was clearly too irresponsible to own a dog. He already had a dog and knew the shelters were pretty full. Still, as the ignored dog sat on the sidewalk, looking miserable, he had to do something. A dog now owned him and he knew what benefits a good dog could provide, also that the relationship needed to be a two-way street. He turned toward Kyle. "Your kids need a dog?"

Kyle shook his head. "My kids would love a dog but Michelle would probably leave us. Got enough trouble as it is."

"I'll just be a minute."

Burgess shoved the truck into park and got out. He approached the woman on the sidewalk, still immersed in her phone, and stopped just inches from her. "Ma'am," he said loudly. "Put that phone away."

She looked up at him, then jumped to see such a large man so close. "Get away from me or I'll call the police," she said.

"I *am* the police." He watched her process that and recognize she might be in trouble.

Of course, she said what everyone said. "I didn't do anything." There was a tattooed design on the hand holding the phone. She wore shower shoes and plaid pajama pants. An oversized gray hoodie.

"Exactly. You didn't have your dog on a leash, as the law requires. You weren't paying attention when the animal wandered out in front of my vehicle. You didn't even bother to attend to your dog, or the situation, when I called it to your attention."

She sighed, like being held responsible was a huge burden, shoved back a thicket of uncombed blue hair, and said, "What am I supposed to do?"

Seriously?

"You're supposed to have your dog on a leash. You're supposed to pay attention to your pet when you're walking it." He looked down at the pile of poop the sad dog was depositing on the sidewalk. "And you're supposed to clean up after your dog."

She shrugged like it was no big deal. "I forgot to bring the poop bags."

He figured she always forgot to bring poop bags. Was one of those people who still expected mommy and daddy to take care of things. Or the city. Or the designated poop collector. Kyle often joked that he wanted to be reassigned to dog poop officer and that he'd be a great one. The city would be far cleaner and far richer from all the fines. Kyle *would* be a great poop officer, but Portland had other, more important uses for him.

"Then you scrape it off the curb into the gutter and try to remember for next time."

Another indifferent shrug, like what he'd said was only a suggestion and she was rejecting it.

Burgess had more pressing things to do but her attitude annoyed him.

"Clean it up. Now," he said.

"I really don't…"

"Now."

Sullen, she stomped across the sidewalk and gingerly put out a foot to scrape the poop away. That task done pretty pathetically, she glared at him. "Satisfied?"

Burgess was rarely satisfied but there was no reason for her to know that. "And put your dog on a leash."

She held out her arms like she was waiting for him to search her. "You see a leash anywhere, Officer?"

"Do you own a leash?"

The dog was watching their interaction with interest, eyes going back and forth like the animal was watching a tennis match. It was medium sized, multi-colored, and looked intelligent.

"Tell you what," Burgess said. He hesitated. "What's your dog's name?"

"Andre."

"Okay. Here's what's going to happen. I'm going to take Andre with me to the police station. When you show up with a leash, and proof that he is licensed and has had his shots, he will be returned to you. Ask for Detective Sergeant Burgess at the desk."

She looked at him in total disbelief. "You want me to do what?"

Her eyes, he noticed, were almost the same color as her hair.

"Come to the station with his leash, his license, and proof of shots, and you can have him back. Better bring poop bags as well, as evidence that you're normally responsible about that. Got it?"

She burst into tears. "You can't do that. Make me do that. It's not my dog. It's my boyfriend's dog. And he's going to have a fit when he hears."

Burgess supposed he ought to be sympathetic. Maybe the boyfriend was abusive or made her walk the dog. But he was the meanest cop in Portland, and if that occasionally meant being on the meanest poop squad, he was okay with that. The dog deserved better.

"Then send your boyfriend." He knelt down beside the dog. "Okay, Andre, You're coming for a ride in a police car. Think you'll like that?"

Andre must have, because he trotted obediently beside Burgess and jumped willingly into the backseat.

"Looks like you've joined the poop squad," Kyle said as Burgess climbed back in.

"Yeah. Someone's got to do it."

"That was supposed to be me."

"You can take the next one."

"And there's always a next one. I'll text Stan and tell him to meet us in the conference room."

Burgess nodded. "He's a good dog," he said. His dog, Fideau, was teaching him about the excellent qualities dogs could have.

"Maybe he wants to join us in the conference room. We could use a clear head."

The bottom line was that both he and Kyle were in pretty sour moods. It had been a long day full of bad stuff and raised questions they couldn't answer, and that snotty attorney and the shocking state of the fake ambulance had been disturbing. What if the hospital had released her without checking?

Maybe when they got back, Stan would have something for them. Or the stolen license plate or the one for that business the Mercedes was registered to would lead them somewhere. Or Wink and Dani would have found another valuable clue. Or some helpful citizen would have called with a useful piece of information. He did still have those messages on his desk from callers who wouldn't identify themselves. There might be something there.

He parked in the garage and he, Kyle, and Andre went inside. Andre was in heaven with dozens of new things to sniff.

Kyle, watching, said, "I wish I were so easily pleased."

"And if you were, you probably wouldn't be very good at your job."

"Be a great poop cop, though."

Burgess stopped at the desk to inform them about someone coming to reclaim Andre, and then all three of them went to the conference room. Andre curled up in a corner and went to sleep and Burgess, Kyle, and Perry started throwing what they knew up on a white board.

They started with names. At the center, there was a single name: Colleen. Lots of space left to add information as they learned it.

Then Margaret Briscow, the owner of a 2013 Subaru registered to an address where there was an empty house, who had gone to the hospital looking for a missing girl. Glen Briscow, driving a Subaru with plates from a Prius registered to Edwin Hall. The registration on said Prius listed his address as the property owned by Tobias Jones, who was married to a woman named Elvira Clemens.

Briscow had come to the station to report a missing girl and given a lot of incoherent or false information.

Edwin Hall might be the son of Elvira Clemens.

"It's a freaking tangle," Perry complained.

"As it often is. What have you learned about Edwin Hall?" Burgess asked.

Perry shrugged. "He's a ghost. Other than that address where the Prius is registered, there's nothing. No driver's license. No property owned. No criminal record in Maine. No marriage, divorce, or death."

"What about that empty house where the address was used on the Subaru's registration? We know who owns it? Or any purchase information involving Margaret Briscow's Subaru?"

"Didn't get that far."

Burgess added the hitchhiker seeds that might give them a location.

The name and address of the Connecticut business to which the Mercedes was registered. The owner of the stolen plates that were on the fake ambulance.

"Lotta work and very few answers," he said. He looked at his watch. The rest of the day had slipped away. Time flies when you're having fun. Or dealing with jerks. Or any other time. He was tired. He was hungry. His team was tired and hungry and Stan needed to get some rest no matter how scared he was of facing Lily. "Let's call it a day. Or a night. Or whatever."

He looked at Andre, curled up in the corner. It looked like Andre was coming home with him. When the boyfriend showed up, the desk could send him on to Burgess's house. He wondered how Fideau would react. Would he think he was being replaced or be happy to have a friend to play with? He did know how the rest of his family would react. Chris would be displeased, Nina and Dylan indifferent, and Ned over the moon.

"Seriously?" Kyle said. "You want us to quit for the day?"

It was five-thirty and dark out.

"I do," Burgess said. As they continued to stare at him, he added, "Who knows how soon we'll get called back in. Gotta take our family time when we can."

"What about the dog?" Kyle said.

"He'll come home with me. I can't leave him here. They can send his owner along when he turns up with the necessary equipment and documentation."

"You seriously think he will?"

"Or he'll send her, she of the blue hair and vacant mind. He's a good dog. Why wouldn't someone take the necessary steps to retrieve him?"

"Because people are jerks," Perry said. "Anyway, I, for one, am glad to go home. My head is killing me."

They returned to the detectives' bay. Kyle and Perry grabbed their stuff and left. Burgess, with Andre following, stopped at his desk, which was newly decorated with message slips. He looked at the dog. "You mind if I take a look at these?"

Andre settled down beside him.

One of their assistants, who should have been gone for the day, stopped by. "You're here late," he said.

"Yeah. Had some affidavits to type and they took longer than I expected because I couldn't read the handwriting. I get used to it after a while but today. I don't know whether it was me or the writing." She shrugged. "So, you got a new dog?"

He told her Andre's story.

"He looks smart," she said. "You think they'll show up to claim him?"

"More hope than think."

She nodded. "Well, if they don't, we are in the market for a dog. The kids have been begging and my husband has finally agreed. So...let me know, okay." She bent and patted the dog's head. "What's his name?"

"Andre."

"Like the seal up in Rockport?"

"I guess."

"Well, let me know."

Then the office went quiet, just a few murmurs in the distance. He sorted the messages. Nothing that couldn't wait until morning, but one was another of those messages with no name asking him to call.

Chris and the kids were waiting for him to come home for dinner and family dinners got interrupted enough that he went home when he could, so he tucked the note in his pocket, and he and Andre left for the day. He stopped at the desk to let them know where Andre's owner could pick up his dog once he'd shown the proper documents.

Andre, like his dog Fideau, liked to sit in front beside Burgess. He briefly imagined himself becoming one of those crazy animal hoarders who filled their houses with stray animals. Meanest cop in Portland becomes Dog Whisperer. The truth was, though, that the dogs were the whisperers and Burgess the listener.

Besides, his partner Chris would have a fit, and keeping her happy mattered, even if the woman refused to marry him. He looked over at the dog. "Think she'll ever agree to marry me?"

Andre's smart, dark eyes studied him. Then, as though the dog understood the question, he nodded.

FOURTEEN

On the way, to make efficient use of the time, he called the number on the message slip. A woman answered, and when he identified himself, said, "Well, it's about time."

Ah, the public. Once again making him feel appreciated. He said, "What can I do for you, ma'am?"

She sighed and said, "It's too late now."

"Too late for what?"

"Too late to catch them at Rosie's old house."

"Catch who, please, and where is Rosie's house?"

In the garbled explanation that followed, he figured out that Rosie's house was the empty house where the mailbox had been used to register Margaret Briscow's car. Rosie was in a home now, her mind gone with "that dementia thing" and his caller, who had finally given up the name Shirley Bufford, was a neighbor. She'd called because there was a car parked at the house again. Well, actually not a car, but a truck with a cap on the back, and no one was supposed to be there.

Crap. If she'd left a name and a message yesterday, this wouldn't have happened. But of course, it was all his fault. Still, he might learn something, so he asked, "Can you tell me anything about that truck? Make? Color? Whether it had a Maine plate?"

"Black," she said. "Chevy pickup. Maine plate. I've got the license number, too, if that would help."

He forgave her everything. Some people objected to nosy neighbors, but in his business, they could be goldmines. "Give me a minute while I pull over," he said. He parked, got out his notebook and said, "Okay. I'm ready."

She gave him the plate and said, "The driver was a man. Late forties or early fifties, I'd say. Graying brown hair. Needed a haircut. He was wearing green, like he was a warden or a guide or something but there was no insignia on the shirt, and nothing on the truck."

"Tall? Short? Heavy set, regular, or thin?"

"Medium tall. Regular but heading toward heavy."

"If I showed you a photo, could you tell if it was him?"

"Well, Detective, I may be old but I'm neither blind nor stupid. You wanna bring a photo by and show me, I'll know."

"That would be very helpful, Ms. Bufford. If you can give me directions."

"Mrs. Bufford. Married to my Ernie almost fifty years. I don't much hold with that Miz stuff. So I'm the house next door to Rosie's. On the right as you're facing the house. Tomorrow morning would be good. I'm about to watch my favorite TV show, so now would not be a good time."

Which was fine with him, because he was about have dinner with his favorite people. "Tomorrow morning is fine. What time is good for you?"

"Any time after eight and before eleven, when I'm going to a lunch at the senior center. Making Ernie's favorite chicken casserole. Man never could get enough of that. I had to make it at least twice a week. You like chicken casserole?"

"Yes, ma'am, I do." Voices could tell him so much. That she was older. That she was lonely. That she was curious about what was going on next door. That she tried to be a good citizen. That she missed Rosie, who had probably been not just a neighbor but a friend. "I'll see you tomorrow. And thank you for being a concerned citizen. We always appreciate the calls."

There was a hesitation. He figured she was about to ask if that was so, why had he waited to call her back. She said, "I expect you've been busy," and hung up.

Burgess drove home, wondering whether his second mysterious caller might be equally helpful. Maybe after dinner he'd return that call and find out.

He parked beside Chris's car and Dylan's, let Andre out and waited while some sniffing and peeing took place, then said, "Andre. Come," and he and the dog headed inside and up the stairs.

Chris was about to greet him with a kiss when she spotted Andre and stopped. "No. Joe. Absolutely not. Not another dog."

Ned appeared behind her with a huge grin. "Oh, boy, Dad. Another dog for Fideau to play with."

Fideau appeared behind Ned and studied the newcomer, then came to greet him.

"We're not keeping him," Burgess said. "I took him away from his careless owner when he was off-leash and ran into the street in front of me. I said if they wanted him back, they had to show up at the station with a leash, his license, proof that he'd had his shots, and poop bags. They hadn't shown up by the time I left, so I brought him home with me. If they don't show up tomorrow, I've got someone who wants to adopt him."

Chris visibly relaxed. "Okay, then. Dinner is ready. Ned, why don't you get…" She looked at Burgess. "What's the dog's name?"

"Andre."

"Why don't you get Andre some water and put some kibble in a bowl. Then wash your hands. And call your brother and sister for dinner."

Burgess went to change out of his jacket and tie. Fideau followed him, giving him a skeptical look. Fideau couldn't talk, but he could definitely communicate. Right now he was saying he was worried he was about be displaced, and didn't Burgess know he was Fideau's person? And what about some loyalty, huh?

"Don't worry," Burgess said, getting down to Fideau's level and looking him in the eyes. "I know I am your person. Andre is just a guest, and we are supposed to be polite to guests."

Fideau, the world's cleverest dog, nodded and trotted away.

Dinner was Swiss steak with peppers and onions, and Chris's marvelous mashed potatoes, and spinach with toasted nuts and balsamic vinegar. Burgess had never been big on eating his vegetables, but Chris was a wizard at making them appealing. He was pretty sure, if his human nose was right, that there was going to be something chocolate as well.

When they were all settled at the table, he said, "So, Ned. Tell me about this career fair your school is doing tomorrow night."

Ned looked at his plate and his ears got red. "She called you?" he said.

"She called me."

"Uh oh, little bro, I think you're in trouble," Dylan said.

Ned looked at Burgess. "Am I in trouble?"

"No. But I may be if something comes up at work and I can't make it when your school is counting on me. What did you tell them?"

"That you were a police detective," Ned said. "That's about all. But she was excited. I guess because she had a lot of the people coming who have regular jobs. I mean, she said 'cool' when I told her about your job. She asked me if I thought you'd be willing and I said you were very busy and never knew when your job would take up all your time." He looked down at his plate. "I told her it was okay to call you." He looked up. "Was it okay?"

"It's fine. It's just…" Burgess looked around the table. "You all know how it is. We'll have plans and then some bad guy or gal does something and I have to miss them. Right now, we've got a really strange one and we're not getting anywhere."

He realized he rarely talked about his work at home. Cops liked to keep their families protected from the ugly stuff they saw. It was a constant balance between keeping his family aware of his world and its dangers and protecting them from the terrible things people did to each other. Ned and Nina, of course, had seen plenty themselves, beginning with their father killing their mother in front of them. So he made a special effort to keep things upbeat for them.

"Are you going to wear your uniform?" Nina asked.

"Detectives don't wear uniforms, except for ceremonial occasions," Burgess told her. "Unless a jacket and tie constitute a uniform." He didn't add that a lot of those ceremonial occasions were police funerals.

She nodded. "I think they do. Sorta. Too bad you don't have time to get a new jacket. Yours are looking kind of tired."

Burgess looked at Chris, who was grinning. "Do my clothes look tired?"

He watched her try to find something neutral, or supportive, to say, and fail. Finally she said, "You could use some new clothes."

He was reviewing his schedule for tomorrow. A day, like most, that was already too full, and that was before he started chasing down new leads like the call from Shirley Bufford. "If only I had the time. It's not like I'm sitting around watching sports on TV when I'm not at work." He knew he sounded defensive.

"I can run out tomorrow at lunch and see what I can find," Chris offered.

It was a generous offer. He shook his head. "You already do way too much for me, and believe me, I know how lucky I am."

That got him a big smile. He'd learned how important it was to treat people well, and she was still surprised to have found a guy who did. Give compliments. Do your share. Some of his lessons had come from his mother, who had taught him to notice. Some of his lessons had come from seeing all the ways things went wrong, and how badly people could treat each other. This home, this family—after years as a confirmed bachelor afraid he'd inherited his father's violent temper— these were gifts, and gifts were not to be taken for granted.

Dinner over, the kids went to their rooms to do homework, and he helped Chris clean up.

"So, Terry is afraid Michele is going to leave him if he doesn't marry her soon," he told Chris.

"He won't find someone better. She loves him. She loves the girls."

"And she wants a baby."

They moved around the kitchen in the ballet they'd perfected, getting things done while not getting in each other's way in the small kitchen.

"Is that a bad thing, Joe, her wanting a baby? I wanted a baby. Wanted one very badly, but life doesn't always cooperate." She held up a hand as though he was about to protest. "The thing is, Nina and Ned are plenty of family, and Dylan is the frosting on the cake. I've got the family I always wanted. But you…" She paused while she put something in the refrigerator, then said, "You never wanted a family."

"It wasn't a matter of want or not want," he said. "I was afraid to have a family. You know that. I was afraid…probably still am…that my father's temper is in me and might appear at any time."

"You are not your father. He wasn't a good man. You are."

They both paused as Fideau joined them, followed by Andre. Fideau was leading, seeming to say to their visitor, "See, it's okay. My people are good people."

Burgess gave them both pats and treats, then said, "I should take these beasts for a walk. Do we have a spare collar and leash?"

"We do. I'll find them." Before she hurried away, she said, "Want some company on your walk?"

"If it's your company, yes. Always."

She mock punched him in the arm. "Must be time for me to show more of my mean side. The one I inherited from my mother."

They both laughed. Chris's mother, Doro, was a wonderful woman. She backed them up when they needed someone to stay with the kids, or to pick up a kid. She'd stepped into the role of grandmother with great delight.

"Anything you've inherited from her is fine with me."

"We all try, don't we."

She disappeared, returning a moment later with a collar and a leash. She put it on Andre while Burgess fastened the leash on Fideau. The two dogs waited impatiently by the door as he and Chris put on their coats, and they headed out.

The night was crisp and clear, with bright stars overhead. As they walked, they passed many others out also walking their dogs. Fideau and Andre had to greet each one, except, of course, for the shy and yippy ones.

"Must be dog o'clock," Burgess said.

"Dogs are very good at helping people get exercise," Chris said.

"Is that a hint?"

"You're fine." A pause. She said, "But this is fun, just us, away from the kids." She slipped her arm through his.

He'd put his phone on vibrate so it wouldn't disturb their walk, and it was dancing in his pocket. Too bad. He was always interrupting their time together. Not him, personally, but work. That was the job. But right now, it was too pleasant just strolling and talking.

Chris said, "I've been thinking…" She stopped and he wondered if those were dangerous words or something good was coming. "I've been thinking that a small Christmas wedding would be nice. Just family and close friends. What do you think?"

He thought it was about time, but didn't say that. "What changed your mind?"

"Nothing changed my mind, Joe. I've always wanted to marry you. I just …well, your life is so hectic. I wasn't sure I could live with it. With you in danger like you often are. I just…well, I just needed to give it some time. Ponder on it. See how it was over time. Whether I could stand it. No, that's not quite right. Whether, on balance, I would rather be Mrs. Burgess or Almost Mrs. Burgess, the one who could walk away when things got tough."

There was a pause while they greeted other humans and the dogs greeted other dogs, then they strolled on. "I guess I realized that I was never going to walk away from you, Joe. I wouldn't want to."

Burgess was feeling a kind of boyish elation. She'd said yes to his proposal, but then refused to set a date. The phrase "almost Mrs. Burgess" had been tossed around a lot, a term that always frustrated him. He was trying to remember whether Kyle had said something about a Christmas wedding, and whether he'd be stepping on toes, and decided he didn't care. "I'm thrilled," he said. "Are you going to want all that wedding stuff?"

"All what wedding stuff? You mean bachelor and bachelorette parties and rehearsal dinners and a bridal shower? Because you know me, Joe. The answer is no. Just a simple ceremony and a party after with friends. Maybe a meal. I really haven't thought about the details. I just woke up this morning thinking 'why haven't I married Joe?' and knew it was time."

Long past time, but he didn't say it. It wasn't as though their lives were going to change. They already lived together. Already had the kids. Aloud, because he wondered what her take was, he said, "Do you think anything will change?"

"Oh. Things will change. Everyone will call me Mrs. Burgess. The ones who don't already."

"You'll still be Chris Perlin. I'm not expecting you to change your name. Why would I?"

She sighed. "It's not what you expect, you're pretty evolved for a cop, it's everyone else. But you know what?" There was a teasing note in her voice. "I really don't care. I'm marrying you, not a name or a rank. Just a good man who goes out of his way to make me happy even when he's too busy."

His phone buzzed again. He ignored it again but said, "We should be getting back. There are kids to yell at. And I think the dogs are getting tired."

"Unless it's Joe Burgess, the man who works too hard."

"It's the job."

"Yadda yadda. Like I don't know that?"

Back home, the dogs went for water and food, Chris went to check on the kids, and he got out his phone. The message he'd ignored was that a man was at the desk looking for his dog. He didn't have a collar or a license or proof that the animal had been given required vaccinations. What he did have was a trainload of attitude and a willingness to blame his lack of said items on his girlfriend. They'd sent him away and told him to come back tomorrow with the leash and paperwork if he wanted to collect his dog.

Burgess called them back and thanked them.

Then, because the phone had buzzed twice, he checked for other messages. The second one was more relevant. The retired cop in New Hampshire had called and said he was sending an email with the photos attached.

FIFTEEN

B urgess could open attachments on his phone. Well, he probably could. But he wanted to see them on a large screen where he could study the photos without going blind. He never understood how young people could spend all their time staring at their phones, even reading on them. By the time they reached their thirties they'd be blind from staring at screens and deaf from being constantly plugged in to loud music.

He was definitely becoming an old fart.

The old fart decided the photos could wait until morning. He was having such a pleasant evening with Chris he didn't want to spoil it by saying he wanted to go into the office. Not when he didn't need to. He sent the email on to Rocky Jordan, asking Jordan to print the photos, then concentrated on being present at home.

He opened his calendar and looked at December. It was right around the corner, for planning purposes, even if they were going to have a small event. When she came back from looking in on the kids, he'd check with her and find out what she meant by small. While he waited, he got a bottle of white wine from the fridge, opened it, and poured them each a glass.

He carried the glasses into the living room, went back for the bottle, and turned on the gas fire. Turning the unused fireplace into a gas fire had been one of Chris's innovations and one that was giving them a lot of pleasure. He realized as he sat on the comfortable sofa and stared at the flames that he was rarely home enough to enjoy it. There was always something pulling him away. If he was home, he was usually so tired he was staggering to bed.

This night—the kids without catastrophes and he and Chris able to spend some peaceful time together—was a treat.

She joined him on the sofa, sipped her wine, and rested her head on his shoulder. "If that damned phone rings, Joe Burgess, you are not going to answer it, okay?"

He said, "Okay."

They discussed wedding plans. Small did mean small, just their families and closest friends, and it didn't absolutely have to be in December. Though she had sighed wistfully about how pretty a Christmas wedding would be. They agreed they'd each make a list and she would check out some venues, since their yard wasn't the right place for a winter wedding.

Somehow, through some miracle, his phone didn't ring. None of the kids came to them for homework help, social help, or the pleasure of their company, and the evening crept quietly away.

Morning came too early, as it always did, with the usual family commotion. Ned reminded him three times about the career night and Burgess said he would do his best to be there. The answer wasn't satisfying but Ned accepted it. He'd lived with Burgess the Cop long enough to know how things went.

Dylan was cheerful, chatting about the upcoming end of the football season and the Thanksgiving Day game. Nina was quiet but it was a smiling quiet, not one of her these days too-frequent funks. Burgess was sure there was a boyfriend she wasn't ready to talk about, one who seemed to make her anxious. Plus, she was still recovering from a harrowing experience with a boy at school who wouldn't take no for an answer. He and Chris watched her carefully but let her choose what she wanted to talk about.

Burgess ate a bagel and drank his coffee. Kissed Chris and said goodbye to everyone before heading out into the cold morning. Said goodbye to Fideau and Andre and told them to be good dogs. As he backed out, Dylan and Nina were getting into Dylan's car. Having a son who could drive was a huge relief. He was always struggling to fit the time to drop them off into his crazy mornings. He knew, though, that he'd miss a lot, not getting to be a fly on the wall—or behind the steering wheel—and hearing their conversation. There was something liberating about talking in a car instead of being face-to-face.

As usual, his desk was papered with messages along with a stack of reports that needed to go into the case book. On the top of those reports were printouts of the photos Finnegan had sent. He decided those had priority and bent to study them; many were twenty-five years old. Sometimes people aged in ways their earlier photos predicted and the matches were clear; others aged more slowly or so rapidly, or gained or lost weight so that they bore little resemblance to their earlier photos.

He started with that of Edwin Hall. The man looked familiar. After a moment, he pulled the surveillance photo of the man who'd shown up at the desk asking about a missing girl. When he put them side by side, it was clear the man who called himself Glen Briscow was Edwin Hall. That might explain why Edwin Hall's criminal career had ended. But did Glen Briscow have a record? A Maine license? Did Margaret Briscow?

A quick search revealed that both of them had Maine licenses and—big surprise—that the address for both licenses was that empty house. He checked the issue dates and both licenses had renewed in the last year using that address.

Interesting. He really did need to go and see Shirley Bufford this morning. Get her information on comings and goings at that house and the license number of the truck she'd seen. He wanted to know what facility her former neighbor Rosie was in and whether Rosie was competent to be interviewed, though he'd likely also see for himself.

He might use "old fart" as a pejorative with respect to himself, but over the years, he'd found older people to be extremely helpful. He got a lot of information from those older ladies who sat in their living rooms and looked out the window. Who paid attention to their neighbor and were willing to step up and do their civic duty instead of not wanting to be bothered. It looked like Shirley Bufford was going to be one of them.

He filed the various reports in the case book, then turned to his messages. Stan Perry would be in late, they had to take Autumn to the doctor this morning. Terry Kyle would be late. He had a conference with his younger daughter Anna's guidance counselor this morning. Burgess hoped the counselor would have some insight that could help Kyle understand what was bothering Anna.

Ah. The life of a family man. At least his obligation was for tonight, not cutting into their workday. Only recently becoming a family man himself, he was slowly learning the challenges of balancing work and family. And "challenges" was the right word. Because he was big and tough and unintimidated, he was often called in—by Chris—to handle situations where he might need to back someone down to protect his kids. He didn't like it about himself that he was good at being intimidating, at least not when it didn't involve bad guys or reluctant witnesses, but he rose to the occasion when it was necessary.

Not so long ago, the matter had been Nina not coming home from school and not answering her phone and Chris was tied up at work. That had led to a very scary scene, a teenage male without boundaries or a conscience, and a dramatic rescue. Before that it had been Dylan in trouble for protecting a girl in a headscarf who was being tormented. The school had regarded Dylan as the troublemaker until Burgess forced them to follow their own rules. He would be fine without any more of those, thank you. At this point, the principal pretty much hated him.

As he was about to return to the rest of the messages, he remembered the second message, or second non-message since a request to call wasn't actually a message. He'd taken that one home with him, so he checked in his briefcase. pulled it out, and dialed.

All he got was a brusque answering machine message telling him that he knew what to do. He did. He left a message with his name and number and that he was returning their call. Then he went back to sorting messages.

Sometimes, as he surveyed the sea of pink that piled up on his desk when he was out doing detective work, he wished there was a Burgess mini-me who could triage the darned things and return necessary calls so he could get his work done. But as he often reminded younger cops, you never knew when slowing down and paying attention was going to lead somewhere.

As there had been yesterday, there was a message from Dani, asking him to stop by the lab. He could do that right now and avoid dealing with all this pink. But suppose something important was lurking here, like the message from Shirley Bufford, so he forced himself to look through the rest.

In the end, there was the same pile as yesterday. Urgent or Important, Might be Important, Could Definitely Wait until Later.

He returned a few calls that didn't lead him anywhere. Then, because one of the messages was from Rocky Jordan, who had been trying to get a read on the license plate belonging to the woman who claimed to be Colleen's mother, he dropped by to see Jordan on his way to the lab.

"I've got that plate for you, Sarge," Jordan said, offering Burgess a couple of sheets of paper. "Took some doing, though. You've got a name and address here. I hope they lead somewhere." Jordan sighed. "Thinking about that poor girl and what was done to her, I wish I could help more with this. Got anything more for me?"

Burgess had a bunch of photos he'd been wanting to try photo matches with and hadn't gotten to. Nor had Stan or Terry. He said, "Want to try some photo matches? See if anything comes up?"

Jordan brightened. "Sure. Bring 'em on."

"I'll grab some from the file. Be right back."

He got the file of photos and took it back to Jordan's office. He laid out a copy of the photo of the woman claiming to be Colleen's mother. "This is the woman whose plate you've been tracing. Love to know more about her." Took out photos of Glen Briscow a/k/a Edwin Hall and Margaret Briscow, and gave Jordan the background. "Those are the priorities right now. Be grateful if you could learn something."

"Happy to help." Jordan was already turning away, eager to get to the task.

Burgess continued on to the lab. Wink wasn't there but Dani was bent over a microscope. She looked up when she heard his steps and smiled. "The biologist came through. It's quite a rare plant and is only found in a few places." She handed him a couple of sheets. "I listed the areas where it grows. I hope it will help."

"You're a wonder," he said. "Thanks."

"I'm only the crime scene tech, Joe. The botanist is the wonder. He was actually quite excited about helping to solve a crime."

Something else to go in Burgess's gratitude diary.

By the time he got back to his desk, Kyle and Perry had arrived, and there was a message from the hospital that the girl had briefly regained consciousness. He updated them on what was new and shared the photos that the New Hampshire detective had sent. "Rocky is looking for matches. But I am sure that this guy," he tapped the photo of Glen Briscow, "is actually Edwin Hall."

"Explains why Hall's criminal activities came to a halt. Anything on Briscow?" Kyle said.

"Not that I've found. But maybe he's just gotten better at hiding it. So…hospital says the girl was briefly awake, so I'm going to head over there and see if she's able to speak. One of you needs to learn all we can about that empty house where the Briscows have registered their cars. The woman who owns it, I understand, is in a nursing home. I'll have more information about that when I've spoken to the neighbor."

Which reminded him that the clock was running. He'd better visit Shirley Bufford before she left for her lunch, then go to the hospital.

He filled them in on what Dani had learned from the botanist. "I've got her notes on my desk about areas where this particular plant can be found in Maine. Maybe you two wanna divvy them up and make some calls to the local sheriffs, see if they've noticed anything funny going on. Secretive compounds, rented houses where the residents seem to want to stay hidden. You know what to ask."

"It'd be kinda cool," Perry said, "if the case was solved by a plant."

Burgess offered a handful of pink slips. "There are calls from people who may have some information for us. Probably most of them cranks. We all know about that. But maybe there's a gem of information in there somewhere."

He divided them into two piles and gave one to each of them.

"Off to interview the woman who lives next to that empty house. If I don't return or call in two hours, come looking for me."

He meant it as a joke, but only a half joke. Their adversaries, whoever they were, were people without consciences, which made them very dangerous.

At least in mid-morning, the traffic was light. Out-of-staters claimed it was always light and Portlanders complained about traffic so light it was nothing, but there were intersections that routinely jammed up. He was headed out of Portland to the west, to the area where the city petered out and farm fields began to appear. Bufford's house and the one involved in their case were on the road that led to his favorite farm stand. If he had more time, he'd have a standing date with himself to go to the farmer's market on Saturdays.

It wasn't his nature to get carried away, but he could easily be seduced by baked goods, fresh tomatoes, and the visual magic of multi-colored mushrooms. By getting to buy fresh cheese and homemade pasta, and his fish directly from fishermen's wives. It was most fun when he took Chris, because they took turns being lured into buying something and always came home with a trunk full. The kids, of course, were most interested in the baked goods. He could set a bag of fresh cinnamon rolls on the counter and it would be empty before he finished putting the rest of the food away. A smart man, he always got a second bag that he left in the trunk.

Just before he got to the vacant house, he put on his blinker and pulled in the neighboring driveway. It was a small one-level house, white with green shutters. Well-maintained with burlap-wrapped shrubs for winter and flower gardens that had been put to bed. He went up the short walk and knocked. Waited. Then knocked again. She'd told him she was going out later in the morning but she should still be home now.

He was starting to worry and hoping there wasn't bad news on the other side of the door, when it was opened and a small, sparrow-like woman smiled up at him.

"You must be the detective," she said. "You look like a detective. I'll bet people have a hard time keeping things from you." A tilt of the head as she said, "Am I right?"

"I guess I'm pretty good at what I do," Burgess admitted. "May I come in?"

Flustered, she shook her head and said, "Oh dear. Where are my manners? Of course you can come in." She stepped back and gestured toward a doorway on the right. "We'll go in the living room, if that's all right."

Burgess followed her into a small, neat room with dark furniture and a lot of cushions. Also a lot of crocheted doilies, which reminded him of his grandmother, whose hands were never still.

She gestured toward the sofa. "You can sit there, please. Feel free to move some of those cushions. My older daughter Angela, who isn't very good at gift giving, brings me them and because she tries, dear girl, I don't have the heart to throw them away. Actually, when new ones come in, I try to put the older ones in a closet. But it's a small house with small closets. I'm afraid I've run out of space."

"Mrs. Bufford——" he began.

"I know. Living alone like this, when I've got someone to talk to, I do go on a bit. Would you like some coffee? Or tea? I've made some nice banana nut muffins."

"Coffee. Black. Would be great, ma'am, if it's not too much trouble. And I'd love a muffin."

She bustled off, leaving Burgess in a sea of cushions, studying the small room. Like many cops, he spent a lot of time in places that were neither clean nor neat, so this place, which smelled faintly of lemon polish, was a treat. He moved some cushions to give himself more space and got out his notebook.

She was back very quickly, carrying a tray with two cups, two muffins, and two small, flowered napkins. She set it on the coffee table and slid one muffin and a cup toward him.

"This looks great," he said.

She smiled. "Now, about that vehicle I saw. Since my memory isn't what it used to be, I've taken to writing things down." She reached into her apron pocket and pulled out a sheet of paper, which she handed to him.

He saw that she had printed the information and her printing was neat and precise. He read what she'd written. The vehicle was a Toyota Tundra truck with a cap on the back, green like a game warden or forester might drive. She gave the plate number and listed the dates when she'd seen it parked at the house.

"If he came again, I was going to go over there and challenge him. Ask what he was doing there. If Rosie had given someone permission to use the house, she would have told me."

"He's not someone you recognize? A relative or a friend of your neighbor?"

She shook her head. "Rosie has two daughters. Sandra lives down in Massachusetts. Elaine lives in Brunswick. And neither of them is married. Well, right now. As far as I know. I suppose it might be one of Elaine's boyfriends. She goes through men like I go through paper towels. But Rosie hasn't mentioned a new fellow and Elaine usually keeps her informed." She hesitated. "If informed means calling up her mother to bitch about how hard her life is and how she keeps making bad choices in men. But usually Rosie tells me about that and she hasn't. But of course, she isn't herself these days. We used to joke together when we were forgetful or had trouble finding a word and call it 'old timers' but now it isn't a joke."

"How bad is her condition?"

Shirley Bufford shrugged. "There's good days and bad, is all I can tell you. Of course, it's bad when an active, engaged person like her is afflicted like this." Her voice dropped. "We were best friends for more than fifty years."

She picked up her muffin, stripped off the wrapper, and broke off a piece. "Go ahead and eat, Detective. Please. I made these specially for you."

He mentally contrasted this woman, willing to bake for a cop's visit, with the smirking kid down in the park refusing to give up the necklace. Then gave himself a mental kick. Not all young people were bad, and not all older people were good.

Burgess remembered that he had copies of the photos of the man and woman who'd been looking for the girl. "If I showed you a photo, would you be able to tell me if it was the man you've seen?"

"I can look," she agreed. "He wasn't very distinctive, you know. Just medium. Medium tall, medium build, medium weight. And I only saw him from a distance."

Burgess took the photos from his pocket and handed her the one of the man. She studied it, then turned on a light so she could see better.

Finally, she said, "I think that's the same man, but I can't be sure." Her gaze dropped to the other photo he was holding. "What about that photo? Am I supposed to identify it, too?"

He shook his head. "A woman who is a person of interest in our case."

Undeterred, she held out her hand. "May I see it?"

He figured "why not?" and handed her the photo.

She studied it a minute, then sighed and said, "Oh, dear." Then she looked at Burgess, a very sad look, as she said, "That's Rosie's daughter, Elaine. The one who chooses bad boyfriends. If she's somehow involved in harming a child, it will be his fault. Elaine is a follower. Always has been, despite Rosie's efforts to get her to think for herself. She's always looking for someone to tell her what to do. If she's involved in what happened to that girl, she's picked herself a doozy this time."

"You're sure this is Elaine?"

She gave him an 'I may be old but I'm not stupid' look. "Known her since she was born. Of course, I'm sure."

He realized he didn't know Rosie's last name, nor had he asked what facility she was in. But first, Elaine's last name.

"Elaine's last name?" he asked.

She gave him a half-hearted smile. "I'm really not sure. See, Elaine doesn't just pick bad men. She marries them, so I don't know what her name is right now. But Rosie will know. Even on her off days, she's usually clear about Elaine. I guess you can't spend so much of your life worrying about your child without that worry getting embedded in your mind. She always talks about Elaine, and it's usually some concern about what Elaine is up to."

He got Rosie's last name, Harmon, and the facility where she was staying. Then asked, "You said Elaine lives in Brunswick?"

"Was living. She could be anywhere. Not only does she pick bad men but she's quick about moving in with them. Then when it falls apart, Rosie has to bail her out, come up with another deposit on an apartment, buy her new furniture, and help her get back on her feet. It would be comical if it weren't so sad."

He'd gotten all he was going to get here, and he wanted to swing by the hospital and see how Colleen was doing. But as he thanked her and rose, he realized he should check out the house next door while he was here. See if there was anything it could tell him about why it was being used as a mail drop.

"Is there a hidden key somewhere I could use to take a look at Rosie's house?"

"None that I know of, but I have a key."

She went to a drawer in the sideboard and got it for him. A shiny silver key on a bright red ribbon.

Ask and you shall receive, Burgess thought. "I'll bring it right back," he said.

She shrugged her narrow shoulders. "I'm going out soon. Why don't you leave it in the mailbox. My mailbox."

So Burgess took the key, moved his vehicle so she could get hers out, and went next door to see if there *was* anything the house could tell him. He'd come out here not expecting much and gotten a lot. Who knew what else he might find?

SIXTEEN

The house had a musty, unused smell and the air coming at him was surprisingly cold. Most people left some heat on in an empty house to protect the pipes. He zipped his jacket and headed inside, closing the door behind him. He was standing in a hallway with a stairway to his left leading to the second floor. On his left and right were a pair of identical rooms. What must have been, long ago, the two parlors—the one the family used and the one that was reserved for special occasions. The sheet-draped furniture looked ominous and ghostly. The undraped furniture was dark and heavy. Although the house wasn't occupied, the shades on all the windows were drawn.

Despite the cold, the house was clean and neat. No signs of the rodents who quickly invaded unoccupied houses or the spiders who infested empty corners. There were a few books and old magazines about, but no mail, notes, or anything that might give a clue about how the house might have been used by Glen or Margaret Briscow. But there was some reason the house was so well kept up. Was it simply because that was what Rosie Harmon wanted and her daughter complied? Another question to ask.

The refrigerator was empty but still plugged in. Dishwasher empty. The stovetop clean and crumb free. Rosie might be in a home but someone was caring for the place. Caring except for the inadequate heat. Was it supposed to be the daughter's responsibility and she'd fallen down on the job? A question he probably needed to ask Shirley, although he'd try to ask Rosie Harmon first.

The half bath under the stairs was clean.

He climbed the stairs, already thinking this might be a futile operation, but needing to be thorough. Upstairs there were three bedrooms and a full bath. Two of the bedrooms were as pristine and unused as the downstairs. The third, though, was a surprise. Instead of the usual bedroom furniture, as in the other rooms, this one, the room farthest away from Shirley's house, had a lock on the outside of the door. The room was dark, with light-blocking curtains drawn closed. Against one wall was a mattress with no covers or pillows. It was the only item in the room.

There were some small stains on the mattress that might be blood. Depending on how things developed, he might bring an evidence tech back here to check that out. He needed to know more first.

He opened the closet. Empty.

Seeing echoes of that fake ambulance—only a mattress and rings to fasten a recalcitrant occupant—Burgess took a few photographs of the room, the mattress, and the lock, and went back downstairs.

He was leaving when something crinkled under the front hall rug. He bent, flipped back the rug, and found a rumpled, dirty brochure. Aimed at parents with stubbornly defiant teens, it offered "a comfortable, secure residential program where your children can reconnect with nature and the simple country life away from bad influences and the temptations of their regular lives." There were photos of a group of smiling teens on a hike, another of them sitting around a campfire, a third showing some of them in canoes. All of the teens looked absurdly happy. Burgess figured they were stolen from a genuine camp brochure.

Maybe this was what he'd been looking for. He thought it was peculiar that there were no names and no addresses, just a phone number to call to learn more. A call best made from Terry Kyle's burner phone.

He put the brochure into an evidence envelope, returned the key to Shirley Bufford's mailbox, and drove to the hospital.

At the nurse's station, they told him that the girl's moment of consciousness had been fleeting and there hadn't been any since.

Discouraging. They were circling around something that eventually they'd get nailed down, but she could probably have answered many of the questions they were laboring to answer. Still, he was building a picture in his mind of what had happened. He had no clue, though, about how to find the place where this girl and, the brochure suggested, others were held—possibly sent by desperate and well-meaning parents looking for a solution for managing their out-of-control teenagers.

Actually, he had one clue. A very small one—those hitchhiker seeds. It wasn't much to help him locate a secret camp for wayward teens in the huge state of Maine.

He ought to head back to 109 and see if anyone else had had a breakthrough. He ought to go and visit Rosie in her facility and see if she could tell him her daughter Elaine's address and current name. If that failed, he'd have to call Shirley back and press her on where he might find Rosie's daughter. See if she remembered anything else that might help.

He was feeling discouraged but reminded himself that he now had identities for both the man and woman who'd come looking for the girl. That was a big step forward, yet he worried these people would turn out to be impossible to find. Certainly Glen Briscow, a/k/a Edwin Hall, knew something about evading law enforcement.

He also wondered what the state police were up to with respect to the very dead Tobias Jones or the missing Elvira Clemens. Had she come home to find her house and yard swarming with police or had she joined her son wherever he was? Had she been a participant in what was done to Stan Perry? These were questions he couldn't easily ask the investigators.

There had been nothing in the papers.

He had other questions for Elvira Clemens, too. Like, was she involved in some way with the place where the girl had been held?

He rubbed his forehead as though it was a magic lamp that would summon some answers. Then, before he moved on to his next task, he went into Colleen's room and sat beside the bed.

"Who did this to you?" he asked the still figure. "Are there others at risk who need to be rescued? We really need you to wake up and talk to us."

He waited a while, simply watching the rise and fall of her breath, until he finally rose and headed back to his truck. Maybe tomorrow she would surface. For now, it seemed he was going to have to figure this out himself.

Back in the truck, he sat staring out the windshield, as though somehow this gloomy, gray afternoon was going to give him answers. Likely fruitless, he knew. His city only spoke to him when it wanted to.

While he was out driving around, he might as well pay a visit to Rosie Harmon.

He parked in an area marked "Visitors" and went inside. All of these places were alike in some ways. They might have nicer furnishings, better lighting, real flowers, and kinder staff, but they were all depressing, with fragile people nodding off in wheelchairs; they often smelled of old age, cleaning products, and pee. Given a choice between ending up here and dying in his bed, he wanted to die at home.

Of course, his history would suggest he'd probably have neither option. Some bad guy would be quicker or more ruthless or crazier or something. The ever-present danger was one reason Chris had refused to marry him. She'd live with him and love him but--? But what? Did she want to be free to walk away if he was crippled but not dead? No. Chris wasn't like that. She was loyal. She had struggled to live with the risks of his job but also didn't want to leave. Maybe their time together, and jointly caring for the kids, had helped her decide in his favor. Because now, it seemed, there was a change on the horizon. She wanted to get married.

If she wanted a Christmas wedding, that's what she should have. He didn't care for any of the wedding folderol but evidently, to some small extent, she did. Maybe the ceremonial part was to make it more real. License, officiant, witnesses. Burgess shrugged. He didn't know.

He dragged his thoughts back to where he was and to the task at hand and went to the reception desk. "Detective Sergeant Joe Burgess, here to see Rosie Harmon," he told the bored woman.

She opened her mouth to say something rote, like it wasn't visiting hours or did he have an appointment, then registered the "Detective Sergeant."

"She's in her room, I believe. I'll have someone take you there."

She picked up a phone, held a brief conversation, and told him, "Maryam will be out soon. You can sit over there." She indicated a row of chairs. "I'm afraid Rosie is having a bad day."

She wasn't alone, Burgess thought as he took a chair. Bad day. Bad week. Bad year? God but their summer had been awful. Even his vacation had dumped him in the middle of a crime. He was a big, scarred, cynical crime magnet.

Some days he could physically feel time slipping by, and this was one of them. He wasn't naturally patient. He was more of a charging bull than a watch-and-wait type, but often enough the cases that came his way required more of the latter. He'd learned to live with it. No choice in the matter. But there were still days when he wanted to tip the world sideways and shake something loose. This case felt like they were building toward a solution with teeny, tiny Legos.

He realized a woman was standing in front of him, waiting for his attention. She was a petite, dark-skinned woman with a shiny black braid down her back. "If you come with me, please, I will take you to Miss Rosie," she said. An accent he couldn't place but one that was very pleasing. He thought the patients must love this little woman with her ready smile and gentle voice.

"Sorry," he said, and stood.

"I think maybe they told you at the desk that Miss Rosie is having a bad day. She really isn't. She's just…well, she gets lonely. Her daughter was supposed to visit today and she didn't come. So Miss Rosie is sad."

"This was Elaine?" he said.

She nodded. "I think she tries to be a good daughter but she's not very organized. Or something like that. I know she sometimes promises to come and then she doesn't, which makes things more difficult for us."

"What's Elaine's last name," he asked. "If you know."

She paused, considering. "I think she has recently married and changed it. I don't know the new name but before she was Elaine Hawes."

"Would the facility have an address for her?"

Another pause. "Yes. But should I be telling these things to you when our residents are entitled to privacy?"

"You should, because there are activities going on at Rosie's house and we need to ascertain whether a family member is involved or these people are strangers. I will ask Rosie, of course, but her friend Shirley says she may not be clear about what is happening."

The small woman sighed. "That is true. And Miss Shirley is a very good friend. She visits often, which makes Miss Rosie very happy. It is hard for our residents, you understand, having to leave their homes and live here, away from friends and usual activities. Even though we try to make them comfortable."

She started walking again, saying, "They miss their homes."

"Of course they do," he agreed, as she paused before a closed door and knocked.

There was no answer.

"Wait here," she said. "I will make sure she is awake and able to see you."

She slipped inside and closed the door behind her. He heard the soft murmur of voices and then she reappeared. "She is ready. Please try not to upset her." She opened the door wider to admit him, then followed him inside.

SEVENTEEN

Rosie Harmon was sitting by the window. She had wayward white hair, some of which had escaped a small braid. She wore a pale lavender housecoat with faded pink roses on it, loose gray track pants, and dirty, fluffy pink slippers. Her hands were clasped in her lap. She gazed up at Burgess as he approached and asked, "Are you Elaine's new husband?"

He pulled a chair closer to her, so that he was in her line of sight, and said, "No, ma'am. I'm sorry. I'm a detective with the Portland police department."

She shook her head and looked at the woman who'd brought him. "Maryam, did we call the police?"

The small woman moved closer and put a hand on Rosie's arm. "No, Miss Rosie. The detective is here to ask some questions about your house."

Instantly, the old woman looked alarmed. "Has something happened to my house? My daughter, Elaine, is looking after it for me. She hasn't said anything about problems."

She turned to the small woman and said, "Maryam, why is this man here? Has something happened to my house?"

To Burgess she said, "Who are you and why are you here?"

The woman called Maryam patted her arm and said, soothingly, "It's okay, Miss Rosie. The detective just has a few questions for you."

Rosie Harmon said, "Is my house okay?"

"Your house is fine," Burgess said. "But someone has been getting their mail there and may be using the house. We wondered if you know who it was?"

"That will be Elaine." She turned to the aide and said, "It's probably Elaine, Maryam, isn't it? I think she said something about…only I can't remember what she said." Rosie Harmon rubbed her head as though, like Burgess earlier, she was trying to summon some answers.

"We can ask Elaine directly, if that would be easier for you," Burgess said.

The old woman shook her head sadly. "Elaine is…my daughter is… she's not very—" She searched for a word and Burgess, who had a bad habit of wanting to fill in other people's conversational gaps, restrained himself and waited.

At last she came up with "responsible" and then lapsed into silence.

"Why don't we ask her what's going on with the house?" Burgess suggested. "Would that be easier for you?"

She nodded.

"If you can tell me where to find Elaine."

"Oh. You know…I…" Long hesitation. At last she said, looking mortified, "I can't remember." She reached out a thin hand laced with purple veins. Her nails needed cutting. "Don't get old, Detective. It's a miserable thing."

She looked so small and fragile, so troubled by the failings of her mind. Burgess felt guilty for doing this to her, even though his work often forced him to be less kind than he liked to be. He looked at the aide. "Mrs. Harmon, do you think Maryam might be able to help me with Elaine's name?"

"I don't know." It sounded like an admission of defeat. The thin hands knotted as she looked at the aide. "Maryam, do you know how to find Elaine?"

"We probably have some records in the office, since she's your emergency contact, Miss Rosie. If you say it's okay to share that with the detective."

Rosie Harmon nodded. "It's okay. I'm happy people are keeping an eye on my house. I hated leaving it. I hate it here." She started to cry. "I just want to go back to my home and live out my life the way I was supposed to."

It was heartbreaking to see. Burgess put one of his big hands over Rosie Harmon's small one and said, "We'll keep an eye on your house, ma'am. I was there this morning and everything looked fine."

She gave him a wavering smile. "Good luck finding Elaine. She's supposed to keep this facility updated but as I said, Elaine isn't always very responsible. And now she's gone and got herself married again and I don't know his name or anything about him."

"You've never seen him?" Burgess asked.

She shook her head. "No. Well, yes. Uh…She did bring him here once so I could meet him, but he was restless and didn't stay long."

It was a long shot, given her poor memory, but Burgess took it. He said, "Do you think you'd recognize his photo?"

Rosie Harmon tapped her temple, saying, in a small voice, "My memory is very poor, Detective."

She wanted him to go, he knew. Wanted to be freed from being forced to reveal her flawed memory to an intrusive stranger. He got out the photo of Edwin Hall, now calling himself Glen Briscow, and showed it to Mrs. Harmon.

She took it in trembling fingers and brought it close to her face, then held it away at a distance, and shook her head. "I just don't know. I'm sorry."

He thanked her for her time, gently shook her hand and rose to go. The aide, Maryam, followed him out, calling back, "I'll just take him to the office and see if he can get Elaine's address, Miss Rosie. I'll be right back."

When the door was closed behind them, she said, "She'll need some calming down, you see. Anything out of the ordinary upsets her." She paused and held out her hand. "May I see the photo? I was here that day, the day Elaine brought her new husband to meet Miss Rosie."

Burgess gave her the photo. She studied it much like Rosie had, holding it close and then at a distance, and said, "I can't be sure, but I think this is the man."

She left him at the office after explaining what he needed. Before she left, he got her information, in case he needed to speak with her again. The office had an address and phone number for Elaine Harmon, or Elaine Wise, as she'd been when Rosie entered the facility. They didn't know if that was still her name or her address, but the phone number had worked recently when Mrs. Harmon was sick and they'd needed to contact her.

Burgess thanked them and left. He might be getting somewhere. Or he might be embarking on another wild goose chase. Or a wild Elaine chase. Or a wild Elaine and Glen chase. Still, he felt hopeful as he drove back to 109. Shirley Bufford and the gentle aide, Maryam, both belonged in his gratitude diary.

Despite his morning bagel and Shirley's muffin, he was hungry. He tried to eat a healthier diet these days, shrinking his waistline in favor of his bad knee, but sometimes he needed to eat and today was one of those days. Luckily, he knew just where to go. There was a sandwich shop on his way back where they made fabulous meatloaf sandwiches. If he was lucky, Melina, who owned it, would have some meatloaf set aside for her favorite customers. Burgess was definitely one of those. He thought her meatloaf sandwiches also belonged in his gratitude diary.

When he came through the door, she looked up and smiled, though her busy hands never stopped moving. "Detective Joe!" she said. "I hope you are hungry?"

"When it comes to your food," he said, "I'm always hungry."

"So you are wanting two sandwiches, yes? And what about for Terry and Stan? And will you want cookies? I have oatmeal raisin just out from the oven."

He couldn't go back to 109 with food for himself and not for them, so he said, "Sandwiches and cookies for all."

"How is your family? Mrs. Joe? And your handsome son?"

"Everyone's well. Growing up. Even Ned is in double digits now and won't let us call him Neddy anymore."

"Ah. Children are like that, yes? The days are long yet they grow up too fast."

Not knowing quite why he said it—maybe simply for the pleasure of saying it aloud—Burgess said, "And Mrs. Joe and I are actually getting married in December." As he said it, an idea came to him. "A small wedding. And we will need a caterer. Would you consider—"

She cut him off with a shriek of joy. "Oh, Detective Joe, that is such good news. I will speak with Mrs. Joe...uh...your almost wife...about the food."

Right. Because wedding food was a woman's department. Not that he minded. He thought Chris would be pleased that he had a caterer and happy to work with Melina to plan the food. Now, if he could come up with a venue, he'd be a hero.

Melina's busy hands flew, and in no time, carrying bags of sandwiches and cookies, he was at 109 and heading inside.

He found Kyle and Perry in the conference room, discussing something. They both looked up when he entered, and from their expressions, he understood that Cote had been around asking questions to which they had no answers.

"Hope your morning was better than mine," Perry said. He waved the sheaf of pink message slips. "Can you tell me why the fuck they call and ask us to be in touch and then act surprised when we call back?"

"Because people are idiots," Kyle told him. Then, taking in what Burgess was holding, he said, "Luckily, not all people. You've been to Melina's, Joe?"

Burgess nodded.

"And you have cookies?"

He nodded again. Sometimes it was so easy to make his teammates happy. He handed out sandwiches and napkins. Said, "Anything good happen while I was out?"

"I think I'm getting a handle on what's bothering Anna," Kyle said.

"Autumn is growing perfectly, according to the charts, and took her first shots like a champ," Perry said.

So it wasn't all bad.

"I spoke with the neighbor next to the empty house. Shirley Bufford," Burgess said. "She gave me some information about a man who has been parking at the house." He passed Bufford's notes to Perry.

"And she identified our mystery woman as the daughter of a woman named Rosie Harmon, who owns the house and is now in a facility for people with dementia. Her name is Elaine Wise, but according to Rosie

…uh…Mrs. Harmon and the aide who looks after her, she may have recently remarried and changed her name."

He took out the flyer he'd found under the rug in Rosie Harmon's house. "And I found this."

He laid it on the table and Kyle and Perry bent to read it.

"Holy Fuck!" Kyle said. He stabbed the paper. "This is it, Joe. You know that this is it. Wherever this place is, it's where our girl was being held."

"Our girl." That possessiveness about a victim happened rarely, but it did happen. The rule was don't get attached, but there would always be those cases where they did.

Their challenge, well, one of their challenges, would be try and find this place. Another to locate Elaine Harmon Wise. They had her phone number, one the facility said had worked recently, so they could look for her phone records.

He put the photos of the woman now identified as Elaine Harmon Wise, who might be calling herself Margaret Briscow, and the man they knew as Edwin Hall a/k/a Glen Briscow, on the table. "Elaine Harmon Wise and Edwin Hall," he said. "The two who were looking for the girl on the night we found her. He came into the station, she went to the hospital. And…" He pointed at the information he'd gotten from Shirley Bufford. "We've got his truck make and registration. We know he had a Prius registered at his mother's place. I wonder where the truck is registered."

"On it," Perry said, picking up the paper and heading for his computer. At the door he paused, did an about-face, and came back to the table. "Sandwiches and cookies first," he said.

"Right," Kyle said, "an army marches on its stomach."

"I always found that weird to imagine," Burgess said, but he joined them at the table and unwrapped a sandwich. Tried not to inhale it, which was hard because it was delicious.

"Chris wants to get married," he said. "And she wants a December wedding."

He looked at Kyle, who shook his head and said, "I thought I'd called December."

"You did. I'm sure we can work something out. She said she's willing to wait until January, but then she got all dreamy about how pretty a Christmas wedding would be."

Kyle nodded. Said, "Maybe we'd better pick our days now, so we don't have a conflict." A pause. "Assuming Chris and Michelle agree, of course."

"Of course."

Vince Melia appeared in the doorway. He spotted the sandwiches and said, "Melina's?"

Burgess nodded.

"You don't have an extra, do you?"

So Burgess gave up his second sandwich. He was supposed to be watching his weight anyway, right?

Melia joined them at the table, unwrapped his food, and said, "Catch me up."

Burgess gave a quick summary of what they'd learned and passed him the flyer he'd found in the vacant house.

"This," Melia said, stabbing the page just as Kyle had done. "This is it. Now all we have to do is find a needle in a haystack."

EIGHTEEN

After Burgess and Kyle had bent over their calendars, blocked out the first and third Saturdays in December, and agreed that they'd let Chris and Michelle decide between them who got which day, the team got down to work.

"Nobody better kill anybody on those weekends," Stan Perry said, though they all knew that the holidays were catalysts for violence.

"Let's just get this one put to bed," Burgess said, "and worry about December in December."

"Right," Kyle agreed. "We can always hand it off to the B team."

Their imaginary B team, the one they fantasized about giving their cases to.

He said, "When are we going to call that number?"

"I'd like to get a little more information about our players first," Burgess said. "See if we can locate Elaine Wise. From what I've been told, she'll be the weak link. We don't want to play our hand too fast. They get suspicious and they might move the whole operation somewhere else."

"We don't know if there is a whole operation," Perry said. "Right? Whether there's one teenager involved or a dozen. Do we?"

Of course they didn't.

Stan Perry, his food reduced to a pile of crumbs, headed to his computer with the plate number they'd gotten from Shirley Bufford.

Kyle was still working his way through the messages.

Burgess turned to the name and address Rocky Jordan had found working from the plate on the car driven by the woman claiming to be the girl's mother. He went to his computer and started digging.

The rest of the afternoon slipped away. Time flew whether you were having fun or not. He'd gotten a name for the woman, he believed, and was sorting through local photos to see if he could recognizer her, when he looked at the clock. It was almost six. Never mind that he was nose to the ground and on the chase, he had to get home, get spiffed up, and head out with Ned to the career event at the school. These days, with the police so vilified, he doubted if he was going to win the hearts and minds of any middle schoolers, but he could hope, right? After all, his kid was counting on him.

It happened as he was driving home. He'd just gotten off the phone with Chris, saying he was on his way, when it hit him like a bolt of lightning. Sudden. Devastating. So overwhelming he almost drove off the road. What if they couldn't solve this? What if their girl died and they couldn't find the place where she, and probably others, had been held and mistreated? He rarely had doubts of this magnitude. Usually, he was too busy to pause and ponder the possibility of failure, mostly because, since he and his team spoke for the dead, failure wasn't an option. Of course there were those cases they couldn't solve. The ones that haunted them. But that failure and the pain it brought were usually much further down the road.

The grip of this possibility was so powerful he wondered if he was having a heart attack or maybe a stroke, and he pulled to the side until his heart rate slowed and his breathing became normal again. It had been quick—coming and going in a minute or two—but it had left him sweaty and shaken.

Sorry, he told himself, can't wimp out now. There are lives at stake here. As a pep talk, it wasn't much, but he was able to pull himself together and finish the drive home. He was met by two dogs eager for his attention, which reminded him he still hadn't managed to hand off Andre. After the owner had failed to meet the requirements for reclaiming his animal, he'd never returned to the police station. It was probably time for Andre to find a new home and a more attentive owner, for the dog's sake and Burgess's.

He took a moment to give them pats and they followed him inside.

He thought he was hiding it well, but while the kids were gathering at the table for tonight's pizza dinner, Chris took his arm and drew him into the other room. "What's happened? Are you okay? You don't look okay."

Nothing like being told you looked ill to make you feel ill, right?

He shrugged. Might as well tell her the truth. She was a good bull-shit barometer. "Just a weird moment of doubt. About myself. About the case."

She hugged him. "You'll figure it out. Getting justice for the vulnerable? That's your superpower."

He'd never thought about having a superpower before. Wasn't sure he liked it. It came with too much responsibility and he already had enough.

From the other room, Ned called, "Hurry up and eat, Dad. We don't want to be late."

He would love to be late. Or to not go at all. But as he was constantly discovering, parenthood came with a lot of responsibilities he'd never known about. Food, shelter, clothing, love, security, and a moral upbringing he understood. The rest was uncharted territory.

He followed Chris back to the table and joined the family. He wasn't very hungry. Melina's sandwiches, even if he hadn't gotten that second one, were substantial. But he wasn't telling Chris that. Not when he'd vowed to be a better partner.

When their plates were full and everyone was chewing, he offered a new subject. "How does December 7th sound?" he asked.

Chris smiled. "Sounds perfect."

"For what?" Nina asked.

"Yeah. For what?" Dylan echoed.

"A wedding," Chris said.

"Whose?" Dylan again.

"Mine. Joe's and mine. And I suppose that Nina will be maid of honor and Dylan will be best man."

"But what about me?" Ned said through a mouthful of pizza. "Don't I get a job?"

"Oh, you and Fideau are going to be our ringbearers. You'll have to wear ties, of course. Red, I think."

"Neddy and Fideau?" Nina said. "Are you kidding?"

"Ned," Ned corrected.

"Oh no," Burgess said. "We're very serious. We've given this a lot of thought."

"I think I've found a venue," Chris said.

"And I think I've found a caterer." Burgess hesitated. "Actually, since Terry and Michelle also want a December wedding, the two of you are supposed to discuss the dates. The first Saturday or the third."

Chris smiled. "I'm easy. Kinda prefer the earlier date, though. We'll talk. And wow. Now I guess I need a dress. And a guest list."

"Me, too," Nina said. "Can we go dress shopping together? That would be so much fun."

Dylan rolled his eyes. Burgess wanted to but didn't. Fideau put his head in Burgess's lap and gave him a look he read as, "When are we getting rid of this Andre creature? Have you forgotten I am your dog and you are my human?"

He scratched the dog's ears, said, "How could I forget?" and everyone stared at him.

"Fideau's wondering when Andre will be leaving us."

"Dogs can't talk," Ned said.

"This one can."

And then it was time to go.

NINETEEN

Ned was practically dancing beside him as they went up the walk to the gym entrance. Burgess had memories of so many times he'd been in a school gym. It seemed like everything except sports had taken place in his school's gym, and it looked like things hadn't changed. They were surrounded by families with children around Ned's age. Some of the parents were in suits or jackets and ties. Those, Burgess figured, were there to share their featured professions. Maybe he should have worn his uniform.

A tall, pretty young woman in a flowered dress was darting around the room, clearly trying to corral the presenters and steer them to their tables. Every few minutes she paused and looked nervously at the door. A missing presenter, perhaps? But he was a professional reader of people and thought there was more.

He was watching her, waiting for instructions, when Ned tugged on his arm. "You're over here, Dad," he said, pointing toward a table. There was a cardboard sign with Burgess's name on it. And, grateful for small things, he saw that he was indeed correctly designated as Detective Sergeant Joseph Burgess.

He was at the table, ready to drop into the waiting chair, when his phone buzzed. It had better not be a summons to a crime scene or an urgent need to get to the hospital, he thought, because he couldn't leave. He was a big proponent of responding when duty called, no matter the time of day or the weather, but he couldn't abandon Ned now. He's promised. If it was an emergency, Kyle or Perry could handle it.

It was the desk at 109. A man was there again to pick up his dog and this time he had brought the requisite items. What should they do?

Burgess debated. Send the man to his house? Make him come back in the morning? He'd already been in once before, and had managed to procure the necessary documents, leash, and poop bags. It showed the level of concern and responsibility Burgess had been looking for. It should be safe at home, since Dylan was there. But, like most cops, he didn't like people knowing where he lived. He said, "Have him wait there. My son will bring the dog."

He hoped Dylan didn't have plans. He called, told Dylan what he needed, and got a "Sure, Dad. I'm on it," which pleased him. It was a relief to be able to hand things off sometimes.

Then he turned to Ned, who was watching him anxiously. Ned said, "Do you have to go?"

"No, Ned. No emergency. It's fine."

"Did you bring your gun?"

"Not into a school. Not when I'm not here on duty."

"Your handcuffs?"

Yes, Burgess did have those. He'd brought his duty belt with a stun gun, cuffs, all the things he'd worn as a patrol officer. He'd also brought his badge and pepper spray. He figured some of Ned's classmates might want to see those.

The tall woman stopped by to thank him for coming, told him her name was Janice and to call on her if he needed anything, then bustled away. Shortly after that, she announced that the event had started and the rest was a blur. It seemed that many of the students, male and female, were interested in law enforcement and their questions were good. Did they need a college degree? Did they have to study criminal justice? How were police officers trained in Maine, for how long and where? Did cops get trained on how to do that fancy driving they saw on TV? Could a small woman become a police officer? Was his job dangerous?

Of course there was the predictable one: Had he ever shot some-one? To that he gave his usual answer: Most police officers go through their entire careers without firing their weapons except at the range.

He was impressed by these kids. He hadn't even known there was such a thing as a criminal justice program when he was in middle school. There was a lot of criticism about today's young people and how they were always stuck on their screens, but these kids were well prepared by their teachers. They were poised and curious and their questions thoughtful. He wondered if the other parents in the room were getting good questions as well.

Among his questioners was a small boy with hair almost the same red as Ned's, with pale skin and rusty freckles. He lingered after most of the other kids had moved on. Burgess sensed he wanted to ask a ques-tion but was too shy, so he said, "Did you have a question?"

The boy looked down at his shoes, then back at Burgess. "I'm Van," the boy said. "Which my stepdad says is short for 'vanish.' Is it scary when you have to go to a house where people are fighting?"

Burgess nodded. "It is. There are a lot of things we do that are scary, but it's our job. We go into scary situations so people will be safe. That is definitely one of them."

The boy thanked him and moved along, leaving Burgess with the sense that there was something serious behind the boy's question. Some-thing from his own life. Maybe involving the stepdad whose joke was that the boy should vanish? He tried to push his concern away but he'd seen situations where stepfathers did make children disappear.

When it seemed the event had only started minutes ago, Janice clapped her hands for silence and announced that the job fair was over. She thanked everyone for coming. As she was inviting everyone to enjoy cupcakes and punch, a large man appeared in the doorway, a man not dressed for a parents' night at a school. He wore dirty jeans that barely cleared his crotch and an obscene tee shirt stretched over a large beer gut. Burgess saw fear on her face. Whoever this man was, he was someone whose presence she'd been dreading.

Burgess didn't know the man but he knew the type.

"Sir," she said, stepping forward to head the man off.

Stepping around her raised hands and ineffectual pleas to stop, the man made a beeline for the boy named Van. He said, "Come here, you irresponsible little brat. I told you to stay home and watch your brother." He was not using his inside voice, and his words were slurred and hard to understand.

The boy cowered, looking like he was about to cry. In a small voice, he said, "Mom told me I could come tonight. She said you would look after Gabe."

"Well, I told you to stay home, didn't I?"

The man had almost reached the boy.

Grabbing his pepper spray, Burgess quickly worked his way through the crowd, trying to reach the boy before the angry man did.

Without pausing, the man bellowed, "Dammit, Van. I tole you ta stay home. Tole you I wanned ta go out."

The way he slurred his words, it was apparent he'd been drinking heavily. His red, belligerent face agreed.

As Burgess got closer, he smelled the reek of alcohol, so strong the man might have bathed in it.

The shaking boy had moved behind a table and huddled there, trying to make himself smaller.

Burgess got to the man just as he had reached the boy and drawn back his fist.

"Police officer," Burgess said loudly, stepping into the man's path, putting his bulk between the man and the frightened boy. "Whatever you're thinking of doing, don't. You're disrupting a school function and terrifying a child."

"Oh la la la, so I'm scaring this useless brat. Like I give a fuck about that."

At least, that's what Burgess thought he said. It was as though conflict had accelerated the man's intoxication. His words were increasingly hard to understand.

The man balled up his fist again. If he couldn't punch the kid, he was going to punch Burgess and get him out of the way.

"I wouldn't do that if I were you," Burgess said, this time making his voice loud enough for everyone to hear. "You hit a cop and there are consequences."

But the man was mission-driven. He'd come here to make a point with his stepson and he wasn't going to be deterred. He swung at Burgess, who sidestepped the blow so it only grazed his shoulder. He grabbed the man's outstretched arm and put him on the floor.

"Stay down," he commanded as the man tried to buck him off.

"Fuck you."

Burgess planted a knee on the man's back and looked at Ned. "Get me my handcuffs, Ned."

And Ned, who loved to be Burgess's helper, darted to the table and brought back the whole duty belt. He knelt nearby, unsnapped the cuffs, and held them out.

Keeping his knee on the man's back, Burgess cuffed him, then pulled him to his feet.

So much for an evening at Ned's school where he got to be a dad and talk about his career. He hadn't planned on giving a hands-on demo.

As he checked the room to be sure everyone was okay, the cuffed man lowered his head, bellowed, and charged toward the terrified boy.

"That's enough." Burgess grabbed his arm, spun him around, and sprayed him with pepper spray.

The man folded into an angry, yelping heap. Unable to use his hands, he wiped his streaming eyes and nose on his knees.

"Stay there," Burgess ordered. He got out his phone and called patrol to come and pick the man up. To the staring crowd, he said, "It's under control. Nothing to worry about."

But of course now he had drawn a crowd of curious students who had more questions, while their anxious and protective parents were trying to pull them away. He nodded at the boy. "Van, you okay?"

The boy wiped away tears and nodded.

The tall woman, Janice, who had been standing protectively behind the boy, asked, "How can I help?"

"Distract them. Thank me for a hands-on demonstration and remind everyone about the cupcakes and punch."

As she turned to speak to the crowd, he added, in a lower voice, "And let me know if you hear anything from Van about further threats or abuse. We do what we can, but the justice system isn't always as protective as it should be."

She spoke, her thanks to Burgess drawing a laugh, and the lure of cupcakes soon pulled the crowd away.

"You know this guy?" Burgess asked as she lingered behind.

"Van's stepfather. This isn't the first time he's made a scene. The poor boy is absolutely terrified of him. We've notified social services, but you know how that can be. His mother tries, but she has to work and that means leaving the boys with him. Van gets the worst of it, trying to protect his brother."

"This can't go on. She needs to get that man away from her children."

Burgess knew far too much about abusive men bullying wives and children from his own father. "I'll call social services," he said. "Sometimes a call from us makes a difference."

They exchanged a look that said they both knew it probably wouldn't. She put a hand on his shoulder and leaned closer. "We are so lucky you were able to come tonight."

He didn't say, "All in a day's work," because his days were so varied, but 'serve and protect' was definitely part of his job. He stayed with the handcuffed man until patrol came to take him away. As they started to lead the man away, he wheeled toward Burgess and said, "This isn't over, you know. You mess with my family and I'll mess with yours."

When Burgess had first been on the force, no one would have dared to threaten a cop. These days, it was almost the norm.

He shrugged, then joined the crowd enjoying cupcakes and punch.

Burgess gave his cupcake to Ned, who loved sugar. His son was in heaven. Tonight had been a twofer—his dad had shown up for him, and he'd gotten to eat two cupcakes. Maybe a threefer, since his classmates had also seen Ned's father in action.

Before Van left, Burgess took a moment. He said, "I'm sorry that happened to you."

The boy shrugged. "He gets mad when I don't do what he wants. But I really wanted to come and my mom said it would be okay. She said she'd spoken to him and he was fine with it. Only then he started drinking, and once he does, he gets all mean and forgets anything he's agreed to."

"Does he hit you?"

Reluctantly, the boy nodded "Yes."

"Does he hit your brother?"

Another nod.

"And does he hit your mother?"

A slow, sad nod.

Burgess was so sick of weak, pathetic men who built themselves up by terrifying women and children.

"Where is your mother tonight?"

"She works nights. At the hospital. She's a nurse."

Burgess wondered if he knew her. Wondered if she'd been fooled by this man into thinking he was a good match for her or if she'd been desperate for a boyfriend or someone to look after her kids. He was going to find out. Of course he was going to find out.

He got the mother's name, then gave the boy his card, writing his cell phone number of the back. "If he tries to hit you, or your brother, or your mom again, you call me. Can you do that?"

"We're not allowed to use the phone."

"In this case, it's okay. It's okay to protect yourself and the people you love. Remember what we talked about tonight? About how police have to go into difficult situations to keep people safe?"

He got a nod.

"Well, I need you to be safe." He paused, then said, "Will you call me? Promise?"

Another nod, a little more affirmative this time. "I will, Detective Sergeant Burgess. I will."

They gave the boy a ride home. Burgess resisted the urge to go inside and see how they lived. He'd done what he could. Maybe it wouldn't happen again, but he doubted an arrest would deter the man. Bullies like him were slow learners. He could only hope that if it did, the boy would call.

As they finished the drive home, Ned said, "Thanks, Dad. For showing up for me. For letting people know what cops really do, instead of all that stuff they hear about how cops are violent." Silence. Then, "I like Van. I'd like him to be my friend, but he's never allowed to play with anyone. He always has to stay home and watch his brother. It's really not fair."

"Maybe he could come and play and bring his brother. Would that be a plan? You'd be okay with that?"

Ned grinned and sat up straighter. "That would be a great plan."

Ned pounded up the stairs and by the time Burgess got to the kitchen, he was sharing the whole adventure with Chris, Dylan, and Nina. Even Fideau seemed interested.

"And Dad was just great," Ned said. "He stopped the guy's punch and put him on the floor, and I helped with the handcuffs." He grabbed a breath. "And that was important, because the man was Van's mean stepdad who hits him all the time and he was heading straight for Van." Another pause. "Van's kind of small and scared. And now I understand why."

Burgess tried to derail the conversation by thanking Dylan for delivering the dog. But it didn't work. He got a smile and "no problem." Then everyone went back to discussing the events at school, still looking at him like he was a hero, when he'd just been doing his job. He hated praise and fuss, especially at home, and badly wanted to be somewhere else.

For once, the universe agreed. A call from the hospital that the girl was awake sent him back out into the night.

TWENTY

I t didn't happen to him so often now, as he got further removed from those awful days sitting beside his dying mother, but sometimes, coming into the hospital, stabbed by the cruelty of the cold, bright lights and breathing air scented with antiseptic and fear, he was dragged back to that excruciating death watch for a woman whose death could have been prevented. He had to take a moment to shake off the miasma of bad memories before he went to see the girl.

The nurse gave him the usual "only for a few minutes and don't get her upset." Burgess needed all the time he could get and expected anything he asked would upset her. It was the nature of the job. Cops weren't generally visiting hospital patients just to chat. He knew it, she knew it, but he nodded and agreed.

The girl in the bed looked smaller and paler than he remembered, as though the long-term effects of what had been done to her had sapped her youthful essence and were shrinking her.

He pulled a visitor chair close to the bed and sat down.

Those startling green eyes studied him with a mixture of fear and confusion.

"It's okay," he said. "You're safe. I'm the police officer who found you down in the park. Do you remember me? My name is Joe Burgess.

I'm a detective with the Portland, Maine police department, and I think your name is Colleen?"

He'd kept his voice low and soft, speaking slowly so she could process his words, so her reaction was astonishing. She glared at him, yelled, "Colleen's dead, you idiot. They killed her. Or let her die. Or whatever. I'm Maureen." She sounded unbelievably sad.

The outburst seemed to have taken all her energy. She fell back against the pillow, exhausted, and closed her eyes.

Burgess waited to see what she would do next, hoping the nurse wasn't hovering just outside the door and would send him away for upsetting her patient. Her statement threw what they knew, or thought they knew, into chaos. Why had the woman who'd come looking for her daughter told him she was looking for Colleen and never mentioned another daughter? Was this girl in fact someone named Maureen? Were Colleen and Maureen sisters? Twins? Was there another girl out there or was there a body, a crime victim? It immediately amped up his need to move this case forward.

The nurse didn't appear.

The girl didn't open her eyes, as though, if she kept them closed, Burgess couldn't see her. It was like something a small child might do.

"Maureen," he said, still using his careful, gentle voice, "I'm here to help you any way I can. I can do that better if you'll talk to me."

Silence.

"You have been badly abused by someone," he said. "Someone you escaped from. We found you in a city park with only a blanket. Do you remember that?"

No response. Maybe she couldn't talk about it yet. He'd known cases where the victims were never able to talk to the police but went numb every time their traumatic experience was broached. He hoped that wouldn't be the case here. Because of what had been done to her. Because she was surrounded by liars, including a woman who might be her own mother. Because he was increasingly convinced there were other teens at risk.

"We need to know whether there are other girls, or other teens, who are still at risk so that we can rescue them."

Her eyes didn't open but the girl said, "There are. But I can't tell you where I was because I was…because Colleen and I were…we were taken there in a van with no windows. It was a long ride and we were so scared we weren't paying attention to much. Colleen had tried to escape and the man hit her. Hit her hard. I was afraid she was dead. Or would die. I was just lying beside her, holding her. Hoping they'd stop the van and see what they'd done and get her some help."

It was a slow, stumbling reply that seemed to take all her effort. Then she fell silent.

Despite his need to know, Burgess felt like he, too, was abusing this girl. He asked, "Would you like some water? Or maybe a soda?" He wanted to offer food but wasn't sure what she could eat in her depleted state.

"Water," she said.

He looked around, found a pitcher and a glass, and poured some for her. He raised the bed so she could drink more easily. Said, "I've got your water here."

The amazing green eyes opened and she reached out two shaky hands to take the glass. She drank. He took the glass from her.

She said, "Please. I can't…"

"I know this is hard. Let me ask you a few questions. You can nod or shake your head or say yes or no, okay?"

She gave a faint nod.

"This place where you were. Did your mother or your parents send you there?"

A nod.

"You and Colleen?"

Another.

"Colleen is your sister?"

"Twin."

Identical, he would bet. There was something about the twin bond. "Because they thought you were troublemakers?"

He got two words. "Colleen was." Then, "I couldn't let her go without me." Silence. "I can't. I…"

There were probably a lot of things she couldn't do right now. Talk. Think about her sister. Think about where she'd been. She needed to rest and he wasn't helping. He said, "It was supposed to be a fun place?

A kind of a nature camp? A place away from screens and bad influences? That's what they told your parents?"

A nod. She said, "Parent. He's my stepfather. He doesn't care. He wanted us gone."

"But it wasn't a nice place?"

She started to sob. Said, "It was horrible. A prison. We were all... prisoners. Sorry. I can't..."

"How many of you?"

A small shrug. "Maybe twelve."

Burgess the abuser, skilled in pressing people who didn't want to talk, had to leave this girl, this child, alone to recover. But only she had the information he needed. He said, "You need to rest. I'm going to leave you now. There is always someone watching the room so no one can get at you. No one who means you harm. But was there a girl there named Melanie Porter?"

He thought he got a faint nod.

"Can you tell me anything about the place that might help us find the others?"

"It was like a summer camp. Kinda. Maybe long ago? Flimsy buildings with bunks."

Her eyes closed. He thought she might have fallen asleep. But then they opened and she whispered, "There was a lake. With boats."

And she was asleep.

He rose. Patted her hand, said, "Thank you," and left.

How many lakes were there in Maine? Lakes with boats on them? Hundreds. He needed to know so much more. But for now, he had to leave her to rest. He headed out to his vehicle, wondering whether a hitchhiker plant and a defunct summer camp on a lake might be enough to find the place this girl had been held captive. He was oppressed by the knowledge there were so many more who needed to be rescued. By the burden of it. And the challenge.

Then he stopped. Before he left the hospital, he might as well kill two birds with one hospital visit. He went to find Van's mother.

He found her in the ICU, and though he had never known her name, he recognized her from other times he'd been here. She was small and pretty, with hair a few shades darker red than Van's, and she looked utterly worn down. Her name tag said she was Anita Elwell.

He introduced himself and asked for a few minutes of her time.

She smiled and said, "Maybe a few. Never know when all hell is going to break out around here."

"I was at the school tonight for the careers fair," he began.

She visibly brightened. "Was Van there? My son Van, a smallish boy with red hair like me? Did you meet him? He really wants to be a police officer when he grows up."

"He was, and—"

Before he could continue, she put a hand on his arm, gripping it hard, the moment of brightness gone. "Oh, please. Oh no. Please don't tell me Mark showed up."

Burgess nodded.

The woman started crying and it all came out in a burst. "He pretended to be so good with the kids, at first, and now he's shown who he really is and I don't know what to do. I've asked him to leave. It's my house. He just laughs at me. I can't afford to lose my job and childcare is impossible and Van is too young to be responsible for his brother and I know I'm a totally shit mom and…and I don't know what to do."

"You can start with a restraining order barring him from coming near you or your children. That will get him out of the house. We can help you with that. But the childcare thing? Is it not possible to work days?"

She shrugged. Pulled a tissue from her pocket and wiped her eyes. Started with, "The pay is better on this shift." Stopped herself, wiped her eyes again, and said, "I'll have to, won't I?"

Burgess nodded. "During the day, if you need coverage, there are before school and after school programs at the schools, I believe."

But she was already moving on. "So Mark showed up and…had he been drinking? Did he make a scene? Is Van okay?"

A pause. "He had been drinking, hadn't he?"

"Yes, he was drunk and yes, he made a scene. Van is fine. My son Ned and I gave him a ride home. Mark's been arrested. I don't know how long they'll hold him. But for now, the boys are okay and he won't be there when you get home. But this can't go on. You know that. There's too much risk to your children. And to you."

He let her absorb that and said, "You should get that restraining order as soon as you can. Then he can't legally come near you or the children."

Her sigh was eloquent. "I'm ashamed of myself for letting it go on this long."

"Guys like that are good at charming their way into relationships and then they're hard to get rid of."

She tried for a smile. "I guess you'd know."

"I do. Let me know how I can help. Oh, and my son, Ned, wants to know if he can arrange a time for him and Van to play. I suggested it might work if Van could bring his little brother. How old is his brother, by the way?"

"Gabe? He's five."

Burgess didn't know how long she'd been in this relationship, but it might be that the younger boy had spent much of his life in a violent situation. It also struck him, then, that if she was at work and Mark had come to the school, the younger boy might well have been left home alone. At five. It would have been shocking if he hadn't seen it dozens of times before. He could still be shocked, but not by this.

He said, "And Van is ten?"

"Eleven. Just." And then he saw what he was thinking cross her face. Mostly to herself, she said, "He wouldn't. He wouldn't leave Gabriel home alone. A five-year-old? But otherwise, how could he…?"

She wouldn't look at Burgess as she said, "I'll see about changing my shift. And getting that restraining order." And repeated, "I'm so ashamed of myself."

"Balancing a demanding job and being a single parent is hard. Everyone makes mistakes."

"You're too nice," she said, "but I appreciate it."

He left her then, hoping she'd do the right thing, and vowing to follow up. He needed to know whether the five-year-old had been left home alone while Mark made his scene at the school, but that could wait until tomorrow. Right now, it was very late and he was very tired.

He'd just go back to 109 and record what he'd learned from the girl, then head home to get some sleep.

TWENTY-ONE

Back in his truck, he didn't start the engine or drive to 109, but sat in the dark and pondered. If there was a secret camp somewhere in Maine where teens were being held prisoner and abused, it was really a matter for the state police. He should call them, share what the Portland police knew, and hand the case over to a better resourced department. He was reluctant to hand this girl over, though. Colleen or Maureen, whichever one she was. The detectives who showed up might be gentle and compassionate or they might be harsh and mission driven, while he felt so protective.

He was also reluctant because he was attached to this case. To this girl. Probably a wrong-headed, knight-in-shining-armor thing, where he wanted to be the one to break up the nest of vipers holding these children hostage and profiting on the backs of their misery and their parents' incompetence. He ought to get over himself and share what he knew. He shouldn't be one of those territorial assholes he always complained about who wouldn't share because they wanted the solve and the glory.

It wouldn't be easy to hand off because they all had such a stake in the case. The hours, the stories they'd been told. The attack on Stan Perry. All the information they'd developed.

KATE FLORA

What would help out here was if they had someone on the state police they could talk this over with without triggering a whole pissing contest about who had jurisdiction. Most of his contacts had retired. That was what happened when you were a dinosaur who wouldn't quit. Retired or moved so far up the food chain that they would feel their loyalty to their organization meant they had to claim the case as their own.

Kyle, who was a bit younger, might still have a contact he could talk to without having to share everything they knew. He'd ask in the morning. And for help locating that defunct camp on a lake? He did have one contact who might be useful—a game warden he'd met working a case. Wardens knew the Maine woods.

For now, he'd record what he knew for the files and head to bed. Record what he'd learned from the girl and also write a report on the incident at the school career fair.

Of course, when he got home, Fideau thought it was a good idea for Burgess to take him for a walk. Burgess actually enjoyed these walks. Before Fideau, he'd often stopped somewhere between work and home to process the day and file away the ugliness or his anxiety so the family wouldn't have to see it. Now he used these walks for the same purpose. Sometimes, although he worried that he might be becoming a nutcase, he even shared parts of his day with the dog.

Yes, it was crazy. He was probably becoming a crazy dog owner. But sometimes when he told things to Fideau, the dog would stop and tilt his head, like he was considering what Burgess had said. If he thought Burgess needed comforting, he'd press his head up against Burgess's leg.

Chris might not know about the confidences, but she approved of his walks with the dog. He was less anxious and got more exercise. He slept better.

He thought about the saying, "You can't teach an old dog new tricks." It seemed, at least, that this dog could teach an old human new tricks. Fideau could be infinitely patient as Burgess laid out the facts of a particular case. Was attentive tonight to the complicated story of the girl.

"Did you know Chris and I are getting married?" he told the dog.

Fideau nodded. So damned smart.

"And you're going to wear a tie and be in the wedding?"

Another nod.

"Think she'll be happier?"

Fideau stopped and stared up at him. As Burgess read the look, his dog was saying, "Of course, you idiot. Although what she really wants is you in a safer job."

"Well, that's not going to happen."

Fideau nodded.

"We are a ridiculous pair, aren't we."

They headed for home.

Despite the pleasant time he had in Fideau's company, no walk in the dark was ever entirely relaxed. Not for him or his dog. They both saw and heard things that gave them pause, and there were things Fideau smelled as well. If the justice system was its usual self, the man named Mark who'd threatened Burgess's family would be back on the streets in no time. That would amp up his concern for his family and add another element of danger to these walks.

Occasionally, even though he knew the current system was better, Burgess sometimes longed for the old days when someone who threatened a cop's family would quickly learn what a bad idea that was. These days he was a cynic who thought everyone had rights except the cops.

On that bright note, they reached home and both headed for bed. It felt like only minutes before his alarm was bleating like a sick sheep.

He was buttoning his shirt when he thought of the necklace they'd found down in the park. It had had an initial on it. He didn't remember what that initial was, and hadn't gone back to look at it after the woman at the hospital had insisted the girl was named Colleen. He added it to his mental to-do list and finished dressing.

His family was in the kitchen in various stages of breakfast, and Fideau was at the kitchen door, looking for him. He patted the dog's head as he said, "Thanks again for taking that dog down to the station last night, Dylan. It was a huge help. Ned would have been very upset with me if I'd had to leave his career event."

"And there would have been no one to help when Van's drunk stepfather came in," Ned added.

Once again Burgess was subjected to appreciative looks from his family. He nodded and took it because he didn't want to hurt their feelings.

He wasn't feeling hungry, so he just had coffee, pouring it into his insulated mug.

"You coming home for dinner?" Chris asked.

"I will if I can and I'll call if I can't."

"Try," she said, "because I have a dress I want to show you."

"Mom!" Nina protested. "He can't see your dress before the wedding. It's tradition. And anyway, I thought we were going shopping together."

Dylan rolled his eyes.

Ned said, "Why not?"

"Because it's supposed to be a surprise. Because it's supposed to be a very special moment when a man sees the woman he loves coming down the aisle looking beautiful," Nina said.

"Mom doesn't need a special dress to look beautiful," Ned said, and they all agreed.

Burgess slipped away while the spotlight was on her, and headed out into a crisp, sunny morning.

Last night's cold had left the world glazed with a faint dusting of frost. The grass was silver as were the blackened remnants of last summer's plants. It was pretty, glowing in the morning sun, and he enjoyed it as he drove. He always credited his mother for making him a detective, and it had begun with her urging him to pay close attention to the world around him. Since a lot of the world around him was unpleasant, he appreciated it when the world put on a nice show.

He parked in the damp garage, feeling like an especially deep chill rose off the cement as he walked to the building.

Inside, it was warm and bustling. Because that necklace was on his mind, he stopped in the evidence room to take a look at it. He didn't recall what the initial was and hadn't looked closely. Now, tipping it out of the bag and holding it in his hand, he saw that it was a *C*. He thought it was likely that the sister, the twin, probably had a matching one. He wondered if they'd ever find her. Or that necklace. Whether she was really dead or only injured and for that reason kept away from the other teens.

As he pondered, he realized he had no idea how long the girl had been held in the place that purported to be a camp. It was at least weeks; her condition showed that. But had it been longer? He needed to contact the police in the town the woman claiming to be the mother lived, or at least the location of the address on the car's registration. See if there was anything they could tell him. Or anything they *would* tell him. Sometimes he called up and got cooperation. Others times a stonewall. He'd never know until he tried.

He took the stairs and found Kyle in the conference room, holding his report from last night.

"So we're looking for a camp on a lake?" he said.

"Yeah. A defunct summer camp. On a lake. Because they're so rare, you know?"

"Define *rare*," Kyle said. "So how was she?"

"Exhausted. Terrified. It's hard to believe her own mother sent her to that place."

Kyle waved the paper. "But the mother said her missing daughter was named Colleen. And this girl says she's Maureen and that Colleen is dead."

"I looked at that necklace we found down in the park," Burgess said. "It was the letter *C*, not the letter *M*."

Kyle nodded. "What kind of a mother—" he started, then stopped himself. They both knew about those kinds of mothers. About all kinds of mothers who failed to protect their kids, hurt their kids, pimped their kids, killed their kids.

"There's a stepfather who didn't want difficult kids around. Our girl says her sister was difficult."

Our girl. It was such a clear sign that they, or at least he, had become attached.

"Sometimes I think there ought tc be a license requirement before a woman can move a new guy in when she has kids," Kyle said.

Burgess thought about Van and his mother's abusive boyfriend. "Sure would make our lives easier, wouldn't it? You heard anything from Stan?"

Kyle shrugged. "He's on the way. But Lily is making things as hard as she can."

"Pretty much as we expected. Few women are good at putting up with the demands and the hours of our lives. Speaking of women, did you talk to Michelle about a date?"

"She likes the one closer to Christmas. Already got stars in her eyes about how to decorate and what she'll wear. And the girls are over the moon about being bridesmaids. I don't think there's going to be any peace and quiet in the Kyle household until sometime in January."

"And Chris likes the earlier date."

"Well, that's something we don't have to worry about. Which is fine, since we've got plenty here."

Stan Perry came in, carrying a tray of coffees. "Thought I'd better bring a bribe of some sort. I couldn't stand to be in the doghouse in both places."

"Oh, poor Stanley," Kyle said. "Welcome to my world."

Perry handed out coffees and sat. "So, what have we got and where do we go from here?"

Burgess filled them in on all the names he'd learned yesterday. His visit with Shirley Bufford and learning the identities of the woman and man who'd claimed to be Glen and Margaret Briscow. His search of the empty house. Then his visits with Rosie Harmon and the girl who said she was Maureen.

"Busy day," Perry said. "So what's on our agenda for today?"

"Too much?" Burgess said. "Terry or Stan, do either of you still have any contacts on the state police you could talk to on the QT? We need to know what's happening with their investigation of Tobias Jones, that body in the farmhouse, and Elvira Clemens? And we need help locating an abandoned summer camp somewhere on a lake. Which is something the wardens might be able to help us with. And look into the registered owner of that car from Connecticut, the one the woman who claimed to be looking for her missing daughter Colleen, was driving."

"Colleen?" Kyle interrupted. "But the girl says her name is Maureen, right? So what's that about?"

"What's any of this about," Perry sighed. "I can't remember a case where there were so many players using fake names. Can either of you?"

Burgess shrugged. It was always going to be something. "So, I'm going to follow up with the police in Connecticut. Stan, you want to try and track down Elaine Harmon Hawes or whatever her name is now? Maybe Hall, if she's married Edwin Hall. Unless it's Briscow? Maybe start with phone records?"

"Elaine Hawes," Perry said. "Because I've already been looking at the plate on that truck, which, no surprise, belongs to a company called Adventures Away. No record of such a corporation or d/b/a anywhere in Maine. No joy with the address, either. Like that Subaru we looked at, it is registered to the empty house. So maybe Elaine Hawes is a new way in. I might even have to take a drive up to Brunswick." He hesitated, then said, "And pull over and grab a quick nap in the car. I can't remember the last time I slept for more than two hours at a time. I'll start with that phone number, though."

"And Terry," Burgess said, returning to his earlier question. "You still got any contacts with the state police you might ask about what's happening with that farmhouse and the body? And the whereabouts of Elvira Clemens?"

"Got one. Been a while but she might still help." His quick smile came and went. "Gonna take some finesse, that."

"Which you are very good at."

"Hey," Perry said. "I'm good at finesse, too."

"You are good at pulling rabbits out of hats."

"That, too," Perry agreed.

"I'll start with that Connecticut license plate," Burgess said. "Talk to the police down there. Then I'm going to try my friend in the warden service. See if he has some ideas about where to find that camp. Unless some other hell breaks out first."

"Which it will," Kyle said.

Before they dispersed to their tasks, Burgess said, "Had an unpleasant run-in with a kid's stepfather at Ned's school career fair last night." He digressed to ask, "You ever hear of a middle school career fair?"

"Yeah. Have," Kyle said. "The girls' school has them. I think they're trying to get kids career focused early, before hormones totally take over."

"Autumn doesn't go to school yet," Perry said. "What about this run-in?"

"Drunken stepdad showed up and tried to beat up one of the kids. It looks like the usual mess—mom's great new boyfriend turns out to be a drunk and a violent bully. He was supposed to stay with the younger kid so the older one could come to the event. Only he changed his mind and told the kid to stay home so he could go out. The boy had been told by his mother it was okay to attend, so he left."

Burgess paused. "Sorry. Too much information, I know. Here's the thing—as patrol was taking him away, after he took a swing at me and tried to hit the boy—he threatened me. Or rather, threatened my family."

He looked at them and shrugged. "Is it just me or are things getting more dangerous out there for cops?"

"You know they are," Kyle said. "For cops and for kids and for everyone. We're in an epidemic of expressing personal freedom in ways that are very wrong-headed."

"Love that word, wrong-headed," Perry said.

"Anyway, I'm more worried than usual about my family," Burgess said. "The boy's in school with Ned, which means they're in the neighborhood. And we know the courts won't hold him long, despite an assault on a cop. I'm hoping the mom will get a restraining order. That will give us something to work with if he makes threats. Man's name is Mark Hammond."

He made a mental note to get Hammond's booking photo so he could show it to his family. To give patrol a heads-up about the man and the threat. Then he shelved the idea of showing it to his family. He'd get the photo but for now he'd keep it to himself. He wasn't ready to alarm them like that yet. Not when things were going so well and everyone seemed happy.

They all sighed with a shared sense of frustration, understanding it was unusual for Burgess to share a concern like this, and went to their tasks.

TWENTY-TWO

According to the plate that Rocky had deciphered, the vehicle the woman had been driving was registered to a Fiona Cassiday, with a Connecticut address in a town called West Carver. From the map, it looked like it was one of those prosperous southern Connecticut towns with easy access to New York City. Burgess's internet search had turned up two photos of Cassiday at charity events with a man identified as her husband Alan. He'd also unearthed an earlier photo of her with another man, in which they were identified as Fiona and Jerome Mulcahey.

He was sure it was the same woman, unless, like the girl over at the hospital, she had an identical twin. He surmised also that Mulcahey was the girl's father and Cassiday the step. That might give him a surname for the girl in the hospital.

He made some notes about what he wanted to ask and called the West Carver police department. After identifying himself to four different people and explaining why he was calling, he finally found himself talking to someone willing to entertain his questions. The man was a detective. Older, maybe even Burgess's age. And cautious. The man began with "What's your problem?" Not auspicious but sometimes it took a while to break the ice.

Burgess was used to building pictures of people from their voices and their mannerisms. Even on the phone, people had mannerisms. Coughs and throat clearings and tongue noises. The sounds they made as they rearranged themselves in their chairs or shuffled papers or played with items on their desks. The background sounds of the rooms they were in. This man was sitting near, but not in, a detective's bay, maybe in a private office with the door open. He had some seniority, as in the minute or two Burgess had been speaking with him, two people had interrupted with questions.

"Zoo around here. Hold on. I'll just close the door," the man said. "Oh, and the name's Cavanaugh. Harry Cavanaugh."

Burgess had already given up his name. He waited. Heard the door close and the complaining creak of a chair. Like himself, Cavanaugh was no lightweight.

"So walk me through this," Cavanaugh said. "Why are you interested in Fiona and Alan Cassiday?"

"Don't know if I am," Burgess said. "Here's what I have." He described finding the naked, unconscious girl in a city park and that the girl had been badly abused and appeared to have been physically restrained. "She had no ID of any kind and after blurting out, 'don't let them get me, don't let them take me back" she lapsed into a coma. She has moments of consciousness now but her recovery is still uncertain."

He gave the man a moment for comment or questions, and when none was forthcoming, continued with his story.

"The next morning, we received a call from the hospital. A woman was there claiming to be the girl's mother and insisting on seeing the girl. I went to speak with her, since the girl's condition and situation were concerning. She gave me a false name and presented a fake driver's license. When I asked for some proof that the girl was indeed her daughter, she refused to provide it. She reported that she had last seen her daughter two days earlier, which would have been impossible given the girl's condition, unless she had been a perpetrator. Recognizing that I was suspicious, she bribed a woman in the restroom to create a commotion in the lobby. While we were handling that, she drove away. Despite having obscured the plate on an otherwise pristine vehicle with dirt, we were able to decipher it. It was a Connecticut plate that led us to Fiona Cassiday."

Again, he waited for Cavanaugh to say something and got silence.

"Subsequently, a man identifying himself as the family lawyer showed up, claiming to have a court order allowing him to remove the girl from the hospital. He said he had brought an ambulance to transport her. He refused to provide identification or show us the order. The hospital's attorney refused to release the girl without seeing both ID and the order, and without sign-off from the doctors that she could be safely transported. When we inspected the ambulance, it had no equipment, only a dirty mattress on the floor, and no trained medical personnel. After we examined the vehicle and the drivers, the vehicle drove away."

Still nothing from Cavanaugh. For all Burgess knew, Fiona was the chief's sister or the couple were big donors to the department. He said, "Am I wasting my time, explaining all this?"

More silence. Maybe Cavanaugh had gone to sleep. "Thank you for your time," he said, though he hadn't gotten anything of value from the man.

"Hold your horses, young man," Cavanaugh said, which almost made Burgess laugh. "I'm just pondering on all this."

"Well, while you're pondering, let me tell you what I'm calling about. I'm trying to get some background on a couple who would send their twin teenage girls to a camp in Maine where one of them ended up near death and the other may already be dead. Because that's what I'm pondering on. I'm trying to find a way to locate this camp or get better information on the people who are running it because there are other teens there who are at risk. Information Ms. Cassiday must have."

"Sounds like a pretty crazy story to me," Cavanaugh said. "The girl make all that up?"

Right. This guy sounded a lot like the girl's mother, describing the battered and starved girl he'd found in the park as a willful teenager who was a chronic liar. He said, "Until last night, the girl was unconscious and unable to speak. Last night, she managed a few sentences. The condition she was in wasn't something she could have done to herself."

Another silence from Cavanaugh. By now, Burgess knew the man would adhere to the party line about the girl being a troublemaker. He should have understood that from the man's initial "what's your problem?" Detectives always had problems. Solving them was the job. They didn't call each other up with information like this just to chat.

"What's your email?" he said. "I'll send you some pictures." He figured he'd also send pictures of the woman he believed to be Fiona Cassiday.

The man grudgingly gave up his email address and Burgess wrote it down. Then, in case he might pry something out, he said, "So you're acquainted with the Mulcahey twins?"

"One of 'em. Colleen. She was big trouble 'til the parents sent her away to that school in Switzerland."

Confirmation that their surname was Mulcahey. It was something.

"Except that's not where they sent her," Burgess said.

"So she says, according to you."

Burgess was done with this waste of time. "Guess you weren't listening. She hasn't said anything much. We're cops, you know. Detectives. We figure things out." He was going to hang up but added, "She's a beautiful girl despite being battered and emaciated. Raven hair and striking emerald eyes. Says her name is Maureen. Hard to imagine how she hitchhiked from Switzerland to Portland, Maine, naked and bruised as she was. You know?"

He hung up.

It went like that sometimes. You did your best and ran into people who were territorial, or generally uncooperative, or, in this case, had cement between their ears or unquestioning loyalty to rich citizens. *Colleen Mulcahey is a troublemaking liar, so I'm not listening to anything else you say.* He doubted it would do any good, but he sent Cavanaugh several pictures of the girl, vivid ones that showed the extent of her injuries and the deep purple grooves on her wrists. A violation of her privacy, but there was an outside chance it might move the man to, as he'd put it, ponder on what he was seeing. Likely he'd just dismiss it as involving some other girl. Even when there was also a picture of Fiona Cassiday.

He went to check with Kyle and Perry to see if they'd developed anything.

Both of them were gone.

He hoped that meant Perry had sniffed out an address in Brunswick and was headed there, and that Kyle was off having a clandestine meeting with his state police contact.

Burgess decided he'd get that booking photo and find out what the situation was with Hammond, then call his friend the game warden, Hank Boudreau. "Friend" was actually too strong a word. It was more like acquaintance. But the man had been very helpful during the family vacation when they were harassed by malicious teens on jet skis, and together they'd managed to get those teens, and their five-hundred-pound canary father, off the lake and into jail where they belonged.

Boudreau was low key and persistent. If he couldn't help, he'd likely know someone who could.

It had been such a crazy, busy summer for everyone in law enforcement that Burgess wasn't sure the man would remember him. But the wardens knew the woods, the back roads, the places where an abandoned summer camp might be found. He thumbed through his notebook to find the man's number, sat at his cluttered desk, and dialed.

He went to voice mail. Of course he went to voice mail. It was hunting season. Boudreau probably hadn't slept in a month. He left a message with his name and number and that he needed some advice about a case. Then he sat and stared at his desk.

Amidst the sea of pink messages was one that seemed to be trying to slip away. He wouldn't mind if they all slipped away. Except he would. He never knew when something might be important, like that note from Shirley Bufford.

This was a note from Terry Kyle. Stan Perry had a lead on a place Elaine Hawes might be living and after the last time Perry had tangled with this crew, Kyle didn't want him going alone. It was a sensible precaution. Burgess tried to set his impatience aside. He'd be the first to tell a cop that it often made sense to work in pairs, however macho they might feel. He'd done it plenty of times himself, and sometimes regretted that he'd gone by himself.

If he was honest, his annoyance was mostly frustration because they were taking action while he was stuck here brooding about an infuriating conversation with the kind of cop he hated most.

Burgess needed action. He wanted to go out there and make something happen. Trouble was there was no "there" to go to and no way to make something happen. Still, impatience dogged him like an itch or an ailment.

He turned to the lab reports section of the murder book and studied Dani's report about the hitchhiker plant. The botanist had listed the few areas in the state where the plant grew. He took out a map of Maine and located those areas. "Heck," he told himself, "this oughta be easy. It's only hundreds of miles of woods, waterways, and wilderness." People from away, as Mainers called them, didn't realize how big the state was.

No way could he narrow it down without the warden service's help. That and maybe some county sheriffs. And maybe an army and some very good luck. It was a fact that some people came to Maine to get lost and there was plenty of room to do that.

It was that crappy time of year when darkness came too early. He was too restless to stay at his desk and felt the need for action pulling him away. He didn't know what it was, but felt, as he had the other night when he'd found the girl, that his city was calling him. That something out there needed his attention.

He pulled Mark Hammond's booking photo and printed a few copies. Looked up Hammond's record and found priors for domestic assault and malicious destruction. A real prince among men. Then, because his impatience wouldn't settle, he checked the clock. If he couldn't make anything happen with this case, there was something else he could do. School was out. He needed to know whether Van and Gabriel were home and safe. Whether Gabriel had been left alone last night, which could lead to additional charges against Hammond. He wanted Hammond to stay locked up so he didn't have to keep looking over his shoulder while he searched for the place Maureen Mulcahey had been confined.

He grabbed his coat and headed out into the darkening afternoon.

When he was younger, he hadn't noticed how cold the garage could get. It was another aging thing, he supposed. He hated it. Hated that despite Dr. Cohen's drugs giving back some of his energy, he still felt like he lumbered. He felt more like a moose than a wolf.

Dammit! He wanted to grab his head and shake all this negativity out. Replace it with the thrill of the hunt. Of finding the evidence, the witnesses, the clues, that would move this thing. Then, as he sat in his cold car, his city spoke to him again. It said *stop sitting on your ass and go check on those kids.*

The cop gut. Sometimes it sounded almost too fantastic. The first time it happened to him, he didn't believe it but it wouldn't let go. When he told his sergeant that he 'just had a feeling that he had to go into that building' he expected scorn and disbelief. Instead, his sergeant had gone with him, trusting his instinct. And they'd gotten there in time to keep a father from killing his crying baby. So now, even when it seemed unbelievable, he listened.

Of course, when he was impatient to get across town, every light was against him, every intoxicated or otherwise impaired soul had to stumble into his path, and every idiot who shouldn't be allowed to drive was out driving incompetently. A seven-minute drive was taking twice that long. He pounded on the dashboard. Yelled, "Get the fuck out of my way."

By the time he got to Anita Elwell's house, he was deeply certain something was wrong.

He parked where he'd parked last night to drop Van off. A small, neat white house with dark blue shutters. There was a car in the driveway. He hoped that was good news and meant that the mom was home. He was beginning to feel relieved when he saw that the front door was open and the door frame was shattered. He called dispatch and asked whether Mark Hammond was still in jail. Learned that he'd posted bail and was out. Anita Elwell home, Hammond out, and the door kicked in? His heart rate went through the roof.

TWENTY-THREE

He texted his whereabouts to Kyle and Perry, called for back-up, drew his gun, and headed for the house. The curtains were drawn so he couldn't see but instinct said bad things were happening inside. He'd be the first to tell another officer to wait for back-up before heading into a dangerous situation. Why he'd thought it was important for Kyle to go to Brunswick with Perry. But there might be children in there. Children at risk from a violent man. Also perhaps a woman, since a car was there. Anita Elwell or someone she'd asked to look after the kids. He didn't have time to wait. Every second counted.

The door opened into a hall that was cluttered with coats and boots and bikes and toys. A homey contrast to what was happening in this house. He paused there and listened before he announced himself. Three sounds came to him. A woman pleading. A small child crying. Another child bravely saying, "You stop hurting my mom." That would be Van.

All there in a nutshell. They were at the back of the house, probably in a kitchen.

He didn't know if Hammond had a weapon. With his record, he shouldn't have been able to get one. This wasn't the first woman he'd abused. But the laws were lax and guns too easy to obtain.

Quietly, he moved into the room on his right. A living room. Signs of violence everywhere. The TV had been knocked off its stand. The coffee table overturned. A smashed lamp lay on the floor. A game controller on the floor had been crushed. Half the couch cushions were on the floor.

There was a smear of blood on the doorframe leading to the next room.

This was bad. Very bad. He stepped back outside, informed dispatch there was a hostage situation involving children, and asked that patrol arrive without lights or sirens. The last thing he needed was for Hammond to grab the woman or one of the children to use as a hostage.

He silenced his phone and went back inside, heading for the rear of the house.

From the kitchen, beyond the room he was in and a small dining room, came the meaty thud of a blow, a sharp cry, then the sound of something falling. Van's voice, crying out and then silent. Some things falling, he thought. A body and a chair.

Everything fell away except his focus on what was happening in that kitchen. Once he'd ascertained that neither Hammond nor the family were in this room, Godzilla could have been in the room beside him and he wouldn't have noticed. His job here was to handle Hammond without any further harm to Anita and the boys.

He moved through the dining room, skirting an overturned chair and gingerly stepping over a smashed bowl and pieces of fruit scattered on the floor, edging forward until he could see into the next room.

He couldn't see Hammond, but directly ahead, Anita Elwell crouched on the floor, her arms spread protectively, her eyes fixed on someone standing above her. Behind her, Burgess could just see the head of a child lying on the floor. Van. His head was bleeding and he was very still. Somewhere in the room, a child was sobbing. She was saying, "Leave him alone, Mark. I don't care what you do to me, but please, please, leave the boys alone. They're just children. Helpless children. And you're a big man. You don't..." A sob. "You don't understand how strong you are, how you can—"

"Just shut the fuck up, okay." Hammond said. "That stupid little brat got me arrested. Arrested, Anita. I might lose my job because of him. I oughta break the little fucker's neck."

The voice said Hammond was somewhere to Burgess's left. He tried to move to his right to get a better view. Hit an apple with his foot and sent it skidding into the wall with a thud. He froze.

Hammond said, "What the fuck was that?"

Burgess heard him moving toward the door and stepped left. Careful, this time, not to step on any more fruit. His phone buzzed against his thigh.

He'd slipped his taser in his coat pocket when he left the truck, something he didn't usually do. Cop's gut again. Now he got it out, praying that it would work. Sometimes they didn't, as every cop knew, and he'd lose precious time switching from it to his gun.

When Hammond's head appeared in the doorway, Burgess said, "Portland police. Get on your knees," then zapped him before he could turn and grab Anita Elwell and use her as a shield. When a violent man is charging, you don't wait for compliance. You don't politely ask them to stop.

The device sputtered and fizzed and did its job just as Hammond reached him and delivered a powerful blow to his stomach. They both went down, gasping. Despite the blooming pain in his gut, Burgess swapped the taser for his gun and pressed it against Hammond's head. So much was hardwired after all these years.

"Stay down and stay still."

Hammond tried to get up.

"I said stay the fuck down. You really want to make me shoot you? Because I can and I will and the world would be a better place if I did."

Hammond, perhaps finally realizing he was in deep shit, stayed down and stayed still. Burgess kept his gun out. He knew this man couldn't be trusted and was a slow learner. Probably thought he'd shake this off the way he'd shaken off his behavior yesterday. Today, though, he'd injured a child. Even the softest hearted—or softest headed—judge would understand he presented a risk to public safety.

Anita Elwell appeared in the doorway. She was pale as a ghost and clinging to the doorframe for support.

She looked at the man on the floor. At Burgess. At the gun. "I think he's killed Van," she said, her voice barely a whisper.

At that moment, patrol arrived. Burgess explained the situation. Asked them to call an ambulance. An officer stayed with him while two others took Hammond off his hands.

"Search him," Burgess said. "I haven't had a chance."

No gun, but Hammond did a have a knife. You learned to be grateful for small things and Burgess was grateful the man hadn't used it on the Anita or the boys.

He stood, feeling as creaky as an old ironing board as he unfolded from his crouch and holstered his gun. Then he went into the kitchen, past the nearly catatonic woman, to check on the boy. Unconscious but breathing. His pulse was steady. The cut on his head was bloody, but head wounds were. They wouldn't know more until the boy got to the hospital.

Burgess looked at the mom and asked the question he already knew the answer to. "Did you call an ambulance?"

No response.

He said, "You're a nurse. You should tend to him. You're better at this than I am."

No response.

Catatonic was right.

In the far corner of the room, crouched down and pressed against the door was a small boy with the same red hair as his mother and brother. "Gabriel," Burgess said. "It's over and you're safe. Hammond is gone. The bad man is gone and your brother is not dead. He'll go to the hospital and he's going to be okay." Even if it was a lie, he had to say it. Right now, the child needed reassurance, not a range of possibilities. "Can you look after your mother for me?"

After a moment, the small boy crept out of his corner, crossed the room, and wrapped his arms around his mother's legs. He said, "You're okay, mama. You're okay."

Kids could be so amazing.

From the doorway, Anita Elwell said, "Oh my God! I never thought…" Which they both knew was a lie. She bent to wrap her arms around her child.

Burgess thanked his aching gut for its good instincts.

In the distance, sirens signaled the approaching ambulance.

TWENTY-FOUR

Burgess put an arm around her shoulders and led the woman and the small boy out of the room so the ambulance crew could work. The living room was a mess, so he suggested they sit at the dining room table. The boy sat, but she couldn't help herself; she immediately started picking up the pieces of the smashed bowl, then stood there, helplessly, like she had no idea where to put it.

"Gabe," Burgess said. "Do you know where there's a wastebasket that's not in the kitchen?"

The small boy nodded.

"Can you get it and bring it here to your mom?"

With a nod, the boy slid off his chair.

"He shouldn't..." she said. "He shouldn't be waiting on me. I should be...uh...looking after him. It's just..."

"It's fine," Burgess said. "Good for him to have something to do while you pull yourself together."

"I'm not..." She stopped. "I'm an ICU nurse. I'm supposed to be the one who can respond to emergencies. Function under pressure. And I'm...I'm an incompetent wreck." Another hesitation. "I should be with Van. He'll need me. But...I can't leave Gabe."

She dropped the mess of broken crockery on the table and dropped herself into a chair. "I don't think I'm okay," she said. "I can't think. There's something wrong with my head."

It could be shock. Burgess had seen plenty of that. But he asked, "Did he hurt you? Did he hit you? Hammond?"

She nodded.

Her blouse and skirt were torn. Now, processing that, he hoped it didn't mean what he feared it meant. And that that something hadn't happened in front of the children. He said, "He assaulted you?"

The faintest of nods.

"Did the boys see?" A hard question. An unkind one, given her state, but he needed to know how many people in this situation would need therapy. And for what. Half the time, cops were just armed social workers.

She shook her head. Not ready to talk about it. Possibly, she never would. Just like it would be a long time before she stopped beating herself up for creating this situation. And that would be if she got a good therapist and actually went to her sessions.

"You need to go to the hospital yourself," Burgess said. "You're not okay."

She almost smiled at that, which was reassuring. Normal responses were a good thing at a time like this. "You've got that right, Detective. But Gabe?"

"Don't you have a friend who can take him? Or what about his father?"

Her small laugh was bitter. "His father is…just like Mark. Except he's already in jail." She stared down at her hands. "I make such bad choices." A long pause before she said, "My sister will take him. She won't like it. Says she's sick of the messes I get into. But she'll take him."

Her eyes went to the small boy who had returned carrying a wastebasket almost as big as he was. "It's the only one I could find," he said.

"It's great, Gabe," Burgess said. "Thank you. Put it down beside your mom, okay?"

The small boy set down the basket and got back on a chair. He said, "Is my mama okay?"

"We want a doctor to check her out," Burgess said. "What happened was scary."

A nod from the boy. He asked, "Do I have to go to the hospital, too?"

"No, sweetie," Anita Elwell said. "You can go to Aunty Sally's house. You know you always have fun there. You can play with Aaron and Jimmy."

One of the EMTs was in the doorway. "We're ready to transport the boy, Joe," she said. "Does the mom want to ride with him?"

Burgess gestured for her to follow him into the living room. Said, in a low voice, "She should come with but she needs to be checked out, too. I think she may have been raped."

She was a pro. She only nodded and said, "We'll take care of it."

"I'll be along soon. We'll need to make a record of their injuries. The boy's. And the mom's."

"The little one is okay?"

"I think so."

There were footsteps in the hall, and Terry Kyle came in. No "what happened," only a brisk, "What can I do?" from Kyle.

"She's going to the hospital with her older son. As soon as it's arranged, you could take Gabe…Gabriel…to her sister. Then meet me at the hospital." He wanted to know if they'd learned anything in Brunswick, but this was not the time.

Burgess looked at Anita. "Can you call your sister and make sure she can take Gabe? If it's okay, we'll take him there. They're taking Van to the hospital now and you can ride along." He hesitated, said, "You need to get checked out, too. Because if he…if you were assaulted—" He hesitated, trying to find a gentle way to say it. "You'll want a record of that."

She looked puzzled, until he added, "Because you want him in jail for as long as possible, don't you?"

Then she understood. She said, "I'm so ashamed."

"Mark Hammond is the bad actor here. Not you. Remember that. You didn't…and don't…deserve any of this. You don't and your boys don't."

He gave her a minute. She was so fragile right now he didn't want to push her. But Van needed to get to the hospital. He needed to get there, too. The little boy needed to be someplace safe. And he needed to get a crime scene team here to record what had happened. A brutal assault on a child and, he suspected, a violent rape.

They got the sister's address and confirmed she could take Gabriel. Before Kyle left with the boy, he took him upstairs to collect some things. A favorite toy or two and a book and some pjs and clothes in case he had to spend the night.

"I should be doing that," Anita Elwell said, not moving from her chair. But a moment later, when they wheeled the stretcher through, she stood and followed it out to the ambulance.

Kyle left with the young boy. Burgess waited for the crime scene team to arrive so he could give them direction. Then, because he knew they'd need to take Anita's clothes for evidence—all of her clothes—he followed Kyle's example and packed a small bag to take to the hospital for her. Years ago, as a young officer, he might not have thought of these things and certainly would have been uncomfortable going through a strange woman's dresser to get her some underwear.

No one had ever told him that doing such things would be part of the job. Not packing a bag for a traumatized child. Not bringing underwear to the hospital for an assault victim. Not trying not to show how much his gut hurt from Hammond's punch.

Sometimes it felt like the universe had it in for his cop's gut. It sure did take a beating. Sometimes it was things like Hammond's punch. Sometimes it was the knife that tension and anxiety wielded that felt like he was being stabbed from within. Whatever the cause, Burgess was a "suck it up and get on with it" type. You didn't get to wimp out in the middle of a crime scene. "Oh, poor me" was for other people.

Another exciting day in the life of a detective.

He paused in the truck and called Chris to say he wouldn't be home for dinner. She was understanding, as she usually was, but frustrated. "We have so much to discuss, Joe. There isn't much time to plan a wedding."

"I'll be there as soon as I can. I want to help. I really do. But I've got to get over to the hospital. It's that boy, Van, the one I met at the career night? The one Ned wants to be friends with? The mother's boyfriend assaulted him. He's unconscious and on his way to the ER. I want to get over there. See if he's going to be okay."

"The boyfriend?" she asked. "Please tell me he's in jail."

"Detective Burgess on the job, ma'am."

Chris laughed. "You do make the world a better place. See you when we see you."

Then she was gone and he drove to the hospital.

Before he went inside, he paused again. His phone had buzzed while he was in the middle of handling that crisis and then he'd forgotten about it. Now he pulled it out and checked for a message. Too often they were complaints from Cote, looking for updates. This time it was a call he'd wanted. The game warden had called him back, apologizing for not responding sooner, but it was hunting season. He was happy to help and Burgess should give him a call tonight. He expected to be home unless they were called out for poachers or a lost hunter. He added that maybe Burgess could leave him another message, clarifying what he was looking for, so he could ponder on it while he was sitting in his truck watching for poachers.

Burgess called him back and left a long message, describing the case they were working on and what they were looking for. After that, all he could do was wait and hope the man came through with something.

He put his phone away and headed inside. Hoping for good news about the boy and expecting bad. And wondering if maybe Kyle and Perry had turned something up.

TWENTY-FIVE

He found Kyle in the Emergency Room, hovering outside a curtain. They hadn't had a minute to talk at Anita Elwell's house and Burgess was eager to know what he and Perry had learned. But first, their new crime victims. "The boy or the woman?" he asked.

"The boy." Kyle nodded toward another curtain. "Mom's over there. I wasn't here when they were brought in, but I guess she went totally to pieces once they got here. Dr. Cohen is with her, and there's a neurologist in with the boy." He shrugged. "That's all I know."

Neurologist didn't sound good, but maybe they were just being careful because it was a head injury. Burgess would have liked to be in the room, to hear firsthand what was being said and done. The medical staff wasn't always with that program, patient privacy and all. There was a constant tension between their role and the detective's role, each side believing that their way was right.

"You ask for updates?"

Kyle shook his head. "I tried."

"At least we know Dr. Cohen will keep us informed," Burgess said. "You want to get some coffee, since there's nothing we can do here?"

"Feeling kind of like there's nothing we can do anywhere," Kyle said.

This was bad. Kyle didn't discourage easily. Like Burgess, he was a "put your shoulder to the wheel and push" type, toiling quietly and producing results.

Before they headed to the cafeteria, Burgess stuck his head around the curtain surrounding Anita Elwell and told Dr. Cohen where he'd be and that he'd like updates.

"As if I didn't know that," she said, but she said it with a smile. "And I'll let you know about the boy as well."

Over coffee, Kyle said, "Sorry. It's the whole wedding thing. I just don't…we just don't have time for it right now, and there's no way I can say that to Michelle. I don't want to be a bad sport. She's excited about this, as are the girls, while all I can think is that if I had more time and less distraction, I might be able to break something open in this case."

"So, Brunswick? Nothing?"

"She wasn't there. Neighbors seemed pleased to have her gone, or at least him. They confirmed that our photos are of the couple now calling themselves Gary and Margaret Briscow, but said that until a few months ago, she was Elaine Hawes. I guess she was a bad neighbor and he was a worse one. Woman next door said they deserved each other and hoped she'd seen the last of them."

"So maybe we'll get something from her phone records," Burgess said.

Kyle shrugged. "Hope so. Neighbor also said they've never seen any teenagers around. That she drives a Subaru and he drives a truck. No sign of any van. They've been gone a lot lately, which she is grateful for. And that is pretty much it. Confirmation of what we've already confirmed and not a hell of a lot more."

He finished his coffee and set down the cup. "I figure if I drink a thousand cups of this brown water, I may get a slight buzz. Oh, there is one thing. The woman we spoke with said that the neighbor on the other side was closer to Elaine and she might know more." He stared into the empty cup. "Oh. And from time to time a large older woman used to visit them. She seemed nice enough. Neighbor thought the woman was his mother."

His quick, cynical smile came and went. "Referring to the neighbor who was closer to Elaine, she said they were birds of a feather, by which

I believe she meant women who had to have a man in their lives no matter what a loser he was." A sigh. "Way things are going, Michelle may be beginning to think she's tying herself to a loser."

"You just need a good meal and a good night's sleep," Burgess said. "You aren't a loser. She loves you. You're raising two terrific daughters. You have a hard job and sometimes, like with this one, you hit a wall. We'll figure it out. This case and the wedding."

"Sure thing," Kyle said.

Burgess hesitated. "You've got a date. How about a venue? Chris found one for us. Maybe they'll have space for yours as well. And I asked Marina to cater."

"Bet you didn't tell Chris the menu was a lot of meatloaf sandwiches," Kyle said. He stood. "Let's go and see the girl. Maybe she knows some names. Maybe even if the girl's parents, who don't seem to know whether she's Colleen or Maureen, won't help, there might be other parents who will."

It was a great idea and they were instantly on their feet. As they walked to the elevator, Burgess said, "My warden called me back. He's happy to help. You get anywhere with your state police contact?"

"Not yet. She's being very cagy, but hope is eternal, right?"

"Hope is the thing with feathers."

"Hope is a Dumbo's feather," Kyle said. "But I'm too tired to play this game."

They rode the elevator to the girl's floor and checked at the nurses' station. The nurse reported the girl had had a good day. Had been awake more and had eaten. It was clear to Burgess that she'd become a pet for the nurses. They were ready to move her to a regular floor, which immediately concerned Burgess and Kyle. In the ICU, access was limited and monitored. On a regular floor, it would be much harder to keep her safe.

Testing his concern, Burgess asked the nurse whether anyone had tried to visit the girl.

He got an immediate nod. "Woman was here earlier this morning, claiming to be a relative, and asking to see her. We told her that no one could visit the girl who wasn't immediate family and asked for some ID.

She futzed around a bit, searched in her purse, and said she must have left her ID at home, but she was the girl's aunt and the family had asked her to visit."

The nurse, whose name was Susan, shrugged. "I told her we were very sorry but that access was strictly controlled here in the ICU. We hated to inconvenience her, but if she could come back with ID, we'd be happy to let her see the girl. My colleague…" She waved a hand in the direction of another nurse who was entering something on a computer, "asked about the girl's name and her parents' names and which side of the family this aunt was on. She's quick like that, knowing we need more information for our records. The woman said the girl's name was Colleen and her mother's name was Frona Cassidy. And she was Frona's sister."

She shrugged again. "She seemed so hesitant we were suspicious. As if we weren't already, given what someone had done to our girl. Plus, you know, while we don't know much about the girl's family, we do know her name is Maureen and her mother's name is Fiona Cassiday."

A shrug of the shoulders as the nurse sighed and echoed what Burgess had been thinking. "I don't know how they're going to keep her safe once she's moved down to the ward. They're far too busy to monitor who comes and goes. The place is wide open."

"She's scheduled to be moved soon?"

"This afternoon."

Very bad news. The department would do what it could, but they were short staffed. Hospital security would try to do its part, but again, they were stretched too thin to keep a constant eye on the girl.

Burgess and Kyle exchanged looks. "Thanks for the information," Burgess said. "I guess she's been talking to you, then? About who she is and who her family is?"

Again, the nurse gestured toward her colleague. "She's been talking to Maryellen. Mary has a knack for getting people to open up."

She waved the woman over. Said, "Mary, these are the police officers investigating what happened to our girl. They're hoping she may have told you some things that could be useful in their investigation."

Burgess hadn't asked for that, but he appreciated it. He smiled at the newcomer. Maryellen was a sturdy woman with glossy brown skin and wildly curly hair held back with a colorful band. When she spoke, her voice had the lilt of the islands.

"Oh, that poor baby," she said. "I sure do hope you catch whoever did this to her." She paused and studied them, like she was assessing their abilities. She must have been satisfied, because she said, "You will find them, yes?"

"We're trying," Kyle said. "Because it appears there are others… other teenagers…being held in the same place."

Seeing Kyle wanted to take the lead on this, Burgess stepped back as Kyle continued. "Susan says you and Maureen have been chatting. Is there anything she might have told you that could help us locate where she was held or who was holding her? Anything at all?"

The woman considered, then said, "She said there was a boy. Someone she got to talk to sometimes, before they took her away from the others and locked her up because she wouldn't stop asking about her sister. A boy named Silas. Silas Drummond, I think she said. He was a bit younger and scared. She tried to reassure him. But there wasn't much to reassure him about, she said. He wanted his mother. Told her…Maureen, that is…that his new father wanted to get rid of him. There was a baby, and the father wanted to start a new family without the annoyance of a teenager."

It was a lot. She'd obviously spent some time with the girl. But nothing they could use. Unless that name, Silas Drummond, pulled up something. *It was like gleaning*, Burgess thought. *Combing through a nearly empty field trying to find something, anything, that would nourish their search.*

"He's the only one she mentioned?" Kyle asked.

"By name. You can talk to her. She's more awake. But so, so frightened of being found and taken back."

"We're trying to prevent that," Kyle said. He shrugged. "But here? It isn't easy."

"We can maybe keep her one more day," the woman suggested. "If it would give you more time to make a plan."

A day was something. But there wasn't any way to make a plan that would truly protect the girl once she wasn't here in intensive care. They'd done it, or tried to do it, many times and far too often, plans fell through. Guards, either the department's or hospital security, were called away, or took a break at just the wrong time, or their replacements didn't show up and they had to leave. Sometimes Burgess's team tried to do it themselves, but they also had other obligations and needed breaks. And had weddings to plan.

"We'll go talk to her," he said. "Thank you for your help."

"I would watch her myself," the woman said, "but I have five children at home who cannot be neglected." As they started to leave, she added, "You be gentle now."

They headed to the girl's room. She was sitting up and looked much better. They'd fixed her hair and even given her a touch of lip gloss. He could see, beyond the hurt and the exhaustion, that she was a very beautiful girl.

She startled when they entered, immediately looking around for somewhere to hide.

He stopped in the doorway and held out a hand to stop Kyle. Take it slow, he reminded himself.

"Joe Burgess; you remember me, right? The detective who found you?" he said.

She nodded, the amazing green eyes shifting nervously to Kyle. "This is Detective Terry Kyle, who is working with me on your case."

They stayed in the doorway until she beckoned for them to enter. It was only a slight gesture, like she didn't have the strength for more. Probably she didn't.

"It's so odd to be a case," she said as they took chairs by her bed. Her voice was soft and low, like speaking still took too much effort.

"We want to find the place you were held, Maureen," Burgess said. "So we can rescue the others who were there with you. We're hoping you'll be able to tell us something that will help. Maybe even something you don't know you know. A name. Parent's name. Where someone is from. Anything like that."

She appeared to shrink in the bed, as though any amount of pressure was too much, but her expression was thoughtful. They waited, still and attentive, for whatever she might give them. Time passed so slowly Burgess thought he could feel the minutes slipping by.

Then there was someone at the door, and the nurse, Maryellen, came in. She was carrying something. Pudding, Burgess thought. And a spoon.

"Hey, sweetie," she said. "I thought you might be hungry so I brought you some pudding. It's vanilla, which is kinda boring, but all I could find. Could you eat a bit?" When the girl hesitated, she said, "For Mary?"

That got a faint smile. The girl said, "I eat pudding for you?"

The big nurse gestured toward her own body with fluttering hands. "Well, I don't need it, do I?"

With Maryellen in the room, everyone relaxed. The girl ate the pudding, seeming surprised to find herself hungry and it was suddenly gone. She handed the container and the spoon back to the nurse and said, "I could eat another one for you, if you could find it."

Burgess felt a small twinge of pleasure that this girl had someone looking after her. It was fleeting. Later today or certainly by tomorrow, she'd be in a different place in the hospital without this caring nurse. And where would she go after that? When she was ready to leave? Not back to the family who had sent her to that awful place.

Instead of any of the questions he'd been going to ask, he said, "Do you have any relatives you'll be safe with, when you're ready to leave here?"

For a moment, she looked stricken, as though she hadn't thought about it. Then she said, "I can go to my Aunt Emily. My father's sister. My real father, not that big asshole my mother married. Aunt Emily loves me. Which my mother does not." She looked at Burgess, a look that said he had to believe her. "I'll be safe there."

"Is she Emily Mulcahey or does she use a different name?"

"She is." The girl gave them an address and a phone number, and Burgess wrote them in his notebook.

"But you don't want to go to your father?"

"Fat lot of good he would be. He left me with them, didn't he? And look how that's turned out."

Burgess didn't press it. He said, "How long were you at this camp? With the people who did this to you?"

"It's not a camp. It's a prison. And since September. It was supposed to be like another school year, only at a different school. Except there was no school. Just this place where they made us work all the time except when we were being punished. Which was a lot." Her voice caught and she looked toward the nurse, who hadn't left the room. "Mary, can you stay with me, please, while I talk about this? Because… because I can't—" She went silent.

From the door, Maryellen said, "As long as you need me, sweetie, unless there's an emergency."

Of course, this being the ICU, there were often emergencies. Burgess hoped none would interrupt them right now, when the girl seemed willing to talk. He said, "We'll be in touch with your aunt Emily. Unless you want to contact her yourself? You can use my phone."

The emerald eyes blazed. Truly, though it sounded like something from a novel, they did. An emerald-eyed, raven-haired beauty. It *was* the stuff of fiction.

"And how's she going to react if there's a call from the cops?" the girl said.

"Most people would answer it," Kyle said. "Won't she?"

The girl shrugged and said, "Aunt Emily's kind of shy," but she held out her hand for the phone.

"When you're finished talking with your aunt," Burgess said, "can you tell us about the others who were there with you? Anything that we can use to identify their parents or where they came from would help." He paused, and added, "I know that will be hard for you, but it might help us save them."

Maryellen moved closer to the bed, as though Burgess was being abusive and the girl needed protection. Kyle put out an arm to stop her. They all waited for the girl's response.

"I might as well tell you now. What little I know, I mean. We didn't get to talk much. It was discouraged. But I had a friend. Sorta. His name was Robbie. Robert. He was a little younger and very scared. He used to cry every night. His last name was Hillman and he was from a town near Boston. Uh. Dedham, I think. He was Robert Hillman, Jr., so I guess his dad was also Robert Hillman. And there was a girl I was kind of close to. Melanie. Melanie Porter. She was from Connecticut, like me."

"Anyone ever come to the place to visit? To drop off their kids?"

She shrugged. "Not that I saw. I think they all came in vans, like me."

"Maryellen said you'd mentioned a boy named Silas. Silas Drummond?" Kyle said.

She looked stricken. Stared at the nurse. "I told you Silas went away. Didn't I tell you Silas went away?" Silence. Then, "Went away like my sister went away."

God. This was excruciating. Yet they needed her to talk.

"What about the people who ran the place? How many were there, and do you know any names? We've identified two of them, a man and a woman who call themselves Gary and Margaret Briscow. I can show you their photos if that would help."

"There were four people who were regulars. The Briscows. A big woman who I think was Gary's mother. And another man. The meanest of them. He seemed to be the one who owned the place. Or was running it. Or whatever."

"Can you describe him?" Kyle asked.

She described a man in his thirties. Tall, very fit, blond. No one they'd come across in the investigation so far.

"Anything distinctive about him?" Kyle asked. "Scars, tattoos, a limp, a missing finger?"

She smiled at the missing finger, as Kyle had meant her to. She traced a finger across her cheek. "He had a scar here. A big one. Tattoos up one arm. Elaborate ones. All these writhing snakes. He wore lots of rings. Big heavy ones on both hands. Big silver skulls. They left a mark when he hit someone, which was often."

"He hit you?"

She nodded. "Sometimes. When I asked about my sister. My twin. About Colleen. He told me she was dead and to just forget about it." Her eyes filled and tears rolled down her face. She finished with a whispered, "as if I could."

"I think that's enough," Maryellen said. It wasn't a suggestion. It was a command. And Burgess and Kyle complied, rising to leave.

But the girl held out her hand again. "The phone," she said.

Burgess gave her his phone, and he and Kyle sat down again.

Maryellen hovered by the door in case she was needed.

No one said anything but Burgess knew what they were all thinking: *Please answer the phone and please, when you do, give Maureen the support she needs.*

At last the silence was broken. Someone must have said "hello" because Maureen's eager voice said, "Aunty Emily? It's me. Coll...uh... Maureen. I need help." Then the girl started sobbing, unable to speak, and Burgess took the phone from her hand.

He identified himself and explained the situation and why the girl was calling. He listened for a moment as the woman on the other end expressed disbelief, then said, "Well, I don't know these people as you do, but it happened. They abandoned her to this brutal place where she nearly died. She was able to escape and make her way to Portland, where she collapsed. She needs you here. Is there any way you can come to Portland, Maine, as soon as possible?"

He listened some more, provided some more information, and ended the call, turning to the sobbing girl on the bed. "Your aunt is coming. She should be here by the end of the day." He realized he had no idea where the aunt was coming from.

One good thing to come out of an otherwise crappy, unsatisfying day.

The girl nodded and said, "Thank you." Then, "But the others. What about the others?"

"We're working on it," Burgess said, knowing his answer satisfied no one. "Is she in Connecticut, your aunt?"

"New York," the girl said. "But near the Connecticut line."

Again, they headed for the door. Again, the girl called them back. "Wait." In a small voice, she said, "I overheard them talking about moving us. To somewhere else for the winter. They didn't say where, but there was something about an old hospital. But would it make them even harder to find? That's another reason I ran away. Before they moved us all to someplace more secure. Harder to get out of."

Before they left, he asked Maryellen to please call him when the aunt arrived. It was important that he speak with her. And, though he knew she'd do this anyway, said, "Be sure to check her credentials."

She gave him a look and said, "Do I seem like I was born yesterday?"

They checked back in the ER, but there were no updates on the Elwells yet.

As he and Kyle headed out to their vehicles, Kyle said, "We know who the scarred, tattooed guy with the skulls and the snakes is, don't we."

TWENTY-SIX

Burgess agreed. "Now we just have to find the son of a bitch." Which would be a challenge. They were looking at a career criminal who was slippery as an eel. Handsome. Charismatic. A man without a conscience who took genuine pleasure in hurting others, whether it was financial, emotional, or physical. Scam the elderly? Swindle women who thought he loved them? Hire teens or immigrants to work for him, then stiff them when it was time to pay? Sell desperate people used cars that would quickly stop running? Even selling land he didn't own. The man was on their radar but it was like trying to track a ghost.

Maybe this time they'd get lucky.

Burgess reminded himself there was little about this situation that was lucky.

The piece of crap's real name was Clinton Johns. But he'd used so many aliases along the way that he'd probably forgotten what his original name was. Johns was a one-man crime wave.

As if the stakes weren't high enough, this new information amped things up even higher. Brutalizing teens and swindling their parents might not be enough for the man. Burgess's cynical cop mind offered up numerous possibilities, each more awful than the last. He told it to settle down. Right now, he had enough to deal with without imagining far worse.

Still, he drove back to 109 oppressed by the feeling that the very air was crackling with danger. True, if what the girl told them was right, the other kids being held there had been in danger for months. But with winter coming, even if the Briscows had no intention of expending great care for those they were holding, a summer camp with no insulation or heat wouldn't work much longer. Not when the goal, presumably, was to treat the parents as an ongoing source of income. Burgess figured those who'd set up the scheme probably hadn't thought it through. Except for Johns, who, once he got his hands on the money, absolutely wouldn't care what happened to his victims. Knowing he was in the mix made the situation seem more desperate.

If, as Maureen had said, there were plans to move all the teens to another facility, did that mean they should be looking for them in the new place or the old? Two needles in two haystacks? It made his head hurt.

He had two new names from Maureen that might lead him to parents and possibly more information about the place their children were being held. Three, if he included the boy named Silas that Maureen believed was probably dead. "Might" being the operative word. If Maureen's parents were any example, these kids had been shipped off by people so eager to get them out of the way, they didn't care what happened next and wouldn't fret if there was no contact. But could that possibly be true? Or were there some parents who'd been seduced by marketing like that flyer and hadn't asked enough questions? Would any of these new parents actually know where their children were?

He pondered on that as he sat in the cold garage. He assumed none of the teens being held there had access to cell phones. That was probably part of the promise: We'll keep your screen-addicted teens too busy engaging with nature to need their phones. Still, wouldn't most parents want addresses to write to their children and phone numbers to contact the facility they were sending them to? Even if they didn't plan to write, wouldn't they want an address, so they'd know where their children were? Since education was part of the package, wouldn't they want occasional reports on their kid's academic progress?

He hoped so. But maybe and maybe not. There was the norm, where parents cared and were engaged in raising their children, and then there was the world Burgess functioned in, where however unimaginable something in the realm of parenting was, someone had done it.

Maybe the Briscows' cell phones would have some information, including location data.

He headed inside, planning to summon Kyle and Perry to the conference room where they could make a plan about what avenues to pursue next and who would take on what tasks. Today had been another day with a lot of digging and not much to show for it. He figured the one bright spot was that he'd be able to get home for family dinner.

Unless some fresh hell broke out.

He was climbing the stairs when another thought hit him. Thoughts. Some things about the girl concerned him. First was how she'd reacted when he'd mentioned the boy, Silas, the one she'd told Maryellen about. Her explanation didn't quite ring true, that she hadn't mentioned him because she thought he was dead. The second was what she'd said on the phone when talking to her aunt. She'd started to say she was Colleen, then corrected it to Maureen. He wondered why. It could have been something as simple as stress. Or that her aunt favored Maureen, the better-behaved twin. But it tweaked something. He was a detective, after all.

He arrived in the detectives' bay ready to discuss that with his team. He was heading for his desk when Captain Cote stopped him with a peremptory "Burgess!"

He stopped and waited. Better here than at his desk. Who knew what lay there they didn't want the man to see? Except that Cote was coming from the direction of his desk, so any secrets had already been discovered. He was expecting another inquiry about the case, but Cote surprised him by saying, "Your dress uniform clean and pressed?"

A hesitation while he studied Burgess, like Burgess typically wore rumpled, dirty clothes and had gained an unspeakable amount of weight, then said, "And it still fits?"

"Yes. And yes." Burgess waited for enlightenment.

"There's an event tonight. Cocktail party. Something involving a delegation from Ireland." Cote named one of Portland's best hotels. "The chief is attending, and he wants a few of his staff there with him. He particularly asked for you. You and Kyle. I guess there's some law enforcement aspect to the visit."

There were higher-ranking cops who'd jump at a chance like this, so Burgess wondered why he and Kyle had been chosen. Cops with Irish names? Detectives with interesting cases to discuss? Yet another mystery in a life of mysteries.

Cote looked displeased. Burgess had done nothing to incur that displeasure, but being a detective, he surmised that Cote's presence hadn't been requested and his nose was out of joint.

Mentally bidding farewell to yet another family dinner, which irked him, Burgess asked, "What time does he need us there?"

"By six."

Burgess checked his watch. It was already four-thirty and he still had to go home and change. And shower. And shave. And make sure his shoes were shined. He was careful, but sometimes, busy as they were, things like this slipped through the cracks. He kept his "dammit" and other expletives out of his mouth and off his face, but he thought them. This was a distraction he didn't need.

"You told Kyle?"

Cote nodded. "Don't be late, Burgess. And no sneaking out claiming there's an emergency. The chief was very particular about that. Got it? We are entertaining guests from another country."

"Got it," was what Burgess said, but if there was an emergency, of course he'd leave. That was the job.

He found Kyle and Perry in the conference room. Before he could share the thoughts he'd had on the stairs, questions about Maureen's veracity, Kyle said, "Well, aren't we just the darlings of the hour. Michelle is going to pitch a fit. The girls say they never see me. And I honestly don't know whether my uniform is clean and pressed, never mind whether my shoes are shined."

"You can't always get what you want."

"But what about getting what we need, like more time to work this case? Especially now that we're looking for Clinton Johns."

"What about me?" Perry said, in a mock whiny voice. "Why didn't I get invited?"

"Because you have a tiny baby at home who is still trying to bond with your elusive self," Kyle said with a brief laugh.

"As if the department cared about that."

Burgess quickly shared what he'd been thinking, then realized that if he and Kyle were tied up with this silly performance, Stan would need to step up when the girl's aunt arrived, so he briefed him about that. "When I get the call, I'll call you and you can hotfoot it over to the hospital and see what you can learn about the girl's family situation and whether the aunt knows anything about this so-called camp they were sent to."

"Another night without bonding," Kyle said.

"You shut the fuck up," Perry said.

From the exchange, Burgess deduced that his team was getting stressed and wished there were something he could do about it. He said, "I know. This whole thing sucks. But we'll figure it out. It's what we do. And yeah, I know what we all need is a night off. Maybe soon. Stan, you should feel lucky that you don't have to get done up like a trained monkey and go hobnob with bigwigs."

"Oh, believe me. I am."

"Hobnobbing with bigwigs," Kyle said. "I think that's the title of my autobiography. Unless it's 'Slumming with Sleezebags' or 'Hangin' with the Homeless.'"

"Mine is called 'Down with the Druggies,'" Perry said. "What's yours, Joe?"

"Oh, for sure it's 'Making the World Safer for All,' unless it's 'Lookin' for Needles in Haystacks.' Because there are so many needles in our lives. And haystacks. I'm not into that alliteration crap."

He left them to ponder on their books and headed home. On the way, he made the call to Chris that he didn't want to make.

"As if you weren't busy enough," she grumbled. "The kids miss you. Maybe you'll be home early, and we can talk about the wedding."

"I'd like that," he said. "It would be such a nice break from liars, and abusers, and crime."

"Don't spill anything on your uniform," she said. "Because that's what you're wearing to our wedding. Unless you want to rent a monkey suit?"

"I just want to see you in a beautiful dress and have you stop calling yourself 'almost Mrs. Burgess,' okay? I want you to be the real Mrs. Burgess. I'll wear anything you want me to…except a dress. I draw the line at dresses."

She laughed and even over the phone, he could hear her good mood restored.

At home, he found three kids gathered around the dining table, playing a silly board game. It was a heartwarming sight, and he saw immediately that the older two were being kind to Ned. He knew Ned was distraught about the events at the career fair and realized that his son didn't yet know about what had happened since. He wasn't about to disrupt the game to tell him now. Time enough for that when he knew more about Van's condition. Which of course reminded him that he needed to call the hospital and get an update about that.

He absolutely didn't have time to waste on some fancy cocktail party. Not when he had crime victims in the hospital and a visit to another crime victim by an aunt he wanted to intercept.

And he had no choice but to go.

TWENTY-SEVEN

Kyle was wearing his most opaque cop's face and Burgess was doing his best to match it. He felt like the two of them, in their uniforms, stood out in the room like two enormous blueberries at a penguins' party, especially since the chief wasn't wearing his uniform. But what the chief wanted, the chief got.

In his pocket, his phone buzzed. A call he expected was more important than the babble of complaint about some minor crime in her neighborhood that the woman speaking to him was going on about. He forced himself to be attentive, to say the right reassuring words. He even got out his notebook and took some notes, promising he'd look into things when he was back in the office. By the time she finally left to greet a friend across the room, his sense that bad things were happening away from this place was amped up to oppressive levels and he was struggling to keep anxiety off his face.

Before he could get drawn into another complaint session, he headed toward the hall to check his phone away from the crowd. Before he reached the door, the chief stopped him with a brusque, "Hold on, Burgess, there's someone I'd like you to meet."

The chief had a handsome, imposing woman in tow he introduced as Megan Ainsworth. Megan Ainsworth was simply dressed in clothes that probably cost half his annual salary and wore an understated diamond necklace, diamond earrings, and an engagement ring so large he wondered how she could lift her hand. In heels, she was tall enough to look him in the eye and had none of that slump-shouldered posture tall girls often developed.

"Ms. Ainsworth is interested in how detectives do their jobs, and I told her you were the ideal person to answer her questions," the chief said. That was all he said, but his demeanor said, "give this person your full attention." Introductions made, the chief left them.

She watched the chief walk away, then said, "That's not really what I asked him, Detective Burgess. It's more direct than that. It's, well, it's that we have a little mystery going on and I'd love to have your insight about whether I'm overreacting."

She smiled, and it was a lovely smile. "Let me give you a little background. My husband and I have a small place on a lake up in Franklin County. Just a cottage, really, a place to get away sometimes when the stresses of our jobs become too much. And there's something going on in town that doesn't feel right." She hesitated, considering, then went on. "I know that sounds awfully vague, which is because it is awfully vague. I was hoping you might be able to give some advice about how to go about finding out what's going on. Uh…who to ask and what to ask. I don't want to make a fool of myself."

Burgess imagined a woman of her poise and position rarely made a fool of herself. But he could be wrong. Plenty of people had public facades and private issues. In his pocket, his phone was dancing. He had to force himself to give her his full attention.

She made a face. "I'm not just being nosy, Detective. Honest. It's just…well, you know how it is when you sense something's wrong, don't you? The way it keeps gnawing at you and distracting you from…well, you know, everything else? That instinct that something's not right?"

She stopped speaking and put a hand on his arm. "Listen to me babble. I'm sorry. I'm sure you're dying to tell me to get to the point." She studied his face. "You are, aren't you?"

He was, though now he was also curious about why this situation had drawn her in. Something about her demeanor. The way she was reading him just like he was reading her. About the way she apologized and yet needed some answers. There was something here and maybe he could help.

She took a deep breath. Drank some wine from the glass in her hand. She said, "You're not drinking, are you? A pity. Usually these events, however upscale, serve pretty terrible swill. But this…" She held up the glass so the light illuminated the ruby red contents, and sighed. "This is actually worth drinking. Anyway…" She paused, then said, "I don't want to tie you up if you've got important things to do. You did seem to be heading for the door." She ended with a smile that acknowledged his frustration as well as the fact that she'd been watching him.

Something about her—an intelligent openness—made him pretty sure he could tell her the truth and she wouldn't be offended. "I'm sorry," he said. "Afraid I'm not very good company tonight. Yes, I was heading for the door. We've got a lot of things happening in a case we're working, things that are happening tonight. Plus I've got two assault victims in the ER and I need to know their condition. One's a little boy, eleven, assaulted by his mother's boyfriend. It's a head injury. I need to know he's okay and I keep missing phone calls so I have no idea what's going on and, well, frankly," he shrugged, "it makes me distracted and anxious and yes, lousy company."

"Then I won't keep you," she said. She made shooing motions with her hands. "I'm sure my niggling little problem isn't that important."

Burgess couldn't shoo. Not with the chief across the room watching them. With an inward sigh, he said, "Maybe yes and maybe no. One of the greatest assets to us detectives are observant people. Tell me about this situation that has you concerned."

She lifted her glass and took another sip and something about the gesture, so comfortable and yet elegant, made him long for a glass of wine himself. He knew the chief wouldn't mind, since he'd commanded Burgess and Kyle to attend a cocktail party, but out there in the real world a lot was happening that required Burgess to be on his game.

"Not even a single glass?" she said.

He hesitated, then shook his head.

"Your loss. So, about this situation…"

Terry Kyle appeared at his elbow. Burgess introduced Kyle, said, "Excuse me a moment," and turned to see what Kyle wanted.

"They've taken the little boy, Van Elwell, into surgery, but Dr. Cohen says it looks like he'll be okay." A pause. "She hopes. She asked me to let you know."

"And?"

"And Stan is at the hospital with the aunt, but I think we need to talk to her. The aunt. She's going to spend the night in Portland, so we can do that after we're done with this fiasco."

The woman he'd been talking to said, "Excuse me, I'll be right back." She paused, added, "Don't go anywhere," and hurried away.

"What's that about?" Kyle asked. "This a well-dressed and well-heeled badge bunny?"

"I don't think so. I think she's an intelligent woman with a troubling situation she'd like my advice about when she stops dithering about it and gets to the point. And the chief would very much like it if I took the time to give her that advice."

Kyle shrugged. "Hope it's better than what I've been dealing with. All he's sent me are a couple of people who want more poo patrols in their neighborhood. Maybe we should designate one day a week when we take turns going on poo patrol. You almost got another dog out of it." He rubbed his forehead. "Maybe we could start seizing vehicles when people leave their dogs in them. In hot weather, anyway. Or when it's very cold. We could use a few more vehicles for undercover work."

"Sounds like a plan," Burgess said as the woman arrived at his side holding her own glass, refilled, and accompanied by a waiter holding two more glasses of wine. She handed one to him and another to Kyle. "Because you really shouldn't miss out. Which I know because my generous husband, William McCarty, footed the bill for the wine tonight, so I can vouch that it's good." A pause before she smiled and said, "I think he wanted to serve Guinness in wine glasses but I put my foot down."

Burgess introduced Kyle, then said, "About your situation?" He tasted the wine. He didn't know much about wine. He didn't have the budget for quality wine and anyway, his drink of choice was bourbon. But he could tell this was good. It was also the kind of wine that went down too easily, something he definitely didn't need.

"So," she said, with another great smile, "I get two detectives for the price of one?"

"I guess you do, ma'am," Kyle said.

She repeated "Ma'am" and laughed. "That always makes me feel about a thousand years old. All right, so here's the situation. To recap, for Detective Kyle's sake, my husband and I have a small camp on a lake up in Franklin County. A weekend retreat, mostly. We especially like it in the fall, when everyone else who summers on the lake has gone home and things get very quiet. No motorboats. No paddle boards—not that I have anything against paddle boards, only it always seems to be people trying them for the first time with a lot of shrieking and splashing. That and people towed on inflatables behind power boats. In the fall, we can fish or we can kayak or even sit out on the deck and read and enjoy the peace and quiet and feel quite alone in the world. Except lately…there has been something mysterious going on."

A silence as she searched for the best way to describe her mystery. A few more sips of wine to fortify herself. A slight flush. She said, "You'll probably think I'm a total nutcase." And stopped.

By now, though, they were both curious. Burgess said, "What kind of mysterious? Unfamiliar people or vehicles you haven't seen before? Noises in the night? Lights where there ought to be no people?" He was envisioning illegal timber harvesting or one of those cases where someone with a cottage was doing illegal renovations. Or squatters in some summer resident's cottage. Or thieves breaking into those cottages, a popular Maine activity in the fall. Not his area—he was a city cop— but he figured he and Kyle could still give some advice.

She nodded. "All of those, actually. I mean, maybe I'm just being paranoid. Or just being annoyed that someone is disturbing my favorite season up there." A shrug. "But fall has always been quiet and now it's not."

"This is happening on the other side of the lake?" Burgess said.

Another nod. Another sip of wine.

"What's over there? Other people's camps? People who, like you, might have decided to stay later in the fall to enjoy the quiet?"

"Except there aren't any camps over there. Individual people's camps, I mean. There's just a big tract of land that belongs to a defunct summer camp. We've always worried that someone would buy it and turn it into some big development and ruin the place for all of us, but according to my husband, who likes to chat up the locals, no sale has taken place. And yet there are people there. Of course, my husband isn't concerned. He says it's nothing and not to worry about it."

Tiny alarm bells were going off and little light bulbs were illuminating. This might be something. "And you know this how? What have you seen or heard?"

"Lights. At night. And once or twice I've heard someone screaming. At least, I think it was someone screaming. There are animals around, of course, and they can make noises that sound human, but this...I'm sure this was human."

"Tell us more," Kyle said. "How long has this been going on?"

"Since September. Since when peace and quiet should be descending and they aren't."

"Have you seen unfamiliar vehicles?"

She smiled. "I don't know if I'd recognize vehicles as unfamiliar, Detective. I don't pay much attention to cars and trucks, beyond an abiding sense that men in pickup trucks seem more aggressive on the highway. I've seen an...how would you describe it?...an unfamiliar white van around. I mean an unmarked van, in poor shape, while most working vans have some insignia describing what business they are in. But that's not much of a clue, really. And I've seen..."

She tugged at her earlobe as she considered, a gesture Burgess thought usually came with the need to reassure herself those diamond earrings were still in place. But it might also be a way of recalling memories. Or the only sign a usually composed woman was uncomfortable revealing her concerns to large, uniformed police officers despite having initiated the conversation.

He and Kyle waited to hear what she'd seen.

She finished her wine, glanced with regret at the empty glass, and said, "About men in pickup trucks? I've seen one who is around a lot, even though I've never noticed him in the past. I mean, you know how you get used to the vehicles around you. He's always driving too fast and has an unpleasant habit of blowing his horn at anyone he deems to be driving too slowly." She hesitated. "It's a community where the year-round people tend to be elderly, and they do drive slowly. Driving slowly when your reflexes have slowed down is a smart thing to do, in my opinion. He evidently doesn't agree."

"Would you recognize a photograph?" Kyle asked, while Burgess was kicking himself for not having photos of the Briscows with him. But who would think to bring them to a command performance cocktail party, tucked into the pocket of a dress uniform?

But Kyle had his phone out and was scrolling through, searching for something. When he found it, he nodded, then held out the phone to Megan Ainsworth. "Would this by any chance be the man?"

She took the phone and studied the photo, then shook her head. "I'm afraid I'd be a very bad witness, Detective Kyle. I couldn't describe the man. All I can tell you is that he drives a green truck, kind of like the ones the wardens and forest rangers drive? And always has a most unpleasant expression on his face."

Burgess and Kyle exchanged locks. It seemed like her problem might mesh with their problem. They tried not to get their hopes up. It was such a long shot.

Kyle said, "Have you driven over there to check it out, see what's going on, whether it's squatters or illegal building or whatever?"

She shrugged, a delicate shrug that barely shifted the shoulders of her elegant dress. "You probably won't believe this, but I'm actually quite timid," she said. "I asked my husband to look into it, but he's been too busy to get around to it."

She stopped there, but Burgess was sure the unspoken part of the sentence was, "He's always too busy to get around to it or anything I want him to do." Also, that her husband thought she was being silly.

At that moment, the man she'd indicated was her husband joined their group, and without an "excuse me" or asking for an introduction to Burgess and Kyle—who, being members of the servant class, were beneath him—took his wife's arm, saying, "Megan, there's someone I want you to meet." She might have responded that there was someone she wanted him to meet, but she didn't. A lovely bird in a gilded cage, perhaps?

Before she left, Burgess asked for the name of the town where they had their camp. It was another thing to go on their list of items to follow up. Also, perhaps, something for his gratitude diary.

She turned to leave, then hesitated and said, "I have some more questions for you, Detective."

He said, "Call me," and gave her a card.

He put his notebook away, looked around and saw the chief was deep in conversation, and turned to Kyle. "Think we're done here?"

Kyle nodded, and they left before the chief could send them another citizen with complaints. They never met the Irish guests in whose honor they'd worn their Sunday best.

TWENTY-EIGHT

It was mid-evening, and in the interest of domestic tranquility, Burgess really needed to go home, but there were things to deal with first. Without consulting, because they were on the same wavelength, he and Kyle drove to the hospital and parked.

Before they went inside, Burgess checked his text messages. One from Dr. Cohen before the boy went into surgery. One from the nurse, Maryellen, on Colleen's...uh, Maureen's, floor, saying that the aunt had arrived and was with the girl. Another, from Stan Perry, confirming the same thing. All expected messages and no apparent crises, so why had his phone been dancing in his pocket?

He went to missed calls and found the answer. Four calls from Chris. He checked his voicemail. The first message just said she was leaving dinner for him and hoped he wouldn't be too late, as they had a lot of things to discuss. The second, third, and fourth were different—showing growing levels of panic because Ned had disappeared, and anger at him for not taking her calls.

He called over to Kyle. "Ned's missing. I've got to go home. You take over here and keep me posted, okay?"

Kyle nodded. "And you keep me posted, okay? Here if you need me."

Kyle didn't need to say it, but it was the equivalent of "I've got your back," which was reassuring. Not that much could really reassure him right now. Not when they were hot on the trail of four people who didn't care at all about fellow humans. If any one of them knew Burgess and his team were looking for them, they wouldn't hesitate to strike first. There were those four and there was Mark Hammond. He made some calls to ensure that this time, no bleeding heart had set Hammond free despite having raped a woman and sent a young boy to the hospital with a brain injury. It happened. Inconceivable as it was, it happened. But Hammond was safely tucked up in jail.

Anxiety propelled him, his mind filled with images of sweet, trusting Ned carried off to that mysterious "camp" in the woods that was really a prison. Burgess drove like a maniac through the city, using siren, lights, and his horn to clear other drivers from his path. He called Chris to say he was on his way.

He was a sweaty wreck by the time he pulled into his driveway and rocked to a stop, out of the truck almost before it had finished moving. He pounded upstairs and into the kitchen, where Dylan, Nina, and Chris were gathered at the table around an untouched pie, looking solemn.

"Give me the timeline," he said, like a cop, not like a dad. Then he took a breath and sat down with them. "We'll sort this out. We'll find him. You know we'll find him."

"I've called all his friends," Chris said. "No one has seen him." Her eyes were red and she clutched a sodden tissue.

"Take me through the evening," Burgess said. "How did Ned seem? Was he upset about something?"

Fideau came and put his head on Burgess's knee. The dog didn't like it when his people weren't happy. Burgess rubbed the dog's head as his family filled him in.

"He was worried about his friend Van," Dylan said. "He'd called after school to see if Van could come over, and no one had answered. He knew Van's stepdad was violent and he was afraid that something had happened."

Burgess looked at Chris. "Did he say anything to you?"

She shook her head.

Burgess figured Ned hadn't asked for permission because he feared it would be denied.

"Did he eat dinner?"

Chris nodded. "He was his usual ravenous self and was looking forward to pie. We all wanted to save the pie until you got home…if we could. So after dinner, he said he had some homework to do and asked if he could work downstairs in the new room. I said sure." She looked at Burgess. "That's why we built it, right? So the kids could have a place of their own?"

She looked down at her now knotted hands. "So around eight, we decided not to wait any longer and got out plates and forks to eat the pie. I told Nina to go down and get Ned."

"And when I got downstairs," Nina said, "Neddy wasn't there. He was gone. And his coat and boots were gone." She looked stricken. "Dad, do you think something's happened to him?"

"I hope not."

Burgess was calculating how long it would take a boy of Ned's size to walk from here to the Elwell's house. He figured about twenty-five minutes. So if he got there and found no one home, he should have been back by now.

He hated to treat his family like witnesses, but he needed some answers. "Nobody heard the downstairs door open or shut?"

A chorus of nos.

"What about vehicles? Did you hear any vehicles outside that might have been slowing or stopping?"

No one had.

"So he's been gone between an hour and an hour and a half?"

Chris nodded.

"Okay. I'll take a drive over to his friend Van's house and make sure he's not there or walking somewhere between here and there. I expect he is. If not, we'll regroup and call for more resources."

With a reluctant glance at the apple pie, which was golden-crusted and looked delicious, he put on his coat and boots again. Fideau was at his heels, reminding him that it was time for their evening walk. Well, why not take the dog? He had been helpful in the past. Fideau was great at finding missing kids.

He said, "Fideau, come."

"Sure you don't need some help?" Dylan asked. He'd followed Burgess to the stairs.

Lowering his voice, Burgess said, "I do. I need you to stay with Chris and Nina and try to keep them calm. They'll feel safer if you're with them."

His son straightened and nodded. A year earlier he would have protested that he wanted to come along. Now he understood that Burgess wasn't shutting him out but giving him an important task to do.

"We'll be fine, Dad."

Burgess and Fideau headed out into the chilly night, Fideau on the passenger seat beside him. "We need to find Ned," he told the dog, and got that eerie nod of the canine head that suggested the dog understood what he'd said. Burgess thought maybe he did. The dog had amazed him before.

As they drove, Fideau looked out the side window while Burgess looked out his. Recognizing that the dog worked with his nose, Burgess lowered that window, even though it meant letting in the night's chill. From time to time, they slowed as they passed someone on the sidewalk. But at this time of night, those they passed were not small boys. They were mostly unhoused people, and others Burgess recognized as people he wouldn't want anywhere near his son.

Anxiety had filled the truck like an enveloping cloud. Burgess gripped the wheel so hard his fingers ached. Every bush, every shadow, every movement was scrutinized. They slowed for alleys and for long, dark driveways. At one point, Burgess felt something on his knee and looked down to see the dog's paw. It rose and fell a few times in a series of pats, and tense as Burgess was, he had to smile.

"Thanks, Buddy," he said. "Yeah. I am that upset."

Fideau nodded and resumed his vigil out the window.

Burgess was watching a man hunched over in some bushes, probably relieving himself, when Fideau barked.

Burgess braked and pulled to the curb. He couldn't see what the dog was seeing—or scenting—but he trusted that Fideau had alerted to something. He got out and opened Fideau's door, checking for his gun as he followed his dog to the sidewalk and into a dark space between two buildings. He called for backup as he walked.

Barely visible in the darkness were a group of men clustered around something on the ground. It could have been anything. An animal they were torturing. Or a homeless person. But Fideau had alerted, and he would have recognized Ned's scent.

His anxiety level went through the roof as he accelerated toward the group. Fideau was faster. Barking and growling, the dog charged them, leaping into the air to grab an arm that was holding a raised piece of wood. He brought the arm, and the person holding it, to the ground.

Burgess had his gun out as he approached the group. "Police!" he ordered in a loud voice. "Down on the ground. All of you. Right now."

One of the group tried to run. Burgess rarely discharged his weapon, but now he yelled, "Stop or I'll shoot." Both a cliché and a warning.

The runner stopped and looked back, then resumed running toward the street, where flashing blue lights signaled to Burgess that his backup had arrived. They could handle the runner. He focused his attention on the three who remained. Up close, he saw they weren't men at all, but teenagers out for a bit of mischief. Mischief that in this case involved threatening and tormenting a small boy out later than he should have been.

"They won't touch you, Ned," Burgess said in a gentle voice. "Fideau will see to that."

Still cringing, his eyes on his tormenters, Ned eased away from his crouch against the wall and walked to Burgess. A quick assessment showed no blood but that didn't mean his son was okay.

"Stand behind me, Ned," Burgess instructed, curbing his desire to sweep the boy into his arms and run back to the truck. Until his backup was in place, it was his job to detain the three attackers. His job with some help from his canine companion.

The teen on the ground, pinned there by a growling dog, was begging, "Please, officer. Please. Get him off me. Don't let him bite me again."

Two officers had joined him now, one of them with the runaway in tow. "Looks like you could use a little help here, Sergeant," the older one said.

"I sure can, Tim." Before he put his gun away, Burgess ordered the four of them up against the wall. "They were terrorizing this young boy."

This officer, one who'd been on the force almost as long as Burgess, was another dinosaur. But he was a great cop and knew the city inside and out. It would a big loss when he decided to retire.

The younger officer was one Burgess knew well, had known since he was a rookie. He smiled when Remy Aucoin said to Ned, "What's your name, son?"

"Neddy. Uh…Ned," said the small voice behind Burgess. "Uh…My Joe…uh…Detective Burgess is my dad."

In that moment, Burgess realized that Ned, who had always called him My Joe, had stopped doing it and he'd never noticed. Probably around the same time the boy decided Neddy was too babyish and asked to be called Ned.

The teen Fideau had taken to the ground, the one who'd had a weapon raised to hit Ned, was alternately sobbing and screaming. The stick he'd been ready to hit Ned with lay on the ground beside him. Before he called off his dog, Burgess put on a glove and collected it.

"Fideau, off," Burgess said.

In the light from the other officers' flashlights, his brilliant dog gave him a look he read as, "Are you sure about this?"

Burgess nodded. "Off, Fideau. Go to Ned."

Obediently, the dog released his grip on the attacker's shirt and trotted to Ned. Burgess didn't turn to look, but he knew that Ned had thrown his arms around the dog and was getting a serious licking.

When the four of them—baggy pants, hoodies, and expensive sneakers on all—were lined up against the wall, Burgess recognized the boy Fideau had tackled as the same little snot who'd found the necklace down in the park and refused to give it back. Getting a lot of experience in how to become a serious criminal.

He addressed the group, saying, "Your names and addresses, please."

What he got was silence. Then the snotty kid from the park said, "I need a doctor. That fucking dog bit me."

"Search them," he told Aucoin. And to the other officer, "You'd better call for a second car to help transport these gentlemen." He ignored the teen's protests that he couldn't arrest them. Told the snotty kid that if he was injured, they'd see that he got medical attention.

The officer snorted, "Gentlemen?" and got on his radio.

Burgess shifted his attention back to the four as Aucoin started down the row, searching them. From the first kid's pocket he got a wallet, which he tossed to Burgess. Burgess wrote the name and address in his notebook and checked the rest of the contents. Kid had two credit cards and a couple hundred dollars. At that age, he'd been lucky if he had five dollars to get him through the week.

In a second pocket, Aucoin found a packet of pills and held them up. "What are these?"

"They're for my allergies," the kid said. "I got bad allergies."

Aucoin shook his head. "Why does everyone think I was born yesterday? We'll just have these tested and see what allergies they treat." He tossed the bag to the older cop. Said, "You'd better get some evidence bags, Tim. I think we're going to find this crew has a lot of allergies."

The older cop's radio crackled. Backup had arrived and wanted to know where to find them. He instructed them to bring evidence envelopes and directed them to the alley. "Gonna have half of patrol tied up with this pretty soon," he said. "All because four thugs with time on their hands decide to beat up a little kid." He raised his voice so the kids against the wall could hear. "You're pathetic, all four of you. You know that? Getting your kicks picking on a defenseless little kid?"

To Burgess, he said, "Any of my kids did something like this, they'd be grounded for a month. Luckily, they're grown now and all decent people. How come we're still doing this at our age anyway, Joe?"

Burgess said, "Wouldn't know what to do with myself otherwise, I guess."

"Yeah. Me too."

Even while they talked, Burgess never took his eyes off the four teens. On TV, searching people always looks so pro forma, but in reality it could be dangerous. Many of the things they did could be dangerous. He felt the older cop's hand on his shoulder. The man said, "It's okay to be shaken when it's your kid."

"Thanks, Tim. Appreciate it." Which he did, because he *was* shaken. It hadn't been long ago that he wondered when Ned's turn to get into trouble would come. He'd expected acting up at school or staying out too late or maybe a baseball pitched through someone's window. Typical boy stuff. He'd never anticipated this. What if he hadn't gotten here in time? If he hadn't brought Fideau, with his great nose and even greater instincts, he didn't know what would have happened.

Well, he knew something. He knew Ned would have been harmed, maybe seriously. He knew about the trauma that followed such an attack. He knew the way the damage rippled through families. How lives could be altered by an event that on the surface seemed minor or insignificant. He knew that going forward, Ned would be hesitant to leave the house. To do things on his own. To trust people. That he'd shy away from groups of teens. Maybe be afraid of the dark.

Aucoin had reached the fourth boy now, the one Burgess had met before. The tough little poseur was crying. He pulled himself together enough to argue with Aucoin, insisting that the officer had no right to search him.

"Gotta search you, son," Aucoin said. "We always search suspects before we arrest them. Better safe than sorry and all that. You don't have anything illegal on you, you got nothing to worry about."

"I know my rights," the brat insisted. "You've got no right—"

"He's got every right," Burgess said. "And if you don't cooperate, there are other officers here who'll be happy to assist with the search." He decided not to threaten another encounter with Fideau. Kids these days could be such snowflakes that Mommy and Daddy might file a suit for police brutality. Heck, they probably would anyway. It was a sad thing, but cops got used to being sued just for doing their jobs.

"Sheesh," the cop named Tim muttered. "Kids these days. Quick to insist on their rights but they don't even think about it before they pick up a stick and attack a child."

"I'm not a little kid," Ned said. "I'm ten."

"Double digits," Aucoin said. "And you'd better not become a teenager like these four."

"My dad wouldn't let me," the small voice said.

This was good, Burgess thought. *If Ned could interact like this, that was a positive sign.*

"Go ahead," the older cop said. "Tend to your kid. We've got this."

You had to trust your colleagues. Otherwise, no one could do this job. He said, "Thanks," and turned to Ned.

There were some reddish bruises on the boy's face and scratches on his hands. Burgess wouldn't be able to tell whether the boy had further injuries without removing his clothes, something he wasn't about to do here in a dark alley in the presence of the attackers. He knelt and held out his arms. Ned threw himself into them, burying his face in Burgess's shoulder. Burgess reached past the boy and gave Fideau a few pats. "You were a very good dog tonight," he said.

"Fideau saved me," Ned said. "Fideau and you. But how did you find me?"

There was an awful tremble in his voice.

"I'm a detective," Burgess said. "And Fideau seems to be one, too."

Ned laughed at that.

"Are you all right? Do you need to go to the hospital?"

Ned responded with a sob. "You got here in time."

Burgess figured that since he was the dad he shouldn't be the one to ask Ned these important initial questions. He said, "Can you tell Officer Laukka what happened?"

"I was just walking…" Ned began.

Laukka held up a hand. "Not here. It's gotta be official," he said.

"Can you do that, Ned? Can you tell him the whole story, so he has it for the record? So that we know what crimes to charge these guys with?"

Ned started to sob again. "I want you to do it. Why can't you do it?"

"Because I'm your dad, Ned. Your story needs to be taken by someone who isn't related to you. By a police officer who is trained to speak with juvenile victims."

Immediately, he thought about Andrea Dwyer, the woman they called the "kiddie cop." Dwyer would be great at this. But he didn't want to offend Tim Laukka. He needn't have worried. Laukka was a pro and understood the situation perfectly.

"No worries, Joe. I've already called Dwyer and she's on her way. Woman's almost too good at her job. We're running her ragged – patrol – calling her in on things. Be great if we could clone her."

Burgess agreed. Dwyer was great at her job. He returned his attention to Ned. He said, "We've got our officer who specializes in incidents involving juveniles—which is what you are—on the way. She'll be here soon and will take down your story. And you'll like her. She's very cool. She plays soccer."

He added the soccer because Ned had started playing soccer that fall and was really into it.

"But I want you," Ned insisted.

"I understand. But if your father takes your story, instead of a neutral police officer, it could be challenged in court because I was prejudiced in your favor or slanted the story to make your attackers look worse. We don't want to do anything here that will let them go unpunished for what they've done to you. Do you understand that?"

Burgess knew it was a lot. He'd dealt with plenty of adults over the years who couldn't comprehend the rules of police procedure and the intricacies of the legal system. Also with plenty of crime victims whose trauma made it hard for them to process anything. Now he waited for Ned's response.

"Okay, I get it. It's all about police procedure, isn't it? About…I'm not sure how you'd describe it…making a record?" Ned's response was calm, and he seemed to understand, but Burgess really wasn't sure. He said, "When you give your statement to Officer Dwyer, you can have your mom with you if you want. The rules are okay with that. Do you want me to call her?"

More tears, and the boy said, through his sobs, "But mom is going to be mad at me for sneaking out, isn't she?"

Yes, of course, they both were, but that wouldn't be foremost on her mind, Burgess knew. He said, "What your mom wants to know is that you're safe, Ned. That's what parents worry about. You know. You've seen how upset we got when your brother got stabbed and when your sister was taken away by that mean boy and Uncle Terry and I had to rescue her, right?"

He got a faint nod.

"So, let's call your mom and see if she can meet us here, okay?"

Another faint nod.

Another patrol officer had joined them and was assisting Remy Aucoin in searching the fourth teen, the one who'd objected to being searched. As with the other three, they'd come up with bags of pills. This kid also had a knife. All four of them had fake IDs, pretty bad ones. They'd also found a set of car keys. Burgess figured there was at least alcohol in the vehicle, and probably more drugs, if the amount of money each kid had correlated with illegal drug sales. Maybe the four of them just had really big allowances and these bags were only for personal use. They'd figure that out.

He wanted to get a warrant to search the car. More careful procedure. He didn't want to lose any evidence which might lead to further charges against these four. That they'd find it fun to terrorize and beat a small boy made him sick.

He called Chris, and she answered with a breathless, "Oh, Joe! Did you find him? Did you find him? Please tell me you found him."

"He's right here with me."

"Is he okay?"

"He's okay. Some bigger boys were picking on him, but Fideau took them on and stopped it." He paused to see if she had questions, then went on. "We've got Andrea Dwyer coming to take his statement. You've met her. She's our juvenile officer. And Ned would like you to be there, if you can."

"I'll be right there." He heard quick footsteps and the jingle of her keys as she picked up them. Then a pause. "Where am I going?"

He gave her the name of the street and told her to look for his truck.

"I'll be there as soon as I can," she said. "Oh, Joe. The poor little guy!" A hesitation, then, "Is he really okay?"

"We got there in time."

As soon as he said it, he wished he could take it back. Joe Burgess didn't blurt things out, and something like this could amp up both her anxiety and her annoyance that he hadn't been home sooner. It was the balancing act of his life—learning to be part of a family while still doing his job. Things were more complicated right now with a wedding to plan.

"On my way," she said, and disconnected.

If she had something to say about his not being home, he figured he'd hear about it later. For now, they both had to focus on Ned.

"What do you want us to do with these four?" Tim Laukka asked.

"Take 'em downtown and keep them separated until they can be interviewed," Burgess said. "And get a warrant to search the car. I have a feeling there's more to be learned about these kids and the car may have some answers." He recalled that as he approached, one of them had had a phone out. Maybe taking photos or videos of the assault. "And their phones."

From a distance, he heard a woman's voice, calling, "Hey, Joe. I'm here," and Andrea Dwyer followed her flashlight out of the darkness.

She headed right for Ned, and knelt down so she was on his level. She held out her hand. "Hi, Ned. I'm Andrea Dwyer, and I'm here to talk with you about what happened tonight. Can you come with me now? We'll sit in my car and you can tell me about it."

"But I'm supposed to wait for my mom," Ned said. Burgess heard tears in his voice.

"She's on her way," Burgess said. "Should be here very soon."

"Great," Dwyer said. "That's Chris, right?"

"Right."

"Okay," Dwyer said, "we'll go sit in my car, and when your mom gets here, she can join us. Would you like Fideau to come, too?"

That was a smart move. Ned would feel more comfortable with Fideau there. And Dwyer had seen in a previous case how useful the dog could be.

"Yes, please," Ned said.

Dwyer rose and said, "Come with me." To Burgess she said, "Never interviewed a victim with a dog present before. But that's some dog."

She headed back toward the street with Ned and Fideau behind her. Ned's hand was on Fideau's head.

When they were gone, Burgess felt his concentration sharpening, like his emotions had had double vision as long as Ned was there.

"Cute kid," Tim Laukka said. "I didn't know you had kids. Or were married."

"Not married, yet," Burgess said. "Trying to find some time in all the chaos to get married. As for kids? I've got three, two teens and Ned. It's a long story." He shook his head. "I think you've got five or six, right?"

"Five. It's never easy. But as I said, mine have turned out well."

They both shifted their focus to the four kids still lined up along the wall. Aucoin and another officer were giving them instructions about their arrest and what would be happening next.

"You spare some cuffs, Joe? Tim?" Aucoin asked.

Burgess and Laukka handed theirs over. Then the two officers led their four prisoners away.

For a moment, Burgess and Laukka stood together in the now quiet darkness, sharing a moment. There was no need for conversation. They were just thinking about the years, and the criminals, the job and family. Then, again without speaking, they headed back to their vehicles.

TWENTY-NINE

Chris's car was parked behind his, and she was just getting into Dwyer's cruiser when he came out of the alley. He stepped back and let her get into the vehicle without seeing him. He wanted her focus on Ned right now.

Back in the alley, he said to Tim, "Don't want her focus on anything but the boy right now," and got a nod.

"You want me to get those warrants?"

"I'd be grateful. You got all the names and addresses?"

Laukka nodded. "You know how we are. Belt and suspenders, yeah? So, you want the car and their phones, right?" He stroked his chin thoughtfully. "We oughta put someone on the car 'til we get that warrant. Once Momma and Daddy know their little darling is in trouble, one of 'em is gonna be here with the car keys and then we lose chain of custody plus whatever's in the vehicle."

God, he loved working with competent cops. "Once they're all stowed at 109, maybe get Aucoin back here to sit on it?"

"Nah. I'll get someone else. You'll want Aucoin for the interviews. Lad is coming along well, despite his uncles' interference. He's good. That youthful appearance can be deceptive."

Aucoin was coming along well. And yes, despite having two doting uncles on the force who'd kept trying to intervene back when he was a rookie. They'd learned to back off and let Remy blossom into his own man and own kind of cop. Not that having two uncles on the force hadn't also sometimes been a help.

"Great. Appreciate it," Burgess said.

Laukka left and, still lurking where Chris couldn't see him, he got out his phone and called Kyle.

"Did you find him?" Kyle asked.

"Yeah. In the famous nick of time. And with a little help from a clever dog with a good nose."

"And?" Kyle said, because he was reading Burgess's voice.

"And he was about to get beat up by four teenagers with mischief on their minds and no sense of boundaries. One of them was that useless POS who found the girl's necklace down in the park and refused to give it back. He doesn't get slapped down hard now, there's a lifetime of bad behavior ahead."

"How's Ned?"

"Doing pretty well. I haven't had a real chance to talk to him yet. I didn't want to taint things. He's doing his victim interview with Dwyer right now, and Chris and Fideau are sitting in."

"I'll bet that's a first for Dwyer. The dog, I mean."

"So she says. What's going on at the hospital?"

"Wait," Kyle said. "Before we leave the subject...Were Ned's attackers arrested?"

"They were. Cooling their heels at 109, waiting to be interviewed."

"You need me there?"

"Probably. Depends on what's going on at the hospital. Did you get a chance to speak with the aunt?"

"I did. She's flattened by what's happened. I guess she and the girls were very close. Evidently the mother sold their disappearance as just what the frauds who set up that fake camp did, as a place for troubled teens to get away from bad influences and reconnect with nature. Aunt blames the new stepfather. Says he's a piece of work who never wanted the girls and the mother is an idiot."

"So, she's going to stick around for a few days?"

"Yes. And take the girl home with her, get her an attorney, and get custody. She's real fired up about that. But she keeps asking what about Maureen, which is confusing since our girl says she is Maureen. And this woman isn't the type to simply confuse two twins, especially not twins she's known all their lives. So I'm back to thinking that this girl is Colleen. But why she insists she's her sister, I don't know. Unless—" Kyle hesitated, but Burgess was already filling in the blanks.

"Unless Colleen was the rebel, and did something that got her in trouble and they punished the wrong girl," Burgess suggested.

"Or unless the good twin took the rap for her sister." Another hesitation. "We don't know that she's dead. Only what the girl says. We never got a timeline for that, did we?"

"I think she said it was while they were being transported. So, September?"

Burgess had a thought about the aunt. "Maybe she could call her former sister-in-law, say she wants to send some things to the girls, and see if she can get an address? Think she'd do that?"

"I think she would," Kyle said. "She's furious. Appalled. Ready to help in any way she can. Probably best to wait until morning to do it, though. You think?"

Burgess agreed.

Kyle switched subjects. "Now that we know it's connected to the Briscows, did we ever get a team out to that empty house, see what prints we could pull?"

"Not yet. I guess we should have but things were jumping and since the house was empty, an optimistic cop named Burgess must have decided it could wait."

"Well," Kyle said, "as we get closer and start rattling their cage, I think our friend Clinton Johns, or whatever he's calling himself these days, and his pals the Briscows are gonna get worried and start destroying things and destroying that house might be part of covering their tracks. Think I'll put the local PD on it, get them to watch the house. That okay with you?"

"It's a good idea. We ought to also alert the neighbor, Shirley Bufford. She's a friend of the owner and keeps an eye on that house. And she's right next door. Probably too late to make that call now."

What Burgess wanted to do was drive by Bufford's house, see if there was a light on, and pay her a quick visit if there was. Actually, there were a lot of things he wanted to do, like go to 109 and start interviewing those teenage thugs. Take their car apart and see what he could find that they could be charged with. What he needed to do was wait until Dwyer was done with Ned and then go home to his family. Chris would take his head off otherwise, and he'd deserve it.

Sometimes balancing the job and family was like trying to keep his balance on tippy rocks across a boiling spring river.

"We wouldn't have it any other way, though, would we?" Kyle said. Because after many years working together, Kyle could read his mind. "Don't worry. We've got this. I'll call Stan back in and grab Sage Prentiss. He's always eager to get involved."

"Okay. Good plan. Timmy Laukka suggested we include Aucoin as an interviewer. He was at the scene. Did the arrest. So maybe call in Sage and let the new daddy get some sleep. Or some baby duty. Uh... we found baggies of pills on all four of them. We'll send those to the lab for analysis. And a bunch of cash. You might get the drug guys involved, see if they have history with any of these kids. The kid from the park had a knife. He was the one who was about to hit Ned. Or maybe already had. Ned was bruised and scratched. I'll fill you in more once I've had a chance to talk with him."

"Stuff like this really pisses me off," Kyle said.

"Yeah. Doesn't matter how much bad stuff we've seen. It can still get to you."

"Especially when it's your kid," Kyle said.

"Or any kid. I keep telling the universe not to send me any more kids. My weary old self can't take it."

"And yet the universe sent you down to the park, or else our girl would probably be dead."

"Damned universe," Burgess muttered. He peeked around the building and saw Chris and Ned and Fideau getting out of Dwyer's car. "Gotta go. Keep me up on this, okay?"

"You know I will."

Kyle went off to organize the interviews and some surveillance on the abandoned house. Burgess went to rejoin his family.

He met them on the sidewalk, Fideau dancing back and forth

between him and Ned. He patted the dog and said, "You did a good job tonight." He found a treat in his coat pocket and gave it to the dog, then opened his arms to Chris and Ned.

She was sputtering all her concerns: "Oh my God, Joe, what if…" and "What if Fideau…" and "What if you'd been any later?" Burgess just held her more tightly, while Ned patted her arm and said, "It's okay, Mom. It's okay. You shoulda seen Fideau. He was amazing."

"And I thought I didn't want a dog," she said. Then, "Ned, you are riding with me. Fideau, you go with Joe."

As Ned climbed into her car, he said, "Thanks, My Joe, see you at home."

Fideau climbed into Burgess's truck, in his usual spot in the passenger seat, curled up, and fell asleep.

"I guess being the alpha dog wears you right out," Burgess told the sleeping animal. He should know. He was kind of an alpha dog himself. Whoever would have thought, on that dark, wet night outside a cottage where his son was being held prisoner, that he'd end up with a crime scene dog, never mind such a great dog?

He drove home through his quiet city, willing anyone who needed help to stagger out into the path of another Portland cop. Overhead, the sky was a clear, inky black. Despite the lights of the city, he could see some stars. He worked on his breathing so he could be calm when he got home. The shrink said it was supposed to help and he needed to be calm. It had taken extreme self-control to hold back from sitting in on that interview and hearing Ned's story of what had happened. Now he needed family time. He needed to process. He needed to ensure, with his own eyes, that his young son was okay.

THIRTY

Back home, Burgess, the man who'd lived like a solitary monk for much of his adult life, found himself engulfed in a giant family hug. Three kids, one almost spouse, and the world's best dog. It felt foreign and it felt amazing. He was surprised to find the calming breaths had really worked. Something else for his gratitude diary. Actually, the whole business of rescuing Neddy was for the diary. He had plenty of experience looking for people, but finding Ned without Fideau's help would have taken much longer. And might have likely resulted in a lot of damage to his son.

His son. He could still hear Ned's small, shaken voice saying, "My Joe, uh, Detective Burgess is my dad." It amazed him how they were coming together as a family. As he often did, he wished his mother was alive to see this. She would have loved her grandchildren so much. "Live in the now, Burgess," he reminded himself. Yes, honoring her memory mattered, but right now, his job was to be present for the people right around him.

"So, little bro," Dylan said. "Are you okay? Really okay? Did they hurt you?" Asking the question Burgess had been about to ask.

"A little," Ned said. "They grabbed me off the sidewalk and dragged me down into the dark between those houses, and I tried to get away and one of them hit me. Then they shoved me up against the wall and wanted to know if I had any money. Which I didn't because I was just walking to Van's house to see if he was okay." He looked at Burgess. "Van wasn't answering his phone and I was worried."

No sense in keeping things from Ned. Not at this point. Not when his concern for his friend had already led him out alone into the dangers of the city night. Burgess said, "You wouldn't have found anyone home. Van's in the hospital. His stepfather struck him and he fell and hit his head. Hammond has been arrested. He's in jail."

"Will he be okay? Can I go and see him tomorrow?"

"The doctors think he'll be okay. We'll know more tomorrow and if he can have visitors, I'll take you. But right now, we need to know that you're okay," Burgess said.

They'd moved out of the family huddle and were sitting in the living room.

"I'll be right back," Chris said.

Burgess heard the clink of glasses in the kitchen. She came back with a tray on which there were three glasses of chocolate milk and two glasses of bourbon. It was such a moment that Burgess almost laughed. But only almost. Things would not have gone well if he'd laughed at her gesture.

The kids grabbed their milk. Before Burgess could continue with his questions for Ned, Dylan said, "Did they threaten you?"

Who was doing the interview here? It looked like Detective Burgess had to take a back seat to big brother Dylan. He found he didn't mind. He liked that his family—the two abused kids Chris wanted to adopt, and the son he'd never known about—were bonding. Calling each other bro and sis and calling him and Chris Mom and Dad. People always talked about how lucky kids were be adopted by nice parents, but he and Chris were also lucky to have been adopted by nice kids.

In the end, it seemed that Ned had been punched once or twice, and dragged by his wrists into the alley. He showed off his bruises with a kind of shy pride, like he'd survived an ordeal. Burgess thought it helped that the questions had come from Dylan, who was bristling with anger that someone had dared to touch his little brother. He had the information he needed.

Dylan said, "I wonder if I know any of them, Dad. You got pictures?"

Burgess didn't, he hadn't taken any photos at the scene, although soon he'd have access to booking photos. He said, "I can show you some tomorrow. Be interesting to know if they have a reputation. But don't..." He hesitated about how to word this. "Don't take upon yourself to avenge this attack on your brother. Please. Let us handle it. They've been arrested."

Dylan shrugged and didn't commit.

Then Chris hustled Ned off to bed and Dylan and Nina retreated downstairs.

Alone with his bourbon, Burgess felt the weight of the evening, and the very long day, descend on him. He was trying to summon the energy to start planning their investigative agenda for tomorrow when Chris returned.

She plunked down beside him and picked up her glass. "Sometimes, a little bit of bourbon is a very good idea." She put a hand on his knee. "So, how are you?"

"A lot like you. Shaken. Relieved. Struggling with my urge to yell at him when he's already traumatized enough. Enraged at those four thugs."

"His friend Van's really in the hospital? Is it serious?"

"He's having surgery to reduce swelling in his brain, so yes, it's serious. I tried. But I didn't get there in time."

Her warm hand stayed on his knee. "Maybe in time to keep it from being worse." She sipped her drink and said, "Is this an okay time to talk about the wedding?"

"Sure."

She got out her phone and said, "I've made a list. We have a venue and a caterer." A hesitation. "Can your caterer make the cake?"

"I think so. I'll ask her."

"My minister can marry us. The kids will be in the wedding. I've asked Michelle to be my maid of honor. Did you ask Terry?"

"I did. He's on board. He wants to know whether we're supposed to wear our dress uniforms." It was only then that Burgess remembered he was wearing his and felt a twinge of gratitude that it hadn't suffered during the arrests. Cop's clothes, even detective's clothes, took a beating.

"I'm fine either way, Joe. It's whatever makes you more comfortable. You're used to wearing a uniform…" She let it hang. "I want to show you a dress. Oh, and we need to get a license. And there are invitations. So you need to give me a list. And I need to make a list. And we have to decide how many people…who's in and who's out. And that we need to do now, because the holiday season is crazy busy."

He could handle a crime scene with all its chaos while this seemed overwhelming. All he wanted was Chris to be his wife. But it mattered to her. He said, "I'll make that list tomorrow. Show me the dress…only, isn't it supposed to be a secret? A surprise that will knock my socks off when I see you? Not that you don't knock my socks off all the time anyway."

The hand on his leg tightened its grip. Then lifted as she scrolled through her phone and showed him a picture. Burgess didn't know much about women's clothes. He could describe them when giving details about a suspect or someone they were trying to locate. In his line of work, far too often the women they dealt with were underdressed or undressed. He studied the dress. It was floor length and made from heavy, creamy fabric. The sleeves came just below the elbow and the neck was what he believed was called cowl. It looked elegant and slightly medieval in the way it draped.

"It's lovely," he said. "It will suit you."

She put her arms around him and hugged him. Whispered "Thank you" in his ear.

With that, they went to bed. Chris asleep almost instantly, exhausted by the stresses of the day, and Burgess, after perching on the cusp of sleep long enough to wish for a quiet night with no calls and no emergencies, followed her.

He slept, only to be awakened a few hours later, overcome by shakes so powerful he thought he was in the grips of a sudden flu. As he lay there trying to control it and not wake Chris, he realized it was the aftermath of the attack on Ned earlier in the evening. Suck it up and take it. Take a licking and keep on ticking. Bull your way through it. That had always been his working MO. Burgess, after decades on the job, was tough as nails. Having a family at risk changed the equation. He couldn't be dispassionate. One small boy in danger had wormed his way behind Burgess's defenses. It had shaken him, but he'd failed to recognize it or give himself a chance to process it.

No wonder Kyle had asked him if he was okay. At the time, he'd thought it was whether he'd physically been involved in the altercation. It was a truth among cops that sooner or later, they'd go home hurting. This was different. This was the emotional response of a father charged with caring for, and protecting, his family.

Wow.

He slid from the bed, went into the bathroom, and stepped into the shower, letting a blast of icy water pour over his head and his shaking body. When he stepped out, the emotional shakes had been replaced by just plain cold shakes, and he felt more like himself again. He toweled off and headed back to bed.

From the darkness, Chris said, "It's powerful stuff, having a family, isn't it. I never imagined..."

"Nor I, even though I've seen the impact on so many people."

"Not the same," she said. "The love. The fear. The fierce protectiveness. It's all new and it landed on us all of a sudden. I think it's different if you've grown with it, and with them, since birth. Not lesser. Just different."

They slid together in the middle of the bed, arms wrapped around each other, settling into the warmth and comfort that happened when they were together.

"We'll get through it," Burgess whispered. "You know we will. And Neddy will be okay."

There was no small voice in the darkness to correct that Neddy to Ned. He would always be Neddy to them. Just like Burgess had relished "My Joe."

Eventually, sleep overtook them again. And far too soon, it was morning and Burgess's phone was blowing up.

THIRTY-ONE

The first call, predictably, was from Captain Cote, looking to be updated on the girl's case. Burgess let Ned, who relished the task, take that call and offer to take a message. The whole family enjoyed watching Ned deftly handle Cote, who found it hard to bully a young boy. The second was kind of a surprise, and immediately dragged Burgess back into the case. It was a call from Megan Ainsworth, asking if they could meet for breakfast and finish their unfinished conversation from the night before.

So much had transpired since their talk at the cocktail party that Burgess had nearly forgotten who she was. But her voice was an immediate reminder, and since her query suggested it might be related to their quest to locate that abandoned camp, he agreed to meet her and named a time. He also agreed because the chief wanted him to humor her.

He'd barely gotten through that and picked up his toast when Kyle called, saying he was going to meet with the girl's aunt this morning and sit with her while she made the phone call to the girl's mother. Did Burgess want to sit in?

He did. He told Kyle he was meeting with Megan Ainsworth, and about the feeling he'd gotten that there might be something in her story that connected to their case. "But that's later. I've got time to sit in on that call. How'd it go with those four thugs last night?"

"What you'd expect. Tough guys until they meet real tough guys. Then they folded. It was so pathetic I almost felt sorry for them. And here's the amazing thing. Not one of them asked for an attorney or a chance to call their parents."

"You're kidding. They always want to call their parents. They always lawyer up."

"Dunno, Joe, but that's what happened."

"What about the car? Find anything?"

"Oh yeah. Car belongs to the tall one, not the little crybaby like you might expect."

"Crybaby injured?"

"Not so's you'd notice. Fideau has a talent for biting without leaving marks. Love to know his story," Kyle said. "Wouldn't you?"

As though he'd heard his name spoken, the dog came and put his head in Burgess's lap. Phone still to his ear, Burgess stroked Fideau's head with his free hand while he continued. "About the car?"

"About what you'd expect. Drugs. A few items that appear to have been liberated from their owners without consent. Cell phones and such. And…" Kyle hesitated, aware of the impact this would have on Burgess. "And a gun. We're checking it for ownership and prints. None of them admit to having it, but it was under the driver's seat. It'll match up to one of them."

Burgess felt a frisson of last night's chills. They'd gone after Ned and they'd had a gun. Things could have gone far more badly. He also thought about four sets of parents evidently ignorant of how their teens were spending their time, getting serious wake-up calls now that their sons had been arrested. Teens could be pretty good at fooling their parents. But drug possession, possession of stolen property and probably theft, and possession of a handgun? He wondered if the gun belonged to one of the parents and whether they'd kept it properly secured. From a police point of view, people were shockingly lax about how they stored their firearms, especially when there were children in the house. Probably from a general public safety and child safety standpoint as well.

He had no time for this. They had no time for this. They were on the track of bigger things. But then, were there bigger things than four thugs driving around his city with guns and drugs randomly attacking young children? They had no way of knowing whether this was a first-time thing for this crew. Had they attacked another child? Someone elderly or intoxicated? An unhoused person? They'd have to check patrol's reports. It often went this way. You might be working a case that required all your attention, but that didn't mean other bad things wouldn't happen and also demand your time and energy. Often several such bad things.

The clock was running but he had one more question. "What's Stan up to today?"

"Working his way through Elaine Hawes's phone records. Following up with the neighbor who was supposedly close to her, seeing if there's anything there. Going out to that empty house to supervise an evidence team. Enough to keep him busy. Says he's grateful he didn't have to put on his dress uniform and go dance and sing for the bigwigs."

Following up reminded him that he needed to follow up with his warden, see if the man had any ideas about where to find that abandoned camp. He thought he'd meet with Megan Ainsworth and get some more details about the lake and location of her camp first.

It was time to go. He'd finish his toast in the truck. When he came into the kitchen, Ned had slunk away. He went and knocked on the boy's bedroom door. Got a teary, "Come in."

Before he could say anything, Ned said, "I'm sorry, Dad. I know I shouldn't have gone out without asking, but I'd called Van so many times and he didn't answer and no one else answered either. I knew things were bad with his stepdad and I was worried and you weren't home and I didn't know what to do."

"Next time, ask us for help, okay? Mom and I aren't ogres, you know."

That brought more sobs.

Chris appeared behind him and slipped into the room. "It's okay, Joe. I've got this. You go to work. Ned's going to be okay." A pause. She said, "I'm taking the day off and Ned's not going to school. We're going to find out how Van is, and if he can have visitors, we'll go and see him. Otherwise, Ned's going to help me with wedding preparations."

When Burgess didn't respond, she said, "Seriously, Joe, I've got this. We'll be okay. I'm good at taking care of people, remember?"

He knew. Remembered how, when they'd first met and he'd been injured, she'd appeared with soup and her incredible warmth.

She hugged him and turned her attention back to Ned. Their kids had no idea how lucky they were.

Burgess put on his coat, told Dylan and Nina to have good days and stay out of trouble. "Mom's going to stay home with Ned today. He'll be okay."

He snagged his toast and headed out.

It was one of those blah November days, the world all gray and brown. Rusty leaves filled the gutters and people on the streets already wore the pinched, huddled look they would wear until April. No sun to lift their faces to, and a fierce wind off the water that smelled of salt and turned their noses red. The weatherman was talking about the possibility of an early snow. Somewhere in the north woods, there were a group of captive teens either freezing in uninsulated cabins or moved to some other bleak place to house them. As if it didn't already feel urgent, the increasingly cold weather, and the promise of an early snow, amped up his need to find them soon.

Although he needed to get to his desk to check messages and update the case book, he headed to the hospital to meet Kyle and the girl's aunt. Kyle had arranged for a conference room where they could strategize about the phone call. Then the aunt would call her sister-in-law, and they would observe. Burgess wanted to follow up on what the girl had said about Maureen's whereabouts and the mystery of which girl they were actually dealing with.

The aunt, whose name was Emily Mulcahey, had dark red hair and bright blue eyes. She said, "I'm so grateful that Colleen called me. I've been worried sick about those girls and their mother has refused to tell me anything. We used to be so close, Fiona and I. Even after the divorce from my brother. But once she met Alan Cassiday, she drifted away. I was lucky she still let me see the girls."

"We're glad you're here. Glad she has somebody," Burgess began, unsure how to word this. "So...uh...we're wondering about the girl. Your niece. She's told us that she's Maureen, but yesterday I understand you expressed concern to Detective Kyle about locating Maureen. So can you tell us which twin our girl is and how you know?"

The aunt shook her head, as though one of the twins telling tales was a familiar thing. "The girl here in the hospital is Colleen. I have no doubt. They look alike to most people but I've known them since they were born, and although the term for such twins is 'identical,' in some ways, they never have been. Colleen is the more adventurous one. In her mother's words, the more difficult one. Maureen has always been the one to clean up the messes and look after her more reckless sister."

He flashed back to finding that necklace on the ground beside the girl. When he'd checked it later, it had the letter *C*. C for Colleen? He interrupted before she could reply to ask, "Did the girls have gold necklaces with their initials?"

The aunt nodded. "I gave them those for their thirteenth birthday." She fished in the bag for a tissue and dabbed at her eyes. "Do you know anything more about Maureen? Is what Colleen says right? That whoever took the girls has killed her? That she had a head injury and she died?"

She paused and corrected herself. "Whoever my careless, narcissistic sister-in-law sent them to without checking?"

Kyle said, "Your niece says that she's Maureen, not Colleen. But you don't agree. Can you think of a reason why she'd claim to be her sister? Why she'd lie to us?"

The aunt's smile was sad. "Probably because it was Colleen who caused the trouble and Maureen who took the blame. As usual. And now Colleen is feeling guilty about it. She's always been an awful liar. It was…it was kind of amusing when they were little. Colleen would do something bad and then say she didn't do it, and Maureen would say she wasn't telling the truth. People don't believe this, but identical twins can actually be very different. Maureen was the older, by twenty minutes, and Colleen always resented that. As if that made any difference. Maureen was more compliant, Colleen more willful."

She shrugged. "I don't have any children, so the girls were as close as I came. I've always…always been very attached to them. Maybe more so because their mother wasn't all that interested in parenthood.

If she could have laid an egg and walked away, she would have. It was Jerry. Her first husband, my brother Jerome Mulcahey, who wanted children."

She stopped and shrugged. "Of course, then he pretty much abandoned the family when he saw that families took work. He couldn't handle the challenge of living with Fiona and two fussy babies. But Fiona wasn't family oriented, either. She was boy crazy from the age of thirteen. And still is. Currently crazy about Alan Cassiday. But that could change tomorrow. I've always tried…and evidently failed…to be a stable presence in the girls' lives."

"Did your sister-in-law talk to you about her decision to send them away?" Burgess asked.

"Of course not. Because I would have asked hard questions. I would have tried to talk her out of it, because it would be so hard to see them if they weren't close. But I was traveling in September." She sighed. "Taking my dream trip. Three weeks in India. I was working like crazy leading up to it. And then when I got home, I was so busy at work, catching up. Uh…I'm an architect. I'd built that break into my schedule, but you know how it is when you go on vacation. You always come back to chaos and crisis."

Burgess thought about his attempt to take a vacation back in the summer and how chaos and crisis had come with him. He also thought about how, although he hadn't become a priest, as men had in earlier generations of his family, he was hearing confession. This woman felt supremely guilty about abandoning her nieces to the inattention and selfishness of their mother, with one of them possibly now dead. But there was something else going on with this woman. Something elusive he couldn't put a finger on.

Maybe it was no more than the guilt of having gotten so wrapped up in her own life she'd been too busy for her nieces. And now this had happened.

He'd been focused on the story. Now he looked at the woman more closely. Despite the vibrant hair and bright eyes, she looked ravaged. Dark circles beneath those eyes said she hadn't slept and her skin was dry and pale.

"It wasn't your job to raise those girls," he said.

"But it was!" Almost a cry. "It was because I know what kind of a person Fiona is and how easily she could neglect them. And now this. Now I've let this happen."

"You've agreed to call your sister-in-law and see if you can get any information about where the girls are," Kyle reminded her. "Anything might help. An address would be best. Phone numbers or names of the people running the place. Say you miss the girls and want to mail them some things. Some warm, winter things. Ask whether they'll be home for Thanksgiving, and if not, whether you should visit them since they'll be feeling homesick. You know her. You'll know what to say."

"Thought I knew her. Even the lazy and selfish person I know Fiona to be wouldn't do this to her daughters. Except she has." She looked from one of them to the other. "It's Alan, of course. He wanted Fiona. Has no time for or interest in the girls. And frankly, though I hate myself for saying this, once they both proved to be beauties as they matured, Fiona saw them as competition, not her children. She needed them out of the way before Alan saw it, too. The contrast between what she had been and what she now was."

She mopped her eyes. "Sorry. I'm sorry, babbling on like this. It's the shock, really. Of seeing Colleen. Of knowing how shamefully indifferent my sister-in-law has been." She got out her phone. "I'll make that call now."

"Put it on speaker so we can hear," Kyle said.

She nodded and dialed.

It was less than seconds and yet the tension in the room as they waited was palpable.

Then a voice said, "Hey, Emily…it's been ages. How are you? How was India?"

"India was fabulous. Reentry's been awful, though. You know how it is when you go away on vacation, Fee. I'm still catching up. So, speaking of catching up, I wanted to send the twins some things for winter. You know…sweaters and socks and fleeces and stuff. Can you give me their address?"

There was silence.

She said, "Fee…are you there? Is there something wrong with our connection? It's just been such ages since I've seen them. I thought I'd send them some things. You know how much I love buying them stuff. It's odd...but I've called a few times and they never answer, which isn't like them. It got me a little worried. You've been up to see them, right? They like the place? They're doing okay?"

More silence. Then Fiona Cassiday said, "I don't have an address, Em. Sorry. I've got to go." She hung up.

Emily Mulcahey looked at Burgess and Kyle. "I wasn't expecting that. That she'd completely blow me off. Some lies, maybe. And some dissembling. But this? Never."

Burgess said, "I should fill you in on something. Maybe you can help us understand it. The morning after we found your niece down in the park, naked, in terrible shape, and nearly comatose, a woman showed up at the hospital claiming to be the girl's mother. She could produce no documents proving that she was the girl's mother or who the girl was. She showed us a false driver's license and gave us a fake address. When we questioned her and demanded documents, she bribed a woman in the bathroom to create a scene, and fled while we were dealing with that."

"Did she see Colleen? Does she know how badly injured she was?"

He shook his head. "We gave her some details about the girl's condition after she insisted the girl was fine."

Kyle interrupted, "She insisted her daughter was just a difficult girl with a history of lying and running away. It's when we gave her details about how badly abused the girl was and how she couldn't possibly leave the hospital that the woman ran."

Burgess got out his phone, scrolled to the woman's photo, and showed it. "Is this your sister-in-law?"

Emily Mulcahey nodded. "My God," she whispered. "This is so much worse than I imagined. No wonder she won't speak to me. I was thinking she'd been naïve or careless about this. You know, putting her head in the sand. But this means she knows—"

She broke off and looked at Burgess. "But how could she know and not do something? How could she run away like that? And using a fake license? I mean, who even knows how to get one of those."

Burgess and Kyle could have answered that plenty of parents were that cruel or indifferent. And that information about fake licenses was all over the internet. It wouldn't help here.

"You're sure she won't talk to you?" Kyle said. "Maybe if you called her back?"

Emily Mulcahey made a sound somewhere between a snort and a sob. "No way. Not if she knows. I mean, if she knew and she cared, she would have immediately demanded that Maureen be sent home. She would have stayed at the hospital until she was sure that Colleen was okay. She would have called me to look after the other twin while she kept vigil here. But she didn't, did she?" She looked defeated, like this was a struggle she'd been engaged in for years and had lost.

Kyle had another question. "She knew to come to Portland the same night that Colleen escaped from wherever they're being held. Which means someone must have called her. Which means…" He trailed off, leaving it to her to finish his sentence.

"That she knows what's really going on and who is doing it?" Emily Mulcahey said. "That she certainly knows how to get in touch with them, whether or not she knows the actual address of the place, right?"

Burgess and Kyle both said, "Right."

Time was slipping away. He was due to meet Megan Ainsworth soon and this was getting them nowhere beyond confirming, with depressing certainty, their suspicions about families that would send their children to this "camp." Before he left, he thought about the bullying lawyer who'd also tried to take the girl away and found that photo. "Do you recognize this man?"

She took his phone and studied the photo, then handed it back, shaking her head. "Sorry. I don't know him. Who is he?"

Burgess quickly summarized the visit from the lawyer claiming he had papers authorizing him to remove the girl. The fake ambulance. His refusal to show the hospital's attorney the supposed judge's order.

With every detail, she looked more upset, but all she said was, "Wish I could do more. I'd like to get back to Colleen now, if that's okay."

It was okay. They watched her head for the girl's room. When she was out of earshot, Kyle said, "Something fishy going on here. I think she knew who that guy was."

Burgess agreed. He said, "Stan checked her credentials last night, right? We have her information?"

"I assumed he'd done it, so I didn't ask when I got here. I'll call him. Make sure he did and got that info. If he didn't, I'll get it myself. I mean, she's obviously related to the girl. She cares. Knows the family history and about the girl's character. But still, I'd like to know what the backstory is. And what she's hiding."

"Okay. You call Stan and get him to forward that info to both of us. If he didn't get it, you get it. We need her photo. Her license. And what she's driving. I'm not having another of these women come here, pretend to have an interest in the girls, and then slip away. Because this one might slip away with the girl."

He stood. "I've got to go see Megan Ainsworth, let her finish telling her story. I don't know, Terry. There might be something there."

"Agreed. So do you need me here to babysit or can I get someone else over here and get back to 109? We've got a ton of stuff to do."

"Confirm the ID, then get Sage over here." Burgess hesitated. "Make sure he's briefed about our concerns so Auntie Emily doesn't just waltz out of here with the girl."

"On it," Kyle said. Then, "You okay, really?"

"Sort of okay."

"I know all about that. How's Ned?"

"Also sort of okay." Which reminded Burgess he needed to check on Van's condition, and on Mrs. Elwell, before he left the hospital. "I hate this place, Terry. You know that?"

"Known it for a long time, Joe. But our jobs never seem to take us to fancy hotels or swanky bars that pour good drinks, or the elegant living rooms of nice people who are glad to see us. And speaking of fancy hotels and swanky bars, you getting the wedding stuff squared away?"

"Tonight, we're making guest lists. Chris wants the invites to go out this week."

"Funny, that's what we're doing tonight, too. Ain't we got fun?"

"Nope. But we've got fine women, and that is something. If this is what they want, it's what they'll get."

"Yeah." Kyle sketched a wave. "See you around."

"Count on it."

Burgess went to the information desk to learn where Van Elwell was. He got a room number and the slightly snippy admonition that it wasn't visiting hours. Right now, he was kind of tired of being admonished and told what he couldn't do. He was going to the room to check on the boy because he was an investigating officer, not a visitor. He showed his badge, said, "Police business," and headed for the boy's room.

THIRTY-TWO

Anita Elwell was dozing in a chair beside the bed, still clutching Van's hand. Van also appeared to be asleep. While Burgess was standing there, wondering whether to wake them or get his updates from the nurses, a nurse bustled in. She stopped, as he had, at the scene of devoted mom and injured boy both looking peaceful in sleep.

"I'll come back," she whispered.

Burgess followed her out of the room to get his update. He identified himself and asked how the surgery had gone and whether the boy was expected to make a full recovery.

She smiled at his questions. "Surgery went well, Detective. And yes, it looks like Van's going to be okay. As long as he takes it easy. We all know his mom, of course. She works here. And so we're rooting for him. Nothing but the best pudding and all the Jell-o he can eat."

They both smiled at that. He said, "And Anita?"

Instead of a health report, the nurse, whose badge said her name was Sonya, said, "We take an oath about caring for people and doing no harm, but I'd like to kill that SOB. Who does this to a helpless woman and child? Please tell me the bastard's locked up and will stay locked up."

"I can vouch for locked up. We're doing our best, but whether he stays locked up is up to a judge." He didn't elaborate on his opinion of judges.

Nurses read people, and she nodded at what he hadn't said. "We'll keep an eye on them, Detective. It would be kind if, in the awful case he gets released, you let us know. Us…the nurses…and security. Please."

Burgess agreed he would, which of course depended on whether he was notified. Then, not wanting to be late for his meeting, he sprinted down the stairs and drove to one of the city's better hotels. Portland was on the upswing, becoming more of a tourist destination every year. Regular people were being pushed out as houses and apartments became gentrified and used for short-term rentals. The restaurant scene was also growing popular, which made downtown more crowded as the bar-hopping crew in the Old Port vied for parking with those who came into the city to dine.

There were clashes. Fancy cars to break into. Late night crowds on the often-slippery cobblestone and brick streets and sidewalks.

Stan Perry said it was a good thing because it meant job security. As Portland grew fancier, there were more people who expected to be kept safe and more pressure to keep them safe.

He parked—November being a month when tourists didn't flock to Portland and parking was easier—and took the elevator to her room. He would have preferred to meet her in the lobby or a coffee shop. He didn't like being alone in a hotel room with an attractive woman. But she was a woman used to getting her way. She'd said she would order breakfast. She'd said they were staying in Portland because the party would run late and they didn't like to drive home in the dark when they were tired. She hadn't given Burgess a chance to argue.

Now he stood outside her door and knocked.

She opened the door with a smile and waved a hand for him to come in. It wasn't a hotel room. It was a suite. In the sitting room, in front of the window, was a table with a white cloth and lots of silver. Chairs were drawn up on either side. She hadn't been kidding about breakfast.

"Sit," she said. "Take off your jacket and sit. I assume you drink coffee. Black, right?"

And just like that, he was sitting across from her as she raised one of the warming covers to reveal a plate loaded with eggs, bacon, a blueberry pancake, and some hash brown potatoes. She lifted her cover. Her plate had a pathetically skinny omelet, a small bowl of fruit, and what looked like a blueberry scone. Beside her plate was a glass with some thick, greenish substance he assumed was some kind of healthy smoothie.

She shrugged off his scrutiny. "You reach a certain age and your metabolism goes to hell. I'd much rather have your breakfast. But I expect you've skipped breakfast and already been at work for hours. Am I right?"

He felt like he was being run over by a steamroller. Or whatever they were called these days. "You're right."

She smiled. "I'm a pretty good detective."

"Yes. You are. So what else did you want to ask me? Or tell me about your mystery?"

"Eat something, and I'll tell you."

The man who was used to being in charge obediently started eating his breakfast. It wasn't cold or tasteless, as hotel breakfasts often were. It was warm and delicious.

"Yes," she said. "They do a decent breakfast here. It's all those foodie tourists who've made Portland a destination. Hotels have had to up their game. So...our place is in a town called West Cabot and our lake is named Harmon Pond, though it really is a lake. I know because I looked it up once, the difference between a lake and a pond. We're on the east side. Across the lake, on the west side, is where all this mysterious stuff is taking place."

He had his notebook out, awkward on the overcrowded table, and he made a note of the town and the pond. Or lake. Said, "Have you spoken about your concerns with the local sheriff's department?"

She laughed. "Detective, I wasn't born yesterday. Of course I have. And I've gotten the full 'let's be nice to the summer lady who's imagining things out in the woods' treatment. Maybe it actually works with some people, but I know when I'm being politely brushed off."

A statement and perhaps a message to Burgess that he shouldn't try to brush her off. He already hadn't. He was here, wasn't he?

His phone rang. He said, "Excuse me," and checked. It was Cote. He said, "Sorry, I have to take this." To Cote, he said, "I'm in a meeting with Megan Ainsworth. The chief asked me to address some concerns she has. Can I call you back?" Because of course, if it was what the chief wanted, it was what Cote wanted, and he wouldn't persist in his usual fashion.

As expected, Cote sputtered out a "You call me immediately when you're done," and Burgess put his phone away.

"Sorry," he said. "My captain looking for an update on a case."

"Why do I think you're not very fond of this man?" she said.

Burgess thought she would have made an excellent detective. "I don't know if I can help you much," he said. "But why don't you tell me more about what you've seen and heard."

"Seen? Very little, except for that snarling man in the truck. And lights at night, through the woods, in a place where there isn't supposed to be anybody. I asked the sheriff's man about that and he said it was probably just people camping. But I've driven over there, and the road has a gate and lots of no trespassing signs. Which, I'm afraid, I pointed out to him. He wasn't pleased. But it didn't get me anywhere. He just said, 'Ma'am, we're not concerned about it,' which was a clear brush off. So I let myself be brushed off."

"So, lights at night in a place that's supposed to be empty. And voices across the water, including what sounded like someone screaming?"

She nodded. "I told the sheriff about that, too. He said a lot of people confuse the sounds of coyotes howling or raccoons mating with human cries. Frankly, it was so insulting, and so infuriating, I gave up."

"What about people you've seen? Or vehicles? I know we talked about this, but this time I'd like to get some things written down."

"There was the snarling man in the green truck. And the battered, unmarked white van."

"Maine plates?" he asked.

She nodded and ate a little more of the pallid omelet. Drank some of the green stuff, leaving an almost endearing strip of green above her lip, like a kid trying on lipstick, except it was green. He fought the temptation to reach over and wipe it off. Bad enough to be alone with her without that. Instead, he said, "Uh…you've got…" and made a gesture with his finger.

She grinned and wiped her face. "What else? What else can I tell you? And what are you going to do with anything I tell you?"

"So, let me be sure I've got all this. You shared this with the sheriff and got nowhere. You've asked your husband to look into it and he's taken no action. Right so far?"

She nodded. Said, "My husband thought I was overreacting. Told me to calm down and leave it alone. Which—" She made a self-depre-cating gesture. "Which frankly made me more curious."

A revelation that made Burgess curious about why she'd shared it. He said, "When you drove over there to check for yourself, you said you found a locked gate and lots of no trespassing signs. Did you see any signs that other vehicles had been using the road? Fresh tire tracks? A lack of vegetation in the road itself? Anything?"

"It looked to me like a frequently used road." She paused. Looked down at the mostly untouched omelet on her plate. "Thank you for taking me seriously. And detective, I'm afraid I misspoke when I suggested my husband was too busy to look into it. My husband was affirmatively against my looking into it. More adamant, in other words, than his usual indifference." Her tone was a combination of anger and regret. "I'm not a child to be comforted with bland statements like 'calm down' and 'don't worry about it.'"

She drank some more green stuff and carefully wiped her lip. "So now it's your turn. Why are you so interested in my story? Do you think there's something going on over there?"

Burgess did something he rarely did. He told her about the case, and the girl, and the possibility of other teens being held in an old camp in the woods. Kids at risk without families who cared what happened to them.

"So you think it might be across my lake?"

"Honestly, it could be anywhere, Ms. Ainsworth. But this is definitely worth checking out."

"Megan. Please. Call me Megan. And how will you check it out? You're going to drive up there yourself?"

"If I have to. I'll probably start with the county sheriff, see if I get more satisfaction than you did. Ask the warden service. They know a lot about what's going on in the woods. And take it from there."

"But I get the impression the situation is urgent," she said, once again demonstrating her detection abilities. "So when are you going to do all that?"

He was enjoying her company and a good breakfast and hoping her information might lead to something, but he didn't need any more pressure from anyone. She must have read it off his face—meaning he'd been careless and let his guard down—because she said, "I'm sorry. I know you're busy and I know you're worried about those kids. I guess I'm just..." She smiled her nice smile and made a self-deprecating gesture. "Truth is that I'm used to getting my way. That's probably why I was so annoyed when the local cops blew me off like that. It's not like we don't pay enormous taxes and the only service in town that we use, besides the roads, is public safety."

Ah, the old 'I pay your salary' argument. He'd heard it a million times. And yet he didn't find her as annoying as most of the people who used it. She had apologized and she was pretty self-aware.

"Yes, I am worried. And yes, I am busy. It would be great if this were my only case, but other things happen and they need attention, too. But I promise you I'll look into it, sooner rather than later, and that I'll let you know what I find out."

She nodded. Sipped the vile green drink and ate some fruit. Most of the pallid omelet was untouched, while his was almost gone. With an utterly unselfconscious gesture, she reached over with her fork and speared the last of his, then snatched the last piece of bacon. "God, I get so tired of eating slimming, healthy food. I bet you never have to worry about that."

"Not true," he said. "I just lost about forty pounds. It takes the pressure off my bad knee."

She laughed out loud. "Honestly, Detective. You are so refreshing and I appreciate it."

She ate the rest of his food and put down her fork. "I'd offer you some of this vile green stuff, but I know you'd refuse and you'd be right. Kale may make us live forever, but it's kind of like forever in purgatory."

On that note, he finished his coffee, thanked her for breakfast, and left. They'd been getting along too well. There was a subtext in the room that he read and chose to ignore.

He went back to his truck and called Hank Boudreau.

THIRTY-THREE

He got a gruff "Boudreau" with noises in the background, identified himself, and asked if the warden had time to talk.

"Kinda bad time, Detective. Sorry. Got a clusterfuck here of the first order. Why don't you gimme an hour and I'll call you back."

Since Burgess knew all about situations like that, he agreed and disconnected. Then, because it seemed like he'd been loitering over breakfast for far too long, he called Kyle to make sure everything was squared away at the hospital.

"Copacetic, Joe," Kyle said. "What's the matter? Don't you trust me?"

"More like I don't trust me. Or anything that's going on right now. You at 109?"

"On my way. Wasn't going to leave until Sage was there and briefed and he took a while. But he's careful, so things should be okay. How was breakfast?"

"Delicious. As for her information? I don't know. I think this place she's referred to is something we should check out. I want to ask my warden about it but he's in the middle of some crisis and has to call me back. I'll be at 109 in about five. See you there."

He put his phone down, then immediately picked it up again and called Chris. She answered, "He's fine, Joe. We're going to Burger King for lunch and then going to see Van." Another person who could read his mind. She said, "Do you know how he is?"

"Unconscious when I saw him a little while ago, but they say the surgery went well and he should be okay. His mom, Anita, is with him, so if you visit, you might bring her something to eat. You know how hospital food is, and anyway, she's going to be reluctant to leave him. You'd be that way."

"I would."

She sounded good, like spending some time with Ned had been reassuring, as had making the plans for their wedding. Probably neither of them had realized how much it weighed on them, even though it was something they wanted.

"You home for dinner?"

"The usual. Hoping to be there. Depends on what happens here."

"Right. You be careful, Joe, okay? I don't want to be a widow before I'm even a bride."

"You, too," he said.

She laughed.

He pulled into the garage and parked. Kyle pulled up beside him and got into his passenger seat, then said, "Had a call from the local cops. There was someone suspicious at that empty house last night. Neighbor called it in. Person was gone before they got there, but the neighbor said it was a green truck, same truck she's seen there before. Evidently, she went over to check it out and the guy jumped in his truck and drove off. Almost hit her. So they'll step up patrols. But the real alarm system is that neighbor."

"Shirley Bufford. Yes. She's a good friend. Sounds like our suspicions were right. We've rattled their cage and now they're getting panicky," Burgess said.

"Wonder if the girl's mother was in touch with them after Emily Mulcahey's call?"

"You mean alerting those who possibly killed one of her daughters that the cops might be getting close? That's hard to imagine."

Kyle shrugged. "Thought we could imagine pretty much every horrible thing people get up to."

"There's always something new. But maybe you're right. I mean, if she was a concerned mother, she wouldn't have run away after learning that her daughter was in serious condition. I don't think Mulcahey's statement that her sister-in-law has always been a selfish narcissist covers it."

"Agreed." Kyle said. "Though I don't know what we do with that. So we're hanging out here in this cold, smelly garage because if you go inside Cote will grab you?"

"Something like that," Burgess said. "And because it's easier to think when people aren't asking me dozens of questions and I'm not staring at a desk that looks like a pink hailstorm just happened."

"Pink hailstorm," Kyle mused. "That might be your most poetic yet." He hesitated, then said, "But you're feeling it, too, aren't you? That things are closing in. That if we spook them, there's only a short window before those teens are harmed or they disappear again."

"Yeah, I'm feeling it." You didn't have to believe in the supernatural to sense badness coming in their business. It was like a dark cloud that followed them around like an unwanted pet.

They left the truck and went inside. Kyle went to the conference room. Burgess figured he'd better see Cote and get it over with so he could concentrate on important things. First, he checked his desk. His pink hail analogy hadn't been off, except that the hailstones were huge and numerous. He sorted them into the usual piles. Not a lot in the urgent pile, for once, and no intriguing messages from people who thought they had some useful information. The rest could wait. He went to see Cote.

"Well, that was a heck of a long breakfast," Cote said. He was wearing his look of lewd speculation, which Burgess ignored. Instead, he lobbed the ball back into Cote's court.

"Yes. That hotel does an excellent breakfast. One of the rare perks of this job is having to have breakfast with someone and having it actually be tasty." He couldn't remember ever speaking the word "tasty" aloud.

"She all squared away?"

That look again, like Burgess had taken the time to "square her away" in the manner that Cote was implying.

"I'm not sure how much we can do for her. Mostly, she was looking for advice about some unusual activity near her cottage up in Franklin County. The local cops had ignored her concerns. I think she wanted someone to listen and take her seriously. I mean, I suppose I could drive up there myself and check it out, but it's two and half hours each way, not our jurisdiction, and we're very busy here."

Cote frowned. "But you could do that, if it would put her mind at ease and please the chief, right?"

Yes, you brown-nosing fucker, I could, Burgess thought. *If I didn't have the girl at the hospital still surrounded by mystery, and all those teens at risk, and an injured child at the hospital who's just had a risky surgery, and a wedding to plan.*

"It's a little late today," Cote said. "Could you do that tomorrow? Take a ride up there and check things out?"

As Stan Perry was wont to say, when he forgot himself, Burgess almost said, "Holy Fuck, Captain. You want me to do what?" But he kept it to himself. Most of the time, Cote was trying to keep them from doing what they needed to do. But now, when Burgess was thinking checking that place out wasn't a bad idea, especially if his warden confirmed it might be a place of interest, he was practically being ordered to do it.

"It's possible. I'll have to see where we are in the investigation. If I go, I'll need to take Kyle with me. In case there's more to this than some squatters or campers."

"I don't see——" Cote began.

Burgess said, "I'll need Kyle." Not adding that if it connected to his case, it was a place where a group of teens were being held in unsafe conditions by a group of conscienceless adults with nothing but profit on their minds. Definitely violent and quite likely armed. He stood. "Is there anything else?"

Cote made shooing motions with his hands and Burgess shooed before he was ordered not to take Kyle. He would anyway. Of course he would. But in the endless battle of Burgess vs. Cote, he liked to choose his spots.

He found Stan Perry hunched over a large pile of printouts and Kyle on the phone.

"Finding anything?" he asked Perry.

"I think so."

"You catch up with Elaine Hawes's friend?"

"Yeah. Such a flake I'm amazed she remembers her own name. She knows that Elaine got married to some guy. Name of Edwin or Glen. Or maybe both. She's not sure. Thinks they've moved up north somewhere. Unless it's into her mother's house. Unless it's not north but maybe west. She wasn't sure. Says Elaine quit her job and has a new one, something like a counselor for teenagers, which she thinks is hilarious since Elaine still acts like one herself. She had a phone number, which is the one we already have, but thinks Elaine has a new one, which she's written down somewhere. She'll call me if she finds it. If she remembers."

Perry shrugged. "In short, pretty much a dead end. Is Ned okay?"

"Seems to be. So far. Kid's already been through too much, so we're watching him closely. You know how it is. Sometimes the trauma doesn't show up right away."

"Yeah," Perry said. "That's how it is with me. I'm just a little snowflake."

"So, little snowflake, you took a team out to that empty house today?"

Perry did a mock salute. "Not yet. Morning got away from me. But that is the plan, sir."

They both laughed.

The conversation reminded Burgess he wanted to look at the reports about last night's incident involving Ned. Details about what they'd found in the car. The interviews. Whether there was any information back about the gun. He wanted to put the boys' names in his notebook so he'd remember them. Before he called Kyle and Perry into a strategy meeting, he went back to his desk to see if there was anything about the incident there.

Nothing. Tracing the gun and analyzing the pills would take time. Time when the less-than-fabulous four would be out on the street again, possibly not sufficiently chastened and likely to seek revenge. It was too common—the bad actor blaming their victim for getting them into trouble. Personal responsibility had mostly gone the way of the dinosaurs.

Chris wouldn't like it, but he thought it was time to take Dylan to the range and teach him how to use a gun. Then, realizing he was being a sexist jerk, he corrected that to time to take Dylan and Nina to the range. Chris would like that even less. Especially since the purpose of their range training would be keeping the family safe, which meant keeping a firearm in the house. Definitely not something he would suggest before the wedding. They didn't need any more stress right now.

His phone rang. A voice with a strong Maine accent said, "Hank Boudreau. This Burgess?"

"It is."

"Got that damned thing sorted. For now, anyways. You know how the courts get all kindhearted and let these fuckers go. Though our judges up here are pretty good with illegal hunting stuff. So, how can I help?"

Burgess described Megan Ainsworth's mystery and named the town and the lake. "Do you know it, or know someone who does?"

"I know it. Not my area, but I've been there, helping out on searches and all. You want to check it out, I could meet you there. Bring along a local warden who knows the area."

"That would be great," Burgess said. "Would tomorrow work?"

He could hear the rustle of a jacket as Boudreau shrugged. "I can probably make that work. Gotta make it early, though. Hunting season. You know. A lot going on."

"That would be great. Actually," Burgess said, "we're looking at a big problem that might or might not involve this place Ms. Ainsworth mentioned." He described the situation with a group advertising an outdoor camp for troubled teens. Their finding the girl in the park and what they'd learned from her and their investigations. "Winter coming, they're gonna have to move those kids. Hoping to find the place before they do. Any places you know, places other wardens know about, all of that would be helpful to us. We don't know the woods."

"Yeah. You don't," Boudreau said. "Almost fun sometimes to take the state police out. Kind of a babes-in-the-woods situation. And they ain't...aren't very good listeners, either. You a good listener?"

"I try to be."

"I'll bet you are. You don't sound like a youngster with something to prove. They're the worst. 'Course, we've got 'em, too. Guess every organization does. So. You sure you can't come today? Today would be better."

Burgess looked at the clock. Almost noon. Said, "It's two, two and half hours up there and dark comes early."

"After dark can be good, though. 'Specially if you anticipate trouble. They don't see you coming. You aren't afraid of the dark, are you?"

The half-serious, half-teasing tone of someone comfortable in the woods and aware of others' unfamiliarity. People liked to own their expertise, occasionally wave it in the faces of those who didn't have it. In this case, it was part of the traditional rivalry between various public safety agencies. Boudreau was staking out his territory. Burgess didn't mind. He'd been known to do a bit of that himself.

But jumping in the truck right now, with all that needed attention here? Burgess sighed. Boudreau was right. By tomorrow morning, something might have come up that would mean they'd need to postpone and it felt like every day mattered.

"Okay. Today. Give me two and a little and tell me where to meet you."

Boudreau gave him directions and Burgess wrote them down.

"One other thing," Burgess said. "Don't know if it matters, but the blanket the girl was wrapped in had a lot of hitchhiker plants attached. State botanist thinks it's kind of a rare plant. We thought it might be a clue to the location."

"Don't know about that, but the local warden might," Boudreau said. "See you soon."

Burgess put the phone away and turned to Kyle. "We're going on a field trip. You got warm clothes in the car?"

"Does a bear?" Kyle said.

"Hey, what about me?" Perry complained. "Don't I get to go?"

"You really want to go tromping around in the Maine woods after dark with maybe snow coming when you could be at home with Lily and Autumn?"

"Yes. Yes, I do."

"Jeez," Burgess said, "and I was trying to be kind. We need you here. We need someone who knows the case to be able to respond to the hospital in case they…the aunt or anyone else, try to take the girl away. In case someone makes an attempt on that vacant house. To take a team out there to get fingerprints. The next-door neighbor, Shirley Bufford, has a key. Here to see when Van Elwell, the little boy who was knocked unconscious by his mom's boyfriend, wakes up and take his statement. To get a statement from his mother about Mark Hammond attacking her. So, a whole lot to keep an eye on right here."

Perry brightened. "In that case, then, okay. I'll sulk about being left behind, but I'll stay."

They discussed what Perry needed to do, then Burgess and Kyle grabbed what they needed from their lockers, and left.

"Oh boy. I can't wait. I've got new waterproof hiking boots," Kyle said when they were on the road.

After that, they fell silent. It was a long drive, and while they couldn't know whether this was a lead or a wild goose chase, they both felt like they were heading toward something.

After a while, Kyle said, "Maybe we should have brought an army."

More silence.

Then Burgess echoed, "An army."

There was a bite in the air that suggested snow, and the weather forecast now confirmed that an early season storm was possible. They drove on through a gray afternoon, down a gray road, heading toward they didn't know what—maybe nothing, maybe something—with the weight of perhaps a dozen teens at risk pressing on them.

THIRTY-FOUR

Boudreau was meeting them at a general store in the target town, and Burgess pulled into a space beside a green truck at exactly the two-hour mark. It had taken the occasional lights and sirens along the way. The more rural you got, the more you ran into people whose entire day consisted of the long, slow drive to Walmart. They didn't follow his parents' generation's rule about pulling over for faster cars and often didn't bother to look in their rearviews. That was why he used the sirens. Today he could celebrate not scaring anyone into a ditch, as sometimes happened.

Boudreau climbed out of the truck with a grin. "Guess when you set a time, you mean it, Burgess."

Burgess shook the outstretched hand, said, "I try," and introduced Kyle.

Boudreau introduced another warden who'd come around the truck as Kenny Packard. They shook hands as well. Packard said, "I'm new to this area, but I'm happy to help. Put in a call to the warden I replaced. He said he'd been wondering about what was going on over there but hadn't had a chance to check it out." He shrugged. "Guess there might be something." He paused, then said, "And I asked him about that plant you mentioned. He said yeah, there's a bunch of it out there. In case that helps."

"We can take my truck," Boudreau said. "One vehicle's lot less noticeable than three." He paused, then said, "We expecting these people to be armed?"

Burgess said, "We don't know. But two of them are career criminals, and they're holding a bunch of teens against their will. So, I expect so."

Boudreau said, "You guys got long guns? Because if you do, you should bring them. If we find what you're hoping to find, it's better not to be outgunned."

"We do," Burgess said. He and Kyle got their gear.

Boudreau studied them, the professional assessment of someone who knows what gear is important if you're going into the woods. More so if you're going after bad guys. The wardens were involved in a lot of searches with the state police and so familiar with working with other public safety agencies. He nodded, which Burgess took as approval of how they were dressed and what they were carrying, and they moved it into the warden's truck.

They climbed in the back seat, the two wardens got in the front, and they were off. It was a little after two in the afternoon. Maybe two and a half hours of daylight and then some time before the light completely faded.

Boudreau drove through the quiet town and out a narrow, winding road. At one point, the other warden pointed to a fire road. "That's where your friend Ms. Ainsworth and her husband have their place. They may call it a cottage, lotta rich folks do, but it's nicer than most of the houses in this town. I did some asking, though, and they aren't the kind of folks who throw their weight around. People like them. At least, they like her. Guess he comes across as kind of a stiff."

They drove on, past numerous fire roads, until they were on a dirt road that ended at a wooden gate with a giant 'No Trespassing' sign in bold red letters.

"We walk in from here," Boudreau said. "But hold on a minute."

He left the truck and slowly walked the road to the gate and then past it, studying the ground. Then walked slowly back, looking at the hinges on the gate and the lock. He did something with the lock, then returned and motioned for them to get out. "Plenty of traffic through here. A heavy truck. Something with narrower tires. And maybe a coupla cars. We had rain up here two days ago and these tracks are since then. Good thing we're here today. That snow comes, it'll make a hash of things."

Maybe a lot of traffic because they were moving the teens?

Burgess hoped not. But they'd done all they could. Couldn't have been here sooner. Wouldn't have been here at all if it hadn't been for that cocktail party and Megan Ainsworth. If they'd gone generic, asking the warden service for possible sites, they might have had to search, or had the wardens search, many in different parts of the state.

They grabbed their gear and started walking.

"It's maybe a mile to where the old camp is," Packard said. "Or so's I'm told."

There's always that sensation you get when you might be close to a find, Burgess thought. *Hope that you will, with all those implications, warring with hope that you won't.*

They knew about four players—the Briscows, Glen Briscow's mother, Elvira Clemens, and Clinton Johns. But it was likely there were others involved as well. Four people, who were coming and going and would need to sleep and make trips out for supplies, were not enough to contain a dozen teens. Unless they were always restrained, as Colleen seemed to have been.

If they'd been walking in the woods, their approach would have been noisy with all the crisp fall leaves under foot. On the road, passing vehicles had blown those leaves away. There was only the crunch of gravel. The wardens, accustomed to long walks in the woods, had set off at a breath-taking pace and Burgess cursed himself for forgetting his knee brace. Warm clothes. Warm socks. Waterproof shoes. And nothing for his bum knee.

Those were the breaks. They were here. The place was obviously being used for something. And every twinging step was bringing them closer to whatever it was.

Abruptly, Boudreau, who was in the lead, stopped and put out his arm. They gathered around him and leaned in to hear.

"Looks like the first building is just up there. There's a green truck parked beside it." He pointed to a thicket of trees where only the faint brown of a roof was visible.

Wardens. Christ. They could see in the dark and hear a pinecone fall a mile away. They could walk on sticks without making a sound. Burgess, who was good at city searches, hadn't seen it. Give him a warehouse any day. Or even a dark alley. For a moment, he wondered if he should have brought Fideau. But it was a long drive with who knew what at the end. Hard on a dog, plus even a great dog required attention, and Burgess needed all his attention for the mission.

The man who was used to being in charge waited to be told what to do. And Boudreau didn't hesitate. He said, "We go off the road now. Circle around and come at this place from the woods. If they are expecting someone to show up, they'll be watching the road." Without waiting for agreement, he headed into the woods.

This time, Packard let the two cops go first and then brought up the rear. Like leaders on a hike. Maybe he was afraid Burgess and Kyle would get lost.

The ground underfoot here was soggy. Not a bad thing, since it damped down the leaves and made their progress quieter. Boudreau moved through the woods like someone from a Fenimore Cooper book, though he politely held back branches that otherwise would have snapped back into Burgess's face.

Neither Burgess nor Kyle said anything. They'd put themselves in the hands of professionals and had to trust that. From time to time, Burgess did check his handgun with the hand that wasn't holding his shotgun. Patted his pockets for shotgun shells and the pouch on his belt for spare magazines. Behind him, rustling sounds told him that Kyle was doing the same. The air felt thick with danger. Anticipation. Dread. Something that filled the silent afternoon and made it difficult to breathe.

Off to their right, they heard a truck start up and the sound of tires crunching on the gravel road. Someone was leaving. Likely someone they wanted to locate. To find at this place. Burgess recalled that the warden's truck was parked in the road facing the gate. He wondered if that was deliberate.

"Want to go back?" Boudreau asked. "See if we can catch him while he's opening the gate?"

Burgess was torn. Letting any of this crew—if indeed these were the people who had brutalized Colleen—get away was troubling. If this was the place. But now that they were this close to the camp, he needed to press on. To see whether this was what they'd come for and if the teens were still there.

Feeling like he was making a bad choice, he shook his head.

"Kenny can go," Boudreau said. "Kenny and Kyle."

Offering a compromise. Burgess nodded and the two of them set off toward the gate at an even faster pace than before.

As he and Boudreau turned back toward the camp, Boudreau said, "I kinda mucked up the lock on that gate. You know. Just in case."

Because wardens no more wanted their suspects to get away than the Portland cops did, and their suspects had a lot more latitude for escape with hundreds of acres of woods to get lost in.

He and Boudreau resumed their nearly running pace until they came out of the woods between two shabby-looking cabins. Boudreau rose onto his tiptoes to peer into the windows of one while Burgess checked the other. There were mattresses on the bunks. And pillows. Signs of recent habitation. But no people.

"Someone's been here," Boudreau said. "They're gone now. But shit, look at this." Burgess joined him at the window as he pointed to heavy metal rings in the walls beside each bunk. "They chained them up?"

Not something you'd find in a summer camp. Not even in an abandoned one. Summer camps were for all the fun, outdoorsy things that fake brochure had advertised. Not for chaining kids to walls. This was the place. But unless those kids were somewhere else on the property, they were gone.

Burgess was too late.

THIRTY-FIVE

They searched the rest of the camp. There were signs of occupancy everywhere. One large cabin had insulation and heat and covers still on the bed. A refrigerator, still plugged in, though empty. A stove still connected to gas. A stove so filthy it turned Burgess's stomach. There were dishes and glasses on the shelves, with packing boxes ready to accept them. Trash outside in the cans. Trash that would have to be searched.

As they worked their way through the camp, the mantra that beat steadily in Burgess's head was "Too late. Too late. Too late."

Kyle and Kenny had returned empty-handed, reporting that as they came out of the woods, a man who'd been bent over the lock ran back to his truck. The truck accelerated and drove right through the closed gate.

"We got the plate, though," Kyle said. "It's Briscow. And there's front end damage, so it'll be easier to spot. We've put out a BOLO."

"But they're gone," Burgess said. "So where do we look next?"

Boudreau put a hand on his shoulder. "Relax, Burgess. Maybe we'll find something here."

They still had to finish searching the camp and go through the trash. Maybe there would be clues to where the teens had been taken. There was one more thing Burgess thought he needed to search for what he didn't want to find. A grave. Or graves. Places where Maureen Mulcahey and possibly others were buried. That was something he hadn't shared with Boudreau when he'd asked the man for help. Now he felt he had to.

He said, "Our witness...the girl who escaped from here more dead than alive...she says they killed her sister. So something else we need to look for, now that we're not searching for the living..." God, he was suddenly inarticulate. Unable to utter the word. A word he'd used so many times over the years.

Luckily, Kyle stepped in. "We need to look for graves."

The two wardens exchanged looks. "Search dogs would be better for that," Boudreau said. "Especially now, in the fall, when the leaves have covered everything. You want me to make a call?"

He did. And he didn't. Momentarily, Burgess felt like the child who puts his hands over his face and assumes he can't be seen. He had that childish desire to stop right here before they found something awful. But he was no child. They were here and they might as well finish the job. "Yes. Please. That would be good."

"Gonna be a while."

The afternoon was already growing late. A while might mean working in the dark. Burgess shrugged. "Better to know if they're willing to come."

"They is us," Boudreau said. "And yes, we'll come." He turned away and got on his phone.

When he was done, he said, "Maybe an hour. Better than I thought. Kenny and I will go do a walk around. You can come with or—" He gestured toward the trash cans. "Be my guest."

Burgess and Kyle took the three trash cans inside the one cabin that had heat and lights, turned on the heat, and started spreading out their contents on the floor. "How many times you think we've done this?" Kyle said.

"Too many to count."

"Yeah. By now, we are experts at reading the trash. It's like those ancient Greeks, or was it Romans, who read entrails as a form of prophecy. What do you prophesize we'll find here?"

"Food scraps. Used paper products. Tampons and pads. Empty cans and bottles. I'd say maybe some cleaning products but it's clear no one ever cleaned the kitchen or the dining area. And the bunk houses were likely only swept out the door."

Burgess put on gloves, got on his knees, and began methodically searching. His bum knee informed him that this was a bad idea.

They worked in silence through the first can, which was a total bust. So was the second. The third didn't look promising. A couple of crumpled receipts for groceries and other purchases. Then they hit something that might have promise. Bundled together with an elastic band, and not too badly stained from the other trash, was a bunch of letters. Different handwriting. Different recipients' names. All sent to the same address. It was a post office box. But there were ways to get the owner's information, plus they could stake out the box.

It was something. Something that would involve more paperwork and more delays, but having the names of some of the other teens might also be helpful. If not in locating them now, in any subsequent prosecution. And they could hope that some of the families had been more diligent than Colleen and Maureen's.

"We gonna read 'em?" Kyle asked.

"When we're done here."

"Yeah. Because we wouldn't want to leave a single trash can unturned, right?"

"You may aspire to the poo police," Burgess said. "I do not aspire to be the trash police." He considered. "Well, the litter cop, maybe. Stop every idiot who tosses cans, bottles, fast food wrappers, or lottery tickets out the window. If the department could keep the money, we'd be rolling in it."

"Litter and Poo. Sounds like a British TV series. Litter's the old, wise cop, cranky and set in his ways. Poo is the cheeky young upstart with good insights who constantly has to be reined in." Kyle grinned. "I get to play Poo."

They finished searching that last barrel, replaced the trash, and took the barrels back outside. The room now smelled of rotten food and damp cardboard.

"Did we check the bathrooms?" Kyle said.

"Not thoroughly, just a quick check to establish there was no one there."

"I think we should. And give those cabins another check. If these kids knew they were being moved, one of them might have left something behind. A message of some sort." Kyle stopped. Said, "Well, I can hope, can't I? And we should do it before it gets any darker."

It appeared that there was a girls' cabin and a boys' cabin. They searched in and under each of the mattresses and found nothing, until Kyle reached down between the bottom bunk and the wall and came out with a single sheet of wrinkled paper.

The writing was in pencil, and was shaky, and the message was short. "Moving us to a new place. In case you find this, in case Colleen did get away…don't know where but heard empty hospital? Please. Find us. We're hurt and we're starving."

Given how Colleen said they were treated, someone had risked a lot to leave this message.

They checked the bathroom, hopeful after the note, but found nothing. Then, before it got fully dark, they walked around the camp. The lake, in the dusky gloom, looked dark and unfriendly, the waves slapping the shore sounding like a giant cat lapping up a bowl of cream. They stood on the shore and looked back at the camp—the weary cabins and dining hall—everything painted a dull brown. In summer, with green grass, some flowers, clotheslines adorned with bathing suits and towels, and boats pulled up on the shore, it might have looked inviting. Now it just looked sad.

"Boathouse," Burgess said. "We didn't see a boathouse. There must be one. It's a summer camp on a lake."

They started walking the shore, away from the camp and the road, feet crunching on leaves, until they saw a small brown building so neatly tucked into the trees it was almost invisible. The door was padlocked, but it was a flimsy one Burgess broke off with a rock. They slid it from its hasp and opened the door.

Despite the cold, the scent of decay that rolled toward them was overwhelming.

Hands over their mouths and noses, they staggered back, coughing.

Then, because detectives don't get to wimp out just because something smells bad, they clicked on their flashlights and stepped inside.

Two kayaks and a sailboat were against one wall. Against the other were two bundles wrapped in what looked like nylon sails. Both bundles were bound with rope and a lot of duct tape. Despite the fact that they looked more like mummies than humans, both men knew what they were looking at. The smell was sadly familiar.

They stepped outside, drawing in lungfuls of the cold, crisp air.

Boudreau was coming out of the woods as they did. He looked at them, then stepped in through the door and immediately stepped back out again, saying, "Oh fuck! You know what this means, don't you."

He didn't mean that they'd found bodies. He meant they'd found a crime scene that could not be disturbed. It meant their case blowing up and into the hands of the state police.

It meant two dead bodies, one of whom might be Maureen Mulcahey. And a very long night ahead of them.

THIRTY-SIX

After a brief minute or two of cursing, Burgess got his phone out to call the state police. Then he hesitated. Once this became someone else's crime scene, he and Kyle would just be witnesses, forced to hang around until someone had time for their stories.

Before that happened, he wanted to take another look at those bodies. Not to unwrap them, which is what he really wanted to do, but just to look at the size. He wasn't going to mess with the crime scene and all it could tell. Just study the scene. Take some photos. Start his own crime scene investigation even though he'd soon be edged out.

"Take your time," Boudreau said. "This is what you were afraid you'd find, isn't it?"

Burgess nodded.

"And now you're gonna get sidelined and you're not gonna like it much." Not a question this time. The wardens worked with the staties pretty often. It was usually a cooperative relationship, but all public safety organizations are territorial. They got used to seeing their expertise sidelined when their knowledge could have helped.

Burgess stepped back into the fetid room. Kyle, reading his mind again, followed and used his flashlight to illuminate the bodies so Burgess could get some pictures. One of the bundled bodies was thin, as you'd expect if the kids were being starved. The other was surprisingly large. Burgess had an unpleasant theory about that.

Then they both stepped back outside.

"Our girl is small," Kyle said. "So her twin will be, too. Neither of those bodies is the right size."

"Which either means she's not dead...which is what we've been hoping...or her body is somewhere else."

"Definitely hoping," Kyle said. "And the large body. You thinking what I'm thinking?"

"I am."

No excuse to stall any longer. Burgess made the call to alert the state police that they'd been searching for a missing girl and found two bodies. That done, the four of them adjourned to the one warm cabin and settled in to wait.

"Think I should call off the dogs?" Boudreau asked. "Or are we still looking for another body?"

Burgess shrugged. He didn't know. He supposed, in the interest of being thorough, that they ought to get the cadaver dogs in to make sure there weren't more bodies out in the woods. Or in some other structure they hadn't yet found. "I think we are."

"Guess we can't leave either, since we're your ride," Boudreau said. "And now we've all gotta wait for the staties."

"We got our people coming, it would be nice to have some food," Packard said. "It's gonna be a long night. And coffee. You'd think there'd at least be coffee here, but there's nothing."

Mentioning food and the long night reminded Burgess and Kyle they'd better make calls to their families, saying they wouldn't be home for dinner. They stepped back outside into the chilly night. A wind had come up and the trees were swaying and sighing and the last remaining leaves filled the air with a dry rustle.

"We going to tell the staties about that note we found?" Kyle said.

"Christ. I don't know. We should. We'd be pissed if it were our case and they were holding things back."

"And how many times has that happened?" Kyle said.

Which Burgess couldn't argue with, because there was 'territorial,' and there was 'who's the big dog?' and the staties were always the big dog that didn't like to share. He said, "And the letters?"

They stood in silence, each pondering making a choice that went against their ingrained commitment to justice. Would keeping things to themselves be more or less likely to get those kids found before additional bad things happened?

"It'll be a while before they get here. Why don't we read the letters and take notes, then turn them over?" Kyle suggested. "We'll still have our information but less guilty consciences. Ditto with the note. We can take its picture, so we'll have the words. The handwriting. Because even if we share what we know, they aren't going to be embedded in the case the way we are. Right?"

Burgess sighed. "Right."

The decision made, they called Chris and Michelle to say they wouldn't be home and called Stan Perry to update him about what they'd found. Perry said things were quiet at the hospital and he'd start digging into possible places the teens might have been moved to. He didn't sound sorry he wasn't along, which was surprising. Probably exhausted from caring for a newborn. Then they went back inside to read the letters. Burgess figured he'd better explain what they were doing to Boudreau and Packard. The wardens seemed cool with it. So Burgess and Kyle started opening the letters and reading them.

It was a heartbreaking task, reading messages from family members who seemed to believe that their kids were having a great time at a nature camp in the Maine woods. They noted names and address and the names of the kids the letters had been sent to. Sent to but never delivered.

"Do you suppose they eventually deliver these and force the kids to reply?" Burgess said.

"Maybe they used to. But if that was the case, why throw these away unread?"

"Maybe their original plan, to repeatedly milk the parents for money, turned out to be too much trouble and now they don't know what to do with these kids," Burgess said. "A couple dead kids, or dead bodies, definitely complicates things."

Burgess was eager to be gone, to work on finding possible sites they might have been moved to. It was on him like an unscratchable itch.

They had no answers. They couldn't leave.

Time passed.

Wardens with dogs arrived and were sent off by Boudreau to look for more bodies.

The state police arrived, already grouchy because they'd had to work their way around Boudreau's truck, the other wardens' vehicles, and the broken gate. As the detective sergeant in charge stomped into the room and demanded that Burgess and Kyle tell their story, Kyle put a hand on Burgess's arm and whispered, "Hang on to your temper. We want to get out of here before sunrise, okay?"

Burgess favored Kyle with a sweet smile. "Sure thing, Boss. I will do my damnedest."

They turned over what they'd found, doing their best 'reluctant to part with it' act. Told the story of what had brought them to the camp—the girl in the hospital and Megan Ainsworth's concerns that their chief wanted them to take seriously. Eventually they were deemed of no further use and sent on their way, along with Boudreau and Packard.

The search dogs hadn't found any more bodies.

Boudreau drove them all to a diner that opened at five a.m. By then, even though the wardens had brought coffee and donuts along with their dogs, the four of them were ravenous. There was nothing like a meal heavy on carbs after a long night to dull the senses. By the time they paid the check and rose, Burgess wondered whether he'd be able to drive without falling asleep at the wheel. That kind of behavior by public safety personnel was frowned on.

They got in the truck without speaking. The forecast snow hadn't materialized, except for a few flurries, so the road was clear. A good thing for a weary driver. Burgess was able to put himself on autopilot and focus on the case.

There was so much they wanted to know that would have to wait for the state police to share it. And so much weighing on them about the fate of the remaining teens. Although they'd shared their concerns about them with the staties, they hadn't felt a shared urgency to find where they'd been moved. They hadn't seen Colleen that night in the park and didn't know the whole story about the players involved. Clinton Johns must be known to them, yet the mention of his name as someone possibly involved hadn't seemed to raise the level of concern.

"Of course," Kyle said, as though Burgess had spoken all this aloud, "they're used to playing it close to the vest just like we are. So maybe once we were dismissed, they got all excited and put things in motion."

"We can hope. They've certainly got more manpower, uh…more personnel, and resources to search than we do."

"But they don't care like we do," Kyle said.

"So, why did they kill Elvira Clemens?" Burgess wondered. "Was she showing an attack of conscience and became a weak link?"

"Dunno. We don't even know if that is Clemens and not just another one of the teens."

"But we speculate, don't we."

"It was speculation," Kyle sang.

"Jesus. You are too damned lively, Terry. You know that?"

"Sometimes if you act a certain mood, you can make yourself feel it. I'm acting chipper because I feel like crap. You know how you're always saying you're too old for this shit? Well, I'm getting too old, too. Too old to balance cases like this with raising a family and planning a wedding. Did I tell you that Lexie has a boyfriend? I can already tell I'm going to be losing sleep over that."

"Yeah. Nina's pretty secretive but we know there is someone. And we're worried precisely because she's being secretive. I never pictured myself as Daddy Bear, but I'm definitely becoming one."

"You've always been a Daddy Bear, Joe, for all the waifs you've collected over the years. This is just a new chapter."

"Papa Bear and the Waifs. Sounds like a children's book."

"Or a rock band."

They drove on in silence. Then Kyle said, "I'm glad we ate, or I'd feel even crappier. You got any ideas for how we find the place they've moved the kids to?"

"Not yet. I'm going home to consult my crystal ball. You got any idea what the story is with Maureen Mulcahey?"

"You mean where she is?"

Burgess made an affirmative sound.

"Our cases aren't all straightforward, but sometimes they're like walking a maze blindfolded," Kyle said. "We're used to being lied to. Goes with the territory. And the aunt did give us a theory for why she might have lied. But I, at least, have been hoping that the 'good' sister is still alive. Only why wouldn't Colleen know? She said her sister was killed while they were first being transported to the camp, and she was there until her escape."

They had nothing but guesses.

Speaking of guesses, Burgess guessed that pretty soon he'd have to let Megan Ainsworth know what her suspicions had led to. Over the phone, he thought, since there was something in the air between them he didn't want to deal with. It was flattering to have an attractive woman interested in him, but he'd never been the play around type, not even back in the day, when he was young and badge bunnies were everywhere.

But thinking about Megan Ainsworth had him reviewing their conversations. And, as sometimes happened when the brain was full of disparate aspects of a case, some things she'd said suddenly did, and didn't, make sense.

He turned to Kyle, half-asleep in the seat beside him. "Megan Ainsworth's husband dismissed her concerns that something might be going on across the lake. If the cottage was their special, quiet place and this was troubling her, why would he do that?"

THIRTY-SEVEN

"You've met her," he said, as Kyle came awake. "Did she strike you as ditsy? As someone who imagined things or overreacted? And why wouldn't the sheriff have humored her and at least taken a look at what was going on there? Unless—"

"Unless her husband put in a word and suggested it not be followed up?" Kyle said. "Her husband or someone else. But it sounds like the husband actively discouraged her from exploring the place."

"And why would he do that?"

"I can think of a few possibilities. What do we know about him? Anything?" Kyle again.

"We know he's an arrogant snob, just from that brief encounter at the cocktail party. Beyond that? Nothing. We know his name isn't Ainsworth. She mentioned her generous husband William McCarty, right?" Burgess said. "Didn't introduce him, but told us his name? Perhaps her comment was intended to suggest that he liked to use his money to impress people?"

"So, if I'm thinking what you're thinking, we want to know if he has any interest in that property, right?" Kyle said. "And possibly that camp for teens project was a way to use it until he could make plans to develop it?"

"And if he owns that property, could he own any other property that might…" Burgess paused to search for the right words. Finished with, "Might be a place to stash some teenagers?"

"Definitely a thought. Unless it's just a wild-ass guess because we're stuck and desperate. That note, if it's authentic, tells us the kids are desperate, too," Kyle said. "And we know such guesses have paid off before."

Burgess nodded. "So we go with our wild-ass guess while we also look into other things. Let's get Rocky Jordan on it. See what he can find out about McCarty, his finances, and any property he, or companies or partnerships he's involved with, owns. Then we can dig in when we get back to 109."

Kyle made the call. Burgess concentrated on driving now that they were closer to Portland. It was early, but already the roads were filling up with morning commuters. People in Maine often had very long commutes to their jobs.

"Guess I'll postpone that call to Megan Ainsworth," Burgess said. "Though Cote will want to know what I've found. Of course. How he feels about our getting the state police involved? I don't know which way that will go."

"Do you suppose she's involved?" Kyle said. "Ainsworth?"

"I don't. Why would she put us onto the place? Doesn't make sense."

Kyle agreed, but said, "We've had plenty of cases where things didn't make sense. Until they did. Plenty of people ratting out their partners. Maybe they had a disagreement. Maybe it was his thing and she's never liked it, or he hid it from her, she has her suspicions, and she damned well wants to know what's going on."

"Or maybe we're tilting at windmills."

"Or maybe we are."

"Something else I'm wondering about," Burgess said. "Which of them has the money, McCarty or Ainsworth? Ainsworth sounds like money, doesn't it? What if this is his play to get some money? Tuition and room and board, if this were a legitimate program, would be steep. Some parents will pay a lot to have their problem children taken off their hands. Or maybe he's always getting into shady real estate deals with her money, or losing money, and she's tired of it?"

It was all speculation. They had rules about that. Speculate all you want as part of figuring out what's going on but reach no conclusions until they can be backed up by facts. They were pretty short on facts.

They drove the rest of the trip in silence, each man speculating like hell about possible paths forward. As they drove, the already gray day darkened to match their moods. By the time they drove into the cold gray cement structure that was the garage, they were both feeling dark. Both exhausted from a tense night without sleep. From finding bodies when they'd hoped to find captive teens. From the mystery of what had happened to Maureen Mulcahey.

Upstairs, they found Rocky Jordan deeply immersed in one of the internet searches he loved. Burgess's desk had experienced the usual pink snow squall. On top was a message from Sage Prentiss to please call as soon as they got in.

Kyle read it over Burgess's shoulder and said, "I hope this doesn't mean what I think it means."

They were on the same page about that. Sometimes you got cases that just kept kicking you in the head.

When he called, Sage didn't answer. Burgess figured he'd give it a few minutes and try again, but left the message they were back and Sage should call them. Then he tried the aunt and got no answer. No answer from the nurses' station, either. It was an ulcer-inducing information void.

Then, with visions of the girl and aunt gone back to Connecticut where it would be hard to reach them again, he went into the conference room and grabbed a pad of paper. At the top, he wrote: Wedding Guest List. If he couldn't move the case, he wanted to do something right. Trying to force his other concerns from his mind, he made the list Chris was waiting for. Across the table, Kyle was bent over a similar pad, and Burgess speculated that Kyle was engaged in the same task. Who knew when there might be another quiet moment, particularly if their speculations were true and Jordan ferreted out a location.

In truth, it wasn't a quiet moment. It was a highly anxious one, and he and Kyle were just postponing facing that for a few minutes. He picked his head up and said, "Done," at the same time Kyle did. And at the same time that Rocky Jordan appeared in the doorway holding some printouts, and Burgess's phone rang.

He took the call and got Sage Prentiss's unhappy voice declaring that there had been a commotion at the nurses' station and when that was sorted out and he returned to the girl's room, she and the aunt were gone. They searched the hospital, but they weren't there. He was heading down to security to look at footage, see if he could spot them leaving and learn what the aunt was driving.

"Crap!" Burgess said, followed by a string of harsher expletives. "Dammit, Terry. They pulled that 'cause a commotion' thing again and did another disappearing act. I should have warned Sage not to leave her even if someone was being murdered outside the room."

"It doesn't make any sense," Kyle said. "Why would they need to do that?" A pause, then, "The aunt. There was something. Something off about her. She said the right things and told the right story but...I don't know. Cop's gut, I guess. It didn't seem entirely genuine. Or there was something more to it, something she was holding back. But Stan watched her with the girl and thought she seemed okay."

He looked around, as though Stan was somewhere in the room, ready to be summoned into their conference about what to do next.

"Stan went to get fingerprints and all from that empty house. The techs got tied up with something else yesterday," Burgess reminded him, then offered a possible explanation. "Maybe, despite what she said—the aunt—she's still very close to her sister-in-law and is taking the girl back home."

"Christ. Didn't we have a restraining order to prevent anyone from removing the girl from the hospital?"

There was silence as they considered that. Then Burgess said, "We do. It would violate the judge's order that the girl not be removed from the state."

Dammit. He was losing track of the pieces.

Rocky Jordan, waiting patiently in the doorway, cleared his throat and said, "I may have something here."

Burgess motioned for him to come in, and said, "Give us a minute, okay?" To Kyle, he said, "Call Sage back and remind him about the order. Tell him to get data on the aunt's car and put out a BOLO. And let us know what's happening." Then he turned his attention to Rocky Jordan, who'd approached the table and was laying out some papers.

Jordan opened his laptop and pulled up a map. "This," he said, pointing to the first paper, "is a deed for what I believe is the parcel you were interested in—the place you found where those kids were being held?"

Burgess and Kyle leaned in. It was a deed from a family trust conveying the four-hundred-acre parcel to Megan Ainsworth and William McCarty. It was dated six months ago.

Burgess stared at it. "No way! This doesn't make any sense. If she owns it, why is she deterred by a gate and a lock? Why wouldn't she have a key to the gate? And why wouldn't she know what was going on over there? Why approach us with some crazy story about lights and screams?"

"Unless she doesn't know she owns it," Kyle suggested. "Unless he was doing this behind her back."

"And what? Forged her signature?"

"Like we've never seen that before?" Kyle said. "We can get an expert to analyze that."

Jordan cleared his throat again, then set down another paper. "And there's this."

It was a list of properties and their addresses. One of them was highlighted in yellow. Jordan pointed to it. "This seems the most likely place they might stash those teens. It's an old nursing home. Went out of business about five years ago. And your guy, William McCarty, bought it two years ago. He's kind of the king of the bargain sale, looks like." He ran a finger down the list. "Got most of these for a song at auction when no one else bid on them."

"Just McCarty or McCarty and Ainsworth?" Burgess asked.

"Both," Jordan said. "But despite their signatures being notarized, hers are all over the lot, like he brought in some ringer to sign for her and each time it was a different woman. Sure, they're supposed to check IDs before someone signs but 'supposed to' isn't the same as did. And fake licenses are easy to get."

"Thanks, Rocky. This is great," Burgess said. "We're lucky to have you."

Jordan smiled and ducked his head. "Thanks, Joe. Happy to help."

Which he was. He picked up his laptop and turned to go. Then turned back and shifted the papers to reveal a new one. "Here's a copy of the map." Then he left them.

"Jesus," Kyle said. "It feels like we're being tugged in too many directions just when I was hoping for a short day and a chance to sleep."

"Detectives never sleep," Burgess said. "Didn't anyone ever tell you that?"

"Nah. I had dreams of adventure, you know. Shiny badge and catching bad guys and basking in all the glory."

From the doorway, someone cleared his throat. Not Rocky Jordan again, or anyone who was there to be helpful. Suppressing their sighs, he and Kyle turned toward the door.

"You were supposed to call me," Cote said, coming into the room and focusing his glare on Burgess.

"Just got in and then we had a crisis over at the hospital. Are having a crisis at the hospital. The girl has disappeared," Burgess said.

"That girl is too much trouble," Cote said. "What about Ms. Ainsworth and her concerns? Do you have some answers for her?"

Burgess sighed inwardly. Might as well get this over with. "You recall that the girl said she'd escaped from a camp somewhere in the woods where teens were being held? Where they'd been sent by parents who thought they were sending their problem teens to a nature camp/school where they could experience the great outdoors far from bad influences and screens?" he said.

He waited for Cote's response. The captain seemed to be puzzling over this before he said, "About Ms. Ainsworth?" as though a bunch of teens being held in brutal conditions didn't matter.

"It seems that her concerns were well founded," Burgess said. "The property Ms. Ainsworth was concerned about, which is located across the lake from where she and her husband have their camp, turns out to be where those teens were being held. Kyle and I visited it yesterday, as you instructed, along with two wardens familiar with the area. It was the camp where those teens had been held. We found evidence that they'd been there along with two dead bodies wrapped in tarps in a boatshed. We had to call in the state police, and we spent much of the rest of the night bringing them up to speed about our investigation. We don't know whose bodies those were. You will recall…"

Burgess paused to give Cote time to recall or pretend he recalled what they'd learned from the girl. "You will recall that the girl said she was a twin and that her twin had been killed by those who were running the camp. We're waiting to hear whether one of those bodies was her twin."

They weren't, actually. They expected the smaller body would belong to one of the boys Colleen had mentioned and the large one would be Elvira Clemens. But that, for now, was speculation.

Dammit. Now that Kyle had sung it, every time he thought the word "speculation" it came out as song. Cote wouldn't appreciate him bursting into song.

"You called in the state police?" Cote said, as though Burgess had just said that they'd been happily dancing in shit and that was why their report was delayed.

Burgess shrugged. "Had to. Dead bodies. Not our jurisdiction." He didn't elaborate. Cote knew full well who had jurisdiction over dead bodies in most parts of the state.

"Ms. Ainsworth," Cote began, as though catering to the wealthy was their only concern. "You've gotten back to her?"

Burgess smiled. "We've got a few details to clear up first, Captain. Such as we've learned that she's a record owner of that property and so why was she in the dark about how it was being used? Speaking to her without the background wouldn't be sensible at this point. I'm sure you can see that."

"She's the what?" Cote was actually sputtering now. Then, without waiting for a further explanation from Burgess, he said, "Keep me informed," and left.

"Well now, son," Kyle said. "I think you handled that with finesse."

"I think I need some sleep. There are so many balls in the air I'm getting dizzy."

"As long as ours are securely attached and not in the air," Kyle said.

"Oh, and if you put your head between your knees, that sometimes helps."

Burgess deleted "screw" and "fuck" and a few other expletives and was only left with, "You."

"Oh yeah. Me. The guy who needs to finish this thing. And if we go looking for that defunct nursing home, we'll need Stan as well."

"My shining armor needs polishing and my white horse needs rest."

"A policeman's lot is not an happy one," Kyle sang.

"WTF is it with you and singing, Terry. You don't sing."

"Michelle has been listening to clips of wedding bands, and I don't mean the kind you wear on your finger."

At least he didn't have to deal with a band. At least, not that he knew. Maybe Chris would talk to Michelle and she'd decide they needed one. What he needed was sleep. Sleep and some answers. Before he disappeared again into the world of crime, he called Chris for an update on how Ned was doing. As he waited for her to answer, he thought of all the things in that case that needed following up. A policeman's lot and all that.

It was nice to hear her voice. It instantly connected him to the world outside his, a world without bodies and cruelty and children undergoing brain surgery. She said, "Hey, Joe. We missed you. You okay?" and he was seized with the urge to leave this place, go to her workplace, and put his arms around her.

"It's crazy and it's far from over. I've made a guest list, but I don't know when I'll get to drop it off. Maybe in an hour. You want it at home, or shall I bring it to you?"

"Home is good. But..." He froze, thinking of all the bad things her "but" could mean. "But if you bring it here, I can see you. Give you my laser assessment. Put my arms around you. You know. All the things almost Mrs. Burgess needs to do."

"Soon you can drop the almost."

"And won't that make you happy?"

"It will. How's Ned doing?"

"Oh. Kids. They're amazing the way they bounce back. And Van is doing well, too. We're going back tonight, after school and after work, to take him some snacks and books. Ned's idea. You know that our son is such a kind person." She didn't say "too kind" though it was Ned's kindness that had led him into danger. "So, maybe I'll see you soon?"

"I hope you will."

He found Kyle watching him. Kyle said, "Ned's okay?"

"Seems to be." But his moment for home and family was over. "Think we should hop over to the hospital and see what's up?"

"Let's see how Sage is doing. Maybe things are under control. Why don't I give him a call?"

Things were so rarely under control. He nodded. "Good idea."

What he really wanted to do was jump in his truck and go check out the property Rocky had found. Now that the bad guys were aware the police were on to them, he wasn't confident that the rest of the teens would be safe for long. He didn't see how their captors could simply let them go, and what they'd found at the deserted camp demonstrated that those involved weren't averse to killing. Though how could Edwin Hall a.k.a. Gary Briscow allow his mother to be killed? Because he was a grifter who cared for no one but himself?

Of course, Burgess didn't know that she'd been killed. Maybe she'd simply keeled over from a heart attack or something and they'd just disposed of the body.

Across the table, Kyle was on the phone, murmuring something. When he set it down, Burgess said, "What?"

"They've identified the make and plate number of the aunt's car and there's a BOLO out. Not much more we can do. Sage is heading back. He can keep an eye on things here and we can check out that property."

"It's a plan. I need to drop off my wedding list with Chris before we go. I should do that now."

"And I should probably give mine to Michelle. Who knows when we'll be back?"

"Or what shape we'll be in."

"Better be good enough shape to stand up at a wedding," Kyle said. "Your habit of getting bashed by bad guys absolutely will not work in this case. No gunshot wounds. Not stab wounds. No stitches. No visible bruises."

"It's not like I invite it."

Burgess looked around the room. They would take Rocky's map and the list with the property address along. Was there anything else here that needed to be tucked away from Cote's prying eyes? He thought not.

"Okay. We'll go drop off those lists. Come back here and grab Stan, then gear up for battle. Is that the plan?"

"That's the plan."

They headed out to their vehicles and did their errands. Then they stopped at 109, scooped up Stan Perry and the gear they'd need, and headed out.

THIRTY-EIGHT

"This better lead to something," Perry said. "Lily is not happy with all the time I'm spending on this case."

"Didn't Uncle Terry tell you, you gotta set her expectations right from the get go. Otherwise, she's gonna keep expecting you to come home like someone who works a nine to five."

"Oh, fuck you, Terry. You weren't a detective when your girls were babies. You worked a shift and you went home. Like a normal working guy."

"Oh sure, Stanley. Oh sure. Like there was never a shift when I'd have to work a double because we were short, or someone was sick, or I had to go to court or I made an arrest just at the end of the shift and couldn't just drop the bad guy off and go home to play daddy. This is our life. You wanna take a desk job, be a supervisor, go for it. You'll be bored as shit."

"Okay, kids, no fighting in the car," Burgess said. "Save your energy for the bad guys. If this pans out as we expect, you'll need it."

"Sure thing, Dad," Stan Perry said. "Can we stop for coffee on the way? I mean, if we're gonna be real cops, we need coffee and donuts, right?"

They got coffee and donuts and it seemed to calm everyone down.

Not how caffeine was supposed to work; it must have been be the sugar and carbs. And the fact that they'd all been working too hard and missing too much sleep.

He was tired of driving, having already done enough of it today, but the thrill of the chase was kicking in. Still, he felt like they were a woefully small band to take on what lay ahead. He didn't know how many opponents they would be facing. It wasn't a warden's job, but on impulse, born probably of having had Boudreau on the search last night and knowing the man to be trustworthy and smart, he called the warden and got a laconic, "Boudreau. That you, Burgess?" Evidently, like him, the warden hadn't gone home to sleep.

"It is."

"You got something for me?"

Burgess thought Boudreau sounded hopeful. Well, he'd seen the conditions those kids had been held in, and he'd seen the canvas-wrapped bodies. He knew the situation was serious.

"Not exactly. We've got a lead on another property those teens might have been moved to. It's not the big woods, but it's rural and wooded and we don't know what we're facing. Thought you might be up for a little adventure."

"You mean you don't want to call the staties," Boudreau said.

Which was true. Burgess tried to be good at sharing because he got pissed when other public safety agencies—like that one down in Connecticut—wouldn't share info or take things seriously. But he was, much as he hated to admit it, territorial. He didn't want to put in the hours, the days, the gut-twisting anxiety and whatever it took to develop a case and then have another agency step in and shut him out. He had not, for example, heard anything about the bodies they'd found, even though he was a cop, he'd found them. and had asked for updates.

"You got it."

"Where is this place?"

Burgess told him.

"Yeah. I know that area. Gonna be a bitch to sneak up on it, if that's your plan. When you thinking of doing this, because after dark would be better if you can swing it."

They were two hours away and it was after three. Dark would begin around four-thirty. Burgess said, "Planning on getting there around five."

There was silence while Boudreau considered. "Yeah. I can do that. I'll see if I can rope Kenny into joining us. Gonna have to think of some reason for us to be there, though. You got any ideas?"

Now Burgess considered. "Lost hikers? Lost hunter? Lost child?"

"You still a child, Burgess?"

"My partner sometimes thinks so."

"Never mind. I'll think of something. There's a pretty good diner not far from there. Betty's. We can meet there." And Boudreau, more a man of action than words, was gone.

Burgess barely knew the man, but knew he could trust him and his instincts. He felt better knowing there would be more of them to keep each other safe.

That settled, he concentrated on driving. They would make a plan once they got to the diner. Beside him, Kyle's breathing indicated he was taking a nap. The quiet in the back seat suggested Perry was, too. He thought about closing his eyes, too. They were tired and stinging from staring at the gray road for so long. Decided it was a bad idea. His team often jokingly called him "Dad." Time like this, when he was thinking "let the kids sleep" he felt like it.

Time passed. Dark came on, a slow greying out of the afternoon. Just before five, he saw a brightly lit building with a sign for Betty's Diner. The lot was crowded. He spotted Boudreau's truck at the far end of the lot and pulled in beside it.

"Wakey, wakey, kids. We're here," he said as he shut off the engine.

Like the good cops they were, both came instantly awake.

"Where is here?" Kyle asked. He looked around. "We're stopping to eat?"

"We're stopping to meet up with Boudreau and make a plan."

They climbed out of the truck, stretched stiff limbs, and walked to Boudreau's truck. He and Packard were bent over a map they had spread out on the seat between them.

The three of them climbed into the back seat. "What do you think?" Burgess asked.

Boudreau shrugged. "They picked a pretty good spot, from a defensive point of view."

"Can we do it?"

Boudreau opened a laptop that showed an aerial view of the property. It was perched on a hilltop and almost entirely surrounded by open fields. To the north, a thick patch of woods came closer to the building. He put his finger on the screen. "If we come through here, we can get pretty close." He hesitated, turning to look at Burgess. "Do we know if they're armed?"

"Don't know. But we assume they are."

"Right." Boudreau sighed. "Be a big help if we knew what kind of weapons they have. But we're kind of used to going in blind. Operating in a sphere where everyone is armed. Aren't we, Kenny?"

Packard nodded but didn't speak.

With the engine off, the truck was getting cold.

"So what's our approach? Where's the nearest road?" Burgess said.

They leaned in as Boudreau pointed to the map and outlined the plan. "Be better if it were later," he said. "When people are asleep." A shrug. "But we're here now. Might as well get started."

"Everyone's wearing a vest," Burgess said.

They all geared up. Burgess put some of the goodies he'd brought—flash bangs, smoke bombs, teargas, in a pack for Perry to carry, along with some bolt cutters.

They returned to the truck and followed Boudreau through a maze of back roads until he pulled to the side and parked. They parked behind him, grabbed their guns, and got out. The air had the bite that suggested snow might be coming later. They silenced their phones and headed into the woods.

It felt like they walked for an hour, though it was probably less. Trying to move quietly through the darkening woods can make any journey feel longer.

Burgess knew how to dress for the weather. He'd learned that as a rookie out on the streets on patrol. Plus, moving helped to keep them warm. But the wind was rising as the temperature dropped. It was not a pleasant exercise. Burgess hadn't seen, or heard, anything when Boudreau suddenly raised his arm for them to stop. They huddled around him as he said, "There's a small building up ahead that isn't on the maps. We should check it out."

Burgess had already seen what these people did with small buildings. Small buildings where teens were chained up. Small buildings that reeked of the stench of death. Even though they hadn't reached the building that was their goal, the air felt heavy with menace. It was a feeling cops often faced going into dark buildings. You don't know what you're going to find but you can sense it will be bad.

Maybe a hundred feet on, they reached the building. Ahead, through breaks in the trees, they could see the old nursing home that was their destination. First, though—this.

There were no lights visible. The few windows were blocked with cloth. Not curtains but drapes of sheets or blankets. Everyone was silent while Boudreau approached the window and listened. He shook his head. He wasn't hearing anything inside. When they'd worked their way around to the front, they found the door was padlocked. Not for long, as the bolt cutters did their job. Stan Perry did the honors and Burgess caught the lock before it could fall with a clang.

Slowly, carefully, Burgess pushed the door open. The inside was completely dark. He realized he'd been holding his breath as he waited for more death-laden air. But it was only stale and stank of mouse. He clicked on his flashlight and ran it around the interior.

A couple of empty bunks along one wall. A rusty woodstove that hadn't been lit. On the other wall, two more bunks. One of them was empty but there was someone—someone or someone's body—in the second. Quickly, he moved across the room and knelt down beside the figure, shining his light on it. The figure was either in a drugged sleep or unconscious. She didn't blink or flinch at the light. It was Maureen Mulcahey.

He checked for a pulse. Faint but steady. Turned to the others and said, "She's alive."

The other four, who'd been holding their breaths, exhaled.

Now they faced a quandary. Leave the girl here while they continued their mission to the larger building? Leave someone here to guard her? Call for help, which would likely blow their mission and put the other teens at risk? Or what?

Boudreau and Packard held a whispered confab, and Boudreau said, "Kenny will take her back to the truck and call an ambulance from there. If that's okay with you. We don't want to leave her here. Not when we don't know who is around, who might check on her, or what the risks to her would be if that happens." He left unsaid the risks to her if their mission failed and those who were holding these teens came back to get her.

Burgess didn't like it. He felt that they needed everyone for this mission. But he also knew they had a chance to save at least one life and should take that chance.

"I know," Boudreau said. "It's risky. But we can't leave her here and we can't take her with us."

Burgess looked at Kyle, who nodded. Then at Packard, who was a big guy, but it was a mile or more back to their vehicles. He asked, "You sure you can...?" even though he'd done the same thing himself. Done it and suffered from it later. In the moment, they did what had to be done.

Packard shrugged. "You know we haul people out of the woods all the time, right?"

Which probably was half truth and half bravado. "Take her, then. Thanks. And good luck."

Packard handed his long gun to Boudreau, lifted the girl to his shoulder, and disappeared the way they'd come.

Burgess watched until they vanished in the dark. Then, Boudreau still in the lead, they headed for the large building that loomed through the trees ahead. There were lights on there, mostly in a row on the second floor.

"I hope there aren't motion sensor lights," he whispered. It seemed likely, in a building that had been abandoned for years, that they would be turned off or disconnected to save electricity, but this crew could have turned them back on, especially since they had to know the police were searching for them.

Their question was answered a minute later as they slowly crept out of the woods into the open space around the building. A light ahead blazed down on them.

They pulled back into the trees to regroup. Boudreau said, "I've got this." He stepped forward and shot. The light stayed on and Burgess realized he'd shot at a surveillance camera. His second shot took out the light. He stepped back into the trees with a faint smile. "Guess we've rung their doorbell."

Which could go two ways. Those inside would fight back or go into defense mode, with the teens as hostages. Burgess would bet on defense mode, which would make things far more difficult. It was hard to plan their next moves when they had no idea how many they were up against, but they'd never known that. And they were here.

They gathered in a circle and discussed what to do next. Above them, the lights on the second floor went out.

There was no moon or stars. The sky was overcast and a bite in the air said snow would be starting soon.

This, Burgess thought, *was where hubris, or territorialism, got him.* They could have left this to the state police, who'd come in with their armored vehicles and their SWAT team instead of a small group of city cops and one warden.

"Having second thoughts, Burgess?" Boudreau asked.

"More like third. But we're here. No changing our minds now."

"Good," Boudreau said. They all leaned in and he laid out a plan.

The building had three stories, with long wings on both sides leading out from a central building. The entrance was in the center, with other entrances at the ends of the two wings. Fire escapes led up both ends and in the center on the back of the building. They knew, from the lights they'd seen, that most likely the teens and their captors were on the second floor in the wing closest to where they stood.

"We go in on the other end," Boudreau said. "Either on the first floor, through the entrance or up the fire escape. Two of us. The other two take the rear fire escape."

While Burgess was processing that and deciding whether it made sense and was the safest way to proceed, Boudreau moved on. "Burgess, you have smoke bombs and flashbangs, yeah?"

"I do."

"Each team should have those. When we encounter…uh…well, whoever's holding them, start with the bangs and then the smoke, okay?"

"You know how to use them?" Kyle asked. Not unreasonable since wardens probably didn't carry stuff like that in the woods.

"I do. But I'll leave that up to you city cops. 'Kay?"

"Okay," Kyle said, but he looked uneasy, and Stan Perry had pulled a little way out of the circle and was fidgeting.

"So, we'll all go together to the first door in case we need the bolt cutters," Boudreau said.

Burgess liked the man but thought he was enjoying this a little too much. He said, "I think we should start at this end. Going all the way around leaves us exposed for too long, now that we know there are lights and cameras all around."

Boudreau shrugged. "Fine with me. Kyle, you're with me. Burgess and Perry take the back."

Kyle and Perry looked at him, so Burgess nodded. They divvied up the gear from the pack. Then the four of them started moving slowly forward. As they moved, the first snowflakes started falling.

THIRTY-NINE

The uneasy feeling Burgess always had when approaching an unknown and dangerous situation was amplified now by his uncertainty about what lay ahead and Boudreau's eagerness to be in charge. It might simply be that he was used to being in charge. But he was a team player. It was the man's eagerness. This wasn't just an adventure with guns. There were lives at stake. The lives of kids who'd already lived through too much. They were here to rescue them with the least amount of danger. Boudreau knew all that, yet he wasn't sure Boudreau was on the same page.

The knife that slept in his gut was awake now and starting to stab him. He ignored it. There was nothing to be done. It would settle down when this was over and not before. There was nothing he could do to placate it.

They were almost to the door when realization struck him. The people they were seeking were willing to be brutal to captive teens. But from what he knew of Clinton Johns and Gary Briscow, or at least when he'd been Edwin Hall, both men were opportunistic, but cowards. More likely to flee when the risk of capture threatened than stand and fight.

He said, "Their vehicles. We need to find and disable their vehicles."

He was surprised that Boudreau didn't object. They retreated back into the trees and made their way along the edge to where they could see the driveway in front of the building. There were three dim shapes. The white van. What he assumed was the green truck. And a small blue sedan. He couldn't remember what their search had told them about Elvira Clemens' vehicle but thought it might be small and blue.

"I've got the van," Kyle whispered.

"I'll take the truck," Boudreau said.

Burgess and Perry headed for the car.

All three vehicles were unlocked, perhaps in anticipation of a quick retreat.

In minutes, steps had been taken to disable all three. As they gathered beside the white van, Kyle whispered, "Lotta guns in the back."

As quietly as they could, they removed the guns and carried them into the woods. It was too much fire power for the small group they believed were inside. Burgess figured they'd branched out from their scheme to raise money on the teens to gun sales. Guns could be very lucrative, and they didn't need to be fed, clothed, or housed. He felt the chill he always felt when confronted by bad guys with serious guns. These days, the cops were too often outgunned and criminals like these were the reason.

As they gathered to head back and enter the building, a heavy door slammed and four people—three men and a woman—came hurrying toward the vehicles. Intent on their escape and their conversation, they didn't see four men slipping away into the darkness.

Odd, Burgess thought. They must have heard the gunshot and noticed their camera wasn't working. Maybe their plan was to escape before whoever was outside had entered the building.

He had another thought, too, that went with that. One that involved booby traps and explosives. Clinton Johns had used those in the past, so it seemed a likely scenario. Make their escape, leaving the teens behind. Either someone would try to rescue them and get blown up, or they were chained up and would slowly starve and freeze. He could wonder about why Maureen Mulcahey had been confined away from the others when this was over.

From the shadow of the trees, guns at the ready, they watched the four approach the vehicles. The snow had gotten heavier, forcing them to peer through a veil of flakes. It was harder to see but their tracks had been quickly obscured.

Beside him, Burgess heard the heavy knock of one rock against another and Stan Perry's quiet curses.

The first man in the group, a man Burgess believed, from his size and shape, was Clinton Johns, halted and turned toward the woods, holding up a hand to silence the others. He wore a black parka, a black face mask, and black gloves.

Burgess and his team went still, watching as the man drew a gun and began walking toward them. The others, also in black and also with their faces hidden, one with a handgun and two with long guns, followed.

Heart racing, Burgess sent a silent prayer of thanks aloft that the more lethal weapons had been in the van. Not that what they were carrying weren't dangerous enough. Never underestimate a gun. He swapped his handgun for his shotgun, took a deep breath, and stepped out of the trees.

"Police!" he yelled. "Drop your guns and get down on the ground."

The three in the rear hesitated. The lead man kept coming.

Burgess gave the man the warning again, and when he didn't stop, put a round near his feet and repeated the command.

In response, the man started shooting. Those behind him joined in.

A lot of bullets were flying around as Burgess made a rapid retreat to the woods while Kyle and Perry covered his retreat.

From the shelter of the trees, Burgess aimed at the lead man and fired again. This time the man yelled, dropped his gun, and fell to his knees.

The other three, either less bold or less crazy, beat feet for the vehicles, quickly discovering that wasn't going to work. The smallest one, the one who might be Elaine Hawes, jumped from the small blue car and ran back to the building. A man who might have been her husband ran after her, oblivious to the watching cops, screaming, "Elaine! No! Stop! There's a—"

His warning was either unheard or came too late. The woman jerked open the door, ran inside, and the lobby exploded.

"That was meant for us," Kyle said, following Stan Perry and

Boudreau as they approached the yelling man, got him on his knees, and took his weapon. He was sobbing, and Burgess, despite knowing the evil he'd done, felt a moment of sympathy. It lasted only until the man moaned, through his sobs, "Dammit! She was carrying the money."

That had been the loss he mourned.

The unknown man, seeing that there was no escape, surrendered.

Burgess used zip ties on their hands and put them in the van. They grabbed the wounded man and pulled off his mask. Clinton Johns, as they'd expected. His mouth was clenched in pain. A search of his person found another small gun and a knife, and a wallet identifying him as David Briscow.

"Those Briscows are quite a family," Burgess said.

The third man, who had no ID, wasn't anyone they knew or had identified as being connected to the case, but he looked familiar. He refused to give his name but Burgess figured once they had his prints they'd know who he was. He was definitely in the system.

The man who called himself Gary Briscow was curled up in a corner, weeping.

"Booby trap explosives and a gun fight," Kyle muttered. "I'm getting married. I'm supposed to be staying safe. Can we go home now and let the sheriff's office or the state police handle this?"

"I guess we could, assuming we can get a ride back to my truck," Burgess said, looking toward the building. "But the place is on fire and there are still a bunch of teens in there who probably can't escape without our help. There's still three of us. And Boudreau. We can handle it."

"Oh, fuck you, Joe," Kyle said. "Like I have ever shirked on one of your crazy missions."

Which was absolutely true. Kyle was a rock.

"You never have," Burgess agreed, shouldering his pack and starting toward the building. "I wouldn't fault you if you waited this one out."

"Like I ever could." Kyle paused. "I just had to say it, you know?" Kyle was trotting along beside him, with Stan and Boudreau coming behind.

"I'm assuming all the downstairs doors are boobytrapped," Burgess said. "So I say we try the rear fire escape."

"Maybe the fire escape on the end?" Boudreau suggested. "Closer to where we think those kids are."

So that's where they headed.

Because the fire escape was in such crappy shape, they decided to go up one at a time. Getting up that slippery, creaky thing was a bitch. At any moment, Burgess expected it to detach from the building and send him flying.

He reached the top, used a pry bar on the door, and pushed through the shattered wood. It was dark and smelled of unwashed bodies, feces and urine, and fear. He used his flashlight to search for a light switch but when he found it, nothing happened.

He was standing in a long corridor. To his left were a series of small doors presumably leading to rooms. On his right, just one door. He opened it and went in.

He was immediately struck by déjà vu, by the sense that he'd been in an awful place like this before. There were two rows of beds and in each bed lay an emaciated figure covered by a thin blanket. Each one was chained to the wall by a wrist. Some of the heads turned when he came in; others lay there listlessly, no longer interested in the possibility of hope or escape. What the fuck could Johns and his cohort have been thinking? Milk the parents for money and then just let the kids die?

He said, "Police officers. We're going to get you out of here," loudly so they could all hear. Then he took off his pack, got out the bolt cutters, and started cutting the chains. There were already traces of smoke in the room. They didn't have much time to get all these feeble kids out of here and down the ladder, and he figured most of them couldn't walk on their own.

One down. Two. Three. As he moved along the first row of beds, he could hear the others, behind him, moving those he'd freed from the beds and out to the ladder. It was not going to be easy.

A horror show like this, so much cruelty and damage, and what had upset Edwin Hall was the loss of his money. His mother dead and now his wife. But it had been the money. A loss that had literally made him cry.

His anger at the man fueled his efforts, helping him move faster. His shoulder hurt. His hands hurt. He cursed himself as he went. Trying to be a cowboy. Needing to do this on their own. Now they needed a fleet of ambulances for these kids and were alone in the middle of nowhere with captive bad guys and a bunch of disabled vehicles.

Curse. Cut. Curse. Cut.

He started down the second row. God. These kids were in such bad shape. How on earth had Clinton Johns and the others managed to move them here? Maybe it hadn't been only a day or two ago. Or maybe they'd moved them slowly, a few at a time? Not just Clinton Johns, he reminded himself. The person behind all this was William McCarty, Megan Ainsworth's husband.

He figured eventually he'd get answers. Right now, there was only time to keep moving. Hope they could get all ten out before the whole building went up. Already the smoke was thicker and everyone was coughing. He thought the floor under his feet was getting hot. Get them out and hopefully himself.

A race against time. Keep moving. Do what had to be done.

He thought of Chris, finally willing to marry him. Of his assurances that his life had calmed down. Of how he'd back away from dangerous things. A promise he'd meant when he made it. One that was never credible given his history, his character, and his job. Probably she knew that. Would she ever get to be real Mrs. Burgess and not Almost Mrs. Burgess? Would Kyle get to marry Michelle? Would little Autumn grow up without a dad? All because Burgess was on a mission.

The last chain free. But the girl cowered in a terrified bundle. There was no time for this, but Burgess took a minute he did not have to calm her. "It's okay," he said. "I'm a police officer. Colleen, the girl who escaped, told us about you so we came to find you." She only stared. "Colleen," he said. "You knew her, right?"

She nodded.

So much smoke now filled the room he could barely see her.

"She sent me to help."

That finally got a small nod. So tense he could barely breathe, unless that was the smoke, Burgess helped the girl from the bed, wrapped her in the blanket, and carried her to the fire escape, keeping up a steady mantra of "It's okay. You're going to be safe now."

He waited at the top for the person ahead of him, Boudreau, to reach the ground with his burden. Balancing the girl on his shoulder, he stepped onto the first metal step. There was an ominous creak and the whole thing swayed.

He stepped carefully onto the next step. Another metallic screech. Another. He felt the vibrations of the flimsy structure through his feet. There was no going back. There was no other way out of the building. He didn't dare look anywhere but where the next step was, but felt the whole thing swaying more.

Two steps from the bottom, he gave up and jumped to the ground. His bad knee told him what it thought about that and he told it to shut the fuck up. As he hurried away, the thing finished pulling off the wall and crashed to the ground behind him. Not a fucking minute to spare.

As the screeching, groaning metal settled onto the snowy ground, the glass in the windows above shattered and bright tongues of flame poured out. He held the small, shivering girl as visions of his mortality flowed through him.

"Holy fuck!" Stan Perry said in a shaky voice. "Just Holy Fuck!"

FORTY

As he got his breath back, he looked to see where they'd put the other kids, expecting to see them lined up on the ground, realizing that he'd made no plan beyond finding them and getting them out of the building. Instead, he saw Boudreau heading for the parking lot and followed. As he came around the corner of the building, he found not a lot of darkness and three disabled vehicles but a mob scene. Warden's trucks, police cars and ambulances, and fire trucks. He almost collapsed with relief. There were even representatives of the ever annoying press.

As he caught up with Boudreau, the man said, "I figured we'd need some help, so I made a couple calls."

A man in a sheriff's department uniform held out his arms for the girl Burgess was carrying. He surrendered his burden and dropped to his knees, suddenly spent.

"You done good," Boudreau said, putting a hand on his shoulder. "You done real good."

"We did," Burgess said. "We did. It's always the team."

After that, it was a repeat of the night before at the camp. A lot of hours being debriefed, first by the sheriff's department, then, their noses seriously out of joint, by the state police. Burgess had no idea what he said. All he wanted to do was go home, hug his family, shower, and drop into bed. There were so many loose threads that needed to be dealt with. But nothing was going to be dealt with before he got some sleep. Some food would be nice, too.

In an interval, he grabbed a few minutes to call Chris. Said he was okay and gave a brief summary of what they'd been doing. He said he'd be home as soon as he could.

At some point, Boudreau had disappeared but the younger warden, Packard, gave the three of them a ride back to Burgess's Explorer. They put their gear in the back and Kyle held out his hand for the keys. "Okay if I drive?" he said.

Joe Burgess the control freak gladly handed them over. He got in the passenger seat. Stan Perry got in the back, and they headed for home.

"Think we could have cut it any closer?" Perry said.

A question that didn't need an answer.

They'd all turned their phones off during the operation. Now, turned on, they buzzed with messages from Cote. From the chief. From the press. Without discussion, they turned them off again. Right now what they needed was quiet. A chance to process what had just happened. True, their brains would already be planning next steps, but they weren't going to discuss that. Not until they'd put miles, and sleep, and food, between themselves and what had just happened.

There would be news stories. The press had been there with their cameras and their shouted questions. There would be fallout. Likely some shouting matches between their department and others about why the fuck three cops from Portland were conducting an operation without notifying the local police. Right now, none of them cared about that. They'd come to rescue some captive teens and they'd succeeded. It was enough. The fact that their captors had boobytrapped the building said how little those lives were valued.

An hour later Stan Perry broke the silence with, "Anybody asks, I thought I was on a hunting trip."

An hour after that, Kyle said, "I heard there was a great resort hotel there. I was checking it out for my honeymoon."

A while later, as they got close to Portland, Burgess said, "I'd just polished my armor and groomed my white steed. I couldn't help myself."

"That, at least, is true," Kyle said. "You can't help yourself. And a lot of people are better off, or even alive today, because of that."

"I just wish you'd stop collecting waifs," Stan Perry said. "How about stamps or Hummel figures?" He sighed. "You know we're going to be in a shitstorm, right?"

"Yeah," Kyle agreed. "That is why we are picking up our cars and going home. We are not entering 109 for any reason."

They parked where Kyle and Perry could get their cars. Burgess watched them stagger to their vehicles. It took a lot out of you, having gun fights and carrying people down rickety stairs while fire and potential explosions loomed. When they had driven away, he moved into the driver's seat and went home. He wanted to make a million phone calls. To Sage Prentiss to find out what was up with Colleen Mulcahey and her aunt. To get updates on Van Elwell. There was more, though these were the most pressing. But he couldn't. His brain was mush. His brain and his body. It took all he had to steer the Explorer through the nearly empty streets toward home.

It was a little before six when he pulled into the driveway. The house should have been dark and quiet but there were lights on. Odd. He'd texted Chris to let her know that it was over and he was on his way home. Texted so he wouldn't wake her.

Maybe someone had gotten up in the night for a snack and left the lights on.

But when he'd come quietly up the stairs, shed his shoes and coat, and gone inside, he found his whole family gathered around the table. The air smelled of bacon and pancakes and the table was set for five. Chris rushed to him and wrapped him in a hug, and soon he was engulfed in a total family hug, with Ned worming his way to the center with his arms around Burgess's waist. Fideau, not wanting to be left out, worked his way in beside Ned and raised his hopeful doggy eyes.

Burgess patted them all.

"We're all very proud of you," Chris said. "Dylan and Nina have made breakfast and Ned has set the table. Think you can eat before you crash?"

He sat down at the table. Nina pulled a huge plate of pancakes from the oven. Dylan set down a heaping plate of bacon and asked if he wanted coffee. Fideau planted his head on Burgess's thigh.

"Your dog has been missing you. He's been keeping watch by the door all night," Chris said. "He thinks you should have taken him along."

"I've missed you all," Burgess said, stroking the dog's soft head. "It makes a difference, on a mission like this, to know I have my family to come home to. And…" He looked at Chris, "And that I had to keep myself safe because I have a very important wedding to attend."

Even though he planned to go right to sleep, he did want coffee. It just went with this perfect meal and nothing was going to keep him awake. Not after the night he'd just spent.

They all had questions and he answered what he could. After the chill of the night—physical and emotional—it was so good to be inside. Warm. Surround by healthy people whose eyes weren't filled with fear. By his brilliant dog with its trusting eyes.

When breakfast was done, they all went to get ready for work and school. He went to get ready for bed.

The phone rang.

Four people, not including Burgess, dove for the phone. Usually Ned got the phone when it was an early morning call and Burgess wanted to sleep. This time, it was Dylan.

After his deep-voiced hello, he grinned. "I'm sorry," he said. "No. This isn't Detective Sergeant Joe Burgess. This is his son. The detective—my dad—is sleeping. May I take a message."

Of course they couldn't get through a warm and lovely family time without an intrusion from Cote.

Dylan listened for a moment, then he said, "I'm sorry, Captain. My dad's been up for more than thirty-six hours and has organized an operation that resulted a gun fight, in the rescue of eleven captive teenagers, and the arrest of their captors. He needs sleep and I'm not going to disturb him." He grinned at the others and said, "So, is there a message I can give him when he wakes up?"

He listened and set down the phone. "Captain Cote needs you in his office immediately. It's urgent."

They shared a family laugh and Burgess went to bed. Fideau, glad that he was home, settled down to sleep beside the bed.

FORTY-ONE

Burgess woke many hours later feeling not his own age, but Methuselah's. There was a glass of water and some Advil on the bedside table with a little note that said, "Take Me."

Always a slave of duty, he did. Then he pushed out of bed and staggered to the bathroom, moving like Frankenstein on a bad day. The mirror didn't disagree. It said he'd had better days, weeks, months, years. It said going back to bed would be the wisest course of action. It said retirement to an Adirondack chair and some bird watching would be good for his health. Instead, he shaved, showered, and dressed. The mirror said a rather noncommittal "better."

"All you get," he told the steamy glass. "I was never a great beauty." He headed for the kitchen and for coffee, Fideau's nails scritching on the floor behind him. He gave the dog a treat and some pats. "Soon we will get back to taking our walks, okay?"

The dog nodded.

The coffeemaker was already set up. He pushed the button and opened the refrigerator. Bagel and cream cheese? English muffin? Should he fix himself some eggs? He thought his Frankenstein body needed protein so he put the English muffins in the toaster and scrambled some eggs. Another quick check of the fridge said there was some leftover bacon, so he warmed that up and sat down to eat.

His phone rang. He checked the number. Kyle. So he answered.

"You see the news?" Kyle asked.

"Just got up. I'm having a healthy breakfast before I face the world."

"Well, according to the world, we're fucking heroes, Joe. While we're getting kids out of that burning building, the fourth estate are already arriving with their cameras. Pictures of you and Boudreau are on the front page of the paper, carrying out those last two kids. Great picture of the fire escape collapsing, too. Michelle is in a state. Says what if we'd all died."

It felt like too much to process. Burgess said, "Seriously?"

"Seriously Michelle is bent out of shape or seriously we're all heroes?"

"Heroes. You know how I feel about that. But glad you and Stan get to be heroes. Maybe they'll even put a letter of commendation in your file."

"Unless they fire us for insubordination."

"Not a problem for you and me. The union will grieve that long enough for us to retire and you can immediately get a better paying job in corporate security. But then there's poor Stan. It would be hard on him."

"Chris wasn't mad?"

Not that he'd seen. He said, "My family gave me pancakes and bacon and tucked me into bed. They've gotten very good at handling Cote. I let Fideau take the call."

"He freaks Michelle out. Cote, not Fideau."

"Get one of the girls to talk to him. He backs down pretty fast when he's talking to a kid. So far, at least. You at work?"

"About to head in. You?"

"Me, too. Heard from Stan?"

"Not a word. But the young, you know. They're very good at sleeping. He's probably still catching z's."

"With a small baby in the house? He's probably doing double diaper duty to make up for the day he missed."

Burgess finished his food, got his gear, his coat, some dry shoes, and headed down to the truck. He dreaded what he'd run into but had to face it. He was a grownup. He'd brought whatever it was on himself.

As he'd expected, his desk was sea of pink. He was surprised to find someone had already sorted them. His usual piles of urgent, needs response, and ignore, plus a fourth labeled: From the press. He picked up the urgents.

Nothing that really was. But news from Sage that he'd located the aunt and the girl. They'd gone to a local hotel and registered under a different name. The aunt said it was because she was concerned for the girl's safety. There was a phone number to contact them.

Before he made that call, he called the hospital for an update on Van's condition. The boy was awake and doing well.

Sometimes something went right.

He hadn't yet decided whether last night's insanity counted as something going right. Yes, they'd rescued the teens and yes, they'd managed to capture those who were perpetrating the scheme, but they didn't have the true instigator and wouldn't unless one of those arrested talked or they could find a paper trail. Despite it being his investigation, his rescue, the perpetrators weren't in his custody. Among the many messages, there were none from the state police. Fuck it. Let them be territorial and figure it out for themselves. Thanks to him and Kyle, they had those letters which would help identify the parents.

Yes. His language was deteriorating. He'd have to get that in check.

Those thoughts reminded him that he was supposed to get back to Megan Ainsworth, something he planned to do when he knew more about what was going on. But maybe she knew something. Maybe even knew something she was eager to tell him. There had been an air of mystery in their hotel room breakfast. In her getting him and his team involved in the first place. Maybe she'd always known and didn't know what to do about it. It was equally possible, of course, that he'd now, or soon, blow up her happy life.

He was interrupted by someone very nearby clearing his throat. He looked up. Cote was looming over him. Damn. He must be losing it, letting the man sneak up on him like this. He stood, ready to counter whatever crap the captain was about to dump on him. Before he could speak, Cote held out his hand. "Congratulations, Burgess. That was a great thing you did last night. The chief is very proud."

Even as he shook the outstretched hand, Burgess wondered if he'd wandered into some parallel universe.

"I haven't seen the papers yet," he said. It wasn't what he'd meant to say. In fact, he hadn't figured out how to respond to any kind of reporting on last night's events. "I guess the chief has?"

Cote nodded. "As I said, he's pleased. This is probably going national, since those kids were from out of state. He wants to have a press conference this afternoon. You and Kyle and Perry will need to be there. In uniform."

Burgess wasn't sure his uniform was fit to wear in public right now. He guessed it would have to do. He said, "I'll let them know. What time?"

Cote told him the time and then, unable to resist a bit of criticism, since it was in his blood, he said, "You look like hell, you know."

"That's what my mirror says. I'm not a spring chicken, I'm an old fall rooster. Not much to be done about that, I'm afraid."

Cote sighed. "Just be there, okay?"

Burgess nodded and the captain went away.

The investigations bureau assistant appeared with another stack of messages. Though he'd tried to let her know he wasn't scary, she usually approached him like he was about to bite her. Today she was smiling. "I'll just keep telling reporters you're unavailable, if that's okay? Oh, and thank you for inviting me to your wedding. That was very nice. My husband and I are looking forward to it."

He didn't think he had invited her. But of course, Chris would have edited his list and added people he ought to have included. "We're glad you can come," he said.

The next person to appear at his elbow was Kyle, who'd also arrived without being seen. But Kyle was good at that.

"Did you hear?" Burgess said. "We've got a command performance at a press conference this afternoon. And the chief wants us in uniform."

"I think the moths ate mine."

It had only been a few days since the cocktail party. He said, "Very busy moths. Well, son, you gotta wear it anyway."

Kyle yawned. "But we've got work to do. We'll be writing reports on this damned thing until hell freezes over."

"The price you pay for being a hero."

"There's something screwed up about that. So…" Kyle switched into work mode. "Any more thoughts about how we tie William McCarty into this?"

"I've got one thought, and you aren't going to like it."

Kyle's smile was tired. "Let me guess. We're giving it to the staties. Yes?"

"Got it in one."

"I think we've been working together too long." Kyle switched subjects again. "What do we know about the condition of our rescued kids?"

"Like anyone would tell us?"

"Maybe Boudreau knows? He was just doing his job, right? You should give him a call."

"I will. And there's the matter of reuniting the twins. Does the aunt even know that Maureen has been rescued? Sage didn't say anything when I spoke to him."

"I'm guessing that's out of our hands, too."

"Which I mostly don't mind except that we did all the work and information voids kind of make me nuts. And how likely is it the state police will know about the aunt? I mean, what if they contact the mom?"

"Oh, Joseph," Kyle said, mock-fanning himself, "everything makes you nuts. That's why you're such a dogged investigator."

Stan Perry joined them, looking pretty much like Burgess felt. He reminded himself that even Stan wasn't a kid anymore, despite how they regarded him. "Autumn did not like her daddy being away," he said. "How on earth does she know? She's just a baby."

"Because you and Lily are her universe," Kyle said. "You'll learn. They only survive by getting us to care for them, and it's a full-time, 24/7 manipulation."

"Wow," Perry said. "Never thought of it that way. So what's up?

We're spending the day writing reports, yeah? Any news about those kids we rescued?"

"Not that we've heard," Kyle said. "Maybe there's something in the paper."

Sometimes Burgess thought he'd passed too much of his cynicism to Kyle.

"Oh, yeah. Right. We just do the work."

"Chief wants to hold a press conference this afternoon," Burgess said. "You're to be there. In uniform."

"What for?" Perry said, which told them he hadn't seen the news.

"Apparently we're heroes," Burgess said.

The nervous assistant appeared again. "Detective, there's a woman on the line to speak with you. Megan Ainsworth? She says it's important."

"I'll take it," Burgess said, and picked up the phone. He signaled for Kyle and Perry to wait.

Ainsworth's words exploded in his ear in an anxious rush. "Detective. Joe. We need to talk. Right now, please. I'm still at the hotel. Can you meet me in the parking garage?"

"I can," he agreed. "Give me twenty."

He looked at Kyle and Perry. "Ainsworth. She wants to meet. And something smells fishy to me. She's at the hotel but wants to meet in the garage. Maybe so her husband doesn't know? Or maybe something else."

"Then you're not going alone," Kyle said. "Stan and I will take my car. She might have seen yours."

After last night, Burgess was glad to have someone to watch his back. Yes, they all had numerous reports to write and should all stay at their desks. But this woman's information—if that's what she wanted to talk about—was a vital part of their investigation. He couldn't see any value in her leading him into a trap. Everything he knew, others knew as well. But sometimes people just reacted without thinking things through. Sometimes it was as simple and primitive as "that cop screwed me and I'm going to get him for it." In this case, the cop might screw her husband.

"Vests," he said.

"Yeah. We know," Perry said.

Kyle just nodded. Burgess told the assistant that if anyone was looking for him, he'd be back in about an hour. Then they headed down to their cars.

The part of him that liked to say "I don't wanna" was being very loud right now. It was right. He didn't. But if he'd always listened to his stay-out-of-danger instincts, he might have had fewer stitches and less pain, but a lot of bad things would have happened. Still, the dense gray clouds overhead matched his mood as he drove to the hotel. What awaited him? A warm greeting? A sharing of important information? Or a trap set by someone with deadly force on their minds?

FORTY-TWO

M egan Ainsworth was waiting for him beside an elegant dark blue Jaguar. The car suited her. So did her leather coat with fur, real fur, at the neck and cuffs. It was a soft fawn color with darker brown fur. Her boots matched. She looked like what she was—a wealthy woman who enjoyed her wealth.

She waved an arm when she spotted his Explorer and he pulled into a nearby spot. Kyle and Perry drove past and parked in the next row. He heard their doors close but no footsteps.

"This feels very clandestine," he said when he reached her.

She smiled. "That's what I thought. But my husband is upstairs, so meeting in the room would have been awkward."

He didn't suggest there were dozens of other nearby places to meet that would have been better than a cold, dark garage. He waited to see what was coming.

"I think you have some idea of what I want to talk about, don't you, Detective Burgess?"

He nodded. "I may. But why don't you tell me."

"Of course." Her voice low and confidential, forcing him to lean in. "I'm sure that after all you've learned, you wonder how much I knew when I asked all those questions about the camp property. I assure you:

It may make me seem foolishly naïve, which I am not, but I had no idea Billy owned that land. He never told me and everyone else I spoke with must have been in on the secret or thought I was a total idiot." She paused. "My husband, you see, has always liked to portray me as his pretty, simple little wife. I guess I've played along because it made things easier. It's pathetic, really, but the thing is that I love him, despite all of his mistakes and his lies. Usually—"

Another pause. "Usually I know what's going on so I can keep his mistakes within reasonable boundaries. This time I didn't. Maybe it's because our cottage on the lake has always been a special place for us. I couldn't imagine he would do something to spoil that specialness. Especially not something like this. Like duping their parents and holding a bunch of kids in horrible conditions. I mean…" She spread her arms wide, like she was giving a speech and making a point to an audience. "What did he think he was going to do with them when winter came? I expect it was really Clinton's scheme. He's always trying to get Billy mixed up in things. Sordid things. Illegal things. Billy's problem has always been his need to prove to me he could make money."

Another pause. "The sad thing is he can't. He can only waste more of mine. Although that camp property does have great development potential." She looked thoughtful. "Too bad it will ruin the lake for everyone else."

The rule was when people wanted to talk, you let them talk. And when you thought they might talk, you set your phone to record the conversation. He knew that somewhere nearby Kyle and Perry were also listening.

"There's this, though," she said. "Even though he screws up, I love my husband. I love him and you have just come far too close to ruining him. Ruining us."

This didn't feel consistent with the vibes he'd gotten when they had breakfast, vibes that suggested an attraction to him. Maybe his vibe meter no longer worked. Maybe she'd had second thoughts and wanted to preserve her marriage. Or maybe she'd been testing him to see what he'd tell her? But no. He thought she hadn't known about this then, that her husband was behind the events that were the subject of her concerns. Maybe her husband had some hold over her, a slender rope around her neck that he'd just jerked and pulled her back?

"You never suspected your husband was behind this? That he'd bought the property?"

She shook her head. "Not then. When I asked you to look into it, I was genuinely concerned. Puzzled about what was going on there. I was upset that the peace of my sanctuary was being disturbed. And yes, I use the word 'sanctuary' deliberately. It has always been that to me. I thought it was to Billy, too."

Time to get to the point. "Ms. Ainsworth. Megan. What did you want to talk to me about today?"

She shrugged and said, "I didn't want to talk to you, really. When it was a mystery, I needed your help. And meeting you? There was a vibe there and Billy isn't always as attentive as he should be. But now that it's a catastrophe, I need to make sure it doesn't reach us. Doesn't reach Billy. Clinton is the only one of them who knows about Billy's involvement, and he will be taken care of. But there's you, with your clever mind and your suspicions and your determination to solve things. I need you taken care of, too."

There was movement behind him. Burgess ducked down between two cars as gunfire erupted, the ping of bullets hitting the metal of the cars beside him. He fell to the gritty garage floor, his face against the cold cement. He heard gunfire he assumed was Kyle and Perry firing at the gunman, and wondered why she would think that eliminating him would protect her husband? Did she assume he was some kind of Lone Ranger who hadn't shared what he knew with others?

Then, as she screamed and fell, he got it. She'd been duped again by the husband who was always trying to fool her. She thought she was protecting her husband by getting rid of Burgess, but Burgess was just the bait her husband had used to get rid of her.

After the explosion of gunfire, the garage went silent. Eerily silent. So silent he wondered if Kyle or Perry or both of them had been shot. He'd never forgive himself if that was the case.

Then he heard footsteps.

He called, "Stan. Terry. Is the gunman down?" and got an affirmative. He got to his feet, brushing dirt from his clothes, rubbing it off his face. One hand was scraped and bleeding. He found her where she lay crumpled between two cars. She'd been shot twice but was still breathing. "She's alive," he said. "Call an ambulance."

The gunman was dead. No ID. But he'd be in the system, Burgess was sure.

And just like that, their report-writing day became a crime-scene day that kept them busy until it was time to go home and change for the press conference. They did take the time to arrest Megan Ainsworth's husband. They could deal with him later.

FORTY-THREE

L ater, a lot later, they gathered in the conference room. They now knew something about the status of the rescued teens, thanks to the chief and to Boudreau, who evidently had sources of his own. All were expected to live, though some would need a lot of care before they could leave the hospital.

As the following days passed, their cases began to resolve. William McCarty would be charged with murder for hire, and, along with Clinton Johns and Edwin Hall, would be charged with multiple counts of kidnapping and child abuse, financial fraud, and with homicide, once the investigation into the deaths of Elvira Clemens and a boy named Silas Drummond had been completed. The third person who'd fled the old nursing home turned out to be Clinton Johns's son. They were still sorting out charges against him. Charges were also being weighed against the families who had put their teens in such jeopardy.

It was, as Stan Perry had called it, a clusterfuck, but one that had had, for the most part, a happy ending. Not for Silas Drummond, Elvira Clemens, and not for poor, feckless Elaine Hawes. Sad news her mother might, or might not, be able to comprehend.

Megan Ainsworth, once she recovered from her gunshot wounds, would be charged with attempted murder. She was shocked to learn that when one leads a police officer into a deadly trap, just doing what your husband says isn't a defense.

Maureen Mulcahey, once she was well enough, would be released to the custody of her aunt. There was no way the State of Maine would allow her to be returned to her mother. Burgess and Kyle had had another chat with the aunt, who apologized for going into hiding without telling them. She had been responding to her niece Colleen's fear that her mother, or someone working for her mother, would try to take her away again.

"You see, Detective Burgess," Emily Mulcahey said, "that call with my sister-in-law? Where she acted so strange? Then you told me about Fiona's strange visit to the hospital. And then later, after you'd left, Fiona called me again and tried to get me to sneak Colleen out of the hospital and bring her home. When I refused to do that, she wanted all this information about Colleen. Like what room she was in and whether the police were watching the room. I figured I knew what she was planning. So I took Colleen someplace I thought she'd be safe."

"You could have called us," Kyle said. "We were all on the same side about protecting your niece."

The aunt's face got very red. "I know. I was an idiot. I panicked. I'm not usually impulsive or devious. I'm also not used to dealing with something like this…that their own mother—" She gave up and shrugged. "This whole thing is so unbelievable."

Which to most people it was.

Van Elwell was recovering well and his stepfather was going to be charged with attempted murder. A relief to everyone, since it meant he was less likely to be out on the street anytime soon.

The list went on and on. Those four boys who'd terrorized Ned? They'd taken the car without permission. The gun belonged to a parent who'd failed to secure it, and it was a stolen gun the father had bought for protection. All four of them were carrying enough illegal drugs to put them in serious trouble. And all four families were doing the usual "not my kid" and fighting everything instead of worrying about what kind of kids they'd raised.

"Seems like these days, we can't leave the house without running into a criminal," Kyle said. "I'm definitely putting in for the poop patrol."

"Lily wants me to find a safer job," Stan Perry said.

"I'm too busy for crime," Burgess said. "I have a wedding to plan."

The rest of November passed in a blur. The twins Colleen and Maureen Mulcahey were reunited and put in the custody of their aunt. The mystery surrounding why Maureen had been kept separate was solved when she spoke to the investigators. Right from the beginning, Clinton Johns had seen the beautiful twins as a different source of income. He'd planned to sell them to the highest bidder. That had been foiled by the injury to one and the defiance of the other. He'd kept the "good twin" separate while she recovered, letting her sister believe she'd died. The weather, and the move, had interfered with his plans before they could be put into effect.

The man who'd shown up claiming to be an attorney was one of Alan Cassiday's cousins, which was why the aunt had recognized him. Why she hadn't said anything was one of those cases of wrongheaded stupidity cops dealt with all the time. This particular case involved a lot of those.

There were families that felt deep remorse for the mistake of sending their children to a nice outdoor camp experience in Maine. Others that refused to take any blame. Prosecutions on all their cases were likely.

On a cold December Saturday a few weeks later, followed by a feast that didn't include meatloaf sandwiches, Detective Sergeant Joseph Burgess became a married man.

The End

ABOUT THE AUTHOR

Kate Flora's fascination with people's criminal tendencies began in the Maine attorney general's office. Deadbeat dads, people who hurt their kids, and employers' discrimination aroused her curiosity about human behavior. Flora's been a finalist for the Edgar, Agatha, Anthony, and Derringer awards. She won the Public Safety Writers Association award for nonfiction and twice won the Maine Literary Award for crime fiction.

When she's not writing, Flora gardens in the writerly town of Concord, Massachusetts, and on the coast of Maine, and bakes when she gets stuck in writing a story. She's been married to a delightful man for more than forty years.

facebook.com/katecflora

x.com/kateflora